UNDREAMED

PAUL WESTERN-PITTARD

COPYRIGHT

Undreamed
By Paul Western-Pittard

© 2012 Paul Western-Pittard

All rights reserved. No part of this publication may be reproduced or transmitted in any form (electronic, mechanical or otherwise) without the express written consent of the author. This is a work of fiction. Names, characters, places and incidents are either the products of the author's imagination or used fictitiously. Any resemblance to actual events, locations or persons living or dead is entirely coincidental.

You can read more books at: pwesternpittard.com

*To Zandra for your support, encouragement,
forbearance and (well deserved) prodding,
but mostly for loving a crazy writer.*

*To David for that immense deep deep
world of yours and Jason, for your spark
without which the days would be dimmer.*

With special thanks to Annette T. Thomas, Annette Cullen, Jenny Lalor, Adrienne Kreegher, Wayne Bryant and my 'beta' readers for your encouragement and feedback. Finally, a tip of the hat to Pawel G for reminding me this could have been a book after all.

1

THE NECKLACE

Look at yourself. Ink-black hair, green eyes and so, so tired.

I stare at my reflection in a cracked mirror. It's mostly dark, which is a good thing because the place is a dump and I don't want to see what's hidden in the shadows. The only light comes from a broken fluorescent that flashes a kind of weird glow across the bathroom making my movements jerky and unreal. I ignore the Goth girl at the end of the bench, just like I make myself unhear the gasps and panting of the couple fucking in the stall behind her. None of that matters.

Hi Alice, it's Alice. I trace one of my reflections in the fractured glass, turn to examine my profile. I'm looking at a stranger. Is she more real than me? Less real? I still haven't figured it out. Pounding bass rises up from the club, rattling the glass which makes the reflection pop and jump like a bad edit. I get that; it suits my mood. 'Just you and me, girl,' I say to the person looking back at me and drop from view. She doesn't need to see this.

I rummage through my bag and pulling out a compact,

pop it open, flipping it mirror side up. Next, the flashpowder: a special blend of who knows what from Rene. Rene: my personal dealer, oracle, witchdoctor and freak. I pause a moment before emptying out the rest. What the hell, right? As I use my credit card to crush and separate it into lines I catch myself matching the rhythm outside, each tap of the plastic catching a beat. Pulling a small silver straw from the bag, I push back my hair and listen as the music ramps up and the crowd go berserk over a house favourite.

In the flashing light I spot a glint of red: a toy fire engine sitting in a soapy spill next to one of the basins. Its wide smiling face stares at me with a kind of dare. I lash out and knock it to the floor.

'Not tonight,' I say. The Goth turns to me.

'Are you talking to me?' She glares at me and snap-jerks into a pose, prickling in to a sudden bring-it-on attitude. Not scary, just predictable.

I don't need it. Turning away I ignore her and the smiling toy on the tiles. 'Salut,' I toast my on again, off again reflection and lean in, snorting up four lines of Rene's mix. My lips and throat go numb. Lights sparkle behind my eyes. My head explodes. Rene, you've come through again. 'Fuck,' I think I gasp, then push past the Goth who says something surprised, entering the mayhem that I'm about to make my own.

The club is huge, powerfully lit and so loud it's physical. Klieg lights and lasers strobe through the crowd, making silhouettes of us all. Hundreds of us — a crazy marionette theatre lifted away by the swirl and beat of light. Heads and bodies snap from moment to moment with each pulse, our arms raised, moving frames in a film. It's intense.

I throw myself into the churn, letting the light blast away the Mirror-Woman. I dance with strangers and let the music obliterate me, becoming nothing but body. Yelling out, I'm hot and crazy and love every second of it as I spin and laugh, not giving a damn that it's just the drugs. Everything splinters into separate moments.

There — a tall muscly guy, mid twenties and dressed in a tight black satin shirt. I smile and move to him, allowing the tide of other dancers to draw me near, never losing eye contact. He winks at me and comes closer, trying to yell something against the noise but the music drowns him out. I put a finger to his lips, not needing to hear him. Instead I lean into him and as he tilts his head to listen, I nip his ear and disappear into the crowd before he can do anything about it. Lost again I laugh, tasting the electric salt of his blood. I could be a vampire.

I pull off my sweater and throw my head back to stare into the colours, feeling the tight beating of my heart and the pressure of air in my lungs. The room moves, bodies surge, time skips and now I'm dancing alongside a girl, taut spray-on tan and blasted-open eyes and a guy next to her whose face transforms into a leer.

Diamonds of perspiration on her skin catch in the fine hair of her neck, refracting the lights. She's so alive, one-souled and simple. I'm jealous. I move with her, ignoring her friend. Her strange eyes are giant reflections and I flash an equally giant smile. Perhaps she's wearing contacts, they're so amazing. She's wearing a tiny silver dress with a matching necklace. I close in, dancing behind her as the DJ reads my mind and pushes the beats into a new rhythm. One of my hands goes to her waist, the other, higher, over her breast. Her heart pounds under my fingers.

Boyfriend edges closer, so transparent I can read his mind. Not tonight lover. I guide her away to another part of the floor and in the laser light my hand drops to my bag. I know what I'm looking for and find the knife by feel. The blade snaps open with a whisper only I hear.

Still following us, her friend's eyes grow wide in shock as he notices the flash of metal. He opens his mouth as I gently rest the blade against the tip of her spine. I hesitate a moment, wondering which way the night will go. It could be tonight, I realise with excitement rising quick and hot in my body. It really could be. All it would take would be a tiny effort, the first resistance of the skin, then deeper into flesh and perhaps bone. What would it be like to kill her? What would my mirror think? The moment passes. With a quick twitch I cut through the necklace, nicking her skin as the blade travels as far as it needs, then a little further. She spins, her face lit by confusion, anger then shock. The boyfriend lunges for me, but I'm already somewhere else.

God that was so nearly right. My fist clenches the jewellery as I push through a couple dancing close. Someone trips behind me and I laugh; I have to, releasing all that potential into the noise and the heat. A voice calls out causing me to spin. It's the boyfriend again. My heart hammers as I hide out of sight behind a giant bodybuilder type who's watching him pile through the crowd. I could let him find me. That would be real. The room blazes blue and bright as the DJ gears up into a new set and the sounds gets louder.

In his hurry to get to me the boyfriend's pushed a woman over and pissed off her partner. They start shoving and shoving back and in a second they both go down. The girl has recovered enough to be pissed off in her own right and starts slapping my guy. Voices rise above the music and heads turn. The tussle is turning into a fight.

A circle of clear space opens like magic around the three of them. The boyfriend swings wildly and lands a blow on the man's jaw, snapping his head to the side. Now he's angry. I lean out a bit further in time to catch the woman launching herself and clawing at him with her nails. Someone in the crowd yells as he tries to get away, his lips bleeding. In a flash of light money changes hands. Someone's taking bets. Quick thinker. My money's on the boyfriend, smaller than the tough guy but faster. Then a fist connects and he falls.

2

THE FIGHT

Droplets of his blood arc through the air in a trajectory unbound by gravity, lifted by the strobing lasers and the impact of the blow. Time slows and there's a moment of calm. Just one moment, pure and single and simple: a meditation. Then someone else joins in and the moment's gone.

The fight is beginning to pull people in, so brutal it's sexy. But just as it's getting interesting, bouncer types start turning up. They're all the same; muscle wrapped up in entitlement. Someone in the crowd screams. There'll soon be enough of them to force their way into the circle and wreck the party.

As I lean in I catch a glimpse of the boyfriend staring at me. Even at this distance our eyes connect. Maybe it's time to get out of here. His expression jumps a notch as he forces his way out of the fight. I run, losing myself again in the throng.

Something shifts inside of me as I force my way through the press of bodies. There's always a dark flip-side to the euphoria and it only takes a moment to let it in. What has

Rene given me? I have to get out of here right now, so I start looking for a fire escape.

Kicking the door open I explode into the cold air, pinwheel down three ice-slick concrete steps and skid on my ass into a dumpster. Knocked free by the impact, a loose pile of snow sluices over my shoulders, leaving me in a grimy, grey and cold as all hell mess.

'Shit,' I gasp, the word pulled straight from my lungs by the ice in the air. I unclench my hand. The necklace is drab under the single sodium light and I throw it to the ground, slightly disgusted. Something rolls in my stomach and I'm going to puke. So much for Rene's magical mystery powder. I keep it down as I struggle to my feet on the treacherous area around the bin.

I'm locked out. The door, a metal slab layered in years of graffiti has closed.

As the adrenaline slowly loses its grip I have to laugh. With the last of its fireworks in my bloodstream fading, a remnant of Rene's mix thinks it might be fun to get back in and check how the fight is going, despite the problem of the door. Perhaps check up on the boyfriend. Underneath all that macho fighting for his girl act, he had something. Instead I do nothing, staring into the black sky and the endless snow, allowing myself to be calmed by the cold and the quiet. Nearby a siren gets louder. I breathe in. Slowly, deliberately.

I breathe out.

The party was over before it started. Rene. What have you done? I guess I shouldn't let it get to me. I have bigger problems. The thing is I don't even know if I'm here, not for sure. I've got a memory, a show I watched when I was a kid. It could have been a rerun of Kung Fu. A monk is telling this apprentice a story: an old man went to sleep under a tree and dreamed he was a butterfly. In the dream the butterfly slept and dreamed it was an old man. Was the old man really dreaming the butterfly, or the butterfly dreaming the man? And when you get past all the philosophy, it kind of makes you think. I might be the butterfly.

Without looking I pull the knife from my bag and flick open the blade, bringing it close to my eyes. The bloodied tip is black in this light with the almost congealed blood of the woman. I look closer, trying to make out my reflection but it's impossible in the snowbound light.

Slowly, carefully, I run the steel across my palm. No pain yet; that comes later. It's scary and amazing — the skin creases at the pressure of the blade, parting as the edge slices through the outer layer. Now there's pain. I bite down on my lips, press harder, push the metal even deeper as I draw it slowly down my hand. A fine line of my own blood follows the tip, mixing with the almost dry blood of the girl. It wells in my open palm, shining silky-black as a snowflake brushes my wrist. I have to blink back tears but I'm careful to keep calm as I fold away the knife, focusing on the pain and the heat.

I go away, but the sting gives me something to anchor on. It's real, which is more than I can say for anything else. It's not sleep, but a weird, intense restfulness.

Sometime later, long enough for my hand to have turned numb the silence of the snow is broken by a soft click. I snap back as I recognise the boyfriend standing in the light of the door, his face half lit, almost a statue. I watch silently as he waits for his eyes to adjust then takes a second to get his bearings. His lip is bloodied and his cheek shows the faint purple of a bruise in the making. He wipes his nose, his hand coming away bloody as he scans the alley.

'You.' His voice is tight.

All right, I wanted interesting. I look at him silently. My heart races again as the pain in my hand flares, forcing me to clench it tightly. I begin to shiver.

'What the fuck is your problem?' he says. 'Give me the necklace.'

'Go away,' I say, getting colder by the second. Whatever slice of peace I had is gone.

'I want,' he says again, 'the necklace back.'

Lightheaded I nod towards a mound of dirty snow. 'Over there,' I whisper. 'But you're not here for that.'

I wonder.

He hunts around for something to jam the door and finding nothing, pulls off his jacket. Stepping carefully from the fire escape he goes to the necklace, his eyes locked on mine. 'They called the cops,' he says, bending to collect the jewellery. 'They'll find you out here.' Maybe. I doubt it. My shivering gets worse as I remember throwing away my sweater someplace in the club.

He stands with the necklace in hand, mission accomplished, and looks at me silently. I stare back, willing myself to stop shaking despite the waves of pain flowing from my palm, invading the rest of my body. He holds up his trophy. 'This was her mothers. Like you give a damn.'

I shrug. I really don't.

He shakes his head and finally sees the blood falling in long stringy loops from my upturned palm, so obvious now from his new vantage point. He stares at me in shock. 'Fuck off,' I say flatly, ignoring the violent shaking that's returned. 'You're not even real.' He jams the jewellery into his pocket and makes his way back to the fire escape. Sounds of voices grow louder from inside.

'Put down the knife.'

'You came for me.'

He blinks in surprise. 'What?'

'You don't give a damn about the necklace.'

'Bitch,' he says, 'you're messed up.'

'Well,' I say, ignoring my body, quaking from the shock of pain and the cold, 'here I am. Ready and waiting. Come get me tiger.' I smile a ghost of a smile, feeling that my eyes are black, blacker than that Goth girl. I take a step towards him, holding out my palm which is slick with blood. 'This,' I say, 'is real.' And it's the truth.

Boyfriend steps back so quickly he almost trips, and stumbling through the door is gone. I wait for a count of five before falling to my knees; tears of pain running freely down my face. 'Too far babe,' I whisper and try to tear off a strip from my tee, but all I manage to do is stretch the fabric. Shivering, I coil my hand in the thin cloth the best that I can, grab his jacket then get out of the alley.

3

HOME SWEET... SOMETHING

The taxi pulls up directly in front of the entrance of my building on Central Park West. The driver jams the brakes so hard I almost lose it again. I've thrown up three times already. He's furious but I've promised a life-changing tip if he can get me home. Behind the wide double doors of the building, an old man in a trim grey suit looks up from behind a desk where he's been reading a newspaper. He rises and walks out under the awning, crosses the last exposed few feet of sidewalk and opens my door.

'Nice to see you home again, Ms Van de Korte,' he drawls, his soft southern accent still noticeable even after years here.

'Not now, Marty,' I say, wincing as I take his hand and climb from the taxi. 'Pay the man. I'll fix you up later.' Marty looks at me more carefully, sees my hand wrapped in the bloody hem of my tee, only half hidden under the jacket.

'I'll call a doctor.'

'No need.'

He tries again. 'Ms Van de Korte,' he starts, but I shake

my head, ending the conversation. Sometimes his old school southern gent act is bearable, but right now what I need is to get out of this cold. I clamp my hand to my chest and walk past him into the warmth of the marble and brass foyer. Thankful for the distraction that the driver's providing as he realises he won't be getting that tip, I keep going.

I step out of the art deco elevator into my apartment at the top of the building. My mind is wandering. If you believe Arlene McKinner, the saner half of the two spinsters who live below me, once upon a time you could see out across the entire skyline from this place. That doesn't mean much to me; there's only one view that matters. I throw open the heavy brocade curtain and stare out over Central Park for a long time. With the lights switched off, I struggle out of my ruined tee and drop it to the floor.

God, it hurts so much. Going to the kitchen I find some vodka on the counter top. Managing to unscrew it with my good hand I raise the bottle to my lips and scull till I choke, slamming it down on the marble surface. 'Damn,' I cough. All right. I know this is going to hurt. Steeling myself I grab it again and empty about half of the vodka over my palm. For a heartbeat the pain goes away. And then it comes back, drawing a line of fire over the cut. I drop the bottle and stagger backwards into the stainless steel refrigerator.

I stumble past the huge picture window into my bedroom, where I fumble out of my bra and jeans and collapse onto the bed. As I stare at the ceiling, the world spinning around me, I'm surprised to hear my own voice. 'I don't want to do this anymore,' I whisper to the quiet dark room and close my eyes, which are green.

4

SYDNEY

A heartbeat. A breath.

A beam of sunlight. It plays across my cheek and gradually I open my eyes, which are blue. That part's so strange and I can't explain it. Everything else about me is the same.

Ratbone, my small black and tan cat jumps onto the bed and purrs as he rubs against my face, wanting breakfast. 'Give me ten more minutes,' I beg, burying myself deep in the duvet. I wish I could stay here, safe and sound and comfortable forever, but Ratbone will not be denied as he bats at me playfully. I squirm lower and he takes this as an invitation to attack the sheets. I play with him for a bit more then yawn and get up, gently lifting him out of the way. Such a cutie.

Walking over to the full-length pine mirror leaning against the wall I take stock of myself. The same blonde hair (needs a cut), the same blue eyes (too baggy), the same face, same body. I need to exercise more. I straighten the old Donald Duck T-shirt I use as a nightie and nod. It's compulsive behaviour but at least I recognise the ritual for what it is, something Dr Ryan, my psychiatrist has asked me to consider. For a flickering moment I think about what I would do if it were her face in the mirror. I hold my hand to the glass and I can't resist the urge to look at my palm, which is whole and uninjured. She's only a dream but it hurts me that she hates herself so much. I wave to myself. 'Good morning.' Ratbone meows in reply. 'Yeah yeah,' I say, 'I hear you.'

Emerging from the bedroom I walk down the thin hallway of our old townhouse, careful to avoid loose boards as the crazy cat weaves between my legs. I come to the door of my sister's room and can't help but smile as I pass the sounds of restful snoring. I promise myself one day I'm going to record that and finally win our bet. Jen argues until she's blue in the face that she's a silent sleeper.

Sunlight floods the kitchen and makes the air almost liquid as it swirls with my arrival, the tiny currents lifting dust motes and pushing them into beautiful eddies. This is what it would be like to live inside a Monet. I take a moment to enjoy the dusty rays falling through the windows, admiring the way they illuminate the old laminex counters and throw sharp-edged shadows across the floorboards. No matter how hard I — or if I'm honest about it — Jen, cleans the place it always looks this way in the morning: a little bit of magic I quietly adore.

The kitchen's a disaster as usual, cluttered with the debris of one of Jen's late night sessions. Folders full of invoices and financials lay scattered over the table, stacked loosely on one of the chairs and even on the counter-top. The ugly grey lump of her laptop is buried beneath a box of receipts next to the kettle. It amazes me that one person can make so much mess.

I go to the refrigerator and yank it open, fighting the

ungodly tight seal to get the milk. Taking a swig from the carton (Jen doesn't know I do this) I pour some in a bowl for Ratbone, who for the moment quietens down.

I've just dropped two slices of bread into the toaster when she turns up in her baggy pyjamas, still three-quarters asleep. She's taller than me with braided gold-flecked red hair and a crazy lopsided smile that can beam brightly at the drop of a hat. Right now though, she's a portrait of misery. Jen slumps into one of the spindly-legged kitchen chairs and splats herself over the table, hiding her head from the sunlight. She shoves some paperwork aside.

'Busy night?'

'You bet. Party party party.'

I pick up a sheet of paper, glazing over at the columns of numbers. 'I don't know how you do it.'

'What? Working from home or book keeping?'

'Either. Both.'

Jen smiles and the room gets a little bit brighter. 'It's all about the lifestyle, baby.'

'You snore,' I say with a grin.

'And you're crazy,' mumbles Big Sister as she crumples again beneath her arms. She glances up at me, squinting in the brightness of the kitchen. 'Anyway, I don't snore.'

'Do.'

'Don't'

The toaster settles the argument by jamming. I thump it, forcing the thing to disgorge two lumps of only slightly burned bread. Fishing them out, I drop them on a plate and join her at the table, contemplating the day ahead and the hours yawn away in front of me. There's a moment of grace, a kind of false dawn when I wake and everything is open and out there and maybe good. It really could be; I don't believe in fate. But the days bring their own weight of expectations and promises that need to be kept. To myself, to others. I eat the toast.

'Can you look after the shop until twelve?' I ask.

Jen picks up a slice from the plate and bites into it without much enthusiasm. 'Your shrink?' she asks, spilling crumbs across the table. I nod. Jen's expression softens slightly. 'So,' she says, 'how was last night?'

'Bad,' I say quietly. 'She cut herself again.'

Jen takes another nibble, concern in her eyes. 'No shit? That's pretty messed up, even for her.'

'She was out of control.' I find myself fighting a horribly familiar sensation of being overwhelmed. 'She knew she was messing up, but she kept going anyway.'

Jen reaches out and takes my hand. 'She's not you. You know that.'

I can't look at her. 'What if she is? What if all that is really me and this is the dream?'

'Are you kidding me?' says Jen, pointedly staring at the kitchen. 'Well if it is, you need to step it up, girl. For starters I want a mansion with a pool and a couple of mil in the bank. Then I want some tall, tanned, well-hung pool boys to help me pass the day. Three or four. I'm not greedy.' I smile. Jen is, well, Jen. She stares at me then puts down the toast, leans across the table and tries for a hug, but the moment is awkward. 'It's going to be OK. You hear me?' I say nothing, instead I nod quickly and wipe the beginnings of tears from my eyes.

'This really sucks, you know?' I say at last, trying to get a grip. But it's so hard. It's not days, or months. It's my whole life as two people.

'I know baby,' she says leaning back. 'But we'll get through it. You have to hang in there, you know what I mean?'

'It's got to stop.' I say when I finally find my voice.

'It will.' Jen scrapes back the chair and takes her plate to the sink, dropping it into the pile of unwashed dishes and mugs. I get up too and head to the bathroom. 'Hey,' she calls out as I walk away, 'Alice?'

I stop and look back down the hall. 'Yeah?'

'Go see the doc. Keep at it, he's a good guy.' I want to agree, but the words won't come. Not that I doubt Dr Ryan, or don't trust him. Jen smiles. 'It's really going to be all right.'

I nod.

5

THE AIPRORT

But I'm not at Dr Ryan's.

I stand still and light while passengers flow around me like water. I'm an island of quiet, surrounded by people, bags, screaming children, the adrenaline of coffee and excitement. I chose my white and yellow summer dress today because the radio said it was going to be scorching, but the airport is air-conditioned. The dress isn't what you'd wear for a flight like the one I'm looking for.

I don't know and do know why I'm here and its got nothing to do with common sense and everything to do with what needs to be done. Dr Ryan calls this kind of thing compulsive but I'm not an idiot. I have a choice and this is me exercising it. I need to be here. I have to find her.

No. It's the other way around. I have to not find her.

Staring up at the black departures board I watch the yellow text countdown flights. The noise of the airport is everywhere; a mash of chatter and movement, electronic announcements and big terminal-spanning chimes. The flight I need leaves in an hour.

I get she's not real. I've always known that — well,

almost always. But New York is real and I'm drawn to it. When I went there before I forgot that difference, but for some reason I know it won't be the same this time around. Last time I was looking for her, this time I'll be looking not to find her. I know how that sounds but in the dream, her family's practically famous. I'll go and she won't be there because she's not real. There's no truth to her except the city she lives in. Then I'll know for sure. It makes so much sense.

I stare at my hand for the millionth time and for the millionth time it's fine. This morning I realised she terrifies me, real or not. Jen says it will all work out, but there's no reason it has to, unless I make it. So, here I am. I just wish I hadn't chosen this dress.

I join a winding line of passengers queuing at the check-in. Slotting myself in behind a couple who are toting a train of chrysanthemum-patterned cases, I wait my turn.

This is the right thing to do, but I'm nervous. I've got fifteen hundred dollars in a savings account, which is enough to pay for my fare. Breathing heavily, I'm light-headed and excited and certain. I know this time I'm really going to go through with it. Sweat beads and my heart beats faster as the woman at the ticket counter greets me with a professional smile.

'I need a ticket,' I say.

She watches me fumble with my purse and I pull out my passport. 'Sure,' she says. 'Where would you like to go?'

'New York.'

The attendant nods. 'Just a moment. I'll check what's available.'

'I want the next flight.' I point to the departures board behind me. 'That one.'

She doesn't even look up from her computer. 'The flight's closed, I'm sorry.' She types some more and the sound of the keys cuts across the background noise. It's tuned specifically to me. I think of the clitter-clatter of skeleton hands and dab at the moisture forming around my neck. It's too hot in here, despite the air conditioning.

'I really want to be on that flight,' I say, flicking away a damp strand of hair from my eyes. 'It's important.'

The woman pauses from her typing and glances at me. I know that look and begin to worry. Sure, this is last minute, but that doesn't mean I'm wrong to do it. Sometimes you've got to act in the moment or the moment is lost. Her smile flickers uncertainly as she sees I'm not carrying any bags. 'I'm sorry,' she says again, 'it's closed. You can't get on that flight.'

'I'd really appreciate it,' I say, trying for a smile. Somewhere deep inside are the beginnings of doubt. 'Is there anything else leaving soon?' I turn back to the departure board as if it can somehow give me more information than the terminal she's using. 'It's a family emergency.'

The woman clitter-clatters again. She's wearing too much makeup. 'The next flight departs in five hours. There's a stopover at LA so you'd get into JFK around four pm local time. It's showing full but I could put you on standby.' She pauses. 'Are you feeling all right Miss?' I imagine her hand hovering out of sight over a security button as I blink heavily. I'm dizzy.

My heart beats loud and fast as a migraine comes out of nowhere and begins to throw colourful sparks across my vision. Not now. I grip the counter and the woman leans back reflexively. The headache hits me fast and my pulse races. There's a chime and someone behind me shuffles her trolley to the next ticket counter. Somewhere else, a bag slips from the conveyor behind the check-in and a harried attendant rushes to catch it before it falls. There's nervous laughter and after a confused moment I figure out it's me. The momentum's slipping away, replaced by something dark and horribly real. Turning away I try to hide the storm that must be visible in my face. 'Sorry,' I say, fighting to compose myself, 'I'm a nervous traveller.'

'Do you need any help?' asks the attendant growing more concerned. 'Perhaps you should sit down. I can call someone if you want.'

I turn to the departure board again. I'm not willing to give up, not yet. 'How long till it leaves?'

'Five hours.'

It's getting harder to breathe. I recognise the coming panic attack for what it is, but that doesn't help. It's impossible to ignore so I brace myself to ride out the waves of fear I know are on their way. I've missed my chance. I never had a chance to begin with.

I breathe in slowly and admit defeat, grabbing my passport back. 'I'm sorry,' I say. 'I've changed my mind.' Eyes stinging, I walk from the ticket counter with as much dignity as I can muster.

Somewhere ahead there's a row of plastic bucket chairs and I collapse heavily into one of them. Sighing, I rub my face hard, looking up in time to see an airport security guard walk past. He catches my eye before moving on, long enough for me to get the message that I've been noted. I lean back and focus on breathing, letting the waves wash over me.

Somehow I manage to pull out my phone and make a call.

6
WITH JEN

Heat shimmers from the faded bonnet of the car. Beyond, strange oases form above the truck in front, its dual chrome exhausts rippling weirdly against the brutal blue sky. Pale grey overpasses cut deep shadows over the road, offering pools of shade impossible to reach in this slow moving traffic.

Jen's across from me, hands locked on the wheel. The car's air conditioner gasps and hisses, beaten down by the heat outside as it blows luke-warm drafts across us both while the radio plays quietly in the background. I can't meet her eyes, instead choosing to focus on the window and the traffic beyond the glass. It's so hot. I wonder how hot it would need to be for the wheels of the cars to melt. One degree more, perhaps. The migraine is going now but I still have a headache. Jen had to collect me from the airport's first aid station. On top of everything else, it's humiliating.

'I'm sorry,' I say eventually as I stare at a green SUV crawling past us to our left. A kid's face lurks behind one of the tinted windows, watching us with blunt curiosity.

'Don't worry about it,' says Jen, but her hands clench ever so slightly on the wheel.

'I don't know, not for sure,' I say, trying to find the words to explain myself to her, 'I have to find out.'

'We've been through this before. You've gone there, remember? No Van de Kortes, no medical empire, no nothing. And that hasn't changed.' She glances at me. 'It's a dream. That's all it is. The only real thing is New York and you don't have to go there again to find that out.'

'They all feel so real. I need to prove they're not.'

'I know, babe.'

I bite back a reply as Jen sighs then veers left abruptly. Behind us a car honks as the driver stands on the brakes. Jen waves a quick apology then changes lanes again. 'Shit,' she says, 'I've missed the exit.' She looks at me. 'You have to stop doing this.'

'I know.'

'They're going to get you on a watch list, or whatever they call it.'

'I know.'

'Next time they might arrest you or something. They'll think you're a terrorist.'

I wind down the window and let a blast of hot air fill the cabin. It ruffles a small map in the back seat and blows dust and traffic fumes through the car.

'Jesus Alice, shut it!'

I squint in the scorching wind, taking a lungful before winding it back up. The interior becomes quiet and stifling again. This is what it would be like to be buried alive.

'Seriously. You've got to cut this shit out. It's not helping anyone.'

I nod. 'Yeah. I know. Just sometimes this is all so...' I

struggle for a moment as I stare at the painfully bright metal around us. 'Dark. It's weird but it doesn't seem real. I don't feel like I'm here.'

Jen shakes her head. 'Well, you're not anywhere else, I can tell you that for a fact. Stuck on a freeway wouldn't be my first choice for a dream.'

'Yeah. Me too.'

'You have to choose, babe.'

'What?' I look away from the snarl of cars to Jen.

'Choose to wake up.'

'I am awake.'

'Not really.' She sighs. With a twitch of the indicator she guides the car onto an off ramp. 'I mean stop thinking about thinking and live your life. So you don't know what's what. I get it. You're sleepwalking right now and it kills me.'

Great, that helps. 'Thanks for the pep talk,' I say.

'I love you babe, but you have to stop feeling so friggin' sorry for yourself all the time. Try to have some fun for once. You might like it.'

I close my eyes. 'Lets go home.'

Jen shakes her head. 'Screw that. I'm dropping you off at Ryan's. Then I'm heading back to the shop.'

I press my hand against my forehead. Despite the heat the pain is slowly going away. 'How about we play hooky instead? I'll stop being mad and you stop saving me. How does that sound?'

Jen leans across the seat and gives me a gentle push. When she does that I know it's OK, we're back from the brink, yet again. 'Sounds fantastic. But I'm still taking you to Ryan's.'

'I hate you.'

'Yeah.'

'Jen?'

'Yeah?'

'I'm sorry.'

Jen holds my hand. 'Just stick with it babe. Don't bail on me.'

7

MEETING RYAN

Jen drops me off, but we're good again. We have this thing called the half hour rule for when I sometimes lose the plot. It's something Ryan suggested to help us not kill each other when things get crazy. When I get crazy. We get half an hour to vent but after that we both move on. I've promised her I'll talk about my trip to the airport with Ryan and she's OK with that.

The Landeth Medical Centre. Every time I come here it feels like the wrong place. It's a big blocky building in the middle of what seems to be an industrial park, surrounded by walking tracks and dry yellow grass. Three brutish stories tall and ugly, there's nothing welcoming about it at all. I'm not surprised it's mostly empty.

A small mirage shimmers above the car park. The day's already blistering and the arrival of a dusty northerly only adds to the temperature. I start feeling dirty as grit gets in my eyes, wiping the sweat from my forehead and regretting that I forgot my hat. A blast of wind pulls at my dress and I hold it down as I veer towards the shade of some gum trees also getting blown about in the gusts.

By the time I get to the entrance, which is a huge glass double sliding door I'm almost reeling from the heat. I pause to drink from a fountain but the water's tepid and tastes faintly of chlorine: disgusting. I flick off the tap, about to head in when a car horn sounds behind me. A small green nineties hatchback pulls into slot marked staff. Dr Thomas Ryan, my shrink, waves from the driver's seat. It's kind of nice his ego doesn't need a Mercedes or something. Or perhaps they don't pay him enough.

Ryan and I go way back, as far back as my time in the Mayfleur Hospital anyway. He's my government appointed doctor and we've been having weekly sessions, regular as clockwork (Jen calls them dates) for six years. Ever since they let me out of that place. After Jen brought me back from New York I wasn't too healthy and had to stay in the clinic until somebody gave me the all clear. Which was fine, but that same somebody also made it mandatory to visit Ryan every week. If I'm honest, really honest, that's fine too. I like him and it doesn't hurt that he's cute.

'Alice?' he calls, winding down the window, 'Head straight up into my office. I'll meet you there. It's too hot to wait around.'

'It's all right,' I say and go to the car as he leans over to collect a large pile of paper from the passenger seat. I hold the door open for him as he struggles with it. He doesn't notice me as he backs out and trips. A gust tears the papers from his grasp and explodes the loose leaves all across the car park. The pages flick and leap over the asphalt, some caught in hot eddies which spin them skywards while others flitter and limp along the ground. They jam against car tyres or wedge somehow into the kerb. I stare at them and their fluttering escape attempt. I'd have taken it as a sign if this happened before my trip to the airport.

'Ah, shit,' Ryan mutters as he slams the door and scrambles after the whole mess, attempting to snatch what he can from the flurry around him. A page flutters past and I grab for it. Then a second one and soon I'm running after another. In a few seconds I've clawed a couple of handfuls out of the air but most of what blew out is gone for good. As the last of the loose leaves escapes across the grass, Ryan leans against his car, the back of his shirt plastered with sweat. 'Thanks,' he says, ruefully sorting through the crumpled mess, 'perfect start to the day, don't you think?'

His office is a confusion of bookcases, old couches and mementos, a messy collection of furniture and ornaments that somehow work together. Jen would call it random crap. To me it's comfortable, a bit like a lounge room. He uses a replica art deco lamp as a paperweight, attempting to flatten the pile out as best he can. I follow him in, dropping onto a faded leather couch as I look at the framed prints on the walls, mostly sixties movie posters with one exception. I point. 'That's new.'

'Do you like it?' He pulls an old tennis ball from its niche in a bookcase. 'Klimt, The Kiss. Very famous.'

I nod, smiling. I know it.

Thomas Ryan is a nice guy. Jen once told me she had a tiny crush on him. She was drunk at the time but I believe her. I can understand why. Thin, standing taller than me with friendly brown eyes and a ready smile, his longish hair is out of control and needs a trim. He always dresses well, but can't quite pull off that casual look and ends up scruffy. At first glance you'd think he'd be in his late thirties, older than me, but when you pay attention something in his eyes says otherwise. Younger, which is strange considering how long he's been my doctor. He pulls a phone from his pocket and throws it on the desk.

'Why all the paperwork?' I ask.

'Just catching up on things.'

'That's a lot of paper.' I get up from the couch, already cooler and calmer in the air-conditioned room, stretching to get a better view of the messy pile. The chaos of the airport is slowly slipping away. There's enough time to go over that disaster later. 'Have you ever heard of a computer?'

'No,' he says, 'what's that?' He leans back and motions to the mass of printed pages. 'I like hardcopies. Reading screens gives me a headache.'

'You're killing trees,' I say.

He shrugs. 'It's either them or me. Personally, I don't trust them.' I smile. 'So,' he goes on, grabbing the tennis ball and tossing it from hand to hand, 'You're stressed. What's up?'

'Nothing,' I lie, automatically feeling guilty. It's spooky sometimes the way he sees through me. 'I'm just the same old Alice, you know how it is.' I will tell him what happened at the airport, I promise myself, but not right now. It's not what it says about me, or any of that psychological rubbish, the fact is the whole thing's just plain embarrassing. I've had enough humiliation for one day.

He shrugs and goes to a corner nook where he turns on an old percolator, busying himself with the filter. 'Would you like some?' I nod as he prepares the coffee, seeing he already has two mugs out.

'Not much is going on,' I say to fill the silence. 'The shop's doing all right and Jen's fine. She's trying to get me to learn to surf again.' I laugh. Small. Nervous. New York-me would cringe.

'Maybe you should try,' he says.

'Not interested. I hate the water.'

He shrugs, pours the coffee and brings it over. 'Yes, it's good to avoid the things that challenge us.'

'Wow. Subtle.'

He sits opposite and grabs the ball again. 'You were traumatised by water when you were a child. We've gone over that. But you're not a kid anymore. Things change.'

'Yeah, well, I don't.' My cheeks flush. I can feel him reading me.

He watches me carefully for a moment over the steaming cup. 'Something's happened. Tell me about it.'

I sit back. 'How did you know?' He holds open his hands in an isn't it obvious gesture and I gather my thoughts before I speak. 'I tried to catch a flight to New York, but I couldn't go through with it. I had to call Jen to come and get me.'

'When?'

'Just before I came here.'

He pulls a pen from his pocket and makes a note. 'Why did you think you needed to travel to New York this morning?'

I close my eyes and wonder what it would be like to sleep. Really sleep. 'I don't know. The day started normally enough. Nothing bad happened. Nothing good either. After I left the house I began wondering. If I go there I might be able to prove she isn't real. By not finding her, it would be like proving I'm real instead. At the time it felt right.'

'That was a big decision. Has something changed?'

I open my eyes. 'New York-me, she's getting crazy.'

He takes a sip of the coffee. 'In what way?'

'She cut herself again. Almost caused a riot at some sleazy club.' I laugh, another uncertain sound. God, the other Alice would hate this. 'Don't you ever wish you were dealing with her instead? She's more interesting. You'd have a lot more fun.'

Ryan stares at me over his notes, becoming very schoolteacherly. 'That requires me living in a fantasy land, which to be honest knowing my own imagination, would be quite boring. Anyway, you're my client. It would be unprofessional.' He smiles. 'Why do you think she's more interesting?'

'Oh, come on,' I say. 'Are you serious? The girl's a nutcase. It's obvious.' I put down my cup as my attention's drawn back to the pile on his desk. 'You shouldn't print out so much paper.'

He follows my gaze. 'You're avoiding the question.'

'I'm not very interesting,' I say quietly. 'Other Alice does all the exciting stuff. She's crazy, but at least she's doing things. I just thought if I could be more like her and take charge for once, then perhaps...I don't know.' I look away. 'I want this to end.'

He flips a page on the notebook as he checks against some old notes. That's got to be for show; he knows me. 'She's also self-destructive.'

'Well yes,' I say, 'but she's so driven. When I dream her, the world's this dark place, but I'm even darker and I make it mine.'

'Do you want to be more like her?' Ryan sips his coffee again, eyes bright as he waits on my answer. I shift uncomfortably.

'We've talked about this before.'

He nods. 'Yes, but people change. Their emotional situations change, and if that situation is manifested in a dream, it doesn't mean it's less valid.'

'She's not changing though, not really. Sometimes she's extreme.' I find myself staring at the palm of my hand. 'And sometimes she's not. Last night was, extreme.' He's about to say something but I keep going. 'She cut herself, but she's done it before. I've told you that.' I point at the table. 'You'll have the notes. Yes, sometimes I do want to be more like her. She's free. Write that down. It's good.' Smiling, Ryan scribbles something in his book. I lean back.

'Well,' he says, 'from what I hear it doesn't seem like she has any more freedom than you do, possibly less even. You've got the better deal here.'

'Isn't this a bit academic?' I say, staring at the ceiling. 'I'm stuck with this. This is who I am.'

'People can change.'

'Not this people.'

'I think you can.'

I sit forward, feeling the heat on my face growing. It's like being a schoolgirl with him sometimes. 'You think I want to stay this way?'

He regards me carefully. 'No, and that's why you keep pushing. Take today for example. What stopped you from getting on the plane this time?'

'I had a panic attack. I wasn't ready.'

'And how many attempts is this?' he asks quietly.

'You know the answer. This one makes four.'

He puts the pen down on the table. The movement is careful, precise in a way his appearance and office aren't. I wonder, not for the first time, how much of the real Ryan I ever see. 'You keep that up and you'll get arrested.'

'I know.'

'One day you will be ready, but when you are it won't be a spur of the moment thing.'

'Maybe.' I'm not convinced.

There's a long drawn out silence, punctuated by the clicking of his pen as he picks it up and underlines something in his book. 'We may want to review your medication again,' he says. He catches my objection before I find the words. 'Just for the time being.'

I rub my head as memories of years of consultations, tests and meetings flash through my mind. I've run the gamut of professionals from social workers to neuropsychologists and have been diagnosed with everything from Insomnia to Schizophrenia to a rare depersonalisation disorder. My illness made me the poster girl of the psych-scene and if it hadn't been for Jen and then much later, Ryan, I'm sure I'd still be hooked up to FMRIs and other frankenstein machines to this day. I despise it.

'No.'

Ryan takes my hand. His touch is startling, dry and warm. I know what other-Alice would do with those hands. 'It is possible to get through this, if we work together. You can change.'

A moment drags out between us. I look down. 'Why do you say that?'

'Because you're still here. When you go to sleep you dream another life. In one sense, you never sleep. Anyone who can survive that is a fighter.'

'She's the fighter.'

'She's you.'

'It's not that easy.'

Shaking his head, Ryan lets go and leans away. 'Who said easy? Not me.'

I peer at the wall clock, another art deco thing, as I stand. 'No, I get that you're trying to help, but no. No more drugs.' He stands as well as I make for the door, walking quickly. 'Look,' I say, 'it's under control, OK? Don't worry about the airport thing. Just a little flip out.'

'Our session's not over.'

I glance at my watch.

'You have to stop running, Alice.'

'No,' I say from the door, 'it's OK, I'm running late. So, next time, yeah?'

He nods. 'OK. Next time. Alice?'

'Yes?'

'Call me anytime if you need to talk, even if you don't think it's important.'

I leave quickly, watching him watching me as I close the door behind myself.

8

SANCTUARY

It's so hot, even in the bus.

It pulls up at the stop with an engine-clicking shudder, its brakes squealing in the heat. The doors screech open, leaving me standing at the entrance to a furnace. This day has it in for me.

A tattered poster on a wall snaps crazily as the wind buffets my dress again. Small dusty eddies join up to form a whirlwind of trash that races down the street, blowing rubbish everywhere. I follow, turning thankfully away from the road and into the cobblestone lane where my shop is. The wind is quieter here, but it still tugs at awnings and rocks signboards.

The alley is quiet: what few customers we get have been beaten away by this incendiary weather. The lane is called Warehouse Alley, but everyone here calls it Echo Street, due to it being pretty much empty most of the time. It's not as bad as it sounds. We get by. I've only ever seen one junkie. Sandwiched between a bulk goods warehouse on one side and a low-rise shopping centre on the other, most of the shops in the alley are small specialty places, like mine and Jen's. There's Looking Books, a second hand book shop; Michel's Fresh Produce; the Nick-Nackery; and then Brundford Flowers where Jen will be climbing the walls. I detour into Aroma, the bakery/cafe opposite us, and grab an ice-coffee for her.

Loaded up with my peace offering I head to my place, my sanctuary. Coming here is more than special, it's coming home. Every time I open the door I'm struck by the explosion of greens and rich earthy smells, the muted restfulness and the beautiful quiet of it all. The ancient brass bell jangles as I balance the drinks I've bought. Allowing myself a moment to breathe in the richness of the place I feel the stress of the day slipping away. One minute here is worth a week of Ryan. Dusty, diffuse light filters through the riot of flowers and decorative ferns. I turn to watch a few pedestrians move like old blurry prints past the two huge frosted windows at the front of our shop. The sounds and heat of the outside world are softened here.

There's a gigantic red jarrah workbench near the back, almost as wide as our whole building, with just a small space to walk around. Jen thinks it's too big but I disagree — anyway the smell of the oiled wood is amazing. Rows of different coloured roses intermingled with long stemmed Singapore Orchids and gerberas line the far side, making the hard red wood lush. Ferns hang from trellises on either side of the store. I can breathe here.

Jen nods at me briefly as she wraps a bouquet for a customer, handing over the flowers and ringing up the sale on our old electric cash register. As the man heads towards the door she glances meaningfully at the clock above the windows. Jen and I have a deal with the shop. I run it and she handles the bookwork, or at least that's the plan. Sometimes like today she ends up doing a bit of both.

'Sorry. I know,' I say, handing over the coffee, 'the bus was running behind.'

She pops the till open, grabs some cash and disappears into the tiny storeroom out the back. 'Don't sweat it,' she calls out, 'I guessed you'd be late. Did you figure out what happened this morning?' I don't answer. 'Well, I'm off. I'm going to hit the beach. Want to come later?' I smile, dropping my bag on the bench.

'Sure. After I close up.'

'So, how did it go?' Jen asks as she emerges from the room.

I shrug. 'He wants to review my medication.'

'Which means he's out of ideas.'

I think about that. 'It won't happen again.'

She hugs me quickly, sticking a straw into her carton of ice-coffee. 'I say shake it off babe.'

'Yeah.' If only.

'Anyway, Mrs Delmore is due in later to pick up her order. Birthday Arrangement. Don't forget. And I told Ralph Murchison the corsages will be ready for tomorrow morning.' I nod. 'And you'll have to mop up behind the fridge. Damn thing's leaking again and the service guy hasn't turned up. And Alice?'

'Uh huh?'

'I'm going to John's tonight. Don't wait up.' She shuts the door with a slutty grin. I follow her silhouette through the window before settling back to stare at the flowers.

The shop is a magic place. The minutes turn into a heavy sap that flows slow and thick through the day. The hands of the clock freeze for hours then jump when I'm not looking, propellers on a little boat of uneven time. The sun becomes even hotter and there are no customers. This must be like sleeping.

Later on I move slowly to an alcove at the back of the store and turn on our ancient computer, waiting for the tired screen to warm up, fans somewhere in the box whining in the heat. A search engine pops open and I type the same old questions — Van de Korte Health: nothing. Alice Van de Korte: several close matches, but none of the woman in my dream. I follow a digital trail leading nowhere and end up walking away.

Maybe my brain is melting in all this heat. A memory surfaces from the time I went to New York: I could almost touch her, that other me. It sent me crazy: the closeness to her made me feel trapped on the wrong side of a mirror. I remember going to Central Park and scratching marks in a tree, then searching for them as I dreamed my other life. They weren't there, of course. I was scrawling on the face of a perfect, slick illusion that could never be my reality. I got sick and Dream-me was scornful. She even organised a Crazy Tour for a friend and retraced the paths I'd taken searching for her. But underneath all that she was thinking the same thing: she was awake and nothing could ever cross over. Ever. And then Jen flew over to save me.

Shapes of people move outside.

The clock jumps again and I'm staring at the reflection of my eyes in the blade of a utility knife. I'm not afraid of it like I sometimes am. I lower it and redraw the sharp tip over the wet, ridged surface of the bench. The scoring is deep and drops of water reflect darkly in the cut I've made. The shop is empty and silent except for the whine of the broken fridge and intermittent drips from a feeder. Street sounds are muffled and unreal. Pedestrians, silhouettes now in the afternoon light, walk to and fro in front of the windows, oblivious to my quiet observation.

What am I doing? I put the knife down, careful to avoid that keen edge. I'm not back to normal and that worries me. I could call Ryan but I don't know what I should tell him. God, I'm so messed up today. I stare at the clock and it's four thirty. I've lost the day somehow. Closing the shop I clean up, collecting buckets of roses and other flowers. I turn again to the window, distracted by the people-shapes moving past without stopping, thinking they may as well be projections. It hits me that this has to be the dream and if I went outside right now it would be into a street full of cardboard cut-outs. I could scream.

The door opens and I fall backward with a cry. A rounded woman in her mid fifties, loaded down with plastic shopping bags stares at me in shock. I get back to my feet with an embarrassed smile. 'You all right, love?' she says.

'Sorry,' I say, putting down my load, 'I'm fine. I was somewhere else for a moment. Can I help you?'

The woman shoves the door shut. 'The name's Delmore. I'm here for my order.'

Oh.

My heart is loud in my chest and I find myself fighting for a breath. It's the airport all over again. A crazy response and I hate myself for it, but knowing what's going on isn't the same as being able to stop it. I wipe my head, trying not to appear flustered. What is happening today?

'Mrs Delmore? There's been a mix up,' I say, 'it's not ready yet. I'm sorry.' For a strange moment I imagine her going mad in this heat and shoving me against the counter, yelling. It gets hard to breathe. The woman heaves up her bags and looks at her watch.

'I was told it would be ready by two.'

'Yes,' I say trying to force a rhythm into my breathing, 'but we've been run off our feet.' I push inside myself and hold this stupid overreaction down. I can't let this turn on me.

Mrs Delmore looks pointedly around the empty shop. 'Actually,' she says, 'don't worry about it. It's getting late anyway. I'd like my money back please.'

'If you give me a few minutes,' I say putting the buckets aside as I head to the safety of the counter, 'I'm sure I can get something together for you.' I stumble over the words, fighting to appear calm. I know how flushed I look.

'No, it's all right dear. I just want a refund. It's too hot to wait around today.' She pauses, then mops her own forehead. 'This heat is such a killer. You look flushed.'

'I'm OK.' The last thing I want is more sympathy. 'I'm sorry about the mix-up.' I ring up a no-sale. She takes the cash and turns, jarring the bell as she leaves the shop. I pull out a tissue and dab down my face. What a screw up.

As I go back to the alcove and switch off the computer I spot a film of water on the floor near the fridge. 'Damn,' I whisper.

My fingers slide across the smooth paint of the fridge. There's no way I can even budge it, let alone move it away from the wall. The old white kelvinator is packed with stock, solid and heavy as a safe. I grunt again with effort but the thing isn't going anywhere. Giving up on moving the monster I flatten myself on the tiles, hopeful of spotting something underneath. Nothing but water and dark. I listen for a drip. Not even that. 'Damn.'

Cursing, I jam wads of rolled up paper towels under the machine, hoping I'm not about to cause an electrical fire. Should I turn off the power? But then the stock will spoil. I have to leave it on. I don't need to look at the clock again to know it's far too late to call in another repair man.

Well you know what? Today's officially a write-off. I give up, grab my bag and walk to the door, closing it on a very crappy day.

9

BEACH

I love the beach but I hate the water. One of those weird tensions we get in life, I guess. Oily waves curl shoreward beneath a startling red sky, made all the more threatening by towering rim-lit clouds. The sea booms as breakers crash over one another in the dying light. I pick my way over sand that stings my feet with leftover heat towards Jen's usual spot. I can see her kneeling, hair free, wearing her new wetsuit. She waxes her board conscientiously, long rhythmic motions. She looks at prayer.

'Jen!'

She glances up at me and waves as I jog the rest of the way, distracted for a moment as someone offshore yells out. As I squint in the half-light a surfer loses control and disappears into the barrel of dark green wave. Ignoring the temperature around my feet I scan the foam for a sign they've come back up. Nothing. I blink in the wind, waiting. Some part of me is counting. How many seconds can someone stay underwater?

'Alice.'

Jen points to a man wading hip deep through the backwash as he tows his surfboard by the ankle strap, laughing with a friend.

'He's all right.'

Jen gets back to work on her board and flashes me a smile. 'They say you don't really have to wax these things anymore.'

'I didn't know that.'

'Yeah. Well, I say what do they know, right? It's all about feel. Screw 'em sideways.'

I have to smile.

'So how did it go this afternoon?'

'Slow day.'

'Fair enough.' She throws the wax back into her backpack and straps on the leash. 'I've got a surprise for you.'

Oh. I put on my best smile. 'Really?'

Jen grins. 'Yup. You and me, we're going on a date.'

I don't get it. She must see my reaction because she stands and whacks me in the arm.

'A blind date, stupid. I've set it for tomorrow.'

I start automatically making excuses before she's even finished speaking. 'No ifs, no buts,' she says, 'we're doing it. It'll get you out of your own head and do you some good.' Before I can say anything more she nods at the water. 'So, are you going to give it a shot today?'

I won't fight her about the date but there's no way I'm going in the sea. 'Not my thing, but knock yourself out.'

'Go on. Give it a go.'

'I'm not dressed for it.'

'I've got a spare wetsuit in my bag. My old one. You'll fit. Come on. The water's freezing. You'll love it.' She grabs at me. This is an old game. I laugh and let her pull me to the edge of the surf. The water washes clouds of foam up the sand as a surge covers my toes. I scream at the shock of it. It's cold all right.

'Far enough!'

'You're not even in the water,' yells Jen, 'come on!' I stop and, still smiling, back away from the shore, letting her carry on. 'Well, one day you'll see sense,' she calls out as she moves further into the wash.

My smile fades as I backtrack onto the looser, hotter sand. Jen thinks she really will get me in. It's not going to happen, but she doesn't know that. I come here to spend time with her despite it. I love to watch her surf. She's so free when she's in the waves. 'Sorry Jen,' I call back. 'Can't do it.'

'Jeeze girl, stop apologising all the time.'

'Sorry.'

She stops as a surge of foam buffets her legs and drags at the board. 'You sure? It's not as terrifying as you think.'

'It's exactly as terrifying as I think.'

'Well you did OK. At least you got your toes wet.' Jen dips into the water and emerges, hair dripping. The fading sun throws a faint watery shadow away from her almost to my feet.

'Maybe next time.'

'Yeah,' she says. 'got to get in while there's still some light left. Wish me luck for tonight.'

'John?'

'Who else baby?'

She splashes away as I wave. 'Good luck,' I call out but Jen is already gone. That's OK. I go back to higher ground and sit down, waiting for her.

10

THE STORM

Those clouds I talked about earlier turn out to be a storm front. Heavy rain lashes at the windows while lightning spikes the sky in brilliant shotgun flashes. The old house settles with creaks and pipework clanks, echoing the thunder. After a day like this, the storm seems right.

I examine the face in the bathroom mirror, ignoring the light show outside, a toothbrush sticking out of my mouth. My Donald Duck T-shirt is completely out of place on someone with my baggy eyes. I'm exhausted. Rinsing, I grab a bottle, undo it and place two sleeping pills on my tongue, swallowing them dry. That face in the mirror scares me. I sometimes wonder if I'm actually looking at her. The part that freaks me out is she thinks the same thing. Maybe I'm haunted, or possessed. 'Go away,' I whisper. I put my hand against my reflection. 'You are not me.' Before I can change my mind I spill out a fistful of pills, swallowing each of them in turn. I know how much is too much and this isn't it. Not quite. There's still hope that tonight might be the night I get to sleep. I haven't given up.

I walk on autopilot from the bathroom, switching off lights as I go. Somewhere along the way I scoop up Ratbone from the couch, holding him in the crook of my arm like a toy. The cat purrs loudly, enjoying the attention as I drop him on my bed, my head swimming. I blink slowly as I lean against my pillow and stare at the thunderstorm outside. I hope Jen's having a good time.

Rivulets of water run down the glass.

Outside lightning strikes a power pole and the room lights up like it's morning.

11

ACHES AND PAINS

I still hear the thunder echoing when I slip out of bed and go to the curtains, completely forgetting about my hand as I pull them back. The cut opens and I gasp in pain. Outside, the park is so shrouded in low cold cloud I can barely make out anything through the grey. For a second I imagine it sunny and in bloom, thronging with visitors, but the fantasy vanishes as quickly as it came. There's a bloody smear of my handprint on the curtain and turning back to the bed I spot ropey black bloodstains on the linen where I must have got caught up. It looks like someone's been murdered here. The cleaner's going to have a fit.

A dull ache begins to replace the insane pain from a few moments ago but it still hurts like nothing else. I'm relieved I haven't cut a nerve. It was such a stupid thing to do. But even with the injury I've got to smile; it nearly sent Ms Purer-than-Pure right over the edge. I wonder what it would take to tip her over. Not so much, I guess. It could be fun, sending that little mad piece of my unconscious even madder, but I'm not going to do it. I don't mind in principle, only that dedicating time to an imaginary, well, lets not say friend exactly, strikes me as a teeny bit obsessive. Then there's that other thing. She might be right. I may be the dream.

I open a bottle of iodine from the first aid kit in the bathroom and pour it across the wound. Jesus that hurts. The pain I mentioned before? That was a warm-up. The liquid stains my hand a dark and unhealthy orange. For a moment there I might pass out, but I bite down on my lip and concentrate until the fire rilling through my nerves is manageable. Then I do it all over again until the bottle is empty.

I give myself a second to recover before pulling out a gauze bandage and wrapping it up the best I can, bite the end of the material free. Before I know it I collapse back against the wall and force myself to breathe through a dizzy spell. Somewhere along the line I've also picked up a mother of a hangover. The day is shaping up well.

The phone starts ringing in the kitchen, which is as good a reason as any to get moving. Standing, I walk stiffly back through the bedroom on legs that feel like they belong to a stranger, grabbing a tee as I go. Throwing it on, I stop as I catch sight of it in the bathroom mirror. It's an old shirt — one of Gabe's from when he took Jordie to Disneyland. Donald Duck stares back at me.

Shit.

I get a shiver. I'm not into voodoo or I-Chi or signs but for a heartbeat it's like I've been picked up and dropped in the middle of my own dream. It's the weirdest thing. I wonder for a second what Sydney-me would make of this. But only a second. That stuff will send you crazy. I go to the kitchen to find out who's called.

It turns out I've also got a text message from Julian, a guy I work with down at the Collective. It's a small group of lawyers and activists I sometimes volunteer for, mostly concentrating on bailing out protestors and giving some free legal advice. A way to put my expensive law degree to good use, it's also a jab at the embodiment of all-things-commercial: my family. It pisses off my parents no end. I text a reply and promise to follow up with a problem he's having.

The voicemail is from Gabe. I start listening to it; God I love his voice. His accent is somewhere between Paris and Brooklyn; exotic with an edge — sexy. It's the first thing about him that attracted me. I met him at a gallery opening in the Lower East Side where he was showing some of his work. He'd only been in the States a couple of years and we hit it off. We've been seeing each other on and off since then, more on than off. As the message goes on he starts explaining about a problem he's having at his new gallery and begins to sound stressed.

I pause the playback and make myself a strong, black coffee. I'm not ready for this yet. As I lean against the marble counter I bring to mind her kitchen, so different to mine. Everything's got its story, a personal history. I can't even remember buying some of the things here. I probably didn't. When I moved in I hired a guru designer called Sam Millner to set the place up, including getting most of the stuff in front of me right now. After he was done he wanted to shoot it for a magazine and we ended up sleeping together. It was fun while it lasted.

The phone rings again and I ignore it. I haven't finished my coffee yet. I like Gabe a lot but I'm not his mother. Sometimes, like the time I first met him, he burns so bright it's amazing, but at others he can turn moody and dark. Right now he's moving between the two. My cup tastes of old cigarettes and booze. And as for what Gabe sees in me, — that's more interesting.

I glance across the open plan kitchen to the lounge and into my own eyes. My portrait, a grainy moment caught in high contrast black and white, stares back at me. There's a sadness to it. I look like a refugee, half turned away from the lens, frozen in the second between leaving and staying. I keep it there on the wall for him, not for me. It doesn't bother me like it did in the early days, but I still don't like the eyes. One morning after we'd woken up in his apartment, he'd asked me about my Sydney self. I told him and he said I had two souls, then took that picture.

The message plays out in that confused stream of consciousness he gets when he's talking to a machine. He's nervous. He's exhibiting his work in three days and something's gone wrong at the gallery. I clear the message and slide onto a barstool, flicking on the TV in the corner of the room just in time to catch a round-faced morning show host segue into the weather for the city, which will be cold. Of course.

I sit through a commercial before checking out the refrigerator. It isn't looking good. It won't get restocked until tomorrow so it's down to a three-quarters empty bottle of juice or something in a can. I choose the juice. Halfway through fighting the stuck lid I'm drawn back to the show. In society news, a grand gala is to be hosted by Mattiew Van de Korte, founder of Van de Korte Health to mark the imminent retirement of longstanding employee, Olen Canders. The event is invitation only and it's expected the who's who of business, entertainment and politics will be attending. Back to camera B and the co-host quips something about her missing invite. I shake my head. Whoever this Canders guy is, the shindig won't be for him. My parents don't have enough room in their egos for that. I kill the TV, feeling a familiar old slow burn.

It turns out the juice is thick and exactly what I need and I drain the bottle as I head into the lounge, looking at the traces of snow falling outside. To the left, my portrait stares emptily back. 'Screw them,' I say aloud.

Flopping onto a chair, I pull out the phone and hit Gabe's number. The connection's about to ring out when Jordie, his son, answers. Yeah, meeting Jordie for the first time was a surprise. 'Hello?'

'Hey,' I say, forcing a brightness into my voice I don't feel, 'Jordie, it's Alice, is your dad about?' The phone on the other end of the line gets muddy as he cups his hands over the receiver.

'Dad,' screams Jordie, 'for you! Some girl.'

Gabe picks up. 'Gabe, it's Alice,' I say, 'I need a favour.'

'Baby, it's not a great time right now,' he says, sounding exhausted. 'There's a shitstorm going down at the gallery and no fucker's owning it. Someone put reflective glass over the prints and when the lights are on you can't see a damned thing. What am I meant to be, a picture framer now? Jesus!'

'So why did you call me?' I say flatly. 'I'm coming over. We can commiserate together.' The line goes silent for a moment as he thinks about it. I can't believe it. First he leaves a message on my service like some broken-hearted teenager but when I need something it's a bad time. And now my hand is hurting again. 'Well screw you too,' I say.

'Whoa whoa whoa, baby,' he says, colour entering his voice, 'chill lady. Yeah, come over. I was only venting. Relax.'

'Good. I'll come around later then.'

I hang up and slope back into the chair, eyes on nothing in particular. You know what? I could really use a pick-me-up. Plus, my personal oracle owes me a refund. I just wish he lived in a better part of town.

12

RENE'S PLACE

Sometimes you do the wrong thing. You know it's wrong even when you're doing it but you go right ahead anyway. Being here is one of those things.

The taxi driver doesn't waste time getting the hell out after I pay despite the tip I just gave him and telling him to wait. I'm not surprised. The freezing South Bronx air isn't taking any prisoners either as I pull my coat tighter. Regardless of the ice it's not cold enough to hide the stink of piss and dead things coming from the elevated rail behind me and I shiver. I get out a cigarette and light up, trying to look like I fit in.

The sky is the dirty grey of old linen. Low clouds hang above the run-down apartment blocks and either someone's got a movie turned up way too loud or else I'm listening to some guy getting the crap beaten out of him. Across the road a burned-out car stumped up on cinderblocks sits with its hood open. It looks like a mouth. I take a drag and brace myself against the cold. God I hate the cold.

A dusting of dirty snow covers everything, sour looking in this light. There's a mostly abandoned apartment block at the end of the street with broken windows open to the air. I've seen people move around there and I wonder how they survive. The taxi dropped me off near the boarded up shell of an old gas station and I can see gang markings all over it. Someone's pulled off the boards around the windows and moved in. A couple of kids dressed in colours watch me from the concrete apron, biding their time. I get moving. I should be all right.

This is a bad place to be a skinny white girl all by herself. Unless she's on her way to meet Rene, that is. I've no idea how they know, but somehow Rene's guests are out of bounds. Maybe he keeps the gangs on a payroll. Dead or raped clients made for bad business after all. I wonder how deep his roots run in this place and I wouldn't be surprised if he owned half the borough.

A train bursts past, setting loose a surge of brown slush from the line. I step away from the mess which is already refreezing on the sidewalk, ignoring the stink of ozone and metal. As I move, my foot kicks something soft and I pull back, hoping I haven't trodden on a dead animal. But it's not; instead a teddy bear stares at me from the ground, its tiny black eyes shiny and clear in the cold.

I find toys. They find me. Whatever. I don't get how, but it happens. Maybe I'm just sensitive to them. Some people get ghosts; I get toys. Maybe there's a joke in there somewhere but if there is, it's over my head. I talked about it to Gabe once, but all he did was nod like it made sense. He'd been stoned off his face courtesy of another one of Rene's special brews and told me it must have been karma or some shit. Not so helpful.

Perhaps it's simple, one of those situations where the more you try not to see something the more you do. Either way it's been a thing in my life forever. If I searched around right now, I'd find more. They'll be there somewhere, hiding in the shade or poking out from a dumpster, dropped and forgotten on the sidewalk, left on the seat of a diner. They are my personal shadows; bears, dolls, toy cars, windups, you name it. Right now though I don't have time for it. My hand hurts like hell and the hangover is taking care of the rest of my body. The bear can stay there. I kick it away and walk on.

Three- storey tenement houses line the west side of the street, some with flags hanging dead in the cold air. I find the one I'm looking for and head towards it. It's dilapidated and filthy, exactly like all the others except for the small kid standing vigilant and alone on the lowest step. Every month or two Rene relocates. It beats me how he does it, but I doubt I've been in the same place more than three times. The only way to tell is to look out for the boy.

I go cautiously up to him and he stares at me with a strange knowing expression. The kid is new, but his smugness isn't. Dressed in jeans and a thin oversized hoodie, he seems tiny and out of place. 'Hey kid,' I say as I get close enough to be heard. He glares back. 'Aren't you cold?'

'Aren't you hot?' He sounds Russian.

I shrug that off. 'Is Rene inside?'

'Who's Rene?'

'Stop dicking with me,' I say, 'is he in or not?'

'Who's asking?'

'Alice.'

'Alice who?'

'Just Alice.'

He flips open a tattered school notebook and checks a list of names by the margin. 'Rene is always inside,' He says, shutting it before I can read anything. He nods at the door, which is missing its street number. The kid is meant to be a distraction. Once or twice I've spotted someone else in the shadows, lurking in the lee of the drug store or sitting near the abandoned car. I've never seen guns but sure as sure they're there; that kid's schoolbook list can bring down a ton of grief on the poor schmuck whose name isn't in it. I wink at him and climb the steps but he moves quickly, getting under my feet. 'Hey lady.' I stop. He glances at the cigarette. 'Get rid of that crap, it'll kill you.'

'Yeah well,' I say pushing past him, 'this is me not giving a shit.'

'Cynicism is the refuge of the sorrowful,' he calls back as I walk through the door. I stop.

'What did you say?'

He stares at me for a moment, nothing moving but the fog of his breath. 'I said,' he replies, 'get inside biatch.' Freaky goddam kid.

13

PERFORMANCE PIECE

The heat is molten in here and I ditch my jacket in a hurry. I'm in a narrow, dark hallway and I can't see the floor as the only light is from a frosted window above, but that's just as well because the carpet sticks to my feet as I walk over it. I'm glad it's half invisible. A strange mashup of Bob Marley and some techno synth pumps from somewhere up ahead and I make for that. As I turn a corner I pass a man in a bright yellow suit and we avoid each others' eyes. An unwritten rule of Rene's house: no fraternising.

The hallway ends at a blotchy red door and I pause for a moment, sweat already plastering the shirt to my back. What is his deal keeping the place so hot? I suck it up and knock, trying not to be reminded of the heat in my Sydney dream. Coincidences freak me out.

'Alice darlin',' calls a voice, 'do come in.'

The living room is huge, dark and smokey, stinking of weed and other things. It's filled with ancient furniture, odd brass ornaments, lead crystal lamps and struggling, pale plants lining the walls like a miniature sooty forest. The smells come at me with physical force, a jungle of ash, spilled spirits, incense and sex. And there, sprawled in front of me, reclining on the couch and smoking a Hookah is Rene, somehow pulling off that Sheik of all Junkies look he's made his own.

I can't imagine how he manages to survive, living in this darkness. It's not just this place; every house is always the same. Sure the furniture changes, but the stink and God-awful heat doesn't. He can't be human. The thing about Rene is he's not your normal everyday dealer. He used to be a chemist. Now, I don't want to know what he is.

He moves hugely, causing creases of white flesh to fall over one another in a slow ripple of skin on skin. He's wearing a massive, stained Hawaiian shirt that disappears into the great folds of his gut. Faded grey cargo pants split along their seams; defeated by the bulk of his thighs. His feet are clad in tartan slippers too small to be anything other than ornaments. I nod to him, then to be safe, to the pretty things he's keeping either side.

To his left, a dark—haired tightly sculpted guy, mid twenties; and to his right, a woman, same age, I guess. I've got to give it to Rene — he can pick his playmates; they're both beautiful but opposite in every other sense. I get the feeling it's more about aesthetics than sex. The man's skin is midnight black with tight cropped black hair and tighter muscles. He stretches catlike in front of me. He's dressed in skintight latex pants that cling in all the right places. On the other side of Rene, the woman is pale as a vampire. It takes me a few seconds to realise she's humming. The sound gets into my head; a toneless drone that somehow cuts through the music. It rattles me. She's wearing this tiny clinging thing that shows way more than it covers and her body is rounded where her partner's is angular, smooth where his is sharp. She looks blank while the man nods to me with a kind of conspiratorial acknowledgement, the corner of his lips sliding into a sneer. Both their eyes are wide and only just this side of wild, cruising on some heavy shit.

They are mysteries. Judging by the way the guy is staring the feeling's mutual. Again I get the sense this isn't about sex. Rene, bless him, has tried every perversion in the book and that would be too simple.

'Do you like them?' says Rene in a register much tighter and higher than you'd think should come from someone his size. He grins at me, his brown eyes hidden behind small circular glasses, his blonde dreadlocks lolling. I shrug.

'Who are they?'

'Friends.' He gets thoughtful. 'Friends of friends actually. Party people.'

'Get rid of the boy,' I say after a reflective moment, sweat running into my eyes. Shit, my head is beginning to swim. 'He's an asshole.' The man glares at me.

Rene laughs, causing a landslide of flesh to readjust itself. 'And what can I do for you today, love?'

'A pick-me-up,' I say. 'And don't give me any more of the rubbish from yesterday. I don't know what you put in it but it bites.' I wipe my face, trying to focus despite the music that has grown louder. 'I want a discount.'

He shrugs massively, disturbing his two ornaments. 'I'm not a scientist. I brew my potions with love, lovey, but the final trip is always yours. You get me?' He smiles. It isn't a pretty thing. 'Time is a one-way street. No backsies.' He raises his hands, great paddles of flesh. A gesture of hopelessness.

I shake my head. 'Whatever.' The music combined with the mystery-weed burning elsewhere in the house is giving me a headache. I shouldn't have come to him today, not after the last twenty-four hours, but I'm going to need his special brand of help to get through tonight.

'Welcome to the looking glass, by the way,' he continues, previous discussion over, 'do you want them to perform? They are very talented. Better than TV.' I glance around and spot a gorgeous blonde sitting on a small barstool behind me. He's got a notebook, like the boy outside. I wonder what kind of ledger he keeps, because with Rene, it's all cash up front and no favours. 'Don't mind Ezekiel,' Rene says, 'he's being sullen today.' Ezekiel nods silently to me. I've seen him once or twice before and we exchange a weird glance.

My headache's getting worse by the second. 'Look Rene,' I say, 'I don't have time for games today, OK?'

He interrupts, raising his hand. On cue, the woman shrugs easily from her gown and slithers naked across his body towards her opposite who twists to face her. Rene's eyes flare and his expression is unreadable as she strokes the bulk of his stomach.

'Now you're being an asshole,' I say. Rene murmurs to himself as the man carefully and teasingly gets rid of his clothes as well.

On another day, a day when my hand wasn't killing me and a headache wasn't splitting my head open, I'm not sure how this might have played out. Getting messed up with one of Rene's experiments is always bad news and this is double that. 'Do you put on this performance for all your clients or just me?' I could have been a little turned on, I decide.

'Only those with potential,' answers Rene, his breathing becoming faster. Screw it. Today's today and yesterday's a dream. I can get what I want somewhere else without these mind games. I turn to go, the incredible furnace heat of the house and beating music washing over me in waves. 'You may have one of them if you like,' he offers through shuttered eyelids. 'Choose your poison.'

'What's your problem?' I sound angrier than I am. I want to be out of here.

'Hmm,' he teases, 'I peg you for' — ' He snaps his fingers over the woman's head and she turns languidly towards me. Her eyes are a piercing green, almost like my Sydney self. I'm shocked I missed that before.

I blink away some sweat in this insane heat. Rene — always messing with your mind. 'Not interested.'

'What a shame,' and he pouts. 'I'm usually a very good judge of character.' The woman returns her focus to the man who reaches for her breasts, cupping them in his hands.

I notice someone's changed the music and I reach out to steady myself as a wave of dizziness passes. Something inside shifts. I stare frankly at the couple who are now kissing deeply, both of them leaning over Rene, who with head tilted back exposes an acreage of fatty jowls. The woman's hands quest into Rene's pants, groping for a growing bulge. I wipe the sweat from my face again. I should be gone by now, but I'm caught. Watching Rene's peepshow is like looking at a car crash. It's impossible to turn away. 'You know what I'm here for.'

'Yes,' he breathes, 'do you?'

'Fuck this,' I whisper. 'Enjoy your orgy.'

An unpleasant expression crosses his face as he flips his head forward to stare at me. 'Everything in its own time, lovey.' Ezekiel steps quietly in front of me, blocking the exit. Shit. I don't know any way out of here except through that door. 'I have something to show you,' Rene says. 'Ezekiel?' Ezekiel reaches down to a cracked wooden credenza and opens one of the doors. It jams and he pulls hard to get it open. It's difficult to see in the smokey twilight of the room, but I can make out a single plastic bag. I didn't realise my heart was beating so fast before, but now my pulse is loud in my ears. He shakes it, knocking loose some of the powder inside. I reach for it but Ezekiel is too quick, grabbing it before I close the distance.

'So how much?' I ask, more than a little relieved to be finally getting down to business and perhaps not being murdered. Jesus. I promise myself I am never coming back no matter how good his shit is.

Rene reclines, luxuriating in the performance, causing the couch to creak. Both the albino and her friend begin to turn their attentions to him as he sprawls hugely, arms wrapped around either one. He grins like a maniac, sporting a huge boner.

'You're disgusting.'

'Allow an old man his fun.'

'What's in the bag?'

'Rene's very special homebrew. Very, very, very good.'

'How much?'

He leans back even further, staring at the naked bulb in the ceiling. 'Not for sale.'

'You're joking.'

'Yes, you're right. But you can't afford it anyway.' He allows a moan to escape as the man and woman work to undo his trousers. 'Ah what the fuck, we're all friends. Join us,' he breathes, 'and you can have it for free.'

I look away, sick of the games and exhausted. 'Go to hell. You're not even real. You know that? You're just one messed up friggin' neurone getting its rocks off.'

Rene laughs, the clarity of his voice startling his playmates who back off uncertainly. 'Darlin, I'm the realest thing in the room and don't you forget it.'

Yeah, well, I don't care. I push past Ezekiel, my head spinning in this insane heat. He makes no move to stop me, thank God. 'Keep your circus Rene, I really don't need this.'

He sits forward. Without warning he shrugs off the man, kicking at him as he lands on the floor. The woman slides away from him and hits the ground with a stupid, fleshy bump. For a moment they seem scared, then whatever's rocking their world blisses them out all over again. It's obscene. 'You really do, you just don't realise it yet.'

'How much?'

'Like I said. You can't afford it.' He starts laughing. A pure, happy, even beautiful sound. I don't know what's going on, but that's it. It was stupid coming here again but I'm done. I throw open the door, stumbling against a wall as I leave.

I catch a glimpse of him laughing from the couch as his pretty things get off the floor and redouble their efforts, feverish and heated, desperate. Sounds of cloth tearing and a giggle drift after me. 'Come back when you need what I have,' he calls after me in that peculiar high-pitched voice.

I explode from the door, gasping from the heat and stench. As my head slowly clears I notice the kid staring up at me. 'What?' He pulls a small plastic bag from his pocket and tosses it to me. I fumble, barely catching it.

'That's from Rene,' he says, looking bored.

I stand there like an idiot, blinking in surprise, feeling the cold. I shiver, for a moment allowing the chill to wash the weird smog out of my system. He opens his hand impatiently. 'This ain't no charity, lady.'

I pull out a hundred and give it to him, walking away. 'Tell your boss he's an asshole.'

'He knows,' calls back the kid. 'Hey lady.'

'Now what?'

'He's got a message for you. He says you'll know when you can afford to pay for what he's got.'

'And what is that supposed to mean?'

The kid turns away, rubbing his hands. 'How should I know?'

I keep walking, beginning the long search for a taxi. I won't be coming back.

14

GABE AND JORDIE

No surprise: the lift is broken and I have to climb four levels to get to Gabe's floor. The stairwell's hot and airless and here I am sweating all over again. It's starting to turn into a habit.

There's a faint smell of mould in the hallway. Sure this place is rent controlled, but Gabe can do better. I've offered to help him find a different apartment but he says he's set-up here. I walk carefully, watching out not to trip on a tangled ridge of carpet that runs from one wall to another. I was caught out the last time I came and almost broke my ankle. With half the ceiling lights out the hallway's gloomy but not dark; someone's idea of economising.

As I head to number nineteen, Gabe's place, I hold my hand close to my chest. The pain along my palm is back and although I'm trying to ignore it, there's now a throb timed to my pulse. I'm going to need to get it seen to, but not yet. The good news is the heating in the block's out again and I slowly begin to cool down.

I knock on his door and after a second hear the scrape of chains and locks on the other side. A solid punch could break through the veneer. Gabe told me once the security is purely psychological, something for Jordie. The kid still has nightmares from the last time they were broken into.

'Hey babe, that you?'

I stand back and put myself into view of the peephole. The door rattles then jumps on its hinges as Gabe thumps a stuck bolt. It opens and with it comes a pungent wisp of a recently smoked joint. An overblown orchestral score blasts from another room as Gabe turns away. 'Hey Jordie, you turn off the game, eh? You've been going at it for hours.' The music only gets louder. 'I'm not messing around, yeah? Switch it off.' Things quiet down for about a count of ten. Then return as loud as before. He turns to me. 'Kids eh?' I think of the strange boy at Rene's and wonder how far Jordie is away from that. A long way probably, but you don't know.

I reach up, pull his face down to mine and kiss him. He tastes of beer. He's taller than me by five inches, has the body of someone who works out, but never does and looks for the most part like he should be saving lives on a beach somewhere. My imaginary sister, Jen, would love him. His brown eyes match his chocolate skin and he'd be amazing if he ever got dreadlocks.

I walk past him into the tiny apartment. It's dominated by a single living room that opens into a small kitchen off to one side, two rooms and a bathroom to the other. Piles of old vinyl LPs lay stacked against the far wall making temporary tables for empty bottles of whiskey with candles jammed into their necks. It's so dorm-room I could laugh. Lights and photography rigs fill up the rest of the room, which doubles as his studio. There are prints, mostly portraits. Some of them are experimental and I don't get them at all. Leaning against a tripod is a blown up snapshot of myself and Gabe standing arm in arm, taken by Jordie.

The whole thing reeks of hot electronics and weed. I wonder how they stand it.

There's an old couch in a corner and I make for it, collapsing into it with a sigh. I had no idea I was so tired as I throw my feet onto a cigar-burned coffee table and kick off an avalanche of magazines. There's a new work up on the wall showing an ancient couple looking intently past the lens. They're so old their faces are a geography all their own and they're close enough to kiss. Despite being mostly black and white, it has this most amazing streak of colour running through it. Like sunlight. There's something special about this one; Gabe might be getting his groove back.

I remember the Klimt in Ryan's office from my dream. God, today is so messed up. So much of that life mirrors my own. No real surprises there, but despite that it's unnerving. Nothing crosses over but it doesn't stop that fucking nightmare from chasing me. My train of thought is interrupted as Gabe sits next to me. He pulls a half-smoked joint from the ashtray and lights it before handing it over. I take a drag. We sit in silence. I like that about him.

'So,' I say after a while, 'did you fix that glass problem or what?'

He reaches behind him and grabs a bottle of beer. 'Sure did. Cancelled the whole goddam thing.'

I nod, sensing the joint kicking in. 'Well, that's insane.'

'I'm protecting my art, baby.'

'Which no one gets to see now.'

'It's not about that. Anyway, it's all a bluff. They'll fix it and it'll be on again. It's how this shit goes.'

'OK.' I'm not sure I believe him but — whatever, I don't want an argument about it. His art, his life.

The music from Jordie's room swells to a crescendo ending in a fanfare loud enough to rattle the walls. Shortly afterwards he drags himself out, wide-eyed and owlish, looking more shell-shocked than victorious. 'Good game?' I ask. He nods. 'Don't say much, do you?'

'Not much to say,' he admits after some thought.

'Did you win?'

'It's not that kind of game.'

Gabe pulls a small camera from the floor next to the couch and shoots a couple of exposures of Jordie without even looking.

'Quit it, Dad.'

He stops and turns the lens on me instead. 'Hey Jordie man, you should eat something,' He snaps a picture. 'I made you some sandwiches. They're in the refrigerator.' The boy wanders into the kitchen as Gabe turns back and takes another drag of the joint. 'Good kid.' I agree. He looks down and seeing my bandage, concern clouds his face. 'Hey baby, what happened to you?'

I lean into him. 'Some clown stabbed me.'

He takes my hand gently. 'Some clown, yeah?' I nod, becoming a vision of sincerity. 'You've got to stop doing this,' he says quietly, not taking any of my bullshit. 'It's not good, baby. Not in any way, eh?' I don't have an answer. I'm saved by the sound of something shattering in the kitchen. 'Jordie, what's going on?'

'I busted a glass.'

He grimaces then lurches off the couch. 'Shit man, that was our last one.'

'I'm sorry.'

'Don't sweat it. I can get more.'

I close my eyes and leaning back yell out, 'You should get yourself out of here and find a decent place to live.'

'Yeah yeah baby, I'm down with that,' There's a brittle

clatter of glass being swept away, 'but it's not so easy to move, yeah?'

'Yeah.'

'So what's the word from down under?'

'No word. She's the same crazy little mouse she always is.'

'For sure? You sound jealous, eh?'

The one thing I'm not, is jealous. Gabe comes back with Jordie beside him carrying a plate of sandwiches carefully in both hands. The boy heads towards a beanbag but Gabe rests his hand gently on his head, turning him to face me. 'Manners, yeah?' Jordie offers me the plate, but I say no. Satisfied, he buries himself into the bag and digs into the food. Gabe throws him a remote and Jordie starts flicking through channels on the massive TV. 'Keep the sound off, man, I'm talking.'

And then his attention is back on me. He kisses my hand as he holds it up for closer inspection. 'Alice baby, you gotta love yourself. This is no good.'

'Yeah, I know,' I say quietly and flash him a ferocious smile, 'but it beats the hell out of being bored.'

'You need to get rid of your demons, baby. They're eating you up inside.'

'Well,' I say, 'this is who I am. Love me or leave me.' I turn and nip his ear and he yelps in surprise.

'Which is what's so great about you,' he says, rubbing his lobe, 'but you're burning up. You get what I'm saying, eh? You gotta ditch the old ways and find your own way. Be your own thing.'

I sit forward, conscious of Jordie chewing his sandwich, watching TV. 'So Gabe, about this favour.'

He studies me with an uncertain smile.

'What?' I say.

'You got this look going on,' he replies shaking his head slowly, 'know what I mean?' I pull the bag from my pocket and shake it in front of him. Tiny teardrop capsules rattle around inside. 'What's that?'

'A bribe.'

He glances at Jordie, who's totally absorbed by a show. Reaching out to me he opens his hand and I drop a pill into it. I grin and swallow mine dry. Gabe washes his down with a beer.

We give it a few minutes then I feel it, a light-headedness, kind of drunk yet also clear. It's not a rush but a wave and when I stare across at Gabe he winks, like we're on exactly the same page. Maybe we are. He picks up the camera again and takes a shot of his tongue. Freakin' weird.

I take another drag of the joint and blow out smoke, watching as it spreads in a slow ink through the air. It slows down and hangs there like a cloud. If I was tiny I'd live on it.

'I've been thinking about your situation,' he says.

Shit. I thought we were past this stuff.

'You know what you need?' He studies the screen on his camera for a long time.

'What?'

'You need to get hypnotised.'

'Bullshit.'

He holds up his hands and leans across to me. 'No, listen to me. It makes sense.'

The smoke is still there locked into place, a painting in the air. I reach out to touch it but miss. 'OK,' I say, 'go on.'

'You need to go mano-a-mano with this dream-you and sort it right out.'

'So I get hypnotised and somehow I automatically get to meet her. I don't think it works like that.' I know it doesn't work like that.

He taps his head, ignoring what I've just said. 'You got her address. Go there and tell her she's not welcome anymore. Kick her ass out. Awesome, eh?' He leans back, smiling like a genius.

My head is light and I touch my cheeks, just to make sure everything is where it should be. I look at him and close my eyes. Hypnosis. God. 'I'll take it under advisement,' I say. Time to change tack.

I give him my sweetest I-can't-believe-how-lucky-you-are smile. 'My parents are having a thing tonight. I want you to go with me.' Gabe's own smile flatlines. I lean forward and slap his thigh, the sound ringing out in the small room. Jordie peers away from his show for a moment. 'Come on Gabe, balls to the walls.'

'Baby, it's not my scene. You know it.'

'It's not my thing either, but screw it right? New experiences and all that jazz? It'll be a blast.' The lightness has spread to my body and I might float away at any second. I glance up at the ceiling, wondering where I'll land.

He grins at me. 'They won't let me in the door. I'm disreputable.'

'Disreputable?' I love how he says that.

'Then we'll match.' I hold out my hands, painting an imaginary marquee. 'Alice and Gabe, The Disreputables.'

'You're a lawyer,' he says.

I shrug. 'Was.'

'OK,' he concedes.

'Come on,' I say, standing up. 'Get into it. Be there or be square. Don't be a loser.'

Jordie turns from the TV and looks at me. 'He's not a loser.'

'She's joking, Jordie man.'

I'm half joking. 'I need this.'

'Why?'

'Because I'm their daughter.' It's the best reason I can come up with. That, and I didn't get an invite.

Gabe pulls out his serious camera and starts snapping randomly. He's not even looking. 'Do you feel light?' he asks.

'Yeah.'

He leans into me and takes a picture of us, face-to-face. 'What the hell, it'll be great. But only on one condition, yeah?' He's going to want to take the camera, sell some pictures.

'What?'

'Do what I said.'

It takes me a second to remember what he's talking about. 'You mean the hypnosis?' He waits for my answer. 'Sure,' I lie.

Gabe gets Jordie's attention. 'Hey Jordie man, how about we get Latisha over for the night?'

All right, I'm not the jealous type, but Latisha? I've never met her but I hate her. The boy lights up. It's like flicking a switch. I wish I had the same effect on people. 'Yeah, she's cool. I love it when she comes over.'

I raise an eyebrow. 'An old friend,' explains Gabe calmly. Then he winks. 'I owe you one,' I whisper in his ear. He smiles. 'Anything.'

'Anything?'

Now it's my turn to wink.

'Give me a couple of hours and I'll find Latisha for Jordie and get some food in.'

'And a glass,' suggests the boy.

I fish out Rene's bag again. 'More for later?'

'Baby, not so obvious, all right?'

'It's OK,' replies Jordie, still watching the television. 'I don't mind.'

Gabe leans down to him. 'Hey Jordie man, you shouldn't be knowing about this shit, OK?'

He shrugs. 'OK.'

I put the bag away and stand up. 'Tell you what. I'll come back later, pick you up and we can have a party on the way there.'

'Sure. Give me some time to find Latisha. We have to smooth things over, if you get my drift.'

I take his chin in my hand and guide his head to mine, which is about ready to detach. I whisper closely into his ear. 'I don't have to leave right away, do I?'

Gabe smiles, leading me towards the bedroom. 'You are one messed up lady.'

'I know.'

15

A SOCIETY EVENT

I'm lightheaded. I close my eyes as the limo powers through the Long Island traffic on its way to the House in Centerport. I don't know what Rene gave me this time but I'm still horny. Chewing some gum I wink at Gabe, reach over and lightly punch his arm. 'Ready for this, buckaroo?' I nod towards the drinks cabinet. He's so intense right now. Maybe it's the pills. I squeeze up against him and give him a hug. 'Don't worry, they're just a pack of assholes.'

'Not worried baby, but the word you're looking for is wolves.' He flashes his quicksilver smile.

'Assholes, wolves —. Whatever. Drink up,' I open the cabinet, liberating a crystal decanter of Scotch.

He stretches out on the leather, soaking up the luxury. 'How did you score the wheels anyway?'

'Blackmail. I called Mollher, their,' I pause, taking a moment to find the right word, finally settling on Helper. There are so many words I could use to describe him, but this one's the least complicated. 'I told him to send out the car or else we'd show up in a taxi and bring down the tone.'

I give him my brightest grin. 'They have to let me in. I'm blood, baby.'

I gulp down the Scotch, tearing up the second it hits my throat. This is good car booze. 'Holy shit,' I breathe, passing the decanter over, 'party up, partner.'

Gabe takes the decanter and drinks, tries for a second to be unimpressed before giving in. 'Now that's excellent hootch.' He raises an appreciative eyebrow. 'I'll give you one thing. Your people know their liquor, eh?'

I nudge him. 'They're not my people. You're my people.' A faint smile: he doesn't believe me. 'What the hell, anyway. Your people, my people. I hate everyone equally.' I put the crystal to my lips and scull. 'Here's to wolves and assholes.'

He nods. 'Fair enough. So why are we going again?'

I have to catch my breath as the liquor burns. 'They don't want me here.'

The car turns off down a tree-lined drive. It's dark away from the main road and for a second the only illumination is the spill of light from the drinks cabinet. 'Almost there,' I say, noticing the tension in my voice. Gabe squints out the window but the driveway's unlit and all he gets to see is his own reflection. 'Family house,' I explain, 'very private.'

'Got it.' He turns around as the cabin lights up with the glare of headlights from a car turning behind us. 'So,' he says, 'how many people are coming to your shindig?'

I shake out a cigarette from my bag and light up. 'Millions, baby.'

He points at his used-looking rented tux, as close to formal as he ever gets. 'They won't let us in. We're far too cool. Never going to happen.' He turns to me and I get the sense he's about to say something, but he seems to change his mind. 'You look amazing,' he says instead. I smile. I do look good. I'm wearing a red full length tulle-neck dress. It's tight enough to turn heads and I feel sexy. The best part is the dress is a no name thing, something I bought off the web. Chic poor. What a blast.

The car pulls up next to a columned guardhouse, where a man in a liveried uniform speaks to the driver. His face is familiar. He nods towards the back of the limo, then checks off something on a clipboard.

'Not that I mind,' says Gabe, 'but why are we really here?'

'Someone has to keep them on their toes.'

'I don't buy that.'

'Jesus, Gabe. My father's a control freak.' I indicate the looming house. 'Kind of hard to miss. He'll be wondering the whole night how his crazy daughter's going to embarrass him. Anyway, I have a right to be here.'

Gabe pushes himself back into the chair. 'Right. Damn, thanks for inviting me.'

'You know what I mean.'

But I can see he doesn't. Good old Alice screws up again. He takes my cigarette and sticks it in his mouth. 'I got an idea, babe. How about we turn around and blow this thing off. If that's the only reason you're here then it's messed up. What's the point? Give yourself a break, yeah?'

I drop back into the seat. 'Gabe,' I say with a shake of my head, 'too late.'

On cue we round a gentle curve. And there it is: Van de Korte House, all five stories lit by rows of gas lamps, their yellow flames flickering in the faint breeze. Smaller lights shine in blues and greens along the rest of the drive and out into the broad space in front of the house. It makes the place even colder than it is. It's alien. I study Gabe's face closely as the scale of the mansion registers. 'Don't be too impressed,' I whisper to him, 'it's only twenty years old.'

Twenty years pretending to be two hundred. My father's genius does not extend to architecture. The massive stone building with its pompous rectangular plan is crammed with columns, pilasters, and lavish overwrought pediments. The house looms like a christmas-lit mausoleum.

The car joins a queue on the circular drive, quietly idling as it waits its turn. I'm getting fidgety, tapping out a rhythm on my legs, impatient as I stare out the window. I remember the bag in my pocket and the two remaining pills. Screw it. I clear my head, grab Gabe and kiss him, snapping out of it. 'Thanks for being here. Head's up!'

'What?'

The seat whispers with the fabric of my dress as I shuffle across and wink at him. 'Come on. I'm not waiting in line. Move it or lose it.' With a heave I throw the door open and run into the night, becoming a silhouette against the decorative lamps. I wave for him to hurry up.

'Remember,' I say as we crunch over gravelly snow towards the wet stone steps, 'assholes and wolves.' I kiss him. 'I'm in your debt forever.'

'Forever?'

'Longer, baby.'

16

ROSES

With his arm in mine I guide him past a young power couple hurrying from the warmth of their limo towards the mansion's not so subtle double doors. A vision of Versace and Armani, they stare in surprise as we push ahead of them. I nod at the younger of two doormen. 'Yo Macks,' I say, 'so where's the party?'

Macks and I go way back. He grins at me. 'Good to see you, Als,' he says. 'Staying long?' Behind him another doorman, someone I don't recognise, checks the other couple's invitation off a list and ushers them inside. Out of habit, I look around trying to spot the secret service types and bodyguards that must be out there somewhere.

'Just long enough for the old man to kick us out,' I say only half jokingly, pulling his list down and perusing the names, 'Are you going to announce us?'

He smiles, earning a stern glance from Mr Serious behind him. 'Not a chance.'

I nod towards the older doorman. 'Who's the corpse?' Macks shakes his head quickly as the other man eyeballs him again. And that's when I notice a small bulge under his waistcoat. 'Ah.' So with a grin that I know borders on manic, I grab hold of Gabe and push in through the doors of the Van de Korte Mansion. Home again.

The Grand Foyer, like the rest of place, is large and overdecorated, designed to impress. Twin staircases circle both sides of the room to meet at a landing, where well-dressed partygoers survey us with looks of incomprehension, one going as far as attracting the attention of one of the waiters and pointing us out. It's official: cheap-dress girl and rent-a-tux have arrived. I can't help myself and smile sweetly, flipping him the bird.

We stop by the centrepiece, a massive Mediterranean-styled urn overflowing with vines and flowers spilling over trellises. Roses of all colours splash over the glazed ceramic, the only colour in a room otherwise dominated by pale marble and inlays of oak. I pluck a white rose and settle it into the breast pocket of Gabe's jacket. Another, I stick behind my ear. 'There,' I say with a wink, 'we fit right in.'

'Baby,' whispers Gabe, 'you'll always stand out.' Sometimes he says exactly the right thing.

Sounds of Duke Ellington reach us from the ballroom, which has been decorated for the occasion. This is so far over the top I have to wonder what tonight is actually about. A daylight-bright mix of gold and white light plays over the assembled guests who are milling around under huge potted palms. I squint as a ray of faux sunlight outlines the shape of a bird. A rainbow parakeet flies from one palm to another. He's pulled out all the stops. Note to self though: stay clear of the trees.

Gabe grabs me and winks, mistaking my silence for second thoughts. 'Fuck 'em, right?'

So I wink right back. 'Fuck 'em sideways baby.' I realise

too late that's something Jen says. 'Come on, the bar's over there.'

We enter the ballroom and into the throng of well-heeled and genteelly tipsy guests. The band in the corner strikes up Take the 'A' Train as we wheel through the heart of the crowd to a lavish smorgasbord set along the far wall. The party is the usual blend of old and evil sparring with young and ambitious. Expensive scents and silk-sounds of designer gowns mix with lazy chatter and shrill laughter. Gabe follows me to the long wooden table and touches a frond of a palm. 'Classy,' he calls above the sound of the band.

'Nah,' I say. 'See that guy?' I point to a middle-aged banker type with a slight paunch laughing heartily with a young woman. Gabe nods. 'They call him Big Daddy. His company got hit by a class action last year. Made condoms but their quality assurance went to hell. He's looking for cash.' I gesture about the room. 'Most of them are. Think of it as feeding time.'

'You don't like them, do you?'

I liberate some drinks from a waiter who eyes us dubiously. 'You think? Hypocrites, bankrupts, sycophants.' I wave at an old couple who are surreptitiously pointing. 'And gossips.' Gabe looks about, catching the half hidden stares and averted gazes. I hear my name over fragments of other conversation.

'Seems they like you as much as you like them, eh?'

'Look at them.'

'I am, baby.'

He taps my elbow and I spot a formidable woman making her way towards us. I hate to admit it but Mother is stunning. Coifed and dressed in a gown worth more than Gabe would earn in a year of good sales, she still manages to appear understated and elegant. She drifts through the multitude, stopping regally for a quick word or pleasant smile, her presence magnetic. I throw back my drink.

Dismissing Gabe with a glance she turns her full attention to me, pinning me with her gaze. As much as I hated that stare when I was a kid, I hate it ten times more now. 'Alice,' she says pleasantly, 'you came.' I shrug and drop my glass into a convenient pot.

'Mother. How's it hanging?' I manage to keep a straight face for a count of five before winking at Gabe.

With the faintest hint of a smile on her lips, Jeane Van de Korte leans forward and kisses me on the cheek. 'To the left, dear,' she whispers. 'Don't you think you've outgrown your rebellious phase?'

I back away and take a step closer to Gabe. 'Condescension. Nice. Good to see you as well.'

Jeane turns to the buffet and accepts a small dish of fruit from one of the white-smocked chefs staffing the table. 'If your intention was to make a statement, consider it made.'

I give Gabe a quick hug. 'I told you we were a close family.' He drains his drink. With anyone else they'd be sinking into their own skin right now, instead he's fascinated.

'Can we have a word in private?' asks Jeane.

'No.'

This time, her smile is steely. 'You're such a fighter. Your life could be so much easier if you stopped battling us.'

I shrug lopsidedly. 'Yeah, but where's the fun in that?' She hits all my buttons and I can't help it. Mother has the power to magically make me fifteen again.

'Dr. Larrs has informed me you've missed four appointments.'

'Slipped my mind.'

'Don't be flippant. Your father is angry.'

'So why am I talking to you?'

Jeane takes the smallest bite of a strawberry then places the rest delicately back on the plate. 'This war of yours is in your mind, the only person you're fighting is yourself. You know we want what's best for you.' I lift another drink from a tray circulating by, not trusting myself to speak. Mother pushes back a wisp of hair and shakes her head, whether in frustration over my problems or the inconvenience of dealing with me, I can't tell. 'It's time you understood you have to want to get better yourself.'

'Which is code for...?'

Jeane straightens, smiling winningly at a couple who wander past, waiting until they're out of earshot. 'Your decisions have consequences, which is something you don't appear to have learned. I've spoken about this with your father and we've decided to link your fund to certain — responsibilities. Seeing Dr Larrs again is one of those.'

I sip the champagne. 'Wow.'

'We're serious, Alice.'

'It's such a bitch having a litigious daughter. Must bring the name down.'

Jeane shakes her head slowly and I can tell where this is going to end. She's made up her mind about something. 'You're right. It does. But there's no one here we need to impress and your little activist collective isn't the game changer you think it is. You're only hurting yourself.' I clutch my bandaged hand without even knowing, surprised by the sharp pain in my palm. 'This is for your own good.'

'Wow. Another cliché. Double it.'

'I'm not negotiating with my own daughter.'

I nod towards the crowd milling around our periphery, heads turned away and pretending to talk. 'Yeah you are.

Look at them. Wondering about that crazy Van de Korte heir. How are our stocks doing, by the way?'

Mother catches someone's eye and smiles. So much of her behaviour is sheer autopilot. 'I honestly don't know,' she says, exchanging a brief wave with a guest. 'And if you still think people are interested in your rebellion then you really need to read the papers. You've got some stiff competition these days.'

She places her palms on my face and I have to force myself not to push her hands away. 'You'll go to Larrs, regularly, on time and polite. This isn't a negotiation. And you've got twenty-four hours to get rid of your boyfriend. I don't like him.' She steps back, evaluating us both before kissing me lightly on the cheek. 'The announcement will be made shortly. Until then, enjoy the party.'

Gabe shakes his head as she glides into the mass of guests. 'What a bitch.' I put my arms around his waist.

'What was that about?'

'Just her drawing some lines in the sand,' I say quietly, hugging him. 'Don't let the swanky dress and jewellery fool you; she loves a throw-down fist fight. They didn't get their money by being nice.'

I pluck the rose from my hair and sniff it. The sweet smell is surprising; roses aren't usually grown for their scents. This knowledge comes from the other Alice, the girl who runs a flower shop. It's so weird. 'Screw this,' I say, 'I need a real drink.' But Gabe is way ahead of me, already leading me to the bar.

17

CERTAIN REALITIES

I swallow the last of Rene's wild little pills and wash it back with champagne. Gabe does the same with the beer he's drinking. I need to take the edge off. Gabe reaches over and clinks his bottle against my glass. He blinks rapidly in an attempt to focus. 'So when's this big announcement going to happen?'

'Why do you care?'

He swallows a belch. 'Don't want them to run out of beer, is all.'

'Good point.' I raise a finger to the guy behind the bar. 'My man,' I say, focusing on the words, 'you can't run out of beer for my friend here. Got it?'

He nods. 'Yes maam, got it. We're good for beer.'

'Just so,' I say, beginning to feel agreeably light, 'just so.' Straightening myself I swivel to regard the party.

'So did you grow up here?' asks Gabe.

I sip the champagne, this time taking care not to splash. 'Yeah.'

'It's big.'

'Friggin' huge,' I agree.

'So, where's your Dad?'

A good question. I scan the room, faces and sounds coming into sloppy focus as I search the crowd. I see him, that thin, almost gaunt man siting quietly in an Edwardian chair near one of the palms. He's chatting to his coterie; a king at court.

I point him out to Gabe, imagining him through his perspective. Father's long face, his watery eyes restless and quick. Grey, receding hairline parted perfectly, dinner suit new and immaculate, a vision of control, conservatism and security; someone you can trust to captain the ship. You'd think it was some sort of public persona. It isn't. There's a white rose in his lapel and without thinking, I pull out Gabe's. And then, with that amazing radar Father has, Mattiew turns his attention to us, expression unreadable.

'Why doesn't he come over, eh?' asks Gabe.

'We go to him.'

'Sorry.'

'What for?'

'For your messed up family. What do you think?'

'I don't need your sympathy. We know where we stand.'

Gabe plants his beer on the bar and scratches his head. 'All I'm saying baby, is I'd never freeze out Jordie like they're doing to you.'

'And that makes you perfect? I'm not the one leaving my kid for the night with some hooker.'

He glares at me, surprised. 'Latisha's no hooker.' I turn away, regretting my big mouth. 'These days anyway,' he mumbles. He has another drink. 'Shit, whatever. Who's the suit with your dad?' I strain to see. I can make out someone talking to Father, but the man's mostly obscured by the palm. They both start laughing at something. Mattiew reaches across and pats his arm, offering an aside to whoever it is standing next to him. He doesn't seem to be a casual guest.

I shrug. 'Don't know, the plant's in the way. Probably Olen Canders. This is his farewell party.'

Across the room, Mattiew checks his watch and stands. The band dies away as he taps a glass for attention, the sound cutting through the throng of conversation. People stop talking; all eyes upon Mattiew Van de Korte, founder, majority shareholder and CEO of Van de Korte Medical. He waits for complete silence. The moment drags.

Rene's pill is doing its magic and I begin to feel light again. It's strange and freeing. Looking at one of the birds I imagine what it would be like to launch off and leap into empty space, the sensation of the wind. Gently sliding from the stool I stand on tiptoes, measuring my own gravity. I could do it, if I had wings. I giggle.

Mattiew turns his attention to me from halfway across the room. 'Thank you Alice, glad you made it.' Damn. Quiet murmurs fill the uncomfortable silence. He stares at me for the briefest moment before making his way to the stage. He accepts a microphone from an assistant and motions for Jeane, who joins him, smiling benignly.

'Friends and family,' he begins, 'where would we be without them?' Some gentle laughter drifts from the audience and encouraged by a small laugh of his own, grows louder.

'Nice,' I whisper.

Mattiew raises his hands and the amusement dies away. 'My esteemed guests — my friends. Welcome.' He graciously acknowledges the few glasses raised in salute. 'Van de Korte Medical has redefined health care over the past twenty years.' There's a scattering of applause. 'Well,' he goes on, 'you ought to know. You own it.'

'Look at them,' I say, careful to keep my voice low, 'he owns them.' Gabe scans the crowd and it's true; almost everyone's attention is on Mattiew. I nudge him. 'You can tell the secret service types. They're the only ones not looking at him.' I wink at a thin athletic man who's secretly examining us. The agent turns away, furious at being sprung.

A wave of lightness washes through me and I grab the bar convinced I might actually float off. With a small smile I glance around to check if anyone noticed. No chance; instead I find the almost-satisfied eyes of people who know they're being courted and expect to be better off for it. A flash lights up the stage as a photographer captures the moment.

Something catches Gabe's attention. 'Hey baby, that guy's staring at you.'

I search the mass of faces but don't notice anyone in particular. 'Who?'

He points. 'That guy. The guy your dad was talking to earlier.'

I look again. Gabe indicates somewhere near my parents, but another palm tree is in the way. Leaning to the side I try to get a better vantage point. 'What's he like?'

'Old. Dressy.' He squints. 'You sure you can't see him? He sure as hell can see you.'

I stand, scraping the chair back on the parquet flooring. The sound carries through the ballroom, drawing angry stares. 'Well, let's go say hi then.' From the stage, Jeane glances in my direction with a flicker of annoyance.

'I've had the pleasure of working with many of you directly during that time,' continues Father, ignoring the disruption, 'and I can say although the organisation's had its trials, we grow stronger, together. The strength of this company lies in its people, their passion and ideas.'

A swell of applause fills the room as I walk away from the bar, looking where Gabe pointed. Yet again my view's blocked. I take another step but my body is strange and awkward and I'm forced to reach out and snatch Gabe's arm for support.

'You OK?'

I shouldn't have taken that last pill. 'No. Something's weird, Gabe,' I say, trying to shake a sudden rush of vertigo. 'Just need to walk it off. Where is he?' Gabe turns me to face the old man standing by the stage.

'He's still looking at you,' he whispers.

I stare. 'I can't see him.' God I feel like shit. I might throw up. I blink again but can't find the guy he's talking about. A bird is in the way, then another branch of one of those ridiculous trees.

Gabe ducks down to match my height, sighting the man from as close to my point of view as he can get. 'The old guy. White hair. Very tall.' I shake my head.

'No. What the hell is wrong with me? Why can't I see him?'

'He's right in front of us,' insists Gabe, sounding uneasy and sobering by the second.

'I know it's a cliché,' continues Mattiew from the stage, 'but Van de Korte Medical is a family. That's how we started. And although we've grown substantially and have clinics in thirty-eight states we are still at heart, that family.' I brush away the beginnings of tears. What? Why am I crying? 'Speaking of family, Dr Olen Canders was with us right from the start and it's with mixed feelings of gratitude for his service and regret that he will be no longer with us, that I inform you he's retiring this year. But despite that mixture of emotions, one thing is clear: his outstanding dedication to this family.' He pauses to clap his hands in Olen's direction. Applause swells as Mattiew invites him to join him on stage.

'There, that's him,' points Gabe.

I shake my head. Bad idea; the floor yawns away from me in a straight drop and I feel like I'm falling. Forcing myself to look at the stage, focusing all my attention on the two men; I can spot my father, but I can't focus on Olen. I crane forward, sick and furious at myself but refusing to give in to this stupid dizziness. With a furious amount of concentration I'm finally able to make out Olen. I see his clothes, even his awkward posture, uncomfortable at being the centre of attention. There's an old pocket watch chain looped under his jacket: a startling detail. But his face is lost in shadows. Light falls away the closer it comes to his features, leaving nothing than the shape of him. Shit this is so crazy. My stomach lurches.

Mattiew leans into the microphone conspiratorially. 'If you don't know the man, you'll know his work. People, passion, ideas, remember? The T7 Infuser was Olen's brainchild, as are the improved micro-magnetic blood filtering systems we use today, but most importantly we owe him for the Cander's Ventilator.' The crowd clap with genuine enthusiasm. 'That ventilator,' confides Mattiew with a smile, 'is a real lifesaver in more ways than one. It kept us going through some tough times, let me tell you.' Laughter.

I shake my head, trying to clear it as Gabe holds me tightly. 'This isn't right.'

'What's wrong? Alice, what's happening?'

'I can't see him,' I say. 'Everything else is fine — but I can't see him!' He guides me towards a chair. 'I don't need to sit down, I need to know what the fuck's going on! Who is he?'

Back on the stage, Mattiew places an arm around Olen.

'As I said, Olen will be retiring this year, but not before supervising the completion of our brand new clinic. And,' he adds, 'that's just the beginning. There's another reason I've asked you all here.' He waits, teasing them. The room sucks in its breath. 'The other purpose of the evening is to announce a round of capital raising to grow the company to a First Tier health provider. Ladies and Gentlemen, we intend to open another twenty clinics not only locally but overseas in the new year.' There's a pause as the guests realise they're going to get richer. Mattiew smiles that politician's smile of his. He just got their vote. He accepts a glass of champagne from a waiter standing ready. 'To family!'

'Family,' choruses the crowd. 'Now please, enjoy the entertainment and have a fun evening.' With a wave, he walks from the stage. The room lights up again as the photographer records the moment for posterity. As I blink stupidly into the press of bodies, I'm blinded as another flash goes off right in front of me, then another as Gabe shoves him away.

The band strikes up again as the mood turns festive, the party breaking into excited, chattering knots. A huddle forms around the bar as people start shouting out their orders. As I move away to find some space I'm buffeted and separated from Gabe, and as I search for him my gaze falls instead on the shadow-shrouded figure of Olen.

My heart beats strong and loud in my ears as I try to push away, finding myself backed into one of the palms. Back on stage the band shifts gears into something modern. My head's reeling and I'm sure I'm going to throw up as Olen comes closer. I squint, wiping sweat from my forehead. 'You,' I say, 'stay the fuck away from me.' People nearby turn to stare but I don't give a shit. I don't care if I'm tripping — I need to get away. Olen moves his shadowy face towards me.

'I'm not joking,' I say. Loud. Too loud. Now I'm sounding crazy. Somewhere someone giggles and time falls apart into loose, disconnected moments.

I sway as images and sounds come to me in snapshots; the frond of one of the palms; a rainbow parakeet squawking against the noise of the room; a startled guest. From a great tunnelling distance a glass of champagne shatters on the floor. And that dark, faceless shape of Olen as he moves even closer. His movement is half frozen in a weird, slow time; inevitable as a glacier. Someone screams. It's me. I stare at my hand, white knuckled as I grip the handle of my knife. The cut in my palm has opened again and my blood drips slowly to mix with the spill of champagne.

Someone calls my name but sounds are muddy, like I'm hearing them underwater. I spin in slow motion to see two bulky men running towards me. More flashes light the room as the photographers close in.

Blackness grows around me as the two security guards pry free the knife. Someone recognises blood and screams. Shadows flicker around Olen and I scream as well. In the distance, Gabe throws a punch and is swatted down.

18

DRUMBEATS

Drumbeats. Heartbeats. Lights flash by. Stairs. Someone whispers urgently. I blink, finding myself half walked, half dragged somewhere upstairs and out of the way. I recognise the doorman from before. Gabe's yelling. For a moment his voice gets louder, stopping abruptly as something thuds down onto the floor. I think he's dead then he begins to moan. I breathe. Gabe isn't dead. At least that's something. OK.

My head lolls and I wonder if I'm going to vomit. It would ruin the carpet and for some reason that annoys me. The two men drag me through a door and sit me on a bed, switching on a light to reveal an elegant room. I look around, which is a mistake and I have to close my eyes as a flood of nausea overwhelms me.

Someone taps me gently on the shoulder and I try to recognise them, blinded by the glare of the room lights. No, it's not that; something's different. The light flicks away, then back. A voice, so familiar. 'She's OK, but she should stay here and sleep it off.' Hands poke and prod, then I feel my own hand lifted. Turned. Examined. 'When the fuck did this happen?' Someone else mumbles a reply. They don't know. In the distance a woman weeps softly to herself. 'Well it needs to be cleaned and re-bandaged. Somebody get a suture kit. Jesus.' This time the voice is angry.

Ah. Father. Of course.

I wait for my eyes to focus as I blink away tears from the light, still seeing dull purple spots dance on the edge of my vision. Sitting up I rub them and make the problem worse. 'What's going on?' I ask, sounding thick and slurred. One day, one of Rene's special pills will kill me. I wonder how bad that would truly be.

'Well that's what we all want to know.' I turn to face Father, my hands clenching the thick cover of the bed. My fingers close around a small stuffed bear.

'Leave her be,' says another voice, the person holding the light. 'She needs to be sedated.'

'You don't know what she's been on.'

'A mild sedative,' argues the voice. 'She should sleep.'

'I want to get out of here,' I say. I try to make it sound imposing but all I can manage is a croak. As I stand the world falls away in a waterfall of sparkling light. 'Shit.' I thump back down on the bed.

Someone hands a first aid kit to the man with the penlight. I stare at him again and even after all this his face is still hidden. I'm not afraid — the numbness and strangeness have won out over fear and remade me into a cotton wool thing. I'm a doll in a woman-shaped body. Even so, I'm curious. 'Who are you?'

The voice murmurs, 'Hello Alice.'

'Who are you?'

'I'm Olen, Alice. You remember me.'

'No.'

His face emerges from the shadows, frail, thin, wide blue eyes. A tentative smile.

'What are you doing to me?'

'Nothing. It's what you've done to yourself.' He turns away and comes back with a hypodermic.

'Get away.'

'It's just a sedative,' he says with a weird catch in his voice. 'Harmless.'

'Get away from me!' I push myself to the back of the bed but heavy hands grab hold and force me still. From the corner of the room Jeane starts crying while Mattiew stands arms folded, white-faced and furious.

Olen leans in and for an insane moment his face flickers in and out of focus. He pulls out his old pocket watch, the silver chain catching the light in a dull gleam. He flicks it open with a sound that reminds me of the knife. 'Nine-forty, or thereabouts. Make a note, someone. Nothing else for her for at least eight hours. I know it's been hard for you, Alice. What happened to you as a child wasn't fair, but you're destroying your life.' He hesitates, then pulls out a card and places it carefully in my bag. 'If you want to, call me. I can help.'

'Fuck off!' I look for someone, anyone to stop him but I might as well be surrounded by strangers. Olen measures a dose of the sedative and I stare in helpless fascination as the liquid spills from the tip in the light. 'I don't need anything,' I yell.

'Calm down.' That's Mattiew, relentless in his anger.

'It's all right,' says Olen, leaning in, 'it won't hurt.'

And in truth, it doesn't.

19

AWAKE AND LATE

All right, breathe.

My mind's full of images from the nightmare. Olen. His pocket watch. The jet squirting from the tip of the needle. Her mother crying. It's all so real I could scream, but I don't.

I calm down and glance at the clock on the bedside table. A quarter to eight, which means I'm going to be late again. Outside my room the quiet sounds of the house and early morning do more to soothe me than any amount of breathing exercises. Through the window a work crew in orange vests are busy fixing the blown transformer. They don't seem to be in a hurry, pacing themselves in the growing heat already creeping past the curtains. Somewhere else a bird sings. Ratbone meows plaintively. 'OK' I say, swinging my legs over the side of the bed. 'OK.' I glance at the clock again.

I go to the kitchen where I scoop a spoonful of instant coffee into a dirty mug, pour water from the kettle. I'm tired, so tired I can't begin to explain it. It's not just tonight, it's every night living her life. Ratbone squawks again and I shake a bit of coffee into the cat bowl as well. For some reason he gets high on the stuff, don't ask me why. The cat's insane. We make a good match. I raise the mug to my lips, choking on lukewarm grains gritty and horrible against my teeth. 'Damn it,' I cough, spitting into the sink. My hands are shaking.

I don't bother making another cup, instead I sit down and close my eyes, trying to imagine for a moment how it would be to sleep. I can't do it — my mind's a storm right now. I remember the conversations she's had like they were mine and I guess maybe they are. It's so confusing. It can't go on.

I dial the number for the clinic and wait for the connection, which is eventually answered by a professional-sounding receptionist. 'Put me through to Dr Ryan please, it's Alice Brundford.'

A slight delay before Ryan's voice is on the line. 'Alice, what can I do for you?'

Where to start? I twirl the cord of the ancient wall mounted phone, choosing my words. It's going to sound mad when I actually say it out loud. 'You said you wanted to review my medication yesterday?'

'Yes, have you reconsidered?'

My eyes close. The image of Olen's watch is clear in my mind's eye for some reason. But that's just a distraction; mostly what I'm thinking about is her promise to Gabe.

'Yes. No. I mean — I've got an idea. There's something else I want to try.'

A pause on the line. 'And what's that?'

I clench the phone. 'Hypnosis.'

There are two kinds of silences in a conversation, my

mum used to say. One kind is natural, part of the to and fro of words and ideas, and then there's this. I bite my lip. 'Why don't you come into the clinic today, Alice? We can talk it through.'

'OK,' I say. It's such a stupid idea I should apologise.

20

LANDETH CENTRE

The Landeth Centre is emptier than usual as I pass the deserted car park to the front doors. The day's still hot but not blistering like yesterday. Even so I try to keep to the shade of the trees but all this does is send the local magpies crazy defending their territory. In this weather, everyone's nuts.

There are still a few tatters of paper caught up on the asphalt and I pick one up. It's a fragment from one of Ryan's notes, the ink sun-bleached after a day in the heat. I can barely make out the print, but it looks like a list of drugs I've been prescribed over the years. The names are so dense they're almost meaningless, though I think I can recognise one or two of them. I can't help feeling exposed. Losing all that paperwork, it's unprofessional.

Minutes later I push open the door to Ryan's office. It takes me a second to figure out what's wrong as he glances up at me, red-faced and sweaty. I almost pass out from the temperature in here as a tiny fan on his desk moves the hot air from one place to another.

'Hi,' he says, 'sorry about this. The air conditioner cut

out ten minutes ago. It probably cooked itself with all the heat yesterday. Maintenance says they'll have it working in half an hour or so. We can reschedule if you like.' He hands me a glass of water, beautifully cold and frosty under my fingers. My throat's dry, so I just nod thanks before pulling off my old baseball cap and wiping a sheen of sweat from my forehead.

'No, it's OK,' I say. The heat in the office is crazy. 'Can't you open a window?'

He shakes his head as he walks around the desk. 'No such luck.' He points to the chair and I sit, the warm leather feeling weirdly like skin. 'So. You want to talk about hypnosis?'

I look away and try to find the right words. 'Alice, the other Alice. It's too much. It's got to stop.'

He sits. 'Has something happened to her?'

Everything happens to her. It's a miracle she hasn't overdosed on some pill from her dealer and wound up dead. And if you die in your dream, what then? I drink the water.

Struggling to explain how horrible it was I end up shrugging, loosening a finger of sweat down my back. 'She went nuts. Really insane this time.' Ryan pulls out a handkerchief and starts wiping his face. 'She was at a corporate thing her parents were holding at their house. She wanted to be there for some power trip or something. I don't understand half of what she does.'

'She wanted to go?' asks Ryan.

'Sort of, yes I guess. So she went with Gabriel.'

'Her boyfriend.'

'Yeah, but there was this guy. He didn't have a face.'

Ryan dabs the back of his neck, listening intently. 'What are you saying, that he was injured in some way?'

My heart beats faster as I relive the moment. 'No. It was

like he was standing in a shadow, but the shadow followed him wherever he went. It's not as though he actually didn't have a face, just I couldn't see it.'

'I?'

I shake my head, flustered. 'I mean her.'

'How did it make you feel?'

'Scared. Really, really scared.' My pulse is loud, even though I know it was a dream. 'She completely freaked out.' I control my breathing. Right now, here, awake, I'm experiencing her terror from that moment. Dreamed or not.

Ryan leans forward. 'No, I meant, how does it make you feel?'

I breathe out loudly. 'Scared too.'

He writes something down, his face shiny with perspiration. 'This could be important, Alice.'

I can't take the gross sensation of the leather anymore and stand up. 'I want it to end. I'm sick of her and her stupid games.'

'Why do you suppose hypnotherapy is the answer?'

'You're going to think this is crazy.'

He smiles. 'Job description.' He must notice something in my expression because he switches to his serious face. Am I getting cynical? 'Go on,' he says, 'I'm listening. There's nothing crazy or irrelevant about your ideas.'

I look at the Klimt on the wall behind him, wondering how to put the idea to him without sounding totally mad. I give up. It is mad. 'So you know about Gabe.'

He nods. 'Yes, Alice's friend.'

'Eff-buddy.'

Ryan leans forward. 'Excuse me?'

'It's what she calls him, her eff-buddy. Not a boyfriend, only someone to spend the night with.'

'Not so great with relationships, your dream self, is she?'

'He's serious if you ask me. She thinks it keeps it simple but it doesn't. He loves her and she should understand that. Even I can see it.' Ryan raises his eyebrows but says nothing. 'Yes. OK. I get how it sounds, I need to keep things separate. I can't be two people, not when one of them isn't even real.'

'Not commenting,' he tells me, 'just listening.'

I go on. 'So they're talking and Gabe says he's come up with an idea about the dreams. Alice is used to it so it doesn't bother her as much as it bothers me.'

Ryan flicks through some notes. 'But she's still getting treatment.'

'She gets, what are those things, MRIs, every six weeks or so and regular check-ups too. I can't understand why she bothers; she seems bulletproof. It's all kind of situation normal for her. I don't know how she does it.'

'She doesn't,' Ryan says, 'she's probably addicted to any number of barbiturates and judging from what you tell me, borderline psychotic. That isn't dealing with it so well, if you ask me. Of course she does have the advantage of being imaginary.'

'Maybe.' I rub some sweat from my eyes, leaving them stinging. 'God it's hot. Anyway. Gabe is fascinated by what's happening to her.' I pause, thinking it through. 'By me.' Even as I say the words it feels surreal. My dream self's boyfriend wants to know me. Does he sense some of the real me when he looks at her? I wonder for a second what I would say to him if I could. Be there for Jordie, I decide. Don't leave him to himself. I get what growing up without parents is like and it really sucks.

I catch myself — it's so easy to fall into that trap, even after all this time. He's not real. They're not real. I snap back to the moment.

'He doesn't know for sure if it's some game she's playing,

but I think he thinks it is real. He's an artist — photographer, so he's mad for taking portraits of her, something about cameras and souls. Either way, he likes to do it and she lets him. He came up with the idea of her getting hypnotised and facing her demon, which is me I guess. She goes on like it's all a big laugh but it got me thinking.'

I stop myself from talking as Ryan writes something into his notepad. Going to the fridge in the nook I pour some more water, trying to cool down. 'It's crazy but what's the worst that could happen? Another trip to Mayfleur? Things have to change. I can't do this anymore.'

'Change,' he echoes. 'So let me get this straight. Your dream self. Sorry, dream friend of your dream persona suggests an idea for a therapy and even though your persona hates the idea, you think it's worth a shot?'

'I'm an idiot, aren't I?'

He shakes his head with a wry smile, managing to put me at ease. 'No. Not even close. But why do you think this is worth doing?'

'The idea seems right somehow. What if I could actually speak to her directly, get in front of her, face-to-face?' I trail off. It sounded better when Gabe said it.

Ryan puts his pen down and stares at me through beads of sweat. 'What would you say to her?'

I drain the glass and pour another. The cold water only makes me feel hotter. 'It's obvious isn't it? I need to take charge, like she does. Otherwise I'll lose myself. This other me is the dream and I want to tell her to go away and leave me alone.' My voice is swallowed by the heat of the office. 'Told you it was weird.'

He smiles again as he scratches his head. 'Not so much.' He stands and walks to the desk, collecting the huge dossier of my records still there from yesterday, dropping them on a low table in front of me. Notes, hypotheses, prescriptions all fan out; a dense tightly-spaced history of failure.

The words are cramped, written in doctor-speak, a code I can't crack. Nothing recognisable as English. 'Your point?' I ask.

'None of this,' he waves at the pile between us, 'helped that much, did it?'

'What about hypnosis?'

He holds up a hand. 'I'm getting to that.'

'You think it's stupid.'

He shakes his head before waving at the mess of paper on the floor. 'According to these, all the therapies you've undergone, even before your time in Mayfleur have been oriented around controlling or even attempting to stop the dream. Is that right?' I nod, experiencing a strange mix of curiosity and vague dread. 'I've thought about your situation a lot.'

'Yeah, me too.'

He smiles. 'See? A sense of humour. It's a good sign. You understand the difference between when you're dreaming and when you're not.'

'No, wait,' I say, 'I don't know. Not for sure.'

'Do you believe this is all real?'

'Yes, except I can't know. Not for certain, not one hundred percent. When I dream my other self it's the opposite way around. It's just as solid as this. It smells, it tastes, it feels.'

He wipes at his face again. 'Well, if you want absolute certainty, maybe you'd be better off talking to a priest. Or a philosopher. You have to trust your intuition.' He gives it a moment's thought before knocking on the solid wood of the desk. 'See this? I can't prove this is real any more than you can. If it's a fantasy, it's watertight in that sense, but you've got to go with your gut. If it walks like a duck, talks like a duck, it's probably a duck.' He kneels and begins to reassemble the stack of paperwork. 'So back to my first question: do you believe all this is real?'

I stare at him blankly. 'Yes.'

He nods, allowing the word to rest. 'Trying to find irrefutable proof all this isn't a dream is a bit like searching for a god, in my view. You can look and look for proof but in the end, it's a question of belief.'

He's going somewhere with this and I swallow back my frustration. 'So why is it exactly the same when I'm her? Why doesn't she think she's dreaming? It's all real for her too. This is what's so hard.'

He takes a sip from his own glass, leaving fingermarks that slowly dribble downwards as the water beads. I can tell he's choosing his words. 'I'm not sure that's entirely true, from our conversations. Your dream persona might also believe this life here is the real one. Deep down, she probably suspects exactly what she is.' He places the stack neatly back on the desk. 'It's all you of course, your persona, your persona's friends, everything is a construct, a manifestation of your imagination. It's hardly surprising your unconscious mind is sending you signals, suggestions. The real question is why now?'

Such a stupid question. 'I told you. I've had enough. If you're telling me New York-me isn't real, I get it. It's kind of old news. I don't care where I heard the idea, but if Dream-me is tapping out code then I want to listen. I'd like to try hypnosis. Knock me out, put me in touch with her and who knows?'

He smiles, but I can read his disagreement.

'So what's wrong with it?'

The room's a sauna. He wipes his face with the handkerchief again. It's drenched. I notice the sweat stains under the arms of his shirt. 'Barring some sort of absolute certainty, it's clear to me in terms of being able to function in the real world, you have a few blips now and again but otherwise you're remarkably well-adjusted.'

I shake my head in amazement. 'You think so? Because from over here it seems to be a complete mess.'

'You have friends and a job,' he observes.

'Only because my sister spends her life keeping me out of trouble,' I say, surprised at the bitterness in my own voice. 'And not many friends.'

'What I'm leading to,' says Ryan, 'is when you get down to it, the focus of the antipsychotics and the other therapies has only been on two things: to try to shut down the dream and help you know the difference between the two.'

'The second part's never been a problem,' I laugh. The sound is tired, satirical. 'Trust me. You can't mistake it for my life here.'

'Which is the point. You don't walk around the streets hallucinating you're in Manhattan.' I stare at him, still waiting for his answer. 'Did you ever confuse your lives? Unless your records are wrong, you've always been able to tell.'

'No, never. It's the one thing that doesn't change. Everything's different, except my name. We share the same world, same history, but it's like we're two completely separate people. No, I'm always clear about where I am. Nothing crosses over. I'm awake here or asleep and dreaming of New York. That's how it is.'

'The way I read it,' he says after a thoughtful pause, 'is the therapies haven't been successful in stopping the dreams, but in terms of keeping you functioning in the real world we've had some progress.'

'Go on.'

'We need a change of focus.'

I wait. 'OK.'

'We should look at the present,' he says, 'concentrate on making your life as good as it can be. By that I mean taking steps to get on top of your panic attacks.'

'I have my breathing exercises.'

'They're a start, but I'm talking about getting to a situation where you don't get them in the first place.' He seems to measure the moment. 'And we move away from attempting to suppress your dream.'

I lean forward, blinking. I'm not sure I heard right.

21

A PLAN

He holds up a hand. 'Bear with me. We've been going down this track' —' He pauses. 'I know your records. Every one of your doctors have gone down the same path and come up short. You understand the difference between the two experiences, so I'm suggesting forget trying to cancel out the dream and focus on improving life in the here and now.'

'I need the dreams to stop.'

'Yes, but the problem is you're acting like an umpire, attempting to stay neutral as you work out which is which. It's time to hop off the umpire's chair and get in the game.'

'Great. Sports metaphors.'

He smiles, grabs the ball off his desk and throws it hand to hand, as if to make a point. 'We're going to take a red-hot shot at getting rid of these panic attacks and more importantly, get to where you don't just know, but feel,' and he hits his chest for emphasis, 'deep down in your gut this is real. When that happens we might even find the dream unravels by itself.'

'So by trying not to stop the dream, we stop the dream?'

'Well, that's the general idea. It's what I'd like to try.'

I'm quiet, lost for a moment as I attempt to understand what he's saying fully. 'I don't want more drugs.'

'Less. We slowly wind back the Apriplex; flush it from your bloodstream.'

'OK.'

'In fact, I'm talking about getting all the drugs out of your system. Afterwards, we focus on lifestyle and health. Try to let your body find it's own level. When we've found some balance, we explore key moments of the dreams. We seek points of contact, look for meaning in your waking life. This thing with the faceless man,' he goes on 'would be a place to start.'

I try to take all this in. 'So what you're saying is hypnosis might be the way to go then?'

'I wasn't thinking in that direction to be honest. It's not like the movies and it isn't a catch-all.'

'I never said it was, but since Gabe, I mean, I dreamed of it —' I trail off. It was a weird idea to start with. 'Well, it's got to be important, right?'

He rubs his chin. 'I'm just asking you to wait.'

'I don't understand,' I say. 'How can this hurt after all the other crap I've gone through?'

'That's my point. I want you to take a rest from these aggressive therapies. Give it a couple of months and let's evaluate where we stand. If you still feel like trying hypnosis, we can talk about it then.'

I'm not going to last that long. 'A couple of months? What you don't get,' I say, flushed with so much frustration I experience a shadow of Other-Alice's anger, 'is every day for you is two days for me. Two months is four months.' I shake my head. 'Twenty-seven years is fifty-four years. You don't get it, I've lived a lifetime and I don't want to be a passenger anymore.'

He's so quiet I wonder if he's going to explode. Instead he leans forward and touches my arm. 'Sorry. I forget what it must be like for you.'

'You have no idea. Stop being a shrink for a second and help me, OK? I want to try this.'

He rubs his face again and this time I get a glimpse of something a lot like exhaustion. 'All right,' he says softening, 'but understand it's my job to help you. Professionally. We both know it's visit me here or check back in full-time at Mayfleur. I don't want that for you, but I'm not prepared to manage you into old age either.'

'Manage me?' I repeat flatly.

'Be honest with yourself,' he says, peeling himself from the chair and walking to a bookshelf. 'You're here on the public purse because nothing else has worked. You're in a holding pattern. People have given up.'

'Sorry, is this meant to be helping? It sounds like you're calling me a lost cause.'

'I'm telling you what you already know. If you want to get out of this, we need to shake things up. Aren't you fascinated about why you dream about New York?'

'No,' I say, 'I just want it to stop.'

He turns. 'All right. If, and it's a big if, you're susceptible to hypnosis, what are you going to experience?' I start to answer but he holds up his hand. 'You say you need to somehow talk with this other Alice, but what worries me is you're still not entirely convinced this world is the real one. Let's say we have a session and somehow imagine her into the room to talk with you. What happens if she doesn't go down without a fight, if she tries to convince you this is the dream? Are you ready for that?'

'Yes,' I say, but I can hear the catch in my own voice. I'm heavy and sluggish, tired. 'So you're saying no.'

'Of course not. It's your choice, always is. But you told me you wanted to end this. This development with the stranger could be important. It might be the reality of the dream is breaking apart on it's own. Or not. I say we stop our attempts to end it artificially and give you,' He points at me for emphasis, 'a chance to resolve it with your own resources, to come to that belief organically.'

'Why is that so important?'

'Because then you can know it's real,' he says eventually. 'To believe. Not just think.' He taps a rhythm on his desk. 'So, what do you want to do?'

I look at him. 'I want you to help me.' He seems to be waiting. 'Do what you need to do, but I'm sick of tagging along with other people's plans for me.'

He smiles; I'm not sure what at. Throwing the ball from hand to hand once more he goes to the bar fridge and pulls out the jug of ice water again, topping up both our glasses. 'That might be one of the most encouraging things I've heard all year. I understand you want to try this and it seems we're on the same page when it comes to reducing your medication. I'll do you a deal. Why don't we try a little relaxation therapy and see how it goes? Not everyone can simply go deep first time round anyway. Relaxation therapy, it's a kind of hypnosis. Shallow. Easy. No digging. Deal?'

'You're not taking me seriously.'

He sips the water, wincing at the cold. 'Opposite. I'm taking you very seriously. We try my idea and then, if things aren't making progress, we can be ready for yours. In the meantime, we practice so if you still want to do it, it can all go smoothly.'

'All right,' I say quietly, 'but this relaxation thing, do it now.'

'Now. You're sure?'

'Yes. I could do with some rest, believe me.'

He goes to the windows and begins pulling the blinds. 'You're the boss, boss.' That's one thing I like about Ryan. He might go on forever, weighing this and that until you want to poke his eyes out with something, but once he's agreed to do something, he does.

'Don't make me act like a chicken, right?'

'No promises.'

The room descends into twilight and I fight back a breath of uncertainty. I never realised it was this small. It seems to get even hotter.

He drains his glass. 'All right.' He stops for a moment to survey his surroundings before walking the perimeter of the office. 'You don't need darkness of course,' he says as he twists the final venetian blind mostly shut, 'but it helps to have as much of a relaxing atmosphere as possible. It would be better if it were cooler.'

'So what should I do?' I ask as he makes his way around the space, 'lay down on the couch or something?' My voice is quiet and muffled, different in the altered acoustics. A strange coolness begins to creep over me despite the heat. Do I want to stop?

'If you like,' he says, 'or you can sit comfortably. Whatever you prefer.'

'I'm a cliché,' I mutter, swinging myself around so I'm lying back against the skin-hot leather. 'What's next?'

He sits in the chair opposite again, looks at me closely. 'You sure you want to do this?' I nod quickly, not trusting myself to speak. 'OK, The first thing I'm going to do is explain what's about to happen.' You can close your eyes if it helps.' I shut them. 'As you listen to my voice and go into this state, you won't be asleep. You're still going to notice the sound of the clock, feel the texture of the couch, feel the warmth in the air.' His tone is relaxed, conversational. He's already started.

'Instead of resting the conscious mind, I want to wake the other, larger part of your mind. All you're going to do today is relax. And to do that, you can help by focusing on your breathing. In. Out.' He repeats himself and I find myself only half listening. Soon I'm breathing in time to his voice. I want to tell him I'm afraid, but it can wait. I do need a good rest after all.

Ryan continues, unhurried, calm. He talks about a staircase. There are ten steps. I take the first.

22

SCREAM

I scream.
Jerking upwards I gawp in confusion. My hand is killing me and I raise my bloody bandage in the dimness.

There's someone at the end of my bed.

A girl, crawling towards me.

I gasp for air, choking.

Ryan's face looms large and concerned as a white flash from a penlight shines into my eyes.

I scream and push myself sideways off the couch, falling to the floor. I might be having a heart attack. My vision blurs then comes back from the brink. Shaking my head I try to get a grip as I stand up, noticing a strange fog of cold air pouring from the air conditioner vent. I drop back onto the seat, looking around, knowing I've forgotten something.

'Alice,' says Ryan urgently, 'do you know where you are?'

'What happened?' My voice is someone else's; a croak.

'Tell me where you are.'

'Your office. What happened?'

He pockets the pen. 'I'm not sure. Things were going well, then you started screaming.'

'I can't remember,' I say, feeling my abused throat.

He sits next to me. 'Alice. You were conscious through the whole induction.'

I shake my head. 'The last thing I saw was you closing the blinds.'

He breathes out. 'OK. It's all right,' he says, but his face makes him a liar.

Moments later I get my things and leave. He doesn't say anything when I shut the door.

23

THE GIRL IN GREEN

I feel used. It's crazy and it doesn't make sense but that's how it is. As I walk over those loose cobblestones down Echo Street I'm in a fog. I don't know what happened, it's almost as if my dream self set me up somehow. Like I said — crazy and doesn't make sense. On top of it all I went and forced Ryan to do something he didn't want to do and guess what? It screwed up.

This isn't helpful and I know it, but that last blast of cold from his air conditioner has gotten under my skin somehow. I'm carrying the dream winter with me here in the middle of summer. Clutching my bag to my chest, I walk head down like a victim not looking at people, afraid to make eye contact.

Enough, Alice.

The alley is busier than yesterday and I find myself side stepping shoppers as they loiter around windows, chatting broadly over coffees or trudging under the weight of their shopping to their cars. A small dog barks somewhere out of sight and I do my best to ignore it, but that's like trying to not think about something, and the random yapping gets to me even more.

I step around a green bin, ripe and rotten with an overflow of garbage spilling out onto the sidewalk in a stinking mess. It's appropriate: things are rotten today. Rotting. The dog's still barking and without knowing it I swear silently. Almost silently. A woman glances at me and moves away as I shake my head; this day keeps getting better.

A fly follows me from the garbage can, buzzing around my face like a dirty black dot and I swipe at it, feeling a gross little impact as my hand makes contact. I dodge another piece of rubbish, this time a small plastic bag blowing past in the breeze, watching as it twitches in the air like a smudged cloud before gravity gets the better of it and it drifts back down, dropping at the feet of a girl sitting on a wooden bench.

Moments seem magnified, somehow portentous and I try to clear my head, fighting the sense of vertigo that always comes before a panic attack. Right now I'm unanchored and nothing feels real. The shop is ahead but instead of opening up I go into the bakery next door. I need a friendly face.

Passing under the powerful downblast of an air-curtain, the smell of yeast and baking bread slaps me right back into the here and now. There's nothing like gorgeous food to bring you down to earth. The aromas of coffee blends, sweet cakes, breads and pastries drive out the cold and I start feeling better right away. The shop's narrow and deep like most the buildings in the alley, with small tables lining the far wall, many of them occupied. I manage to find a seat and order a Cappuccino from Keira, the owner. Slowly, slowly, the weirdness of the session with Ryan passes. It doesn't leave me completely but I can sense my balance slowly returning.

I smile as Keira brings over the coffee, sliding a small slice of fruitcake over to me as well. 'Thanks,' I murmur.

'Tough day at the office, sweetie?'

I nod. 'Strange day.'

Keira raises her eyebrows and pulls up a chair next to me. 'Tell me.'

I glance at her over my drink. 'Don't you have customers?'

'No. Funny thing. According to my accountant they're called clients. What's the difference? And I pay this guy?'

I laugh, almost choking on the coffee. Keira's great. She sometimes gets free flowers from me and I get a cup on the house now and then from her. She's got no idea about my dream, but it's not something you'd want to go and advertise. It's the closest thing I've got to a normal relationship with someone. We're not exactly friends — comrades perhaps. The drink helps, strong and well made. Keira prides herself on her coffee as much as Dave, her partner the baker, does his pastries. She studies me for a moment. 'You're pale.'

'I'll be all right,' I say, sipping the drink.

A small bell rings, the sound cutting through the crowded conversations, sparing me from trying to explain my day to her. She stands and places her hand on my shoulder. 'Take the week off,' she says. 'I'll clear it with your boss.' I smile. An old joke.

I get a weird feeling as Keira disappears into the depths of the shop and I set the coffee down, glancing about, seeing nothing out of place. I check my bag is still by my feet. Something isn't right. Half standing, I scan the other tables again. People busy talking, sipping their own coffees, someone reading a newspaper. There's nothing out of the ordinary, which somehow makes the sensation even worse. I stand. I need quiet.

Seconds later I get it; somewhere, right at the limit of my hearing someone's crying. The sound is whispery and almost not there at all, but the uncertain, stammering voice of someone choking back tears is real. Grabbing my bag I walk to the door, waving quickly to her as I leave.

The alley's much busier than usual. Workers from one of the nearby office blocks swarm into the lane, blocking my view as I search around for the source of the crying. The strangest thing; there's nothing out of the ordinary, no reaction to the sobbing, only people concerned with their own business. Here outside the bakery, the sound is unmistakable: it's a child. I push through a small knot of shoppers to the chair I'd seen the girl sitting on earlier, but she's gone.

I sense the sound moving and now it's behind me. I spin. Nothing. I breathe out, self-conscious and stupid for the second time today. There's no sign of anyone upset, let alone in tears. I scan nearby faces for any signs they might be hearing the same thing but no — no concern, no slight pauses, nothing at all. I turn to a stranger.

'Excuse me,' I say, 'but can you hear anything?'

The guy, about my age with neatly combed brown hair and a cheap looking suit, stares at me in surprise as his friend studies me with equal curiosity.

'What's up?'

'Crying,' I say and I can't help a flush of embarrassment at it all, 'do you hear it?' The two men swap a glance; then one, followed by the other, shake their heads. Before I can respond there it is again, further away this time. The voice is moving. Leaving them to stare after me, I head towards the sound.

I push through another group of shoppers two doors

down from our business, trying to narrow down where it's coming from. The bricks and close walls of the alley make ghosts of the acoustics, bouncing and redoubling the sobs.

I will myself not to run but I run anyway. I know how it must seem but keep going, ignoring the startled stares I pull in my wake. There's desolation in those choking, snotty tears, real and awful torment. I race past Looking Books and the Nick Nackery before forcing myself to slow down. The crying's louder here, but the people surrounding me are either ignoring it or just not listening.

'Jesus,' I mumble, 'you're losing it.'

Then I see her, the girl from the bench. The child is perhaps seven, even younger. She's clutching a well-used teddy bear close to her chest, staring at passers-by. I didn't notice this the first time but her clothes are filthy, coated with street grime and torn in places, yet I'm able to recognise her school uniform for what it is. From across the alley she spots me and blinks widely, wiping a stream of snot from her nose. She tries to step away but stalls as someone almost trips over her. The guy glances at her and walks on like he's seen her enough to avoid her, but nothing more.

Heart beating hard, I go over to her and kneel by her side, forcing myself to appear calm and friendly. Pulling a tissue from my bag I hand it to the girl, who takes it warily. The girl's face is still as a statue, horrified, her eyes puffy from crying. She blows her nose with a self-conscious grace, weird considering how she looks. Deep purple bruises run down one side of her cheek and I will away my reaction, which I know will startle her. My heart is beating faster by the second.

'Hey,' I say, 'what's your name?'

She stares at me a moment before passing back the used tissue. I take it and stand, holding out my hand. 'My name is

Alice,' I say. 'You look like you need help. Are your parents here?' The girl shakes her head, a tiny, furtive movement that's almost no movement at all. Pointing to the awning further down, I reach a decision. 'And that's my flower shop, a few doors away. Why don't you come with me and I'll find some help?' She glances up and down the alley and I wonder if I've scared her even more. How did she get this way in the first place, by trusting another stranger? Tense seconds later, she holds out her own hand.

I fumble my keys but finally manage to unlock the door, pushing it open and carefully ushering the girl in ahead of me. It's obvious the kid's been beaten up. Emotions coil around each other so tightly I'm not even sure what I'm feeling right now. Pity for the child and a huge screaming mad anger at whoever has done this to her. And also those passive, crueller accomplices in the alley who ignored her.

'Sit here,' I say gently, guiding her to the wicker chair near the entrance. 'I'll get you something to drink, then I'm going to call an ambulance.' The girl sits, calm but wide-eyed and wary. 'Are you sure you can't tell me your name?' I ask again, cautious of pushing her even a little. She shakes her head. 'That's OK, you don't have to talk.'

Hurrying to the rear of the shop, skirting the jarrah workbench, I glance back at the child framed by roses on display either side of the door. With the blurred dark shapes of people outside the window as a backdrop the girl, still hanging on to her teddy bear, looks like a doll.

I fill a glass of water with shaking hands and return to her, motionless, eyes wide and glassy. Kneeling by her side I hand it over. 'Here you go,' I say, 'drink this.' The girl stares at me nervously and takes the water. 'Listen, I don't know what happened, but I want to help, OK?' She sips, spilling some of it. I reach out to steady her but my own nerves aren't much better, slopping it as well. I breathe, calming myself enough to guide her hand as she takes a drink. When she's done I place the glass on the floor where she can get it. 'I'm just going to make a call, OK? Sit tight.' The girl opens her mouth, then closes it slowly. 'Do you want to say something?' But again, she's silent. Standing quietly I return to the counter, pick up the phone and dial triple zero for an ambulance. The line connects after an age and fighting to keep my voice from trembling I try to explain to the operator what's going on. I'm giving the shop's address when the glass smashes. 'I hate you!' she screams.

I glance up in time to catch her jumping to her feet and throwing open the door. A wall of noise from the alley hits me after the silence of the shop and I drop the handset as she races outside.

There's a stunned, stupid second when I do nothing before I regain my wits and dash from the store, looking for her. 'Hey!' I yell. A couple turns to stare. 'A girl, has anyone seen a girl?' Faces turn away, embarrassed or disinterested. Somewhere out of sight, someone laughs.

I race over the ankle-twisting cobblestones as fast as I dare, scanning for signs of the green dress, listening for running feet. Nothing. I run back the other way, passing the bakery and out onto the street, where a gust of hot wind brings dust and tears to my eyes. Whichever way I search I'm met with nothing but ordinary people moving casually through their day.

'Shit!'

24

COPS

I didn't expect the police. One of them is with me as the empty ambulance drives away down the alley. The officer is tall, slim, harried and angry at me. She hasn't said anything directly but she doesn't believe me. Her partner is outside looking for the girl but he won't find her. The constable has her book out, flipping through pages, reviewing what I've told her. Why does everyone I meet need to take notes?

'She was seven, maybe eight,' I say again. The cop's name is Baker and Baker, no first name, seems tired. This is the second time we've gone through my statement. Outside, red and blue flashes flicker past the frosted glass windows, turning the plants odd shades. Baker scans her notes. 'So no one appeared to notice the girl except for you, is that correct?'

'I think so,' I say, feeling the weight of the day. 'Maybe someone else saw her, but nobody did anything about it.'

The constable nods, accepting the information, not necessarily believing it. She shuts her notebook and calls her partner on her radio. A man's voice comes back distorted and loud in the quiet of my shop. 'My colleague still hasn't found anyone who can confirm your story.'

'That doesn't mean it didn't happen.'

Behind her the phone rings.

'Can I?'

Baker nods her head, a quick, annoyed motion. Her day has just been made that much crappier, by the woman standing in front of her and she's not about to hide the fact.

The phone's still ringing but I try to make eye contact. 'OK,' I say, 'I know you don't believe me but it really did happen.'

'Maam, why don't you get the phone?'

I answer it. It's Jen.

'Hey babe, this is your friendly best buddy sister with a reminder. Don't forget we've got dinner tonight with Costa. No backing out.'

I've completely forgotten about Jen's blind date. Baker leans forward over the counter, checking things out. 'Jen, I...'

'Nope,' Jen says, 'no chickening out. Be there or I'm going to come round and drag you kicking and screaming. I know where you live.'

'Jen. The cops are here.'

There's a pause on the line. 'You're shitting me.'

'No.' And I do my best to explain how I found the girl, then lost her all in the space of quarter of an hour. As I talk to Jen, Baker pops open her notebook again and scribbles something new in it. I must look guilty. Thrown by all this I'm about to ask Jen if I can call her back when Baker gets distracted as her radio squawks, turning away from me to answer it. It can't be good: her expression changes, a tightening of the shoulders as she talks to dispatch. She signs off and motions for me to end the call.

'Listen, do you need me to come over?' Jen's voice is tense.

'No, it's OK.' I fight off a flush of anger, a body reaction to being caught in the middle of something I didn't start. And then, as always, that whisper of guilt. 'Look — don't worry about tonight. I'll be there.' I have to make it up to her.

'Forget it.' I can tell Jen has already chalked this one up to another freaky-Alice failure. For a second I get a glimpse of my future, full of failed starts and setbacks, just me and Jen getting older and angrier. I don't want that.

'No,' I say, surprising myself. 'I know you went out of your way to do this. I will be there.'

There's a pause on the line then: 'Sure. That would be great. And give me a call if you need help. I mean it.' She hangs up.

I return my attention to Baker.

'So, confirming you're Alice Brundford, of 34 Morrilla Street Brookvale, is that correct?'

I nod, sensing my mouth go dry, realising things have somehow escalated. 'Yes.' Baker studies me carefully. What is she thinking? I've seen that look before.

'I need to inform you, your name was flagged in our database. Are you currently receiving psychiatric care under doctor,' she checks her notes, 'Thomas Ryan of the Landeth Centre?'

I go cold. I know I should protest somehow, or demand a lawyer, or get angry or indignant like Dream-me would, but all I can hear is my own heart beating wildly and a small whisper of breath. My face burns under the scrutiny. 'Yes.' Then, 'How? What's going on?'

The woman's eyes harden as she puts away her notebook. 'Your name came up on our database.'

'It was the time I spent at the Mayfleur, wasn't it?' Baker

raises her eyebrows but remains silent. Hell. I wonder if they're going to arrest me or something.

Baker, still studying me like some sort of exhibit says, 'There are protocols.'

'Protocols,' I repeat, feeling surreal. 'For what?'

'Someone from Social Services will be calling your doctor.'

'So I'm in trouble?'

'No.'

'But you don't believe me.'

'It's not whether I believe you or not, Ms Brundford.' Her manner has become formal and distant.

'But you'll keep looking for the girl?'

Baker rubs her face wearily before turning towards the door. 'Apart from you, no one noticed the child you're talking about. You say you chased her down the alley, which was packed with people on their lunch break, but the only thing witnesses report is you running and calling after someone. No girl. Only you. And no child fitting the girl's description has been listed as missing.' She holds up a finger. 'I'm not saying you didn't see something. But we've got nothing to go on other than your description and no one else to corroborate your report.'

'So you're not going to look?'

'Honestly?'

'You're not going to look.'

The cop stays silent as she goes to the door. She turns. 'If you remember something new, give us a call.'

I shake my head. 'The girl is real. She was sitting on that chair and it looked like someone bashed her.'

Baker taps her notebook through her pocket. 'We have your statement and we'll keep our eyes open for anyone matching the description you gave us. Like I said. If you remember anything else, give us a call.' And with that she's gone, leaving me alone in the shop, staring at the seat the girl sat in not an hour before.

The phone rings again. I ignore it and look at the people-shapes moving outside the window, trying to let the adrenaline drain from my body. How close did I just get? I haven't thought about it for years, but now the shadow of Mayfleur looms over me like a mountain in the mist.

25

DINNER AND WATER

I check the address again but it's right. Thanks Jen. It turns out dinner's at a seafood place on a pier. The restaurant is right at the end of course, glowing like some sort of deep-sea thing caught up in fairy lights and nets.

It's also a shed over water. This is Jen's way of telling me something. I can hear her voice in my head, all smiles and confidence. Confront your fears, tackle them front on like a crazy bull-headed superwoman; that's Jen's style, not mine. I feel dizzy as I step onto the planks. Sometimes she doesn't get it, but then again, here I am, walking over the pier to the restaurant.

As I walk, the memory of the girl comes from nowhere, her eyes wide and caught somewhere between disbelief and shock, her face smeared equal parts with dirt and fear. I try to put it aside but I can't: it's too fresh. The thought is replaced by Baker and her protocol. What was the girl's protocol I wonder? My stomach churns at the thought of that poor kid running away from god knows what. I should have done more, we all should. I don't understand why the good citizens of Echo Street, my customers some of them, chose not to get involved and pretended she was invisible. A sour thought comes to mind: if they were trying to send me mad — too late.

The pier's wooden slats have been worn smooth by generations of pedestrians. So many feet, so many people. I can almost smell the age of the place as I walk, trapped in the salt of the water and the air and the wood. The slap of waves on the pylons underneath sounds like a memory of all those footsteps above. Maybe Jen's right. I underestimate her sometimes.

I go slowly, making an effort not to make an effort, pushing away the stress of the day as much as possible. There's nothing I can do for the girl right now. I closed up early after Baker left and spent the rest of the afternoon searching for her, but it was like she was never there.

Low wattage bulbs hang from loops in the overhead lines, clinking in the breeze, which bears the sounds of music and conversation. Seagulls watch me as I pass, their wind-ruffled charcoal heads turning to follow my progress. There's something sinister about them; they remind me of those open-mouthed carnival clowns, always moving, gaping, following. I stop and take a moment to get a grip.

Opening the door I instantly spot Jen leaning in close to her boyfriend, a curly-headed musician in a Hawaiian shirt. James, that's his name. Or John. Across from them chatting easily, all suntan and breezy confidence in an open necked business suit, Costa. 'OK,' I whisper to myself. 'Polite. For Jen.' And I wave, putting on my very best smile.

The table is barely big enough for the four of us. We laugh as we tangle up trying to shake hands. Ice broken, ritual started. It's too cramped though and I'm squashed as Costa shuffles over to make room. He smiles pleasantly and comments on the weather. Yes. It's hot. We agree. Jen is enthusiastic and starts acting the perfect host; it all seems very normal. For a moment I forget about my day, happy to lose myself in the flow of conversation and the careless, easy laughter.

Costa is a real gentleman; he's genuinely trying here. He's a good listener, tuned into Jen as she recounts her day: one particular unrelenting client and about his need to get laid before he has a heart attack. John — Jack, her boyfriend, smiles. But as the night wears on I can sense Jen might be regretting setting me up with Costa. Watch out John.

The food is delicious, which for some reason surprises me. Other than the cold black water beneath us, the evening is turning out OK. I haven't a clue how much Jen's told Costa about me, but since he's not treating me as an invalid I'll chalk it up to a good start. The wine is strong, the breeze through the open window cooling, blowing away the last of the heat from the day. I stare out over the water and wonder about the girl again. Jen taps me on the hand. I've missed something.

'Costa was saying,' she tells me, looking at me in that way she has, 'that they've opened up a new building on Cockatoo Island. We should go there some time.'

OK. Stay focused. I have no idea what they're talking about, but the thought of islands is a whole different thing to sitting over ten feet of water. You can't get off islands. I shiver even considering it.

'I'm not sure,' I say. God, how weak. 'You know, the shop.' I stare at her; don't push it. Sitting in a shed over water is one thing, hopping into a boat, no.

Jen looks at me and reading my mind, nods. 'Yeah,' she says, 'you're right.' To the others she explains, 'The shop hasn't been going so great lately and we've both agreed to put in extra time to it. The joy of owing your own business.'

Thank you Jen.

Costa nods, raising his eyebrows in sympathy. 'Tell me about it.'

'Costa owns his own firm,' she supplies.

'Yeah, property law, conveyancing, that type of thing.'

I force a smile. 'You're a lawyer?'

He grins, easy and confident. 'Yup. It pays the bills.'

Alice, that is, Manhattan-me, is a lawyer. Things aren't meant to cross over. They never have before but recently there have been a few too many coincidences. I can't say what it means — could be Ryan is right and it's starting to unravel. If only. I wipe at my head, feeling hot. I'm not myself tonight.

Jen leans over. 'But more importantly, he's a pretty bad surfer.'

'Woah, hang on. I wouldn't go that far.'

Their banter is so easy, guileless. I wonder how they do it.

'I would.'

Jen makes a point of looking at me and then John. 'I was on this awesome wave — the only decent set for the last hour when this guy,' She points at Costa, 'drops in, right in front of me. I didn't even see him and the next second, crash.'

I study John. Jack. He doesn't know where to put his attention; Jen who's telling the story or Costa, who seems to be all easy charm. It sounds like one of those how we met stories told by old couples. John or Jack, you've just been wiped out.

'Now the way I remember it,' says Costa, leaning back,

'you fell off and needed someone to pull you out of the water.'

'Well, anyway,' says Jen. Is she blushing? 'We got to talking and it turns out we both go to the same place to blow off steam.'

'I love the beach,' he says, again with that ease. 'I inherited it from my parents. My father was a fisherman back in Greece.'

'I'm not such a big water person,' I hear myself saying, 'our parents drowned.' What the hell? Where did that come from?

Jen blinks. I can't meet anyone's eyes and eventually focus on my wine. The silence stretches and John rests his hand on Jen's.

Jen's flushed. 'It's not something we usually advertise.'

'What I was saying is I find water — difficult.' Difficult. That's one word for it.

Costa nods, listening carefully. 'Yes,' he says, 'I can understand. Our past forms us, doesn't it? We're all creatures painted by our own history. I'm sorry about your parents.'

Now he's a poet.

'Long time ago,' mutters Jen.

He nods. Costa does this funny thing with his mouth, like he's holding something back and then I see it in his eyes. Damn. I glance down to the plate, wondering how much he knows of the other part of the story. Not that it's a huge secret, but for once it would be nice not to be the crazy one, just plain old Alice, take me as I am.

Costa shrugs and with that smile of his, suggests going to the island another time. We agree. John, Jack, looks like a tagalong. He says something to Jen, who nods, but her eyes are on Costa. This double date is turning single pretty fast.

I'm OK with it, after today. Good on Jen if she can find someone.

Dessert rolls around but I'm not there anymore. I'm tired. I can't help thinking about the girl again. Is she hiding right now? Where are her parents? She didn't seem like a runaway, but what does a runaway look like anyway? She needs help, that much I do know. Tomorrow, I'm going to search for her, make an effort. People can't just disappear.

I've done it again.

'What?' I say, trying to catch up.

Costa leans in towards me with that smile. 'I have an idea how tough it is.' He says.

'Pardon?'

'My sister,' he goes on, 'has bipolar.'

I stare at him. I don't know what to say. Alice would punch him in the nuts. Then again, she wouldn't be seen dead here either. Right now, I want to be her. He's judging me, the prick.

But I don't hit him in the nuts; I get up and go to the bathroom instead. The door opens and there's Jen, bodyguard and bigmouth rolled into one. She starts to say something but I shake my head.

'I get what you're trying to do, but I'm not interested.'

She looks at me and it's hard to tell what she's thinking right now.

'So I'm going to leave, OK?'

'Alice,' she says, 'I didn't say anything to him.'

'OK.'

It's not OK. It's a long way from being OK. Now she's lying. That's a fun new development. I wonder how much crappier this day can get. Actually, I don't. Instead, I head for the door. Jen can apologise to Costa, and JohnJack can play catch up for the rest of the night. It's on her.

AWAY FROM THE water the evening is hot and humid. I drop my bag onto the kitchen table and imagine what it would be like to smoke. Alice enjoys it. Seems to be a good stress relief so maybe I should try. And there it is again; I'm so different right now. The girl is messing me up.

The old answering machine is beeping and I hit play. It's Ryan. The police called him. More protocols. He wants to organise a session tomorrow. Talk it through. I wonder what connection of databases and red flags came together that resulted in him getting the call. I hate that I have a file. Somewhere I am reduced to an annotation. Is that it? Everything that matters brought down to another protocol? I jam the erase button down, waiting for the flickering red readout to go to zero.

Wandering into the bathroom I pull open the mirror. There, sitting on the shelf lined up like little soldiers, are my bottles. Phenolan. Apriplex. Lignatol. And on and on. Jen despises them. Yeah, well, me too. Ryan had a point. Tonight I'm going cold turkey. Just for fun.

Later I drop onto the bed, exhausted. Ratbone claws the thin sheet, purring crazily as he turns in circles. 'Go to sleep you stupid cat.' I lay back on the pillow and sigh. I turn onto my side, staring at nothing, my mind's eye on the ragged beaten girl, framed by roses.

26

MOLLHER'S ORDERS

I slowly get that I'm awake. There's the smoothness of silk underneath one palm and the tight pressure of a bandage around the other. A soft light filters through the air but I don't recognise the delicately carved four-poster bed, the richly folded curtains and art on the wall. Then I figure it out. A guestroom. I lean forward and the fall of the bedsheets reveals baggy pink pyjamas. Nice. My head is throbbing, my arms ache and it hurts when I take a deep breath. Got to stop waking up this way.

As I inch my way down the central staircase the house is alive with echoes of rubber-soled sneakers and the banter of the movers as they pull apart last night's props. I walk down the stairs carefully, leg muscles spasming as I go. Not to put too fine a point on it but I feel like hell and have to lean on a banister for support, cursing silently. I get my breath and looking up again, recognise Mollher at the bottom of the steps, waiting for me. 'Mollher,' I say, wincing as I ease myself down the final stair. 'Get out of my way'

He doesn't move, his wide bear of a face framed by a halo of cigar smoke curling around his features like a special effect. He'd make a great Satan. Officially, Mollher is the Van de Korte chauffeur, which is one of those open jokes nobody seems to call out. He's inevitable as gravity. With a permanent five o'clock shadow, he fills his clothes like a wrestler gone to fat, but you wouldn't want to tangle with him. He carries his weight with a memory of violence.

I can handle the cheap suit, the skin-deep smile, the whole shabby-menace look he pulls off. The part that gets to me is his voice: that of a New England lawyer, measured, educated and smart. Which is why Mollher has been around forever. Thugs come and go but he's a breed above. A meeting with Mollher is guaranteed to ruin your day. 'Good morning to you as well, Alice,' he says, 'pleasant as always.' He swings himself in front of me. 'Stay put. We have things to talk about.'

'Get out of my way.'

'Not until we've talked.'

'Seriously. Fuck off.'

He smiles inscrutably and guides me to a nearby chair, leaning forward patiently as we wait for two movers to push past carrying a potted palm between them. 'What are you doing, Alice?' he asks after they clear the room.

'Going home.'

He sits back and puffs on his cigar thoughtfully. I try to stand but he grabs my arm and forces me down. His grip is painful and effortless and for a flash I think about calling out for help. Like I said, he's not stupid, so I know he won't hurt me. Understanding this he slips down a notch from terrifying to asshole. I learned a long time ago there's only one way to deal with Mollher: show no fear.

The sweet smoke clouds the space between us but I choose not to cough. 'Have you considered rehab?' He brushes some ash from his jacket, raising his eyebrows as the cigar flares then dies.

I give him my brightest smile. 'Have you considered go fucking yourself?'

Mollher laughs loudly, drawing a gold lighter from his pocket. He puffs the cigar again, relighting the end. 'You can do better than that.'

I smile and lean towards him, putting my head close to his. 'This is the dream.'

He blinks slowly, looking intrigued. 'So you've decided again? Well, at least you're being interesting now. You might be right, by the way.' He grins and for a moment I swear I'm staring at the Cheshire Cat before he puffs out another cloud of smoke. 'Bravo on your commitment, though not so good for me I assume.'

I snatch the stub from his fingers and jam it into my mouth. The end is wet with his spit but the tip flares with a satisfying glow. "Course not,' I say. 'Not good for me either. So do me a favour and jump off a bridge or something.' I offer the cigar back but he waves it away.

'You keep it.' He rubs his eyes tiredly. 'You're going to crash. You know that.'

'So?'

He regards me closely, his face concerned. I'm fascinated at the metamorphosis, fast and unconvincing as it is. 'You've upset your parents.'

I lean back and blow a cloud of blue smoke into the air. 'You see, the thing about that is, I don't care.'

He smiles, wry amusement rippling over his fighter's face. 'You're to attend a family meeting.'

I snap my head back. 'Gee Mollher, I thought we stopped doing those when I was sixteen.'

'You were mature then.'

I tap out the cigar, watching the ash as it falls to the floor, a kind of indoor counterpart to the snow falling outside. I'm not truly angry, not even surprised. The encounter with Mollher is reassuring in a bizarre way. Its familiar rhythms are playing out like they normally do, the argument working it's way through to conclusion, its cadence known, the insults understandable and predictable. I've had this conversation in one shape or another a million times before. What really scares me was last night and the hallucination. I've never lost control like that before and the thought terrifies me.

'Where's Gabe?

'I don't know.'

I stare him down. 'I mean it.'

The big man leans forward. 'Your parents want a proper family meeting.'

'Mollher, where's Gabe?'

He shrugs. 'Removed from the house. He was acting the fool.'

'Did you hurt him?'

Something changes in his expression. 'Yes.' He watches me tense up. 'But he'll be fine. Anyway,' he pauses as he plucks another cigar from his jacket pocket. 'You should have known how that was going to play out when you brought him along.' I make to stand again but he holds me down a second time, his hand grabbing my arm painfully. Now I'm angry.

'What the hell?'

'Alice,' he says. 'When they get back, they want a meeting. No messing around, no game playing.' I struggle minutely, fiercely. Maybe my parents' attack dog has finally slipped his leash. All my rationalisations about him not hurting me go out the window as I look into his eyes.

'They've put up with your shenanigans since you were a teenager. Time to grow up and get things straight again.'

I shove my face close to his, despite my fear. 'Things were never straight. Tell me, how do you just drop into a coma, forget who you are and expect things to be straight?'

'Couldn't say.' He lets go.

I stand, refusing to rub my arm as he stands as well. 'You're heading into a bad place, Alice.'

I walk away, frustration making my movements stiff and robotic. 'I'm already there you dick.' I head through the front door, not daring to look back. 'And tell them to talk to me directly next time they feel like slumming it.'

27

GABE CHECKS IN

I pull up short as I walk into my building. Jordie is sitting with his back against a wall playing with an action figure. Adrenaline spikes for a moment as I'm thrown right back to the dream where I met the girl near the flower shop. It's so unexpected. 'Shit,' I breathe. Jordie smiles up at me and the weirdness passes fractionally.

'Hi,' he says, twisting the toy into a new pose.

I glance around, hearing footsteps. Gabe walks up holding a bottle of water. 'Hey.'

'What are you doing here?'

'I came to check if you were OK.'

'How the hell did you get in?'

He seems genuinely insulted. 'Marty. The doorman? You think I maybe broke in through a window or some such, eh?' I look around but Marty's not there. Must be on a break. I hesitate a second before walking up and hugging him. 'Sorry. I'm still getting over last night.' I take in his appearance, noticing for the first time the bruises on his cheek and swelling under his left eye. 'You look like crap.'

'Well, you're no rose either right now.'

Jordie laughs.

I punch a button for the lift. 'Gabe, I'm sorry.'

'Don't worry about it,' he says, but I can tell it's not over. I almost let them in when I put my hand on the door, blocking it. 'I need a couple of minutes. Alright?'

He stares at me, expression caught between hurt and curious. 'You OK?'

'Not really. But give me ten. Just to get my shit together, OK?'

He nods. 'OK. Hey Jordie?'

'What?'

'Up and out. We're going to find something to go with this water.'

I wait for them to leave before heading up to my apartment.

Stepping from the elevator I make my way to the bathroom, where I lean heavily on the basin, heart still jumping. I risk a quick glance at myself in the mirror, turning away from the exhausted face in the glass. This is the last thing I want. I need to decompress, but it isn't going to happen. Turning on the hot tap, I splash water onto my face, getting rid of the coldness I've had since waking up at that damn house.

The apartment is cold despite the heating, despite the warmth of the rugs and the heavy drapes. I wander through the rooms, hugging myself, ignoring the throb of my hand under the bandages, feeling lost. I'm tired. The sensation wraps around me in a cold wet blanket, filling me with a dull ache I can't pin down.

I wonder if life might be better in Sydney. Poor little Victim-Alice in Sydney, always on the receiving end of someone's charity. Forever switching and cutting back over her own tracks searching for the truth. She'd love a visit from Gabe and Jordie; she's big into family and there's one for her, ready-made.

'Shit,' I say to no one in particular, wandering into the living room and dropping heavily onto the sofa. Sensing a lump at my back I pull a plastic lion from behind the cushion, staring at it numbly. Sometimes, like now, I understand this has to be the dream. It's not a guess; it's a bone-deep knowing. I've got no idea where the toy came from but I place it carefully on the coffee table. I don't have it in me to be surprised.

The portrait on the wall is staring at me, hollow-eyed, not real, compelling. Examining my freshly bandaged hand I realise someone must have seen to it last night. And now I'm thinking about it, stripped me off and got me into those pyjamas. I can't even dredge up the energy to be insulted. Whatever they gave me hasn't worn off and I'm still not right. Closing my eyes, I wonder if I can sleep.

I don't.

Twenty minutes later I meet Gabe with Jordie at his side. 'Shouldn't he be at school?'

Jordie shrugs out of his bright red coat and drops it to the floor. He opens up a tattered backpack and pulls out the action figure he was playing with earlier, twisting it into a karate pose. 'No school today. Can I have something to eat?'

'There's a takeout menu in the kitchen. Why don't you go order for all of us? Anything you want.' I check with Gabe. 'Cool?'

He tilts his head. 'Don't get chicken, OK?'

The boy mumbles his agreement, walking away as Gabe sits on the couch next to me. 'So.'

'So.'

I search his eyes for a sense of what's going on inside. If there is an inside, that is. What would a figment of a dream think? Could it really think at all or would it only be a mirror shining reflections back at you? I close my eyes. If I keep this up I'll go insane, wind up in an asylum like Real-me in Sydney. 'I'm sorry,' I say. 'I didn't mean for any of it to happen.'

I lean in to kiss him but he pushes me away. 'I said don't worry about it, yeah?'

I back off. 'Fine. They beat the crap out of you. Sorry for giving a damn.'

'Chill. It was my fault.'

'What do you mean?'

'I shouldn't have gone, not my thing, eh? I told you before.'

I rub my hand. 'So you're saying you're blaming me?' I can tell I sound tired, my voice is strange in my own ears. I wish I wasn't having to deal with Gabe right now. Next time I run into Marty I'm going to kick his ass.

Gabe stares at me, eyes wide and annoyed.

'Just forget it.'

Jordie comes back from the kitchen holding two paper menus. 'I ordered Chinese food. But it's got chicken in it. Is that OK?'

Gabe stands, rubbing his neck. 'No man, it's not OK. I don't want you eating that stuff, eh? It's full of diseases and crap. It'll kill you.'

'Hey,' I say, 'it's cool. Calm down.'

Jordie glances between the two of us like we're his parents. Gabe walks to the window and peers down over the traffic. 'What's your deal, eh?'

'My deal?'

'Yeah. Your deal. Last night — you were so messed up. I thought.' He throws up his hands. 'I thought you might have died or something. And then this big ass-thug goes to work on me. I mean...' He stops, remembering Jordie who's still behind him, holding the menus listlessly. 'Can we do this in private?'

I nod. 'Hey listen,' I say, kneeling beside the boy. 'Here's the control for the TV. Why don't you find some cartoons to watch. Your dad and I need to talk alone.'

Jordie takes the remote and jumps onto the couch. 'All right.' He spots the lion. 'Can I play with that?'

'Sure.'

Gabe walks back and ruffles his hair. 'Sorry man. We cool?' Jordie nods.

I open the door to the bedroom, flicking on the light. The bed is a tangled mess of sheets from the night before, clothes and shoes all over the place, my tee lying in a clot near a corner. I sit on the bed, drained. Gabe sits next to me and the silence stretches out between us.

'I don't understand what happened,' I say eventually.

'You shouldn't have asked me to go.'

'Yeah. I messed up.'

He nods, allowing the moment to pass. 'So what was it all about?'

'I told you I don't know.'

'Bullshit.'

I straighten out a part of the sheet. 'It all went weird, OK? The whole thing got so messed up. One minute they're making introductions and the next, everything's blurry and watery and it all goes to hell.'

'That must have been some wicked shit you were on,' he says quietly.

'It's nothing to do with that. I know Rene. He wouldn't fuck me over.'

He looks at me, astonished. 'Are you for real? You're

telling me you trust your dealer? Jesus girl, if you think that then you are far gone.'

'You had exactly the same as me.'

'Sure,' he says, flushed and angry, 'but what did you take beforehand?'

'Shut up, Gabe.'

'Yeah well, I know what I saw.'

'And what was that?'

He stares at me for a long time. 'Someone who's this far away from being a junkie. You're frying your own fucking brain.'

Something snaps. I don't know if it's the last few days or the tiredness or maybe just a grain of truth that does it, but it's like I'm watching from a distance. I jump from the bed and punch him. 'Get out of here!' I yell.

'Whoa, shit. Calm down!' Now he's standing. He grabs my arms, sidestepping as I kick out. Tears streak down my cheeks. I choke on my own helplessness, breathing hard, gasping as words desert me. He pulls me closer but for some reason all I see is Mollher. 'Listen. You got to get away from all this. It's going to kill you sure as sure.'

I finally find my voice. 'Go.'

'No.'

I free myself from his grasp and run across the room, calling the elevator. Jordie turns away from the show he's watching as Gabe follows me into the lounge. 'What's up?'

'Your dad has to go,' I say, rubbing the tears from my cheeks, voice shaking.

'But we just got here. And the food isn't here yet.'

Gabe walks round me, trying to catch my eyes but I look away. He's about to say something, then changes his mind. 'Yeah buddy. We'll pick up pizza on the way back.'

Jordie shakes his head. 'No, I ordered already. I wasn't even going to eat the chicken like you said.'

'That's cool.' Gabe picks up his coat and bag. 'We got to go right now though.'

I'm blank. I've got nothing to say. Jordie studies at him. 'Is this because someone hit you?' He stuffs his action figure into the bag and grabs it sullenly, slinging it over a shoulder. 'Cos you don't need to take shit from no one.'

I wait for the door to slide open. Gabe puts his arm around the boy, shepherding him out of the apartment, but not, I notice, before putting himself between me and his son. He tries to say something but the door closes and I turn away. I'm burned out.

'Yeah well, screw this too,' I whisper. I give them plenty of time to get out of the building then leave as well.

28

DECISION

The day's cold and surprisingly bright. It catches me off guard; I was expecting snow but instead the sky is clear and this amazing, startling blue. A breeze carries the sounds of people talking over the traffic and I can hear the shrill gaggle of children laughing somewhere ahead. I drop my hood and let the wind bite at my ears, allowing the day to seep in.

I pass a guy sitting on a bench wearing a Yankees T-shirt and eating a hot dog, like it's the middle of summer. He stares at me as I go by. You can always count on the crazies. I wind up in Central Park, heading towards the statue of Alice on sheer autopilot. When I was a kid, I'd been amazed to discover we'd shared the same name and as I grew up I found I could relate to the fate of the girl who'd fallen down the rabbit hole.

Coming here now is like touching a cornerstone, an anchor for my memories. In my dream, (maybe not the dream after all) my Sydney self had come to this place as well, looking for a connection. It had seemed so real, such a thin membrane separating us from each other at the time.

I'd almost believed it, the sleeping and waking lives blurring into one continuous line, distinguished by a point of view that was so close, but never close enough. It just about sent me mad; an existence with no night, just a continuation of new mornings, exploring a world that for my other self held no hint of me, my family or their business. The Manhattan of another planet.

I shrug deeper into my coat, forcing away one memory only to be ambushed by a second. I think of it as a kind of messed-up birthday, my first day as two people. It's strange looking back on it — I've got no recollection of waking up and realising I had separate lives; it wasn't like that at all. It was far more subtle. When I was five or six, perhaps a little older, I was walking down a street. I forget where exactly, but the late autumn reds and browns of fallen leaves coloured the sidewalks like splashes of paint. We passed a hot dog cart and a man in a baseball cap selling soda and there was a long line to a shop we had to walk around. Mother was with me and a younger, fitter Mollher. I stopped to yell at them to catch up and as I turned, it all came to me; I knew about her, simple as that. My other self had been living quietly in my dreams for years, surfacing fully formed, complete with her own history and family.

It was like having a secret pen pal, or being part of the most exclusive club you could imagine. She was amazed in the same way, curious about everything to do with my life and for a while she was my new best friend, an impossible fairy-world creature who had moved into my imagination. We even gave each other tours, walking through our favourite places; read books together and played with toys.

The tips of my ears are freezing by the time I get to the statue of Alice. Back then I'd shared my special connection with it with my dream friend. During those days when we went for walks I loved climbing all over its burnished surface with the other kids, knowing it for the magical thing it was. It never diminished; it was ageless, even as we grew up.

It took a long time for me to understand the Alice of my dreams; my other self wasn't a separate person at all. Slowly as I dreamed and lived the tours she gave of the parks, special picnics on a beach and even those awesome fights she had with her sister, I began to sense a falseness. The sense of familiarity grew overwhelming, until I understood I wasn't narrating an adventure to a stranger, I was talking to myself. It's so hard to describe. When I woke in Manhattan it was exactly the same. Why bother taking your friend on a trip, if her memories are your own, her places your places? It slowly came to me there was no difference between myself and her. We weren't friends. We were one person, and once I finally figured it out, it was like a death.

But if the *what* of my life is this messed up, the *why* totally screws me over. I had meningitis as a kid and it nearly killed me. I slept for days, caught up in a fever and rashes, and when I woke up everything had changed. My first dreams of Sydney-Alice came soon after. Who loses track of reality because of a disease? I don't know; no one does.

Sydney-me has a much better reason to be mad. Her parents died. She remembers the crash, and the irony isn't lost on me that I remember more of her life than my own.

Her memories are blurred and painful, shot through with loss. It's so powerful even I have a hard time thinking about it. It was night and she was falling. Her sister was screaming. The car had gone over a bridge, scraping and leaping the steel barrier before flipping and dropping lengthwise into a shallow creek below.

They're not so much memories as sensations: noise, weightlessness, followed by sudden crushing pressure around her waist as the seatbelt digs in. Jen crying, the almost pretty silence of water as it flows over the roof of the overturned car. And then, sleeping until the shocking loudness of sirens followed by the emergency crews calling to her and her sister to stay calm. She hadn't understood what they'd meant at first, she was calm, until she turned and saw her parents.

I scuff the snow from my shoes as I watch a couple of kids clamber and slip over the statue. Some adults stand to the side, laughing in quiet conversation and taking photos. I push my hands deeper into my pockets, ignoring the ache from my palm. I love this place, even in the winter. Sydney-me found a moment of peace here as well, one of the few things we share.

So who's dreaming whom? The question circles around my head like a mantra, a perfect loop with no way to break out. I sniff coldly and reach into my bag for a cigarette when Olen's card flicks out and falls to the snow. I look at it, white on white. I don't know why he gave it to me. Worse — why I couldn't see him last night. I'm about to walk away but turn back and pick it up, staring at the number.

I pull out my phone.

29

MEETING OLEN

The new Van de Korte clinic stands close to the site of the old one, overshadowed by the three towers of the hospital. It's not due to open officially for another month, but it's been taking 'visitors' for about two weeks. I still get the company memos.

The sandstone building is modern and low key with wings looking out over what would be broad, open gardens, if they weren't buried under all the frozen muddy crap from construction vehicles. It's more like a conservative resort than a clinic, but I guess considering the clients it wants to attract, that's a good thing. I get out of the taxi and pull my jacket tighter wishing I'd worn something warmer. During the trip uptown the icy clear sky has transformed into a dull steel dome, with clouds rolling in slowly straight off the Atlantic.

As I crunch my way down the drive I peer past a chain-link fence to the brownstone building that was the original clinic. I've known about the scheduled demolition for months, but being so close, seeing it standing empty and surrounded by dirty yellow bulldozers still comes as a shock. It's been a fixture forever, before my time anyway and knowing it's going to be pulled down is strange. I get my checkups in the hospital and have sometimes stared down on it from ten floors up. I've watched the slow flow of equipment from the old building to the new one, always distant, but down on the ground, it's real. I'm surprised I actually care.

In the early days my parents virtually lived there as they built their business, so it's not too much of a stretch to say I grew up in the clinic and its gardens. I've got good memories of walking around the ponds and exploring the grounds, finding cool new things for my dream self to remember. I'd bump into some of the older patients every now and then and most of them were good enough to talk to me. The place was always beautiful in summer.

On an impulse I leave the gravel drive and pick my way carefully over the churned mud to push my fingers through the links of the fence, staring at the empty shell. Saying goodbye, I guess. I peer past the warning signs and hazard lights posted along the perimeter and try to imagine it in spring. It won't be much longer until those machines finish their work on the gardens and make their way to the building.

'I find it a little sad.' Says a voice to my left.

I jump, literally jump. Startled, I turn to find Olen standing a few yards away, also looking at the old clinic. He's dressed in a heavy black coat with a green scarf wrapped tightly around his neck. He turns to me and gives a strange little bow. 'Hello Alice.'

I ignore a flashback of the faceless thing from last night. 'Hey.'

He walks along the line of the fence to me, taking care to avoid the muddy holes, but I notice dirty streaks running up otherwise clean, pressed trousers. He holds out his hand and I shake it, feeling displaced. His eyes, bright blue — almost electric — peer out at me from under a dark fedora. Old is the wrong way to describe him; he's got an energy about him. 'Glad you're looking better,' he says, 'you weren't doing so well last time we met.' I try to think of something witty, but he saves me the trouble, holding up a hand. 'No, I'm sorry. This is rude.' He gestures towards the new clinic. 'Let's go inside to talk. It's getting cold out here.'

'Sure.' I follow him as he leads the way back to the drive, pausing to take a final look at the building.

Olen's office smells of metal polish and leather. It's big and warm, filled with brass ornaments, lamps and books, a kind of man-den. An old globe stands in the corner of the room near a huge window overlooking the demolition site. The office is over the top, but I sense somehow in tune with its owner.

He sits easily in a big leather chair to the side of an antique oak desk, lined with pictures. 'It's going to be a shame when it's finally gone,' he says quietly. 'Once the work is complete, new gardens will be planted. Some fountains. It will be quite beautiful. There won't be any sign the original even existed.' He scratches his nose. 'But later I'm sure, if you knew where to dig, you could still poke around and find something left from the old days.' He smiles. 'So how can I help you?'

I lean forward in my chair, taking my time. I stare at his blue eyes, bright and young, set like stones into the weathered map of his face. There's intelligence there and patience. And also a spark of recognition. 'I called you from the park.' He waits for me to go on, not making it easy. 'Because I was thinking.' I take a breath, sorting out my thoughts. I don't know the reason I'm here myself. 'Who the hell are you?'

'Well —,' he begins but I cut him off, surprised at my own emotion.

'And where the fuck do you get off injecting me with some sedative? You're not my doctor.'

He smiles thinly, a flicker over his mouth and not much more. 'Well, I'm sorry about that, I truly am but you were in distress and would have hurt yourself. Mattiew was very worried.'

'I am not some sort of asset in need of protection. I can take care of myself.'

He tilts his head sideways. 'Fair enough. I apologise.' He waits.

'Listen.' I try to connect him to the bizarre creature of the evening before, attempt to imagine his face as it was but fail. The man in front of me isn't a monster or an impossibility. I breathe out. 'I couldn't see you last night.'

'I'm not following.'

'Last night, when you went to the stage. I couldn't see your face. It's not that it wasn't there. It's that every time I tried, I couldn't fix a memory of how you looked in my own head. It was like trying to hold on to water, so messed up.'

He squints, concentrating deeply. 'And now?'

'No problem. But why would that happen? Do I know you?'

Olen blinks and glances up, arranging his thoughts. He nods. It's a quick, definitive gesture. 'Yes. No. A long time ago. Your family and I go back quite a way. I used to own the clinic. Were you aware of that?' I look out the window to the old building. That part of our history's new to me. 'No, not many people do. My family have been doctors for generations. My grandfather built it in the eighteen-fifties, and then I ended up selling it to your father. It was his first major acquisition. Very hard for him, almost sent him broke. I had to sell, of course, but even so a shame to lose it.' His tone is wistful.

'So how do I know you?'

'I spent a lot of time with your parents when you were a child.'

'I don't remember.'

'I know.'

'What?'

'Your illness stole your past. You forgot things, places, people.'

I push myself out of the chair. I'm cold, despite the warm air pumping from ducts in the floor. It's an almost perfect reversal of waking from that insane relaxation session with Ryan. It's dizzying. 'I had meningitis. It was serious. How do you know about me?'

He tilts his head again, quick and bird-like, his blue eyes watery in the light. 'I suppose I was one of those people you forgot. Very sad, that entire business. Things might have gone differently if I could have stayed. But it was a hard time for your family.' He rubs his mouth again.

And here it comes: the stirrings of a familiar displacement, as if my life is being rearranged. I recognise nothing of the man in front of me and yet he's telling me about my own past.

'I used to spend a lot of time with your parents,' he explains, 'and I watched you grow up.'

I shake my head. 'I don't remember.'

'That's the tragedy of your circumstance. The disease stole your early memories.' He leans forward. 'I understand something of the situation, Alice.'

The coldness spreads further as I lose control of the conversation. 'Well, you and a whole bunch of experts.' He nods, conceding the point.

'I spoke with Mattiew last night and he told me about your condition.'

I raise my eyebrows, almost smiling at such a delicate description. 'Condition?'

He shrugs.

'This could all be a dream.'

He nods again. 'Yes, it might be. That's your eternal question, isn't it?'

I push my bandaged hand deep into my pocket. 'I suppose you could put it like that.'

He looks away. 'I couldn't imagine what it would be like.'

'No,' I say, 'you couldn't.'

'To live every day that way, everything the same and inscrutable. No chance of change or breaking through. I don't blame you for giving up.'

I stare at him. 'I haven't given up.' Now it's his turn to look interested. I lean forward as well. 'And things do change.'

'What do you mean?'

'The other me, my Sydney self, she feels it.' I struggle to find my next words. 'She's unsettled. I feel it too.'

'Unsettled?'

It's like being Sydney-me with Ryan. 'Last night for example,' I say. 'In the dream, I found a girl and she was wearing this beat up green dress.' He steeples his hands, waiting for me to go on. 'I've never seen anything like it before. It totally freaked me out. I chased her but I couldn't find her.' I look at him. 'Nothing like this has ever happened before. Like I said. Unsettled.'

He leans back and examines me with those fierce blue eyes for an uncomfortably long time. He's coming to a decision. Alice, he says, 'I'm aware of the drugs. The clinic is equipped to help you. We have the best people.'

And there it is.

'Not you too. Listen, I'm a big girl. If Daddy wants to apply some more pressure then he can do it himself. I'm tired of being handled. Sorry for wasting your time.' I get up to leave.

He stands as well. 'Alice. Listen.'

'No thanks,' I say and I'm already shutting the door.

30

A DETOUR

The taxi smells of vanilla and is as hot as a sauna. I sink back into the seat and close my eyes, trying to shift the weight of the day. The phone vibrates in my pocket. Gabe.

'Hey. About before' —' I start, hoping to unburn at least one bridge before the day's out.

His voice is quiet, hurt. 'I'm not calling about that.'

'OK. What's going on?'

'The gallery cancelled.'

'Shit. That sucks, Gabe. I'm sorry. There might be time to find another one.'

'Yeah well,' he says, his voice tinny and distant, 'it turns out suddenly everyone's booked solid, eh?'

I don't like where this is going. 'You can't get any gallery at all? Did you try De Blanc?'

'Nothing.' There's a pause as he figures out what to say next. 'I shouldn't have gone with you last night.'

'Jesus Gabe, we've covered that.'

'It seems like someone's sending a message, yeah?'

'What are you saying?' I take a breath. I know what's coming next and the problem is he's right.

'I'm saying, baby, that you're out of my league, you getting what I mean? Someone put the word out not to take my work and no one in my world could do that. It's your family. They don't like me.'

'Listen,' I say, 'I'll fix it. We'll hire a warehouse uptown and put on the show ourselves.'

There's another pause. Longer this time, the serious kind. 'Yeah. Well, that would be really great. But the thing is I need some time to myself.'

'I said I'll fix it.'

'That'd be real good.' I can hear he doesn't believe me. 'Alice,' he says, 'I can't let Jordie and me be mixed up in this thing you've got going with them.'

I take a breath. 'Come on Gabe, don't let yourself be pushed around this way.'

'Baby,' he says, 'we can't fight that kind of heavy duty shit like you can.'

I want to punch back at him and call him a wimp, but hold off. 'Yeah, I get it,' I say eventually. 'I'm sorry you were roped into this. But I'll put it right. Trust me.'

'Sure, baby. I got to go.'

He hangs up, leaving me listening to a digital tone. Maybe we've just broken up. Shit, I don't know. God, what a day. I can't tell why my parents are pushing so hard now; it can't just be that thing from last night. Maybe I'm losing perspective and it's their version of tough love. Straighten up and fly right, girly. See the doctor, get better and rejoin society. I can almost hear my mother's voice.

'Hey,' I say to the driver, tapping the plastic. He glances at me in the mirror. 'We need to take a detour.'

An hour later the taxi pulls up in front of the burned-out

car, cold and soot blackened on the side of the street. I get out, not before noticing some kid's left a toy in the back seat next to where I was sitting. I tell the guy to wait before walking up to the strange Russian-accented boy standing near Rene's doorway.

'It's Alice.'

He doesn't bother checking his list. 'He's out.'

'Bullshit.' I shake my head and push past him into the house.

As usual the place is hot and damp, a sauna stench of old sweat and stale human breath. I pull off my jacket, pushing down the dark hallway towards the big lounge room where Rene holds his personal gross-out court. As I walk past an open door I stop short. An old couple stare back at me, starkly illuminated under a bare bulb. They're sitting at a small kitchen table halfway through a game of cards, their expressions unreadable, frozen as they wait for me to move on. Behind them, an ancient kettle stands on a gas stove, venting steam. Someone in the room shuts the door, leaving me in the darkness of the hallway. I try, seriously try, not to be freaked out.

I continue into the lounge, where Rene grins up at me from the depths of his couch. He's alone thank God, his two friends elsewhere. Pale light flickers into the darkened room from the screen of a small black and white television set in the corner. I didn't even know they still made them.

'Alice,' he says, 'weren't expecting you, darlin'.'

'Yeah,' I say. 'Me either. I need a pick-me-up.'

'Yes,' he agrees hugely, 'don't we all now and then?'

'I don't want the normal stuff. I'm after something special.' I glance over my shoulder. No Ezekiel either. It feels like I've accidentally found my way backstage to Rene's circus. Most of the performers are gone, leaving only the star and a few props. The unreality of the day goes up a notch. What about that bag you had for me before?

'I said you couldn't afford it, darlin'.'

'You'd be surprised.'

The big man shifts in his chair and the sound reminds me of skin peeling away from a hot, vinyl car seat. A Sydney memory. The smell of the house is overpowering.

'Well,' he says at last, 'I have a different sweet on the menu and if it's a pick-me-up you're wanting, special is my specialty, love. Are we having an occasion?'

I smile, not pushing the point. 'Sure. Why not? Big huge frickin' occasion. And I'm bringing guests. Want to come?'

Rene laughs and the sweaty walls absorb his sound, making him subdued. 'I am a man of uncertain tastes, my delicious. Perhaps you and I could party, but it might scare your guests.'

I shake my head again. Something is in the air, but what the hell. He seems sexy. Now I know I'm dreaming for sure. I lean in and kiss him. 'Too bad. So, what are you offering?'

'Ah,' he rumbles. 'How about you let me surprise you.'

I pull out a wad of cash and lay it on the table in front of him. 'This enough?'

Rene glances at it then rolls his eyes. 'No,' he sighs extravagantly, 'but we all need to scrimp and save and make do, don't we my darlin'?'

I shake my head, smiling. 'You're a greedy fucker, Rene.'

He smiles, waiting in silence until someone emerges from the shadows and a bag of pills slips into my hand. I make myself not jump. There was another man in the room all along. I don't watch as he loses himself to the dark shadowy parts again. Too fucking freaky.

'Now, one more thing,' says Rene as I turn to go.

'What?'

'If you ever leave a taxi parked right out the front again our business relationship will come to an end.'

I wobble my head, a kind of failed nod as the apartment spins slowly. 'Sure. That's fair enough. What you going to do, kill me?'

He shrugs before waving me off petitely. 'Bye bye.'

I stumble out of the house, past the sullen kid and into the taxi, which by some miracle is still waiting for me. 'Home James,' I blurt, then laugh out the stress as I pull out my phone, speed dialling the first of my contacts.

31

A PARTY

My phone's barely audible over the bass of the music. I'm tempted to ignore it, but it could be Gabe so I stalk through the tight packed crowd of partygoers to the kitchen and answer it. By the time I get there it's rung off. The caller ID shows Olen's number. I don't bother checking for a message.

Turning, I find an almost full bottle of wine resting on the countertop, sitting between some guy and girl deep in conversation. I grin as I reach past them, liberating it.

'Hey Alice,' she says, a young, bohemian arty type I'm sure I haven't met before, 'cool place.'

'Thanks,' I yell back over the music. I hold up the bottle and fill my glass. Most people here are strangers and that suits me fine. I nod and smile my way over to the ancient wooden credenza, where a small bowl brims with a mixture of candy and Rene's party-starters. Think of it as a lucky dip. I grab a couple of the colourful pills, wash them down with a gulp of wine.

Snow drifts gently against the window and I'm drawn by the view.

'Beautiful night.'

I turn to face the voice. It belongs to a tall man, dark shirt, jeans and a thoughtful smile. I might know him but can't be sure. I smile back, wondering randomly how I'd react if I saw Dr Goodlooking Ryan from Sydney standing there instead. What a weird idea. 'Hey,' I say.

He nods at the vista outside the glass. 'I love the way the snow makes everything seem new.'

'It's a good thought.'

He holds out his hand. 'Matt.'

'Alice.'

'Ah, so this is your place?'

'Got it in one.'

He turns around appreciatively, eyes resting on the photograph of me on the wall. 'Interesting portrait.'

I turn back to the window, watching him in the window's reflection. 'I hate it. So what do you do, Matt?'

'Nothing too exciting,' he says, 'just working at a book store down in the Village.'

'Which one?'

'Arabian Nights. It's new.'

I'm starting to feel the effect of the pills kick in. 'You know what, I'm not a big reader.'

He smiles again, raising his glass. 'Me either.'

I glance at him. 'Seriously?'

At least he has the grace to look caught out. 'Sorry. That was a really dumb line. So what's wrong with the picture?'

I drain my glass in one long gulp. 'The guy who took it is a dick.' Everything buzzes pleasantly as I search for another drink. There are bees in my head. It's funny. Spotting a couple of untouched bottles in a wine rack I motion for Matt to stay put, then weave through the dancers in the middle of the room to grab them. I return slowly, stopping to talk with someone I do recognise, but whose name I forget.

The soundtrack changes and the music gets harder and pointier. Maybe it's the bees. I spin and laugh out loud at another surprise from the party treats. People start to lose focus, shifting out of phase as they move, stretching into long flesh-coloured swathes before snapping back sharply. They get so clear they're almost glowing.

'Holy shit,' I breathe as I float through the room, joining a couple of guys as they jump and sway all over the place. I fling my arms into the air and spin slowly, totally absorbed by art-deco mouldings on the ceiling that I've never noticed before. The single hanging light fixture glows and blurs prettily as I go around. From somewhere behind me there's the sound of hysterical laughter; seems like someone else has found the lucky dip.

Something hard and unyielding pushes into my back, blasting the wind out of me. I turn my head in surprise, slowly realising I've fallen onto the floor. It's a strange perspective as the world turns sideways. A shape sits heavily next to me and grabs one of the bottles I'm still holding on to. He pours two glasses, one for me.

'Thanks.'

'No problem,' says Matt. 'Someone found your bowl over there by the way.' He tries to help me sit, but only manages to pull himself over.

'Hey, you know what?' I say at last, spilling some of the wine.

'What?'

'I do like the snow. Do you want to go somewhere?'

He grins, unfocused. 'Where?'

I point upwards. 'The roof.'

'Sure,' he says, then closes his eyes listening to the music. I look at him for a moment before standing up and lurching away.

It takes us a few minutes but we finally make it outside. My body's shivering but I'm not cold, which is nice for a change. I've chocked the door open behind me with an old cinder block I keep handy up here. The wind is gentle and probably freezing, wafting city sounds into the night as I walk past the steel blocks of air conditioners near the edge.

Red and white car lights, the blooms of apartment windows, traffic signals, neons. All of this greets me in one sliding, changing shape as I head to the safety rail. My eyes stay open and the light blurs, turning into a wet prism as they sting and tear up, a merging of everything. This is my place, real or not.

I'm starting to get cold. It must be the winter knocking some sense into my body. Even from my vantage point here on top of the universe I hear the music coming from my apartment. No doubt Marty the Doorman will be on his way up to try to manage the situation. I have to confess; I like situations. I wonder how people would have reacted if Rene had taken me up on my offer and turned up. For some reason it strikes me as kind of funny.

Something moves behind me and I turn. It's Matt, looking cold and a little frightened.

'Hey,' I say, 'what's up?'

'Alice, you're too close to the edge.'

I blink in surprise. 'What?'

He slowly advances towards me, holding out a hand. 'Get back Alice. You might fall.'

I smile dizzily, then look down to the street below. My feet are on the lip of the building. I frown, wondering how that could have happened, when the icy cold steel safety rail presses at my back.

'Alice,' calls Matt again, 'let me help you.'

I giggle, finding the whole thing hilarious. He thinks I'm going to jump.

'Stay back!' I shout, doing my best soap opera voice, 'or I'll do it!'

He crouches even lower, turning himself crablike as he gets nearer to me. I wish I had a camera. I can't help it and giggle again before forcing myself to get serious for a second. 'Do you know how stupid you look right now?'

'Alice. I'm not joking. Get away from there.'

'Stop being so patronising.'

I poke a drift of snow over the edge, watching it tumble and come apart in slow motion until it sprays invisibly into the dark. I wonder what it would be like to fall. Like flying, perhaps. I sweep another drift away with my foot, exposing the icy concrete beneath. I close my eyes. It feels peaceful and a stillness fills me as I marvel at how everything has distilled into this single point. When I open them, there's a tiny smile on my lips. I look down then turn.

Matt yanks me back, grabbing my arms with bruising force. I almost scream but my breath is ripped away as he drags me bodily over the rail.

'What are you, crazy?' he says, panting.

I glare at him. 'I wasn't going to jump, you idiot.'

He shakes his head, refusing to say anything else. Instead he helps me up, then holding my arm in a gentle grasp guides me through the door and down to my apartment. I try talking on the way down, but he stays silent.

'So,' I say, 'that was wild.'

'I've got to go,' he says at last.

'Why don't you stay?'

I think for a second he might say something intelligent, but instead he turns around and leaves. I watch him walk to the elevator, head spinning with what happened. I can't believe he thought I was going to jump. I turn back to where the party is only just getting started, full of thoughts of flying.

32

ON THE BEACH

Sunrise.

The world is quiet and beautiful: a painting. Red-rimmed clouds gather loosely on the horizon and the sea is flat and a perfect mirror. A still fog floats above the surface of the water. You don't get mornings like these very often. I'm the only person on the beach as I walk slowly along the high tide line, sweeping my metal detector in slow arcs. Whistles and beeps sing weird melodies in my earphones which I've got turned down as low as they go.

The walking is automatic as I try to keep my mind clear ahead of the hot day, another in this never ending heatwave. Other-me nearly killed herself. I can see that, even if she can't. Things are changing in both our lives, but I'm not her and I refuse to give in. For the first time ever I understand I might be stronger than her. I've never thought of it that way before. Maybe Ryan was right.

The sound at the shore is a comfortable hash of quiet static; the rythmn of the water, the slap of waves and the foam of the backwash each adding their own bit. The metal detector's another ritual, but we all need our rights and routines. It's comforting losing myself in small victories as I unearth little lost treasures. As I sweep the search coil around again the tone changes and shrills.

I kneel in the cool sand, enjoying the fine-grained squeak as my knees sink in. Pulling a hessian bag free from my shoulder, I dig where the signal was strongest. I don't expect to discover anything valuable, it's mostly flotsam of one kind or another, but you never know, the sea is mysterious. Soon enough, I find something in the cold sand and pull loose an old belt buckle, corroded and wrapped in a fragment of seaweed. I smile. No treasure this time, but I throw it into the bag anyway.

As I continue along my way I spot a figure walking towards me out of the mist. I usually pass the same group of early risers: dog walkers, surfers, joggers, as I follow my path in the mornings, so seeing just one other person today is unusual. I keep my pace as they wave. It's Jen, board in arm.

'Hey.'

'Morning.'

Jen's face is carefully neutral. 'I was looking for you,' she says when we catch up.

I nod, slinging the bag over my shoulder. 'Are you angry about last night?'

She flickers through unreadable emotions before stopping at a strange, quirky smile. 'Yeah — no. I was really pissed to start with. I felt so bad I ended up walking home with him and,' She stops and stares at the flat ocean. 'Well, we kind of hooked up.'

Only Jen could do that. I shake my head, smiling quietly. 'What about Jack?'

'John.'

'Obviously,' she says, 'he's a bit pissed too.'

'A bit?'

'A lot.'

'You told him?'

'I dumped him.'

I'm grinning despite myself. 'I can't believe we're related.'

'Yeah,' says Jen, 'me neither. Oh well, what's done is done.' She drops the board and sits on it, staring at the mirror-flat sea. 'Don't think I'll be catching any waves this morning.'

I sit next to her, carefully placing the detector on the sand.

'I'm thinking of visiting Mum and Dad,' she says, 'want to come?'

I stare out over the silent beach and the strange, still waters beyond. 'And the shop?'

'So, open late again. Not a biggie.'

'It's been ages since we've been, hasn't it?'

Jen nods. 'Over a year. It would be good to visit.'

Yes. Yes, it would. 'Sure. I'd like that.'

The lurid grass inside the cemetery stands out against the crisp burned browns outside. It's a small place; old and tucked away, mostly unknown except to the few visitors like us who come to pay their respects. Rose bushes line the metal fence that stretches its broken rails the length of the street. Their thorns make a better barrier than the rusted ironwork. When I was younger, a lot younger, I used to think it was haunted. Now I have different ghosts. We walk through the gates quietly, lost in our own thoughts.

We continue down the path in silence, both of us relishing the quiet. The grass is plush and smells beautiful. The forecast is for another blistering day and so far there's no reason to doubt the hot winds will come. Gentler breezes, not yet warm, wind around the headstones in the yard, bringing with them the scent of roses. Brushing at a fly,

Jen leads the way down the paved path to a newer section and finally stops at a small inexpensive marker set into the lawn.

I kneel by the grave and pull out a weed, leaving myself a moment's silence. Jen joins me, placing a flower at the head of the stone before sitting cross-legged on the grass. It's special here, peaceful, one of the only genuinely quiet places I know. Jen feels that way too and I'm glad I can share it with her. When we're here it's a little bit like being a family again. I'm able to remember them, free of the sadness these memories usually bring. Perhaps it's because we really are all in the same place, separated by years but not distance.

Their faces come to me. I smile a small private smile. Frank, my dad, was a man who smiled a lot. He always seemed to be jumping in and out of projects. He didn't take many things seriously except his football and even then it was only a passing interest unless his team was winning.

I remember one time when he disappeared for hours on end into the shed at the back of the garden and refused to let anyone in. Jen and I, both very young, were captivated by the sounds of carpentry that came out of there, guessing at the things he could have been building. Finally he called us all together and proudly presented two brightly painted rocking horses. We both went wild, dancing around him and hugging him before trying them out. Rachel, our mum, had this strange expression: pride, tempered by a hint of sadness. Perhaps she knew that perfect moment for the fleeting thing it was.

Our parents weren't without faults, but they were dedicated and loved us, so that's about as much as you can ask for I guess. Mum worked at a bank and was always trying to knock the idea of saving for the future into our heads. She was quiet and strong, the voice of reason, but I know she loved Dad's whims almost as much as he did. It was her influence, her planning that provided for us when they died. The money we inherited along with the house, which was paid for, allowed us to buy the florist. We lived with uncle Jeremy, a widower himself until I was seventeen. He'd made it clear raising us was just an obligation to his sister. Two years after we moved out, we bought the shop with the money our parents left us. It seemed right. Mum had loved flowers.

'I still think about it, you know,' Jen says as a gust of wind blows gum leaves across the path.

'Me too. How much do you remember?'

She pulls out a small tissue and dabs her eyes. 'All of it.'

Of course she does. Jen's memory of the crash is clearer than mine. 'Everything changed that day. That's when I started to dream about Other-me.'

She stares at me in silence for a moment. I'm sure she's going to say something angry but she surprises me. 'Why didn't it happen to me?'

'Pardon?'

'I mean,' she says, 'why not me too? I'm not even afraid of the water. I love to swim.'

I shake my head. 'I don't know.'

Jen wipes her eyes again. 'After the crash you got all this weird-ass shit and for me, it was like it never happened. What's wrong with me?'

I hug her. 'Nothing. You're the strong one, that's what it is.'

'It doesn't feel that way.'

'I'd still be in Mayfleur if it wasn't for you.'

Jen smiles tiredly and picks up the flower she'd laid earlier, smelling it. 'Do you think they can see us?'

I read the inscription on the headstone, so sincere and tragically bland, not much different from all the other words on all the other graves. The lives of Mum and Dad reduced to a chiselled sentence. I can't remember writing them; it must have been Jen. Do they look down on us from some sort of heaven? It feels as though it should be true, even if it's not. I have a different kind of angel looking at me, but perhaps that's my Manhattan dream dreaming me in turn. Perhaps not. I look at Jen, who's waiting on my answer. Like I know anything. 'Yes,' I say, 'I think they can.'

I help her to her feet, dusting bits of grass from my dress. We stand; neither of us wanting to move while the day grows hotter around us, and the scent of roses washes across us both like a tide.

As we walk back to her car, I wonder. 'What about ghosts?'

Jen stops, regarding me carefully. 'Shit this is getting depressing. Is this to do with the girl?'

I open my door, gasping at the temperature. We quickly drop the windows to let out the heat as Jen flicks on the air conditioner. A hot breeze gusts from the vents as the car starts with a gassy cough. She wipes the sweat from her face.

'We almost died,' I say, thinking it though. 'What if that made —' I search for the right words, 'I don't know, some sort of connection to somewhere?'

Jen shakes her head. 'Don't you think you've got enough going on without adding ghosts?'

I glance at her. 'You brought it up. It got me thinking, that's all.'

'Well, I don't buy it. This girl you found, why now? If we, you, made a,' and she does that finger quote thing, 'connection way back then, why has it taken so long to see a ghost? Why not when it happened? And what's the link with the girl anyway? It's too random.' She pulls onto the road, gunning the car. 'Stop trying to join things up. Sometimes shit happens Alice. No reason.'

I stare out the window at the other traffic, busy in the rippling heat. 'Shit happens?'

She nods, attention locked on a truck in front. 'That's right. Bad shit happens to good people sometimes.' She changes lanes. 'This is depressing me. We shouldn't have gone.'

I sit back in the seat, captured by the thought the girl might be more than she seemed. It would answer the question of why no one else saw her. 'No,' I say quietly, 'it was a good idea.'

33

SHADOW OF THE GIRL

I take a moment to breathe in the aroma of the shop when I unlock the door, inhaling the cool scents of the ferns and potted flowers, and just for a second I'm content. Shadows walk outside the window as I switch on lights and ready the displays, going through my routine automatically. As I go to turn on the cash register my shoes leave wet prints all over the floor.

Damn. I'd forgotten about the repair guy. I find a puddle of water leading back to the fridge, which is ominously silent. When I open it I swear; the stems I'd put in there overnight are ruined.

Stupid, stupid, stupid me.

I knew I should have got it fixed yesterday. I scoop out the flowers and trudge over to the bin at the back of the store where I dump them, wondering just how much money we've lost. This'll make Jen's day. It's not like we were doing well to begin with.

A few minutes on the web and I find a repair service. As I hang up from placing the call, I trawl through random sites, fighting the urge to do another pointless search on the

Van de Korte family. Somehow I wind up staring at listings for clairvoyants. The bell jangles as someone walks in and I guiltily flick off the screen, looking up with a smile to greet a new customer, happy for the distraction.

As the woman closes the door behind her I remember that I was meant to see Ryan. Oh Damn. I call him and make an excuse of the fridge, telling him I have to stay in the shop all day, promising to see him tomorrow. He doesn't sound too happy about it but I swear I won't forget. Where is my head at today?

An hour later the repairman, not much more than a kid fresh out of school, turns up. Wearing jeans and T-shirt, with a mop of greasy black hair poking out under his cap, he reminds me a bit of a cartoon I once loved. He's friendly, introduces himself as Arlen and sets to work pulling apart the back of the fridge. He starts chatting to me in an amiable ramble, talking about compressors, maintenance and the quirks of different brands. I call it broken; he calls it a quirk. I lean on the counter and watch the endless parade of shadows.

Arlen's still talking when I stand up — blinking. Somewhere in the pedestrian crowd outside, a small figure has passed by. My skin tingles. I wait, frozen. Moments later the shadow returns, hazy in the light but growing sharper as whoever it is walks closer. It's the silhouette of a child. It leans into to the glass and a girl's face appears as she pushes herself against the window, peering inside.

It's her.

I race around the counter to the front of the shop and throw open the door, scaring the hell out of a woman who's walking by. I stare at the place the girl had been standing, but the footpath is empty. All I can see is the usual morning foot traffic up and down the alley. Shit. I start running then make myself stop. I have to calm down. Breathing through the anxiety the way Ryan's taught me, I walk the length of the street, searching for her. I scan the faces of strangers for signs they've seen something unusual but the girl's gone. Again.

Arlen's finished by the time I get back to the shop, packing away his tools into a greasy plastic toolbox. I take the invoice automatically, not even looking at the price as I go with him to the door.

'Did you find them?' he asks as he leaves.

'Pardon?'

'Whoever you were chasing.' He grins under his cap. 'You're fast on your feet. Totally surprised me when you took off like that. Wicked fast.'

'You saw her?'

'Nah. What did they do, steal something?'

'Something,' I say.

'Well, if I was you,' he says, 'I wouldn't let them get away with that. They'll keep coming back if you do.'

I wave him off and return to the bright, quiet shop. The only sounds are the soft drips of the reticulation system and the hum from the newly repaired fridge, all slowly counting the minutes. I pace, caught up in the wake of my adrenaline and disappointment. The thought of going back to the counter and waiting screams at me.

I return to the computer and turn on the monitor where the listings are still left up from the last search. Pulling out an invoice pad I scribble down a number, folding it away in my pocket as Arlen pokes his head through the door, startling me.

'You were chasing a kid right?'

My heart thunders. 'Yes.'

'I just saw a kid in a green dress hanging around outside.'

'You can see her?' I say.

He looks at me like I'm crazy. 'Yeah.'

I skirt the counter, snatching my bag as I go. She's not getting away from me again. I push past Arlen and bolt into the alleyway, almost slipping on the smooth cobbles as I glance around, ignoring the startled expressions of shoppers. There, further along the street is the girl: statue-still among the surge of pedestrians. She looks like a cut-out. 'Lock up for me,' I call to Arlen, who's staring at me in open-mouthed surprise as I run after her.

I reach the end of the alley moments later but she isn't there. I swear, now knowing better than to ask strangers where she's gone. Instead I dash to the edge of the road, a busy intersection shimmering in the heat, trying to see everything at once. I catch a flash of green on the other side. 'Wait!' I yell, but the girl turns and walks away. She's so fast.

Timing the traffic, I skirt the footpath then race over two lanes, stopping for a heartbeat near a low concrete wall. A truck explodes past, whipping up a gale of rank diesel air and grit that peppers my legs and tears at my dress. With an eye on the figure ahead, I climb over the divider and race to the curb.

The girl is there, thirty metres away. She shows no sign of hearing as I call for her to stop. Instead she turns down a small street. I swear again and follow. Something warns me against running; the girl wants to be found. Plus, the last thing I need is to be seen chasing a child. I haven't lost all my common sense.

As I walk down a quiet offshoot from the main road, my nerves are jangling with adrenaline and excitement. It takes every bit of my self-restraint to hold back from racing those extra metres and grabbing her.

'Who are you?' I call out.

The girl keeps on walking.

'What do you want me to do?'

Nothing.

The houses on this street are tall, old and ramshackle. Long dry grass pushes up against front fences, while the sidewalk is littered with burned yellow leaves. I step over an odd spindly branch blown down from one of the huge white gumtrees and lose her for a second. The street elbows away to the left and the girl's disappeared with it.

'Shit,' I whisper, trotting to catch up.

As I come around the corner she's standing, waiting. I move towards her but she steps back, exactly one pace, keeping her distance.

'Listen,' I say, 'tell me what you want.'

The girl says nothing. Now she's closer I can see the dirt on her skin again, cleaner under the dried tracks of tears.

'Who did this to you?'

She stares, then for the briefest moment her face creases in an expression of pure hatred, so intense I flinch back. I don't quite believe it. I kneel. 'Let me help. You came to me. What can I do?' My voice is shaking and comes close to breaking as the girl's face contorts again, this time in sadness. 'Who are you?' A hot wind blows a shower of dead leaves around us both and for a second the air is full of the sound of their rasping beetle sounds as they flutter down.

My breathing is strained, my heart beating hard and I know an anxiety attack is close. I stand, offering her my hand, feeling stupid and scared and uncertain. 'I'm Alice,' I say. For the first time the girl shows some reaction.

'No you're not.'

'What?'

That snarl of anger again. It washes over her so completely it startles me. 'What the hell do you want?' I yell. She runs and I leap after her, but she's faster, leading me around another bend towards an old playground at the end of the street. I follow, emotions wheeling. The girl dashes past an open gate and disappears through a tangle of bushes.

Moments later I push though the same bushes, stumbling to a halt as I'm momentarily lost in the bustling park. Children scream and chase each other through the playground, hanging on to swings and clambering over slides, climbing gear, rope pulls. I blink at the sudden noise, shocked at how busy the place is despite the heat. I search for the telltale splash of green, but she's gone again.

I walk slowly past a crowd of children riding a spinning disc. Faces and eyes look up at me as I go by and some kids on top of a tall slide turn to follow my progress. I glance from them to another group of children in a nearby sandpit, all dressed in summer clothes. Curious faces stare back from everywhere. Something's wrong.

I head to a drinking fountain and wash some water onto my face and small boy standing nearby laughs. I try for a smile, about to ask him if he's seen the girl when he turns and runs away, impervious to the incredible heat of the day. I turn back to the park and the boundless energy of the kids. Squinting against the light, I look for the green dress, but there's no sign of her. My body prickles with the after effects of the chase, eyes watering in the glare reflected from the metal playground equipment. It's like staring into the sun. That's when I realise there are no adults.

My hand goes to my mouth. Kids are playing and yelling and chasing each other, some even sitting quietly under the sparse shade of the trees. But the parents are missing. I'm the only adult in the playground. A hand tugs at my wrist and I yell. It's the boy.

'Hi,' he says.

I look at him, confused.

'She wanted you to have this.' He offers me a white rose, crushed in his small palm.

'Who?' Although I know who. The boy shrugs. The park slowly becomes silent and I'm aware of every set of eyes on me.

'Take it,' he says.

'I don't want it.'

He hands it to me. This can't be happening. 'She wants you to have it,' he says.

'Where is she?' The boy ignores me. I wipe my face, trying to regain my balance. 'Then who are you?' I shake my head even as he holds the rose closer to me.

Now they're all watching. No noise. Every kid still and quiet and waiting. I back off, retreating the way I came, aware of the eyes of the children following me. Finally I give up any pretence of control and run for the exit, bursting through the gate then onwards down the street, not looking back.

34

THE PARK

I throw open the door and step inside the house, shaking. The hallway is mercifully cool despite the blistering afternoon outside, the house's tall ceilings and thick wooden walls keeping out the worst of the heat. I stand there, my back against the wall, and try to let it all slough away. Slowly, ever so slowly I begin to calm down.

I go to the lounge and collapse into a chair, attempting to make sense of what's happened. I tried calling Ryan's office on the way but he wasn't there. He didn't answer his mobile either and I didn't trust myself to leave a message. I think I'm losing it.

The image of the park and its children is as clear as if I was still standing there. 'This is bullshit,' I say to the empty room, surprising myself at my own anger. 'They were just kids, not murderers. Why do I always run away?'

'Hey Alice, is that you?'

'Jen?'

'Yeah.' Footsteps and Jen emerges from her bedroom. 'What are you doing here?'

I shake my head, hardly knowing where to start. 'I saw the girl again.'

'What about the shop?'

'It's locked up.' At least I hope it is. 'I had to follow her.'

Jen's expression becomes unreadable. 'Shit. Really? So what happened?'

'I need a favour.'

There's a moment as she stares, hands on hips and I expect she's going to have a go at me for leaving the shop. 'Sure,' she says, making that the second time I've been wrong about her today.

The car moves through the heavy afternoon traffic, turning down the street I point out to her. Kuchen, the faded sign says. A couple of hours ago I never knew it existed. In the mix of my emotions there's an odd relief it's there at all. At least I didn't imagine it. What would Jen have done if I couldn't have found it?

I haven't told her about the park because I figure she needs to experience this for herself. We round the two sharp corners and arrive at the playground, as real and present as the street.

Jen follows me through the gate, blinking in the glare of the sun. My sense of relief is even stronger for seeing it all here; the slides, the sand pit, the drinking fountain. A couple of children are playing in the shade of a tree and my pulse quickens. Jen joins me.

'So what's going on?'

'I followed her,' I say, almost whispering, 'but when I came here she was gone and there were all these kids.'

'Well, it is a park.'

I ignore this and look around, walking silently to the fountain. Jen squints, following.

'I was here,' I say, then stop. In front of me is the same

boy I'd talked to earlier. I grab Jen's hand as he points at me. Within seconds other children also glance our way and start calling out.

'What the hell?' says Jen.

'You're the girl who ran away,' says the boy.

I feel cold.

Jen nudges me. 'What's going on?'

I begin to answer when a tall man approaches and puts his hands on the boy's shoulders. 'Come on Mark,' he says. 'No talking to strangers.' He guides the kid towards a climbing frame some distance from us.

A kid to our side points and giggles. 'She ran away.'

'Alice,' says Jen, 'tell me what's happening.'

'I followed the girl here. But there were only kids. No adults. I don't know what she wanted, but that kid tried to give me a flower.'

Jen looks me straight in the eyes. 'Do you hear how freaking insane that sounds?'

I shake my head and run over to the boy. 'Hi Mark,' I say. 'I'm Alice.'

'Hey wait a second,' says the dad.

'The girl in the green dress. Where did she go?'

Mark glances at me first in confusion, then with the beginnings of fear.

'You,' says the man again. 'Leave him alone.'

'He tried to give me a rose,' I say as Jen catches up and grabs my arm.

'Come on babe, let's go.'

I push past and try to get Mark's attention, but he's running off to a woman standing near a picnic basket. Jen clamps down and her fingers bite.

'I don't want to hurt him,' I say. Wrong thing.

The man wheels on Jen. 'Keep her away from my son.'

He means it. Soon he's joined by the woman and another guy, well-built and sunburned. A girl of around six races up and stands behind them all.

'Mum, she's the one I told you about from before. She ran away,' she laughs.

Jen tightens her grip on my arm again. 'We should go,' she says. She's hurting me now.

The mother turns to her daughter, then to me. 'That one?' The girl nods.

'What?' asks Jen.

'Her,' she says, face wary. 'Karla told me she saw her running into the park. She talked to herself for a while then ran out.'

I look around in confusion. 'It didn't happen that way,' I say. I almost tell them I was following the girl but stop before I dig myself in any deeper.

'Get her out of here,' says the sunburned man. His voice is a low threat.

'That boy,' I begin, trying for one final shot at explaining, but Mark is now gone, carried off by his father.

'I won't tell you again,' says the man.

Jen pinches my arm hard and herds me away from the crowd, which is beginning to assemble. I don't resist as we walk out of the park and into the car. Jen starts it in silence, hardly acknowledging me as she backs out.

'I am not making this up,' I say at last.

'I'm not saying you are.' But her voice is tight.

'She really was there. Something is going on. Something's changing and it's important.'

Jen refuses to reply.

I sigh. 'I'm not giving up.' I stare at my sister.

Jen shakes her head. 'I won't give up on you either, babe.'

She reaches over and takes my hand. 'But shit. You've got a gift for pissing everyone off. It's a real talent.'

I sit back and blow a strand of hair from my face. Maybe I should cut it short, just like I do in Manhattan. Like my dream does, I correct myself. I reach into my bag for a mint, instead pulling out the folded piece of paper with the number of the clairvoyant I'd written down in the shop. I stare at it in silence as we drive home.

35

CLAIRVOYENT

It's nine pm when I knock on the apartment door and I don't have a clue what to expect. Sun-blasted palm trees and the white stucco entrance of the courtyard fry under fiercely bright security lights behind me. Everything's so stark. I listen to a series of latches being undone with a strange déjà vu, almost expecting Gabe to open it. The door swings wide, revealing the smiling face of a guy who can't be older than twenty, plaid shirt hanging loosely over faded baggy jeans. Not Gabe.

'What's up?' he says.

'Are you Lavar Curren?' I ask, unable to keep the surprise from my voice.

'Sure am,' he says. His face gets dreamy for a moment. 'You weren't joking, come on in. You're carrying a load.'

I follow him into the apartment and sit on a yellow Ikea chair opposite a mustard coloured couch. The room is cluttered with computer games, speakers and hundreds of wires connecting everything. Other than the seating, furniture is sparse with a few nature prints on freshly painted white walls, a throw rug over the floor and a single fern on a glass-topped coffee table in the centre of it all. It's a cross between a waiting room and a high school kid's hangout. This is not the house of a clairvoyant.

'You want a coke or something?' he offers as he sits on the couch, shoving off a pile of video games.

I shake my head. 'So how does all this work?'

He shrugs, looking younger than ever. 'No rules. You tell me what you need to know and I try and tap into the answer.'

I smile, feeling self-conscious and nervous and more and more like I've made a mistake. 'How long have you been doing this?'

Lavar leans forward. 'Forever. Ever since I was a kid. I have this ability to know things, sometimes before they happen, sometimes things other people don't know. I don't get how it works myself, but it does.'

'So no Ouija boards then?'

He shakes his head. 'No props. So, how about we get it out of the way.'

'Pardon?'

He smiles a big toothy let's get it going grin. It might be fake but I like him a fraction more because of it. 'You want to figure out if I'm the real thing, not some kid trying to scam you.'

'I didn't say that.'

He reaches over to a cleverly positioned bar fridge and pulls out a Red Bull. 'You don't have to be psychic to have common sense. Don't worry, it's cool to be sceptical.' He pops the tab and drains most of the can in a single gulp. 'Love caffeine,' he explains, 'hate coffee. Anyway.' I wait for him to continue as he appears distracted. 'So,' he says, 'you have a sister.' I nod. 'Your parents died a long time ago. A car crash, wasn't it? And something about water.'

'Yes,' I say quietly.

Just like that. There's no build-up and the way he so casually reels off this information stuns me. 'It was a creek,' he says. 'The car blew out a tyre then it landed in a creek. You were in it when it happened with your sister and your folks.'

I nod again as he drains the rest of the can. He squints at me seriously and I'm sorry I doubted him. 'So we good to go?'

'Sure,' I say, wondering how to word the question. 'Do you believe in ghosts?'

Lavar puts the can away. 'Hell yeah.'

I rub my head. 'So tell me about mine.'

'All right,' he says. He reaches for my hands and takes them gently, surprising me at the softness of his fingers. I watch, fascinated, as he closes his eyes and tilts his head fractionally to one side, as if straining to catch a conversation on the verge of hearing. I sit that way for minutes, watching him closely as his expression changes, growing serious. Finally he looks at me for long seconds before letting go. I remain silent as he leans over and pulls out another drink from the fridge. He pops the lid but leaves it on the table untouched.

'You OK?' I ask, wondering if this is some kind of act after all.

He stares at me, almost searching for something. 'No ghosts.'

'OK maybe we're going about this the wrong way,' I say. 'There's this girl.'

'I know.'

'So tell me.'

Lavar stands, that easy smile flickering over his face for a moment before disappearing entirely. He seems at war with himself as he stares at me, seemingly lost for words.

'What's the problem?' I ask, getting annoyed. 'Who is she? What does she want?'

He shakes his head. 'I don't know,' he says quietly. 'You should go.'

'Pardon?'

He gently helps me to my feet and guides me towards the door.

'Listen,' I say, 'I can't pay you any more than we agreed, so if this is about more money —'

'Forget the fee,' he says, voice dead, 'I can't help you.'

Panic rises up but I bite down hard on it, forcing it under control. Manhattan-me would probably punch this guy. I channel some of my anger and use it to smother the fear. 'What the hell is wrong with you?'

He looks at me and I can read his confusion. 'You just have to go,' he says.

'Bullshit,' I say, but he's already closing the door. I stand there like an idiot for a minute, before eventually turning and walking quietly away into the night.

36

A VISIT FROM OLEN

I wake up staring into an odd refraction from a decanter lying sideways on the bedside table. I close my eyes and the light plays over my eyelids, a warm pink swathe of shadows on shadows, like an afterimage from looking too much at the sun. I hold my breath, for a moment lost in transition. I could be either of my selves right now, but the low ache in my palm puts the fantasy to bed. I get up, not surprised to discover a couple of rumpled shapes still sleeping on the carpet nearby. The surprised part comes when I spot another shape under the covers next to me. Turns out it was quite the party, after all. I shrug on a gown and step over the comatose figures on the floor.

Walking into the lounge I'm stunned at how many people crashed the place. They're everywhere; over the couches and chairs, curled around pillows and even under a throw rug. The apartment appears more like a crime scene than a home. Mass murder in Park Avenue; I can see the headlines now. I smile to myself as I kick someone with my bare foot. A groan emerges from the shape. Well, not mass murder then. I scratch my nose, wondering what was in those party treats I'd bought from

Rene. I'll ask him next time, or better yet get him to tone down the dosage. It's going to be a bitch getting them all out of here.

Pulling my silk gown tighter I rub my head, ignoring the pounding drum solo going on in there. Over by the couch, a naked guy is somehow still holding on to a bottle of Scotch, which I liberate as carefully as possible. Maybe I should throw something over him. Scratch that, I can't be bothered.

A buzz on the intercom surprises me. I go to answer it, expecting some random guest who got locked out overnight, but instead find myself looking into the face of Olen Canders.

'Ms Van de Korte,' he says.

I'm still staring at him in surprise. 'How did you get in?'

He takes off his hat, a strangely formal thing to do. 'May I come up?'

I glance behind me at the human wreckage from the party. 'This isn't a good time.'

'I apologise for intruding,' he says quietly in that refined voice of his, 'I have something important to discuss.'

'I told you before, I don't need emissaries from my family. If they want to talk to me, they can do it face-to-face.'

A hint of a smile crosses his features. 'Your parents don't know I'm here. May I?'

I shrug.

Minutes later the elevator arrives and he steps inside, takes stock of the situation but doesn't say a thing.

'How did you find me?' Even as I ask I guess the answer.

'Records,' he says. 'This apartment is a company asset.'

'You could lose your job for this,' I say.

Now it's his turn to shrug. 'I haven't been entirely forthright with you.' He motions to an empty bar stool in the kitchen and I nod, sitting on the one next to his.

I stare at him. 'So what do you want?'

'I'm glad you called in yesterday,' he says.

'I'm not following you.' The throbbing in my hand has become powerful and painful all of a sudden.

'I should have talked to you before you came to me,' he says, 'but I was waiting for the right time. Last night, seeing you, I feel slightly responsible.'

'I'm in charge of my own life,' I say.

He examines the wrecked apartment again. 'Yes. I can see that. I left you and your family at a time when it might have been better to stay. Who knows, another familiar face, another constant in your life and things may not have worked out the way they did.'

I rub my eyes. 'Well, time goes on, right? What's done is done and all that jazz.'

'Very philosophical.'

'That's me. Alice Van de Korte, philosopher gal, living the dream. Excuse the pun.'

He looks at me carefully. 'Alice, I might be able to help your situation.'

I wait, wondering where this is leading. 'Seriously.' He pulls out a notepad and writes a word on a page, passing it to me. I take it and frown over the writing.

'It's some sort of prescription.' I say.

'Not quite. It's a drug, still waiting approval from the FDA. Your family own the patent.'

'And?'

'The medicine is a form of anti-psychotic.' He takes back the notepad. 'A powerful one.'

And I get it. I can almost see my father's shadow in the background. Olen, an old friend, doing him one last favour before he bows out. Maybe getting a kickback for all his extra hard work and Mattiew Van de Korte doesn't need to get involved. Classic Dad.

I stand up from the chair. 'I've got no idea if my father put you up to this or not, but I've been through all this before. No thanks.'

'It stops dreams, Alice. Completely inhibits them.'

I stop.

'It's a side effect of the drug,' he says. 'But it would give you the answer you're looking for.'

'Sure it would.' My voice is unsteady. 'Why are you telling me this?'

'Because I can get a sample. Because I'm an old man retiring in a month.' He stares at me. 'After that I won't be able to access it anymore. I'll be out of the game, so to speak.'

I don't trust it; it's too easy to have the solution handed to me on a plate like this. 'So all I do is take this drug and the dream will go?'

He shakes his head. 'No. Not quite. The medication is strictly short-term use only.' He looks at me levelly. 'Though I suspect once you know the truth the fiction will unravel.'

'What if this is the dream?'

'It isn't.'

'So what's the catch?'

He smiles. 'I like that. You were always a quick one. There is no catch, but you do have to be clean before the drug can be administered.'

'Clean?'

'You understand what I'm talking about. It's new. We think all of the side effects are documented, but there may be some that aren't. I can't in good conscience administer a medicine like this to someone in your condition.'

Bingo.

I nod, a cynical smile on my lips. 'Wow. You are so persistent. You almost got me.'

He smiles also; on him, such an enigmatic expression. 'I'm telling you the truth.'

'OK,' I say. 'Well. I'll just drop into detox and meet you later.'

'You know we have a program at the clinic.'

'I know.' A laugh escapes me, a loud, sad bark. 'Shit. Wow. Goddam, you guys are good.' I open the door for him as the pain in my hand grinds away in the background. 'You know what the really crazy part is? I called you. That's how easy I am.' I shake my head, stunned at the realisation I'm so simple to manipulate. I wait for him to leave then slump on a chair. If Marty lets anybody else in, I'm going to get him sacked.

37

THE BATH

The bathroom is the only place free of human flotsam. As I shut the door I switch on the light and ditch the robe. The room is bigger than it needs to be, but it's paradise. With dark slate on the floor and marble on the walls, a few ferns and flowers here and there it's heaven. A big mirror fills the east wall, reflecting a full-sized claw foot tub with bronze faucets. Screw Sydney-Alice's shop. You can't beat a good bath.

I run the hot water and wait for the tub to fill, examining myself. I don't bother judging, I just observe. Still lean, mostly fit. I almost look normal. Steam fills the room and wipes out my reflection and that's fine.

I let the water hit the rim before gingerly stepping in. The heat shocks me awake, quickly engulfing me, wrapping around like a blanket too hot to feel. It leaves only the sensation of warmth and weightlessness as my body finds its own level. I smile and breathe out, letting Olen out of my mind, sensing my fingertips slowly ease away from the edge of the bath. For no reason I picture the girl in green from Sydney. She's so clear and defined it startles me.

Something slams into my chest.

Water pushes over my face and forces its way into my lungs. My eyes fly open, seeing only foam. The acid bite of liquid running down the back of my throat and nose causes me to cough and I slip deeper. Panic sets in as my fingers skate over the rim, seeking something to hold as my body slides further down into the heat.

I stare upwards in terror as a shape looms over the bath. I try to grab the edge and pull myself up but someone's forcing me down, trying to drown me. I kick my legs, splashing huge arcs of bathwater onto the slate tiles, drum my arms, my hands spasming randomly. Some part of me that's not drowning wonders how this can be happening.

And then the weight is gone.

Exploding upwards gagging and coughing I spin around — madly searching for who did this. The room's empty, silent except for the echo of runoff in the drain and the cascade from my shaking body.

Finally, gasping through fiery lungs I cough out enough water to start breathing properly. I search again but the room is empty. Feeling shaken, balance wrecked, I step from the bath and my foot lands badly on a tile. I can feel myself slipping, then falling almost in slow-motion until my head cracks against the tiles.

38

THE SHORTCUT

I'm at a weird angle, confused. Ratbone stares down at me from the bed. It takes me a couple of seconds before I understand I must have fallen out. I'm scared, but the fear is second hand, carried over from the dream. What came first? Me falling out of bed or her tripping in the bath? I've never had such a close connection with her before, even when I went to New York. Up till now I've been able to deal with it somehow, but since things started echoing each other so closely, I don't know. She's invading my life.

My lip hurts and as I pull my hand away I'm surprised at the smear of blood on my fingers. I climb heavily to my feet, still groggy. Going to the bathroom and checking for damage, I find heavy eyes and a cut lip, a thin line of blood colouring my teeth. I look terrible and it's her fault. Grabbing some mouthwash from the cupboard I spit out the metal taste, ignoring the sting. 'Go away,' I whisper to the reflection, seeing her there instead. 'Leave me alone.'

I GET to the stop just as the Number Twelve heads down the road without me. Great. I check my watch and yes, for the first time in living memory public transport is actually ahead of schedule. Which means I'll be late again for the appointment with Ryan. I take a breath. The day's bright but slightly cooler than yesterday, so I decide to race the bus to the next stop rather than wait the fifteen minutes for the next one. Other-me wouldn't hang around. Why should I?

I shake my head as I walk, knowing how agitated I appear. Crazy chick on the loose, stay away. I don't care; I'm out of control — She's out of control and now her stuff is spilling over. Things have always mirrored one another on some level; for whatever reason it's one of the rules. Like the other rule that people don't cross over. No one from here is there and vice versa. These are the unbreakable laws of my life, my personal charter. Sure my worlds are linked, but also distinct; two bubbles joined yet separate. I rub my lip, still tasting a faint residue of blood: *that* is breaking the rule.

A hot wind rasps through the dry leaves of the trees and I check the time again. Got to pick up the pace if I'm going to make it. I spot a small grass and dirt track, almost an alley cutting straight through a block of houses across the street. Perfect. I head for the shortcut.

It must be a service road or a fire access. There are plenty of them, swathes of unbuilt land separating the blocks of suburban houses. A couple of metres in and I'm overwhelmed by a sudden scent of roses. A hot breeze wafts the perfume down the small space, channelled by the high wood-slat fences either side. The smell is overpowering, but I do my best to ignore it as I follow the track.

Further in I find the track's not as straightforward as I thought. I come to a junction, where it branches to the left and right. Household noises drift past the suburban backyards, invisible behind those fences, but it all seems distant. This is how people go missing, a paranoid voice whispers. I go left.

The alley goes on a long long way, much further than I expected. I keep walking, refusing to let this get to me. I'm still unsettled by the dream and the memory of yesterday at the park so of course I'm a bit jumpy. It's only natural.

The dirt eventually gives way to dried sunburned grass which crunches as I walk over it. There's another T-section a few houses away and my skin prickles, sensing the first tiny signs of what might be a panic attack. Alright. This track isn't right.

I can always go back. I turn around to prove the point to myself, seeing the flattened grass stems behind me. My own version of a trail of breadcrumbs; not that I like where breadcrumb-trails lead in fairytales.

I shake it off. I'm not going to jump at shadows, instead I keep myself busy by focusing on the mechanics of walking. The only thing I should be worried about in this long grass is snakes. I go right.

It's getting hotter in here. Now sweating I push further down the track, keeping up the pace. I pass another house, again blocked by a tall fence. A series of high-pitched shrieks echo off the wood and I jump back, startled by the sound. The screams transform into childish laughter.

Shit. OK, I give in. I shouldn't be here.

I don't bother explaining it. All I want is out. The track veers to the right and I bite back on my fear as it shows no sign of ending. I should be well out by now. And whoever heard of an access trail meandering like this one? Don't think about it. Keep moving.

I walk faster, ignoring the heat and the increasingly sweet perfume hanging heavy in the air. I'm not sure but a few metres ahead I can see the heads of bushes peek over the top of one of the fences. The sound of childish laughter echoes down the wooden walls as a gust of hot wind blows seeds and dust into eddies. My heart is shuddering, my breathing ragged. I close my eyes against the stinging gale and run.

I lose myself in the pounding of my own feet and the cloying stink of roses, squinting through dirt and grit and biting leaves and the sound of those kids laughing. And I keep running.

I run until I can't move another step, staggering to a stop, doubled over as I fight to breathe. Someone walks past looking at me strangely. I glance up, wiping the sweat from my face to find myself somehow out of the alley and in a small reserve, the road miraculously ahead of me. The houses behind me seem normal in the bright summer light, their backyards hidden.

I take a deep slow breath. Ryan doesn't need to hear about this.

39

ABOUT THE GIRL

'What happened to your lip?' he asks.

'I fell...' I almost say, in the bath. I touch my broken skin then smile faintly. 'Do you believe in ghosts?' I do.

He studies at me carefully. 'This is about the girl.'

I try my best to hide the surprise but it still shows. 'Yes.'

'So you think she might be a ghost?'

You know what? After this morning all I want is a straight answer. 'My question first.'

He leans over and grabs the tennis ball from his desk then begins tossing it from hand to hand. 'Do I believe in ghosts?' he muses. 'We've been doing this long enough for you to know it's not about my belief. The important thing is what you believe.' His evasiveness gets under my skin and he senses I need a real answer. 'Probably not. I don't think so. But I'm glad you brought up the issue. You're aware that Social Services contacted me and told me you'd called the police about a girl.'

'They didn't find her.'

He nods. 'Right. According to them there was no missing

child matching your description. And no one saw her even after you said you chased after her.'

I rub my face, feeling some of the grit from the track. 'That doesn't mean she wasn't there.'

'True,' he says, 'but what interests me is the progression leading you to believe she might be a spirit.'

'I didn't realise I was on a database,' I say calmly.

He catches the ball and stares at me seriously. 'Really? I don't think you're naïve, Alice.'

'OK,' I say. 'I always thought it was a possibility. Just never knew for sure.'

'I'm sorry, I thought...never mind. Some patients undergoing long-term psychiatric care are listed. Since I'm your doctor, they called me. Believe it or not it's about keeping you safe.'

'It's about keeping track of me.'

He doesn't bother arguing the point. In his world those two things are probably one and the same anyway. I look away, not sure whether to feel betrayed or satisfied that I haven't been paranoid all along. You're not being paranoid when they really are watching you. 'Well, that's peachy.' Out of nowhere, I have a sudden craving for a cigarette. 'She came back.'

It's Ryan's turn to appear surprised. 'When?'

'Yesterday. I didn't bother calling the cops again. There wasn't any point. What with everyone trying to keep me safe.'

'Alice,' he says, 'we don't need to be combative about this. I don't like it either, but we're here to get through this.'

'Fine.'

He puts the ball away. 'So the girl. Let's start at the start: if you believed she might be a spirit, why did you call the police at all? I'm not sure I understand how you thought they could help.'

'I didn't think she was a ghost. Not at first, anyway,' I say. 'There's something about her though, some kind of connection. And yes, I understand how this sounds, but it's not my imagination. There was a guy fixing the fridge at the shop yesterday and he saw her.'

He raises his eyebrows.

'Her shadow, anyway,' I say. 'So I followed her.' I stare at him, daring him to disbelieve. 'She wants to show me something. I think it's important.'

He pulls out a pen and studies it closely while he listens. 'To be honest,' he says, 'I'm uncomfortable you've started seeing this child.'

I almost tell him about what happened in the park and again today, but if he's freaked out by me meeting the girl then this morning's thing will blow his mind. I should trust him, but I hold back anyway. For some reason he's being really annoying. In fact he's being a bit of an asshole.

Where did that come from? It's something my other self would think.

I compensate right away. 'I don't know what's happening but things are changing. The girl's part of it.' And then, quietly, 'I stopped taking my prescriptions.'

He puts the pen down, concern on his face. 'Alice, when did you stop?'

'A day ago.'

He leans back and pushes his hands through his hair. I've pissed him off, I can tell. 'You realise how dangerous that is.' I don't say anything. 'Listen.' He looks me in the eye, demanding my full attention, 'I know you think you're making progress, but dumping the meds isn't the way to help.'

'It's just a day,' I say.

'That's not the point. When I suggested changing your dosage of anti-psychs, it was going to be in controlled measures.'

'Maybe it needs a shock,' I say. 'It's my body after all.'

'Of course it is, but we need to administer your medication carefully, not go cold turkey.'

'What would happen if I do?' I lean forward. 'I'm changing.'

He absorbs this. 'You might start having symptoms like hallucinations, headaches, hearing voices.'

I glance away, feeling exposed. What happened at the park and again today was real, not a withdrawal side effect. The drugs aren't even out of my system yet, I know. You can't be on some sort of anti-psychotic most of your life without picking up a thing or two about how they work.

'At the moment the anti-psychs are meant to be working against all that,' he goes on, 'our test was to change the dosage, measure your progress, but gently. After all these years this is a substantial biological adjustment we're talking about. You have to start taking them again.'

'OK,' I say.

'I need to be sure.'

'Fucking hell, I said OK.' Then I pause, mouth open, stunned at my own language. He raises his eyebrows but doesn't comment. 'Ryan,' I say, 'I really want to talk about the girl. She's important. My lives are coming together, I know it. And she's connected to it some way.'

He digests this for a long time. 'OK then, lets talk about it.' He turns and reaches for my file, starts flipping through his notes. 'Have you considered the reason the two worlds mirror each other so closely might be the dream is echoing the real world? After all, it needs to get it's substance from somewhere.'

'Yes. Of course. But that doesn't explain why it's changing. The girl is important.'

'How?'

I look at the print over his desk. 'I don't know. She's different.'

'Which isn't proof she's a ghost,' he points out.

'What are you trying to say?'

He shakes his head. 'Exploring possibilities. You can't ignore the fact your first instinct might have been right and she's real. Just because the police don't have a report of a missing girl doesn't mean there isn't one.'

I'm confused. 'I thought you didn't believe in her.'

He shrugs. 'I can't know either way, can I? I'm playing the devil's advocate here, Alice. You asked to talk about her, so lets tease it out, follow where the thread leads. Perhaps you want her to be a ghost?'

'And why do I want that?'

Ryan shrugs. 'Any number of reasons. Maybe because you're searching for an easy answer.' He holds up his hand. 'No — it's OK. I would too, seriously. A spirit who yearns to show you something is a lot more poetic than getting through this the hard way.' He adds quietly, 'And you can't pin ghosts down, people generally can't see them. They can't be proved.'

I stare at him.

'Think about it,' he goes on, 'be open to the possibility that what we agreed to do in our last session is challenging and,' he emphasises this, looking like a school teacher again, 'there's no short cut.'

I hold his gaze. 'The girl exists, ghost or not.'

'OK,' he says, 'I'll agree she might be real if you agree she might not be.'

I shake my head. 'I'm not that kind of crazy.'

'No,' he says, 'but to be honest with you, the second you start cutting out the antipsychotics, you experience this' —' he opens his palms, 'ghost?'

'No. She found me before that. I hadn't changed my medication then.'

He rubs his mouth thoughtfully. It's obvious he doesn't believe me. 'OK. Promise me you'll restart the meds. One day isn't a big deal, but I don't want you going any longer.' I nod cautiously. 'And if you find this child — this ghost — again, call me. Straight away. Got it?'

'Sure.'

'I mean it. We have to go carefully, Alice.'

I glance away, and am startled when a small booklet lands in my hands. 'In the meantime, I've found some relaxation exercises for you to try.' I agree to read it, not bothering to look at it. 'So,' he continues, 'since we've got some time left, let's give one a shot.'

He starts talking again but I zone out. I wonder why I've never seen this in Ryan before. He doesn't want to help me.

40

THE SCHOOL

The fruiterer's is a welcome oasis of citrous smells and shade from that damn heat outside. I wander down the cramped aisles with my basket, slowly collecting the ingredients for a fruit salad. I'm scattered. It's hard to focus as I replay moments from this morning's short cut to the bus stop, all the way to that weird session with Ryan. I know what I know. This life may be a dream but even if it is, the child is just as real as me, ghost or not.

I round an aisle, startled by a boy who's staring at me. 'Shit,' I blurt out under my breath. Am I going to start jumping at every kid I run into from now on? Then he moves away, revealing the girl standing right there behind him. Her face is streaked with tears as she stares unflinchingly at me. She's like a sculpture, a figure caught between daylight and shade.

I drop my basket in shock and she turns away, instantly lost in the small crowd.

'Hey wait!' I call, drawing startled glances. I ignore them and push through a couple of women in front of me but she's gone. Pulling myself up on one of the stands for a better view, I accidentally cause a small avalanche of apples to crash down onto the wet concrete.

'Hey lady!' yells someone. 'Get off that!'

The girl's outside, her green dress bright in the glare of the sun. Ignoring the growing confusion I drop to the floor and bolt from the shop.

She's running down the footpath when I burst out of the fruiterer's and head after her. However old she is, she's fast. I struggle to keep up as flashes of her dress flicker in and out of view ahead of me. I plough through pedestrians and around obstacles and, panting heavily in the heat, put on an extra burst of speed. Someone's going to call the cops, I know it. Puffing and heaving for breath, the girl's racing hard but the effort's costing her. Which is surprising.

With a glimpse behind her to make sure I'm still following, she races down a side street and is gone. Distracted by the effort I almost trip and fall, something that costs me more distance. When I look up she's even further ahead and rounding another corner. I curse and try to run faster, not easy in a long skirt and boots.

I get onto Cooper Street, which is lined with clothes and electronics shops and mercifully — free of cops. She's put more space between us and running even harder than before when I next spot her. Gulping down air, legs stinging, I push on. I will not lose her this time. Ryan and the others be damned, I'm going to catch her.

The girl seems tireless as she ducks down street after street, weaving her way over footpaths and dashing across roads. I follow doggedly, slowly falling behind as I become more exhausted. Finally I stop at a small crossroad, shuddering and red-faced as I fight for breath. I try to get my bearings but I've never been here before and doubt I could find my way back.

The only good thing is she's also slowed down. She's exhausted as well. How can that be? 'Wait,' I call out, 'I'm not going to hurt you. You understand that, don't you?' The girl stares at me through bruised and tear-widened eyes. 'Tell me who you are. I want to help. You came to me for a reason, right?' She turns and slowly begins to run again.

I chase across the road after her and into a broad, coarse-grassed field. The grass reminds me of that alley. For a moment I get a sense of déjà vu, but there are no tracks here, just a huge reserve, one of those massive undeveloped greenbelts in the suburbs.

I ignore the long scraping brambles clinging to my dress as I push ahead, keeping pace with the girl who's slowing down even more. She's finding it hard going through all the tall grass. My head's spinning in the heat and I wonder how it must be for her, having run as far and as fast as me, weighed down by her heavy uniform. As she pushes past weeds and husks of wheat, the seriousness of all this sinks in again. 'Who are you?' I scream out, but she keeps running.

There's a rise ahead and the child makes straight for it. Sweat blurs my vision, clings to my clothes and falls in rivers from my face, but I keep going. The girl has come to me. She'd sought me out for a reason and I'm not about to let go of that. For a heartbeat I lose sight of her as she runs over the low top of the hillock, so I push even harder, ignoring the pain. I finally stumble to the top, gasping as I watch her run towards the fence of a primary school. As I stand there struggling to catch my breath in the unbearable heat, she slips past a gap in the iron bars and collapses in the shade of a tree.

By the time I get close my vision is swimming. I trample down the last of the long grass and stop at the boundary.

The gap she's used is large enough for me to squeeze through, but I hold off. 'I want to help you,' I call to her. Slumped under the tree, she ignores me. She lays with her head on her arm, eyes closed and exhausted. I rattle the bars in frustration, causing one of the kids nearby to look at me. 'Listen to me!' I yell to her, but she's passed out.

The boy who saw me wanders off and I can't find any teachers. 'Hey,' I shout, 'someone's hurt.' Nothing. We might as well be the only ones here. I push open the fence and force my way between the bars, ripping my dress on a burr of twisted metal. 'Damn it,' I say to her, 'what do you want me for?' I gently turn her over. She's so light, it's frightening. 'Wake up,' I say, tapping her face.

'You! Leave her alone!' I glance across to a male teacher running towards me, the boy following cautiously behind. 'I said get away!'

'I'm trying to help,' I explain, realising too late what this seems like.

The teacher's face brightens as he runs. 'Get the hell away from her!'

I lean in to her, guessing how this is going to wind up if I don't get out of here right now. 'Wake up,' I say, 'tell me what you want.' She doesn't respond and it's only by the shallowest movement in her chest I can tell she's alive at all. Then I'm shoved sideways and sent sprawling in the dirt as the teacher leans over her.

'Jesus,' he says, looking at her bruises, 'what have you done to her?'

'Nothing, I just...' I trail off, sensing the world close in as a panic attack begins to smother my words. There — the gap in the bars. I might still be able to make it. I get to my feet as another teacher races in, followed by a growing crowd of children looking on with wide-eyed intensity.

Their gazes pin me down. By the time I try to get up a solid six-foot security guard steps in my way. Bells start ringing in the school.

'Don't move,' he says. I don't. I can't, as I watch the girl being gently taken away.

THE CELL'S TINY. It's barely large enough to hold me and smells of disinfectant. I push myself back against the wall of the cubicle, curling up on the cold bare metal bench. Looking blankly through the smeared and scratched perspex separating me from the rest of the lockup, I can't see much. My perspective is limited and everything's been painted a horrible blue. I've been here for hours and I've got no idea of what's going to happen next. I keep telling myself I've done nothing wrong, but it doesn't feel that way. I know what it looked like — I'd have locked me away too. Someone in the next cell coughs loudly and begins swearing at the top of his voice, but he soon trails off, distracted or asleep.

Back in the interview room I told the old, white-haired sergeant the truth; lying would have made everything worse. I hated to do it but asked them to call Ryan. After this morning's session, I felt like a hypocrite. Later the sergeant returned, attitude adjusted and I could almost read that damn word *protocol* stamped on his forehead.

My clothes are ripped from the fence, reeking of perspiration; my hair's a grotty tangle. There's no sympathy in the eyes of the cop who walks by every half hour; I seem crazy, no doubt about it. I breathe out as I wonder what this will trigger in that database on me. More red flags. Maybe they'll never let me near an airport again. The harder I try to make sense of it all, the less sense it makes. I close my eyes, shutting out the unyielding fluorescent light and the blue painted metal of the cell walls. I'm in so much trouble.

Two quick knocks on the perspex snap me back to the here and now. A cop leans towards me and unlocks the bolt before opening the door. 'Come with me,' he says. I unfold stiffly and follow him out into a coldly bright reception area, where a huge curving counter cuts the room in half. Computers and paperwork fill up the desk; the screen closest to me has my name on it.

'Alice.'

I peer around and find Jen standing there, signing something. Next to her is Ryan, quiet, arms folded. Jen's tears aren't far away. 'Jen, are they letting me go?'

'Yes, sweetie.' I recognise that voice. She used it a lot when I got out of Mayfleur. She nods as a sergeant flips over another sheet, which she signs before turning her full attention to me. 'Are you all right?' I nod, confused about whether I should walk around or if I have to stay still. Ryan steps forward and speaks to the cop, signing a different coloured form from Jen. 'So can she go now?' asks Jen. The sergeant nods.

The same officer who'd brought me from my cell guides me through a door to the side that I haven't seen before and leaves me standing next to her. I begin to shake. 'Do I sign something?' I ask. Ryan shakes his head, expression wooden.

'Remember,' says the sergeant to Jen, 'she's in your care until the hearing.'

I glance at the officer behind the desk then back to Jen who's standing stressed out and rigid, her own face a mask. 'Why isn't anyone talking to me? What does he mean?'

'Come on,' says Ryan, 'let's get you home.'

I didn't realise I'd been locked up for so long. It's dark

when we go through the doors, but still ridiculously hot. Jen leads us to a bench under a tall tree. Cars slowly crawl by on their commute home and the air's thick with a smog that refuses to blow away.

'Thanks for getting me out of there,' I manage eventually. I can't think of what else to say.

Jen hugs me but she's crying and I can tell she's so angry right now. 'You're in a shitload of trouble Alice. If it wasn't for Ryan over there you'd have been arrested and locked up for good.'

Ryan stares at me but stays silent. He's saving up some bad news. 'Alice,' he says at last, breaking the silence.

'I know.'

'You know what?'

'I'm screwed.'

He scowls. 'Why didn't you call me?'

I shake my head. 'I couldn't.'

'I thought we had an understanding. Especially after this morning.'

'It was crazy, it happened so quickly.' I glance at him, his face an unhealthy orange in the spill of the street light, 'It was too important, so I followed her.' I pause, trying to figure out what to say next. 'I didn't hurt her. She wasn't even a student there.' I can't say how I can be so sure, but I am.

Ryan is deeply worried. 'A lot of this doesn't make sense.' I wait for him to continue. 'But you're still in a lot of trouble.'

'I get it.'

He shakes his head. 'I don't think you do.'

Jen hugs me again, her face serious. 'You're so lucky the girl ran away.'

I let the words sink in. Of course the girl ran away, or vanished completely, or got lost. It's what she does; gets your attention then disappears. This can't be random. And someone else saw her too; that's something at least.

'So,' I say, 'you know she's real now, right?' Ryan and Jen share a look. What have they been talking about? Jen starts to talk but Ryan gets in first.

'Yes, I do. I told you before I was open to the possibility of it. But that's not the point. Alice, the only reason they let you out,' he says standing, 'is they can't find her. She went missing sometime after they picked you up. It doesn't mean they're not looking for her right now.' He wipes his face with his hands wearily. My heart races.

'They'll fail.'

'And why do you say that?'

'Because she can disappear if she wants to. That's what I've been telling you.'

Jen takes my hand and tells me quietly. 'They're going to get to the bottom of this. They've told us they'll need to ask you some more questions about it later on.'

They won't find her, but I hold back on voicing my thoughts. I keep saying the wrong thing. 'I'm so sorry about this,' I say looking first at Jen, then at Ryan.

'After I got the call from the police,' says Ryan, 'I phoned Jen to meet me here.'

'Thank you.'

'Don't thank me,' he says, voice cold. I look at him in surprise. His face is unreadable. 'I'm doing my job. Alice. Listen to me, if you keep this up, people are going to take decisions out of our hands.'

My stomach rolls. 'What does that mean?' But I know what it means.

He begins to walk away. 'They'll commit you, Alice. They'll put you back in Mayfleur.'

I stand in silence, watching him go.

'Come on babe,' says Jen putting her arm around my shoulder. 'Let's get out of here.'

I grab her hand, feeling beaten up. 'I need a shower,' I say.

'No problem,' she says in that just-out-of-Mayfleur-voice, 'we'll make sure you take your medication first, then you can hit the sack afterwards.'

41

CROSSING OVER

It's not a headache, it's agony. I stare into a pool of bloody water before attempting to sit up. Not a good idea. My balance is ruined and I fling out my arms to keep from falling over. A scary deep ache in my lungs allows only the shallowest of breaths before a pain stabs through my chest. 'Fuck,' I whisper, coughing. The bathroom is empty and there's no sign anyone else has been in here with me. Water runs down my reflection in the big mirror, a huddled shape in the corner looking back with hurt eyes. Taking another agonising breath I get to my feet and put on my robe. The door's locked from the inside, like I left it. There's no way anyone could break in without also wrecking the lock. I wrap my arms about myself, cold and frightened. After a while I unlock the door.

The apartment's unchanged, still strewn with sleeping bodies. I kick a woman curled around a throw pillow hard enough to wake her up before starting on the rest. Moving from sleeper to sleeper, nudging, kicking, I tell them all to open their eyes and get the hell out. I throw back the curtains, letting in a blaze of cold grey light that instantly causes another round of groans and complaints, then go about the same in the bedroom. Protests bubble up all around while someone else pleads for me to turn off the goddam lights.

With a tight reign on my emotions I go back into the living room and start pulling people to their feet. Some of them I recognise, most are strangers. As I bully them awake I wonder if I'm looking at the one who got to me in the bath. Impossible, I remind myself. The door was locked on the inside. The whole thing's scared me more than I want to admit as I try to figure out what happened. I don't believe in ghosts, which leaves me with — I don't know what. I need quiet and space to figure this out, not a bunch of freeloaders.

By now, most of them are stirring, some sitting and looking around in a post-party daze. I go to them and one by one drag them to their feet and push them out. Many are still too drunk to put up a fight. Ten minutes later the apartment is empty.

As the last of the partygoers, a scarecrow of a guy, rambles an attempt at a thank you, I turn away as the elevator shuts in his face. I lean against it heavily, breathing out. The place is finally empty and my head starts clearing at last.

I walk slowly to the wreck of the kitchen, surprised at a drop of blood on the counter. Then another. My hand goes to my lips and comes away bloody. Just like in Sydney. I grab the bench for support, holding on to its cold marble reality.

Finding some ice I wrap the cubes in a hand towel and dab my mouth. Whichever angle I come at it, I can't think of a way anyone was in the room with me. So what does that leave? Heart attack? Maybe a small stroke? Damn. Still dabbing my lip, I head for my room to get dressed when I notice another message on my phone.

The calm, clipped voice of Mother fills the quiet. I listen with growing anger as she tells me they have made some decisions regarding my future and expect to meet me at four. They'll send the car.

I glance at the clock. 'Fuck.'

The world crawls by, a montage of blues and greys, snow and slush. Mollher's driving and true to Mother's word, he'd been waiting for me even as I got her message. I gently touch my lip, wincing at the sting. I know better than to fight this particular summons. After my run-in with Mollher earlier, it's not unexpected. Anyway, we need to talk. I rub my head, a mannerism I share with her in Sydney, and settle back tiredly into the seat.

'Hey Mollher,' I say. 'Any chance you can swing past this place I know?' He doesn't answer, his only response a glimpse at me in the mirror. 'Guess not,' I say to myself. 'Your loss.'

The car slows.

'What's happening?'

'Roadwork,' he says. 'The street is blocked off. I'll find another route.'

'Yeah. Good work. You do that.'

He waits for a break in the traffic before turning down a street to the left. I stretch back and stare at the misty tops of the buildings through the sunroof. It's going to be a tough few hours so I close my eyes and rest, inventorying my injuries: hand stings like a bastard, lip swollen. The headache is threatening to evolve into an all-out migraine and on top of that, I lean forward to check, yes on top of that the liquor cabinet is empty. I sigh as the limo winds its way through clogged streets, slowly inching through the snarl of cars and buses.

I'm staring blankly out of the tinted glass, mind glazed over when I see it; a splash of green in the grey, gone in a second. 'Stop!'

Mollher doesn't bother turning. 'What's wrong?'

'Just stop the car.'

He shakes his head. 'Not possible, Alice.'

I drop the window and lean out into the cold air, stretching to catch any sign of the girl. I know it's her. My pulse hammers with excitement, bringing the reeling vertigo of the dream. The girl's impossible. Nothing can cross over. And then I see the flash of green again.

'Stop the fucking car!' Mollher ignores me and steers deeper into traffic. I won't let this go. I reach over and grab my coat from the seat next to me, throwing open the door.

The car's only crawling along, but as I jump out I almost trip on the freezing bitumen. Horns honk and blare everywhere as I weave through the mess of traffic heading towards where I saw her. Someone screams at me to get off the road, but I barely hear them in my rush to follow the girl. I make a bad call on the space between two cars and painfully clip the bumper of a taxi, the sudden shock forcing me to get my priorities right and head to the sidewalk. A small, calm part of myself understands this can't be the same child. It's impossible: if my Sydney self is chasing a ghost then what is this? But as I finally make it to the kerb, narrowly missing a bike courier speeding down the edge of the street I'm committed.

Muffled tones of my phone filter through my jacket. No doubt Mollher. I ignore it, racing past the steam of a manhole cover. I try to hoist myself higher on a lamp post, but the icy metal is too slippery to grasp properly. People are beginning to stare, watching me from beneath hoods and jackets pulled high against the weather.

The street's packed with pedestrians, all jostling one another as they move in a tide between shops, making it impossible to spot anything. A snarl of people crowd around a hot dog stand, blocking my way; I dodge round them onto the street, narrowly avoiding a taxi. Back on the sidewalk I head right onto another road, desperation growing with each second.

A splash of colour forces me to stop hard, but the green isn't a dress, only a jacket worn by a kid holding his mother's hand. I'm going to lose her; I know it. I make a decision and run towards an intersection, wait for the lights to change and dash to the middle, jumping on the spot, trying for a glimpse of the girl. Someone pushes as the crowd races across on the green, then time's up and I get off the road. I breathe hard, not from the running but the frustration of it all.

On queue, my cell rings again. 'What,' I say into the phone.

'Mollher's called,' Mother says, talking over me. 'Go back to the car immediately or there will be consequences. We are not playing games Alice.'

Not even bothering to hang up, I turn the phone off. 'Screw your consequences,' I say to the dead handset. The lights change again.

42

STAYING THE NIGHT

The sky is darker and colder and the snow's threatening to develop into a full-blown storm. I'm exhausted. I've criss-crossed half of Manhattan looking for her, winding up eventually in the Lower East Side after having gone almost as far as Washington Heights. I've been chasing shadows. I need to rest, dimly aware of the flurries of sleet falling onto the street, making everything treacherous.

The idea of walking into the train wreck of my apartment any time soon isn't appealing. The warm glow of an Irish pub spills out across the road, too tempting to resist. I'll take a break and figure out what to do next. One thing Sydney-me and I agree on: something's changing. I replay the glimpse I had of the girl in my mind as I insert my card. I saw what I saw. Somehow, impossibly, she's here. I look down at the machine as it hums over my plastic, leaving me to stare trancelike at its screen. Nothing crosses over. Nothing. Sydney is the dream and yet, here she is. I don't understand it at all, but I won't let it go.

An electronic beep draws my attention back to the ATM

and I take a couple of seconds to make sense of the display. My card has been rejected, held for security reasons. I hit cancel but nothing happens. I frown, fishing out another from my purse, only to have it eat that one as well. Then I understand. 'You bastards,' I whisper under the flat light. I cross the road to the pub, hoping that the long reach of my parents hasn't also cancelled my secret, private credit card. Minutes later, I learn it has.

Standing outside the restaurant in the growing evening, watching cars, I'm colder than I can ever remember being. I won't find the girl tonight — I've got to be patient. The girl comes to you, not the other way around. I should have remembered that before and saved myself a day.

As I sit shivering on a bench, wondering what to do next, I spot a toy rabbit staring at me from the kerb. I get up and kick it as hard as I can into the street. The plush vanishes under the wheels of a car. I know I'm crazy. I just don't want to be reminded all the fucking time. Wiping my nose I feel the start of tears but force them back as I start looking for a taxi. Be honest. Gabe was right. My life is a mess.

GABE OPENS the door and looks at me standing in the hallway, wet and bedraggled, hair plastered limply to my head, clothes soaked. 'What the hell happened to you?'

I look at him, not knowing where to start. 'Long story. I need a shower.'

He could kick me out. He could say no. I promise myself not to be surprised if he tells me to go to hell after how we left things. Instead, he steps back and lets me in. 'I'll get some towels.'

I hug him.

Later, sitting next to him on the couch, all but lost under a fluffy brown robe, I try to make sense of what had happened. Now I'm away from the cold and in the bright, sensible light of a living room a nagging, pedantic voice inside me reminds me that I hadn't seen her face. I put that thought away. I'm not going to start negotiating with myself; I believe what I believe.

'So,' says Gabe after some time staring at the TV, 'are you going to tell me what happened or what, eh?'

I lean in closer to him, grateful for his acceptance. Anyone else would have turned me away at the door. He'll bring up our argument later, no doubt, but for now I'm just happy to be with him.

I start at the start, telling him how my Sydney self found the girl and that my dream, which has been so real for so long, has begun to get weird and paranormal. But that still didn't prove Sydney was the dream because people there responded like anybody would react to that kind of news. Her life was changing: they were going to lock her away.

Gabe sits quietly as he absorbs all this, watching Jordie thumb his way through a thick graphic novel on the coffee table. I watch him too; he's listening to what we're saying, absorbing everything, processing it on some level. I wonder what he makes of it all and I feel for him, the shitty life he's been dealt, his vague father with his crazy girlfriend. I rub my eyes, surprised at the strength of the emotion. Until now, the kid has been like a prop, like everyone else in this maybe-imagined world. He's real and physical enough to fill a spot, play a role. But as I watch him, caught between losing himself in the colourful graphics and print and trying to make sense of the conversation going on around him I sense a connection that's never been there before. I wipe my eyes again, surprised at myself.

Gabe shrugs. 'I don't understand why this bothers you so much. I mean the girl's a dream. You're the real deal, not her, eh?'

'Because,' I say quietly, 'she's here too. I just saw her.'

He stares at me; mouth slightly open and eyes full of belief. Another thing about Gabe: he's the only person to have ever accepted my story without question. Always curious, sure, but he never doubts me. Right now that means more than anything.

'Shit.'

'Yeah. Shit. I followed her, but she got away.'

'How do you know it's her?'

I look at Jordie, his hand hovering over a page, pretending like hell not to be listening in. 'She's wearing the same clothes, but it's not that. More a feeling. Fuck me, it's got to mean something, right?' He nods.

'I've got to find her.'

'Why is she so important?'

'Haven't you been listening? She's the only thing that's ever crossed over.'

He looks at me quietly, thoughtfully. 'Baby, there's nothing to cross. Sydney isn't real, yeah?'

'Yeah.'

He leans forward and taps my forehead gently. 'If she's there, it's because she's been here all along.'

'She wasn't in my head today. She's real.'

'OK. So we go find her.'

'We?'

'Yeah.'

He hugs me and for a second I'm back in Sydney, being comforted by Jen. Then its gone. I kiss him, alive with anger and powerfully horny. 'This is real.'

'I know, baby.' He smiles and standing, guides me to the

bedroom. The last thing I see before kicking the door shut is Jordie getting to his feet and heading towards the kitchen.

43

OF LAVAR AND ENDINGS

Jen's sitting in the kitchen, sipping rose tea when I walk into the room. She smiles a hello, but I don't acknowledge her. She actually stood next to me last night and made sure I took the pills, like I was a child. And for a while there I really thought she was on my side. She still won't tell me what she and Ryan talked about while I was locked up but I can take a guess. I'm not going back to Mayfleur.

She's content to sit there as I make some toast and that's fine by me. She can get her own damn toast. I lean against the counter, staring at the backyard through the window. The only addition since our parents passed away is an awful old wicker banana lounge, now broken and long overdue for dumping. Maybe I should move out and get my own place, it might do us some good. The hall phone rings and Jen puts down her cup gently, rising to answer it as I throw my plate on top of the pile in the sink.

'Someone called Lavar for you,' she says.

Oh. Still finishing my toast I take the phone.

'Alice?'

'Yes.'

'Hey Alice, I'm sorry about what happened the other day. It was totally uncool.'

'You could say that. Why are you calling?'

'I'd like to meet up with you.'

I get an odd sensation. 'What for?' There's a pause on the line. 'Is it about the girl?'

'Yes,' he says.

I'm not surprised. I organise to meet him at the cafe opposite the shop and hang up, only to find Jen hovering nearby.

'What?'

She glances away, her face strained. 'You've got to help me out honey.'

'I won't do anything stupid.'

She nods. 'We all love you Alice. Don't wreck it.'

I can't trust myself to reply. I need to follow this to the end. Awake, right here, sensing the growing warmth of the day even through the thick walls of the house it's so hard to doubt the truth of this place. New York is a cold, empty shell, something I don't want. Let this be real, I pray to myself, despite the ghost.

I FIND Lavar sitting at the back of the cafe, the drink on his table untouched. He seems nervous. As I sit next to him, Keira brings over a coffee without me even asking. She's such a sweetie. She appraises Lavar in a glance and winks at me. I cringe, embarrassed like a schoolgirl whose first date has scraped through muster. For a second I'm going to set her straight, then change my mind. Let her think what she wants.

'So,' I say, channelling some of my Manhattan assertiveness, 'tell me what's happening.'

Lavar wraps his fingers around his coffee cup, searching for a way to begin. They're pianists' fingers, I note, surprised at how I even know this. 'I'm sorry about the other day,' he says. 'The life of a sensitive isn't always easy. People are so full of psychic debris.' I wait for him to go on. In the shop light he seems older, his skin sallow and there are bags under his eyes. His movements are slow as he sips his drink; he's aged ten years. 'People want reassurances. Loved ones still watching over them, spirits of pets doing well, that kind of thing. A show. They expect to be a little bit freaked out, but mostly they need to feel better about themselves.'

'I wasn't the one who freaked out,' I say quietly.

'I know.'

'So tell me about the girl.' I hold up my hand. 'And I don't need to feel better about myself.'

He looks pained. 'I can't. That's the problem. She's not a ghost, that much is for sure, but when I reach for her, there's only pain.'

'So she's real? Alive?'

He shakes his head, confused. 'I've never met anything like her.'

I lean towards him despite the thumping of my heart. I need to hear what he has to tell me, not run away into another panic attack. I can't afford this crap any more. 'Did you see her? Did she say something to you?'

'No, but I need to ask. Who is this girl to you?'

I laugh, a bark of frustration. 'I have no fucking idea. That's why I came to you in the first place.'

Lavar moves back, looking worried. 'The two of you are connected,' he says. 'But there's this pain, it fills her and she's very angry at you.'

'At me? Why?' I feel a flush of anger myself. 'I don't know her. The first time I saw her was a couple of days ago. How can she be angry at me, I've done nothing to her.'

'I couldn't say.'

I calm down before looking at him carefully, now wary. 'I'm not going to pay you. So if this is a trick you can stop wasting my time and go.'

He returns my gaze. 'No tricks and I don't want your money. But I need to know — is there anything about her, any information at all you can give me?'

'I thought the way this worked was I asked you the questions. Why is this so important?'

He doesn't answer straight away, instead he toys with his cup, pushing it across the table deep in thought. 'Honestly?' I nod. 'She scares me.'

The coldness gets worse and I imagine myself back in Manhattan. 'Ghosts are your business,' I say levelly. 'You're not allowed to be scared.'

'This is different.'

'What? Tell me.'

I fold my arms, relating to my Manhattan self more than ever. I can almost hear her words. Where do these people get off? If I'm going to be shaken down it won't be by some idiot like this. He should stick to scamming old spinsters. Lavar jumps, startling me. Did I say that out loud? 'It's so hard to read you,' he says flatly, 'and the girl is like that.' I rake my hand though my hair, trying to hide my surprise. Silence stretches between us. Fuck it.

'OK,' I say, 'I'll tell you what's going on.' I take a breath then dive in, telling him about my dream self, reciting the events of my life calmly like the history of a stranger. I explain how my lives are mirrors of each other and I never truly know which is the real and which is the dream. I tell him about the death of my parents and even as I speak, understand another parallel in the emotional death of her parents in Manhattan. I cover the Golden Rule; that nothing crosses over and how, despite that, the girl has turned up first here, and now there. It's shattered everything I thought I knew. As I tell him these things his expression doesn't change, but I sense his concern. 'So I've got two souls,' I say. 'Now what do I do about it?'

'The girl is the key,' he says, absorbing everything he's heard.

I nod. 'I figured that out by myself, but why now? What does she want?'

He opens his hands, helpless. 'I can't tell you those things. But listen to me. I don't like her; she isn't normal. There's death all about her and endings.'

'So I'm going to wake up?'

I fight to keep the hope from my voice but he shakes his head. 'It's not like that. If you wake up, you die. Nothing is real.'

'The dreamer always dies. So which is the dream?' Even as I ask, the cynical part of me waits for the punchline. He has the answer. All I need to do is hand over some money and the truth will be mine.

He rubs his nose, his eyes wide. 'This one.'

So no punchline then. 'That makes you make-believe,' I say quietly. Even as I speak the words I sigh inside, defeated yet liberated at the same time. Ghosts aren't real; the girl is a messenger from my unconscious. But as I follow the train of thought it doesn't make sense: if the girl is a messenger, what's the message? Surely it's got to be to wake up, but if it's only a matter of wanting to do it I would have done it years ago. There have been so many times when I've been completely convinced either Sydney was real, or Manhattan; it can't be as simple as belief. Then there's the small question of the girl being in my New York life as well. This is the dream? It's not that easy. I glance at Lavar again.

'Manhattan as well,' he says before I can say a thing.

'That too?'

He reaches out and touches me gently on the forehead, trying one last time to look at me before glancing away and standing. 'I've got to go.' As he walks from the cafe I follow him into the alleyway outside.

I catch up to him as he reaches the intersection. Trucks and cars rocket by, filling the lanes with peak hour traffic. I grab his arm and force him to turn. 'That's it?' I say, 'You drop something like that on me then take off?'

He stares at my hand awkwardly. 'It's too strange,' he says. 'I thought if I met you again it would make more sense but it doesn't.'

'Well screw you,' I say as I let him go. 'Fuck off then.'

He rubs the spot where I held him but stays where he is, scrutinising me. 'Who am I talking to?'

It's only morning but the heat is unbearable, due to last for the next two weeks. I shake my head, hating the unrelenting glare, the temperature. I look about, confused and awash with emotion, the shadow of her very, very close. What am I doing? 'You're talking to me,' I say after a long time.

'Then keep away from the girl.'

He walks off, leaving me standing next to the traffic lights. I could chase after him but what's the point? Anyway he'd probably call the cops and I'd get a one-way trip to Mayfleur, no questions asked.

Both lives a dream? What the hell does that mean? I turn to go when I catch a flash of a green dress from the corner of my eye. The girl's standing across the road, face teary, bruised, angry. 'Shit,' I say. But I'm not even surprised.

The girl begins to walk away. 'Wait!' I call out after her. I check to make sure the road's clear before following, heart racing.

There's a screech of rubber on bitumen and then, weirdly, flight.

44

THE GROWING STORM

'Have you ever noticed it's always snowing?'

I stare at the fire escape through the kitchen window. The steel is white with a dusting of fresh snow. Gabe hands me a glass of something that appears noxious but tastes amazing.

'What?'

'It's always snowing,' I say quietly. 'Why is that?'

He glances at me waiting for the joke, but I stay quiet, contemplating the window. A blast of noise comes from the other room as Jordie turns on the television and finds the cartoon channel.

'Dude, turn it down OK?' The volume goes down a notch. He pulls out a chair and sits, studying me. 'How are you doing right now? You screamed in your sleep last night.'

I look away from the snow outside, reach out to feel the glass. The kitchen is tiny. An old-fashioned refrigerator takes up what little room there is, with a single basin and oven crammed against a wall. If he stretched, Gabe could almost touch the wallpaper either side. We're sitting at the collapsible table he's managed to jam in, which leaves us very close to each other. This room, this entire apartment would probably fit inside the living room at my place. I'm displaced. Nowhere is home anymore. 'I don't know what's happening, Gabe.'

He reaches across the table and locks his fingers between mine. 'Don't sweat it baby. We'll get through.'

The shock of the dream's still real, almost a physical thing. The stupid surprise on the driver's face, the sound, the sensation of weightlessness. Was I dead in Sydney? There wasn't any pain, but that's not what scares me most. It's carried over here too; the constant throbbing of my hand, the sting on my lip, they're gone. I've been numbed. I can't stop replaying Lavar's words, looking for meaning. What did he mean both my lives were a dream, it doesn't make sense. If I'm not my Sydney self, or me, who am I? I pull away from Gabe and rest my head in my hands.

'I've got to go,' I say.

He waits.

'Gabe?'

'Yeah?'

'I need some money. They've shut me down.'

'They finally went all hardcore on you, eh?'

What can I say? He's not even surprised. How is it everyone else sees these things when I can't? He rubs his chin and nods. 'Don't tell anybody about this shit, yeah?'

I agree, watching in fascinated silence as he pulls the refrigerator clear of the wall. The ancient machine rucks up the linoleum in places as he makes enough space to lean behind it. Tiny trails of fluff and dust puff out as he squeezes into the dark gap and takes out a small tin, which he puts carefully down on the table.

'What is that?'

He pops the lid and pulls out a thick wad of bills. 'Seriously, yeah? No one knows about this, not even Jordie.'

I can't believe he's managed to get his hands on so much cash. It must be thousands, and as I look closer at the wads of bills folded neatly along the bottom I revise that number up. Tens of thousands.

'How did you?' I begin but he cuts me off. On second thoughts better I don't know.

'I need it back for certain, right?'

'Sure.'

'What are you going to do now?' he asks, handing some of the money over to me.

I stand, leaning over to kiss him. 'Find the girl. Then I'm going to wake up.' A part of me is surprised at how calm I am about it. Maybe it's that strange numbness. Whatever. The anger's still there, defining as always, but now it seems muted, like I'm experiencing it from a distance. Let it be a dream, let it be real, either way I will learn the truth.

'OK,' he says, surprising me by taking me by the hand. 'I'll call Latisha and we'll go together. We'll get that ghost bitch, yeah?'

It would be so easy to take more of his help now, but he reads my hesitation. The grand fuck-up of Olen's goodbye party still weighs heavily. He turns away. 'Alright. Just don't go freaking out again, cool?'

'Sure,' I say, not knowing how to thank him.

The flurry of snow that started on the way back from Gabe's has turned into a full-on storm. There'll be no chasing the girl today.

The apartment's cold, as usual. I walk through the rooms

as if seeing them for the first time, pausing at an old ornament I bought with Gabe at a market, running my fingers over the glossy covers of a few magazines I keep in the lounge. The portrait stares down at me from its place on the wall, daring me to examine it closely. I put my palm to the glass, searching the image for signs of change, defying it to reveal something. I don't know what I'm feeling, not feeling. I'm as cold as the snow outside.

On an impulse I go into my bedroom, all the time aware of the bathroom. Opening it I look inside, forcing myself to prove it's empty. No ghosts. There's nothing supernatural about it: I partied too hard, perhaps fell asleep in the tub, not that mysterious. I'm going to kick Rene's ass next time, but I keep saying that, don't I? There's no fire in me now. The room's exactly as I left it, towels on the floor, a small steady drip from the faucet, normal. I shut the door.

The photo album will take some finding; if I remember right it's still half buried under a box full of old books at the very back of the wardrobe. I rummage through years' worth of collected junk, my fingers spidering over a couple of ancient stuffed toys, clothes and a folder of early medical reports before finally touching the embossed cardboard spine. A small cloud of dust falls out as I pull the book free.

Taking it to the living room, I drop it on the couch before going to the window and open the curtains to the heavy snowfall outside. Unmuffled by the drapes, the windows rattle slightly as they bear the press of the wind, the whistle of a bad seal fluting strange music into the quiet room. I pour a glass of wine and go back to the album.

The photos must have been from when I was about five or six, a part of my life I don't remember. Mother gave me this not long after I got sick in the hope it might trigger some memories; it never did. I've hung on to the photos ever since, but the girl in the pictures may as well be a stranger. It's strange, but it's the book, not the images in it that brings back memories now.

Still, she's me. As I flick through the large stiff pages, staring at the snapshots of myself, I don't know what I'm expecting to see that I haven't seen a thousand times before. The child who looks at the camera seems normal enough, privileged but not spoiled. Along with my parents, a younger, fitter Mollher is occasionally in frame, their fixer even then. I turn another page. Holidays: a skiing trip, a trek through Yellowstone, a hot air balloon ride. No beaches though, but young me seems happy enough, showing a glimmer of a smile as she's snapped studying hard at a desk doing some homework. I smile as well for this stranger who was me, turning the page.

Another me, another time. There are no expectations as I stare at the images, just a reaching out. Perhaps I'm looking for continuity. Whatever. I drain the glass and seeing the bottle's empty, uncurl myself to find another one.

The storm seems to be losing its bite and as I glance out the window on the way I can pick out cars pushing through the snow. It takes more than a snowstorm to slow down New Yorkers. I go back to the couch and pick up the album, turning the next page. More holiday snaps, more Alice smiling shyly into the lens. I empty the drink in a gulp and refill it, staring at the images through the prism of the glass. I drain that one as well, then another. Soon I leave to get a fresh bottle.

Somewhere my phone's ringing again. I let the call go to the message service, returning lightheaded but somehow heavy. It's a strange contrast. That sense of disconnection I had before is back in spades. Thumping onto the warm spot on the couch again, I flick over another page and scrutinise the girl in the photo. This time she's beaming, wearing an equestrian helmet and riding clothes, standing proudly beside a chestnut horse. So different from how I grew up in Sydney.

I pause at the next snapshot. Favourite would be the wrong word for it, but it is special. Not because it's the best, to tell the truth it's probably the worst of the book, but it's the first image where I recognise some of myself in her. Alice is surrounded by friends, still with the horse. Perhaps she'd won a competition. If so, it doesn't show. There's something different in her face. Her normally cheerful expression is clouded. She's not happy, no, more than that — she's angry. It's not obvious, but I can see the shape my eyes make when I'm pissed off, the small curl in the lip. I peel back the plastic cover and wiggle the photo from the backing.

I stare at the other faces then blink as I see him. Younger and slightly out of focus, the unmistakable face of Dr Olen Canders stares right back at me. In all the hundreds of times I've studied this picture, I can't believe I've never seen him before. He can't just have turned up. It's impossible.

I empty the glass automatically.

45

AMBULANCE

There's a noise. My tongue tastes of blood. Strange. Something pushes my body and I try to push back, but nothing works. Voices either side of me talk in clear professional tones. They're speaking English but I can't understand what they're saying, their meaning hidden by medical jargon and numbers. I open my eyes. Bad idea. Clamping them shut I block out the harsh white blurs and strange leached shadows looming over me. Someone must have noticed because now a hand starts tapping my face.

'Can you hear me?' asks a voice.

I murmur something, fighting against a thick tongue. I try to turn over, frustrated that I'm stuck.

'Listen to me, this is very important. I want you to open your eyes. Will you do that?'

My eyes flicker open, obedient. I shut them again as quickly. The room rocks and lists and I feel seasick. I can't be on a boat, can I? I need to know what's going on so I fight off the grogginess.

'You had an accident,' says a voice.

Ah.

A flash of green. Sounds of tyres screeching. Of course I had.

'But you're going to be OK. I need you to open your eyes again.'

There are two paramedics in the back of the ambulance with me. One of them studies a screen as the other leans over and shines a light in my eyes. 'You were hit by a car,' he says, flicking the small torch away then back again, 'and let me tell you something. You might not believe it now but you're probably the luckiest person alive.'

As I try to think of a reply I'm overwhelmed by the sensation of falling into a warm pillow. Silky, heavy, comfortable. Somewhere, a world away, one of the paramedics raises an alarm as a machine begins beeping urgently. I smile in my mind, intrigued by the sounds of sirens gradually becoming quieter.

46

THE REAL REASON

And in breaking news, Sydney-me's alive. How nice for her.

As I push myself up from the couch the storm's eased into a heavy fall. There are even tiny breaks in the cloud letting in a kind of beaten up morning sunlight. The bottle's fallen over, spilling a red stain into the carpet. It reminds me of blood, I think as I head into the bathroom, where I splash some of the sleep away.

More awake now, I return to the living room, snatch up the picture and look at it again. Olen's still in the background, as if he's been there all along. So I didn't imagine it. I don't believe I'm even thinking this; people don't just appear in photos. It's as crazy as seeing ghosts out of nowhere. I sit again, weighed down by these thoughts. I know this photo so well, this one better than the rest. There's another possibility; he was always there and I wasn't able to see him before. I can't even guess what that means. Maybe I do have my own ghost after all. Some of my old anger has come back, but it's different this time. I can feel it there, a current that once was my true north, but now?

I stare at the photo again.

Maybe Lavar in Sydney was right and both my lives are a dream, but even if that's the case, something, somewhere must be real. Olen says he can destroy the dream — things are coming together, I sense that much at least. The girl, Olen, everything. It's a guess, but possibly the reason I see him now is I'm ready for it.

THE BULLDOZERS ARE MOVING. Outside the clinic the snow's piled in low mounds along the safety fence. The whole thing is sullen and prison-like in the dim light. Shrouded in plumes of steam and diesel the machines haul away debris from a low wall, now reduced to bricks and shards of structural steel. There isn't much to see and I brace myself against the fumes as one of the dirty yellow diggers trundles past, scoop raised. From somewhere nearby comes the sound of splintering wood.

I walk alongside the fence, part of me curious to mark the progress of the demolition work, but the truth is what I'm doing is putting off seeing Olen. It's ridiculous. I'm here now. He's made the offer and assuming he isn't lying about the drug I can stop the dream. And that's worth any price. I'll do the deal with the devil.

I spot someone on the other side striding purposefully towards the half-destroyed building. I slow down, at first curious then concerned. Whoever they are, they're taking a risk walking between the hardware that way. They're wearing a long coat and no hard hat, so it's not one of the demolition crew.

A siren cuts through the sounds of heavy machinery cracking masonry and a furious supervisor storms out of a portable office, yelling and waving his arms. The bulldozers stop in their tracks and a strange quiet fills the site. The figure goes on regardless, stopping only when he reaches one of the toppled walls, pausing to kick through some of the slushy rubble. The supervisor's now seriously angry and starts yelling at the man. He turns. It's Olen.

I stand quietly, invisible on the sidelines as the screaming plays out. When I say screaming, it's one-sided. Olen stands there still as a statue while the other guy yells at him. I can't say why the supervisor's so worked up but he sure is pissed at him. Eventually he runs out of steam and Olen nods before turning away. The supervisor throws up his hands in frustration and waits for him to cross back to the safe area near where I'm standing, before signalling someone inside the office. The siren sounds again and the bulldozers start up in clouds of rank diesel.

'What the hell was that?' I ask.

Olen watches the work from the fence for a few more minutes before switching his attention to me. 'Meeting this way is turning into a habit,' he says. He nods back to the worksite. 'You need to keep them on their toes, make sure they're doing it right.'

'That guy was pretty pissed off.'

He smiles. 'Yes. I'm becoming, what's the term? A repeat offender.'

I shrug. 'Thanks for seeing me.'

'I'm always here.'

'I'm going to take you up on your offer,' I say, still watching the machines churn across the icy mud.

Olen nods. 'Good. I was hoping you might. Let's get inside.' He puts his arm out and gently guides me towards the welcoming glow of the new clinic.

The office is uncomfortably warm and I take off my

sweater. I catch him staring at my bandaged hand before looking away. He's sitting at the other side of the desk, hands steepled as he thinks about what I've said. In the silence I glance at the neat collection of framed photos, one in particular grabbing my attention. In it a younger Olen is standing next to my parents. Mother's holding a toddler, who I guess is me and all of them are staring directly down the lens. There are spreadsheets with more warmth.

'What exactly do you mean, stop both dreams?' he asks. He'd listened without saying a word as I told him about Lavar and his verdict.

'I've figured it out,' I say. I'm impressed my voice sounds calm and measured, seeing how I'm anything but certain. 'Meeting you, the girl, everything. I don't understand how but it's all connected. If I can stop the dream of Sydney from here and figure out a way to do the same over there, whatever's left over must be the real me.' I wonder for a moment if I'm as mad as that makes me sound. I hold his gaze.

'The real you?'

I nod calmly. 'That's right.'

Olen rubs his mouth and it's clear he's concerned. 'This is real. Like it or not my dear.'

I shrug, looking out the window at the snow covered landscaped gardens, then beyond to the demolition work going on in the old clinic. 'Perhaps.'

'Not perhaps.'

'So this drug you're talking about. Is it genuine or bullshit? Be honest.'

'Very real. The therapy is almost completely pharmaceutical. It works by blocking certain receptors in the brain, but it has some serious side effects.'

'Like what?'

'Potential liver damage if the course runs too long. Weight gain. Nausea. Headaches. Blurred vision.'

'Wow,' I say, 'sounds fun.'

He ignores this and goes on. 'But it will almost certainly not work as we expect if there are other drugs in your bloodstream. This is why you need a clean system.'

I give myself a moment to absorb the information. It will be worth this to realise what's real, to know for sure. 'And how long will that take?'

He opens his palms to me. 'I don't know. It depends on what you've been taking.'

I shake my head. 'No idea.'

'Excuse me?'

'I get my drugs from a guy. I don't ask what they are.'

He gets out from behind his desk and sits next to me. 'Alice. You can't do that.' I shrug. 'We need to run some blood tests right away.'

I don't think so. 'No. I'm talking to you now,' I say, 'everything intact. Do I look like a junkie to you? It's light stuff, nothing serious.'

He reaches out and takes my hand, the bandaged one. I flinch, more from the unexpected contact than the pain. My own reaction startles me. 'Why do you want to help me?' I ask quietly. 'You could lose your license for giving me something like this, or wind up in jail. So don't give me the I used to know you as a child bullshit. I want the real reason.'

He sits back, smiling. 'The real reason? Fair question.' He taps his forehead. 'Smart. You were always smart.' I wait for him to go on as he leans forward and looks at me deeply. 'You don't remember me at all?' I shake my head. 'It's strange,' he says, 'because as you admit, when you noticed me you had quite a reaction. I have to say, you made a commotion.'

'Weirdness is part of the ride, know what I mean?'

'No.' He gets up and goes to the window where he stares at the demolition work going on outside. 'You Van de Kortes. You are an egocentric lot. Must be in your genes.'

'The drug,' I say, thinking it through, 'it's from my parents' company, right?

He nods. 'I told you that.'

'It could seriously hurt them if it was leaked that someone was using it before it was approved.'

He smiles a peculiar half smile. 'Yes it would.'

I catch the tiniest change in his expression. It's a subtle shift of the eyes, a tilt of the head and I know something about the man in front of me I never would have guessed. 'You don't like them much.' It's not a question.

He quickly nods, almost too fast to catch. The mannerism is birdlike, nearly brittle and out of place among the solid wood and metal of this office. 'I wouldn't go so far as to say that,' he says, 'but — ' and he shakes his head, a wry smile on his lips. 'Smart and perceptive.'

'The reason?'

He sighs. 'Believe it or not, it has a lot to do with you. I did know you as a child and right or wrong I do feel responsible.' I wait. 'There is also an aspect of redemption.'

'What?'

He looks at his hands. 'I used to be a doctor. Would still be if the situation had gone differently.'

'What situation?'

'My ventilator. You know it?' I do. The Cander's ventilator had been revolutionary in its day and even now the next generation is in almost every hospital in the States. It's one of the most important products the company owns.

'You were paid to design that.'

He smiles at me from the window. 'Not quite.'

OK. Now I'm listening. 'Well, as a physician, I used to be quite good,' he says, 'extremely good actually. No sense in being modest. Even the first prototypes turned heads. I had a small company at the time and was able to hire in the skills I didn't have. The engineer I found was excellent and turned my ideas into something effective.' He pauses. 'But lets just say back then I was naïve.'

'The engineer. He stole the idea.'

'Not from his point of view, but yes, that's what happened. It all became litigious. The concept and design were mine and I paid for the work. The whole thing eventually went to court and the judgement came down in my favour. But the problem was I'd spent all my reserves on laywers and didn't have anything left over to pay for production. I heard about your father, who was doing quite well at the time and organised a meeting. We came to an arrangement.'

I'm no fan of our company but at least I thought I knew its history. What Olen's saying is news to me. The way Father used to tell it, he'd hired Olen and commissioned him to design the machine. It was all part of the myth of his genius for spotting talent. 'So he bought you out?'

'Your parents are astute business people, but they're not doctors. The ventilator was the tool I was going to use to fund the expansion of my own clinic.'

'But you ended up working for them instead.'

He nods. 'The machine was eventually made and lives were saved, but I traded being a doctor for the life of a salesman.'

As if on cue, a wall collapses outside as one of the giant yellow bulldozers sets to work on another section of the old clinic. I glance out the window, but a cold fog keeps most of the details of the building hidden and I can only make out the lumbering angular shapes of the machines.

'So how does helping me fix that?' I ask quietly.

'It doesn't,' he says, 'but if I have to bend the rules to help someone I once knew very well, at least it's a small redemption. A little dignity before I retire.'

I breathe out. Looking at his blue eyes I sense something else there, something steely and unbending. 'So what you're saying is you can do a good deed and sign off with a big fuck you at the same time.' I know how that one goes.

He raises his eyebrows. 'Well, I wouldn't have put it quite the same way, but yes.'

'What the hell, let's get it started.'

He smiles again, but I struggle to see past those eyes. 'Then I'm glad I came back.' I must look surprised and he holds up a hand to stop me from jumping to a conclusion. 'Before you ask, it had nothing to do with you. Your father asked me to return. Probably thought I'd be sentimental seeing the old clinic go. Ever the diplomat.'

'So what's next?' I ask. 'My family are all over me at the moment.'

'Don't worry about your family,' he says, turning to the window. 'I'll deal with them. Check in first thing tomorrow. We need to get started immediately.'

I stand and nod. The pain in my hand is excruciating, but I have a plan. Even if it is someone else's.

47

HOSPITAL

Faces. Strangers lean over me in an odd halo of concern before moving away, talking to one another. I blink slowly, feeling bruised and stiff. My skin is tight against my eyes, throbbing and delicate. And then there's a dull headache that's going to be here for the long haul. I wiggle my fingers, test my arms and legs as I take an inventory of my pain. I can move. No numbness. Nothing broken. The people hovering about me seem uninterested that I'm watching. 'What happened?' I'm surprised at my voice, low and hoarse. I sound like my other self after a big night.

'You were hit by a car,' says a doctor, another anonymous face. He's young, probably too tired, which isn't reassuring. 'It could have been much worse,' he adds almost as an afterthought. 'Mild concussion and bruising, but from what the paramedics say, you should have died.' I try to nod but the muscles in my neck seem to be locked. 'So you'll be OK,' he says, 'we need to keep you under observation for a while yet. Generally speaking though, you were incredibly lucky.'

'People keep saying that,' I say quietly, but he's moved

on, turning his attention to the patient in the next bed along.

The hospital smells. Not rotten, just in the way that hospitals always do, the strange cloying mix of detergents, starches, floor cleaners. It's an abattoir for bacteria. For some reason that's funny and I try to laugh. Bad idea. Instead I close my eyes and ignore the sounds of the ward, trying for some rest. It doesn't happen: I end up staring at my eyelids for hours.

'Well, you look like shit.' It's Jen. I didn't hear her come in.

'Did you get the number of that bus?' Lame joke but I don't care. I'm so relieved she's here I could cry. Her face is at first a weird mixture of worry and anger before giving over to a sad kind of smile.

'Hey sis,' she says.

I try to give her a small wave then think better of it as pins and needles run up and down my arm. Instead I grin back.

'The doctor reckons they need to do a couple more tests and if everything pans out, you'll be good to go.'

'Great.' I mean it; I can't wait to get out of here. I remember mum tucking me into bed and bringing sandwiches on the few days I had off school. There's a kind of safety about being at home in bed and right now that's what I want.

Motioning for her to help, I surprise myself by ignoring the twinge in my back and sitting up. Pushing it even further I get up and limp gingerly across the freezing tiles to a beige wardrobe at the end of the bed. Now I'm up, moving around is easier than I expected. The doctor could be right, considering all the bruises and scrapes I should at least have broken something. Best not to look gift horses in the mouth.

'You might want to wait for the all clear,' she says as I fish my clothes from the wardrobe. They're crumpled and smell of sweat. My blouse is torn and feels disgusting as I put it back on, but it's better than wearing that horrible thin hospital nightgown thing.

'Hello Alice.'

It's Ryan. 'What are you doing here?'

'I called him,' says Jen. I'm about to say something when she cuts in. 'He cares about you. We care about you.'

'Thanks,' I mumble, struggling to respond. It's weird, but I can sense my other self surfacing, almost like she's not ready to go back. Some of her anger spills into me. What am I talking about? Some of her anger is me. It doesn't matter who's dreaming whom; we're still the same person. I pull at my plastic ID bracelet and wonder why I'm only realising this now.

'Alice,' says Ryan, 'the police are here, waiting outside. They need you to answer some questions.'

'Great.' Still staring at Ryan, I say, 'They shouldn't be talking to me, they should be chasing the cocksucker that ran me down. Did they find them?' I catch the uneasy glance that passes between them. 'What?' I ask, feeling my blood rise. 'It's not fair I'm the one being treated like a criminal. I got run over, remember?'

'The driver stopped right away,' says Jen walking over to me. She takes my hand gently in hers. 'They say you walked out in front of them.'

I free my hand. 'Who told you this?'

'The police,' he says.

It takes me a couple of seconds to fill in the gaps, but their faces confirm it. 'They think I tried to commit suicide?' Other-me wouldn't be surprised. Of course they do. 'Maybe New York-Alice,' I say, 'not me.'

Jen leans closer, whispering. 'You know,' she says, 'it might not be such a good idea to tell them things like that.'

I sit back on the bed and sigh. 'Fine.' I stare at them both. 'I didn't try to kill myself, OK?' They want to believe me, that much is obvious at least.

The curtain pulls back a third time, revealing a couple of waiting cops. With no idea what to expect I brace myself for another grilling, but before anyone can get a word in Ryan steps up and introduces himself as my doctor, telling them he needs to talk to them first. He opens his arms and herds them out of the room for a moment, talking in low tones.

They return after a few minutes, something in their demeanour changed. As they run though a checklist of questions the whole process takes on the air of a formality. I'm careful not to mention the girl, but honestly, I don't think it matters much. I could be talking about purple elephants for all they seem to care. They're only interested in getting my statement down and moving on. That worries me.

The word *protocol* raises its ugly head again, but Ryan seems to be in control and the questions pass more quickly than I expect. As the older of the two cops closes his book, Ryan nods professionally to him. I glance at Ryan again. That expression is out of place coming from him. He hasn't said a word to me since arriving and I know he's angry, or disappointed, or whatever. Then as easily as they entered, the cops leave. They don't even look at me as they walk out of the room.

'Are you going to tell me what you told them out there?' I ask him after we're alone again.

He nods with professional courtesy, nothing more. The anger from before lingers like a shadow. It wasn't my fault. I did not walk in front of a car. Jen, who's been waiting quietly throughout the whole interview puts her arm around me but stays silent. Any more of this kid-glove treatment and I'm going to scream. As I open my mouth to speak, her phone rings. She nods a few times, mumbles something low then hangs up.

'Sorry,' she says, 'Kiera sent one of her girls to hold down the fort, but the fridge is leaking all over the place again. I need to go and sort it out.' She kisses me on the cheek. 'I'll come back. Two hours at the most, then we'll get out of here, alright?'

'OK. But we need to talk.'

'Yes,' she says, her voice full of excruciating gentleness. 'Yes we should.' She turns to Ryan and it seems like she's going to hug him, or more, but she holds back. 'Thanks,' she says before leaving with a quick wave. I stare at him then at Jen as she disappears behind the curtain. Is there something going on between them?

'Come on,' he says, pointing to a sliding door. 'Let's get some air.'

The balcony is barely wide enough to fit us both, but it's a break from the room. Outside it's stifling, but that's the least of my worries. Ryan studies me seriously, his mop of scruffy hair wilting in the heat.

'Thanks for being here,' I start. I catch myself. It isn't what I want to say at all. I try again. 'So, what happens next?'

He doesn't smile. 'Just need to make sure my number one client makes it through.' Which isn't an answer. He stares out over the balcony to the parking lot and beyond that a road. 'So what happened?'

'I went to meet that clairvoyant,' I say, 'well, he came to see me.'

'That's a bit ironic, don't you think?'

'Pardon?'

'Should have seen the accident coming. Sorry. Bad joke.'

'I was asking him about the girl.'

'The child who might be a ghost?' I nod. He's humouring me, but I don't have the energy to make an issue out of it right now. I want to go home and he'll either choose to believe me or not.

'Ryan,' I say, 'I'm seeing her in New York as well.' He reacts to this news though I can tell he wants to bring up something else.

'Alice. We'll talk about that later. The fact the dream's reflecting what you experience here isn't surprising. You keep saying your lives are parallel.'

'But never this close.'

He turns away. He's concerned. He waits for a moment, distracted by the hot wind blowing around us both. 'Alice,' he says again, 'it's my job to ensure your situation doesn't deteriorate.' He stares at me, commanding my attention. He's so intense right now. 'I want to be honest with you. You're crossing lines here, seriously. You're lucky to be alive.'

'So they say.'

'I have a duty to the community as well.'

'Where are you going with this?'

'When you're under my care I need to make sure you're not hurting yourself, but also that you don't pose a threat to others.'

'Threat? What kind of threat can I be?'

'You're not the only one lucky to have survived the accident,' he says. 'The driver could have run off the road and crashed. He didn't, but he could have.'

'I'm not a danger to people,' I say, feeling a surge of anger again.

He shakes his head. 'Maybe,' he says at last. 'We need to consider checking into Mayfleur.'

'Like hell,' I say flatly.

'Voluntarily.'

'I said fuck off.'

He stares at me, probably thrown by my language. I don't give a shit.

'I want you to consider going back there for a short while. Think of it as a break. It'll be a chance to take some time out and collect yourself.'

'I said no.'

Judging by his expression this is a long way from over.

Worry begins to worm its way into my mind. He can force it if he wants. I know he can. My lungs ache and the cold, familiar claustrophobia slowly starts creeping in. I work through the process of trying to calm myself, but the thought of returning is like dying. I breathe over it, force my heartbeat into something normal, try to let it wash over me. A panic attack is a kind of drowning, and a cold despair threatens to overwhelm everything. I let the air in, out, focusing only on the rhythm. His voice is small and distant, an insect.

'Breathe,' he says, 'flow with it; don't fight it. Accept what's happening to you, but don't forget it's going to be OK.' I glance his way, embarrassed and hating him at the same time. 'Alice, you have to hear this from me. You need to understand how serious all this is. The school incident, now this. Very soon things will be taken out of my hands.' I nod, wanting to be alone and close my eyes.

When I open them again the girl is standing across the road. I jam them shut refusing to believe it, but when I check a second time she's still there, impossibly motionless in the shimmering heat.

Barely able to breathe, I grab his head and turn it in her direction. 'Look,' I say, 'there she is.' She's tiny in the distance, a small figure flickering in and out of view between the traffic. Ryan says nothing, but his face registers complete bewilderment, then something else. I won't get another chance like this so I swing over the balcony and drop half a metre into a dry flower bed. Ryan stares at me in disbelief before returning his attention to the girl.

'Come on,' I yell and run for the road. All I can think of as I go is that he's finally seen her.

48

THE CHASE

He calls for me to stop. There's no way that's going to happen, he's too far behind. He had to wait for a break in the traffic before crossing, where I managed to get through ahead of him. The girl's just in front of me, keeping her distance, exactly like last time. As I chase her down a winding old road she veers into an adjoining street and I'm lost. With Ryan behind me I feel safer, not exposed as I was before. He's given up calling — he's saving his breath. Something loosens inside as I run. Now he's seen her, he's going to have to change his tune about Mayfleur.

The air's a furnace and the leaves hang long and still from the trees, but I push on. For a while the three of us are strung out like beads as we sprint down this new street, but Ryan seems to get a second wind and slowly makes up some ground. There's no point calling after the girl, so I save my breath too.

She turns down a small road marked out by an old-fashioned sign on the corner. It all seems familiar and I soon recognise the houses with their overgrown gardens. Long dry grass spills out of fences and onto the footpath and in my distraction I almost trip over a half-covered branch. She's taking me to the park again. We cut through an access track and for a moment that nightmare of the shortcut comes back to me, but we're out in seconds. I know where we are now. There at the end of a cul-de-sac: the rose bushes and painfully bright metal glints of the play equipment. I have to follow.

'Hold on,' calls Ryan from behind, 'stop.' I don't stop; I don't even turn my head. Ignoring the burn in my lungs and the ache of my legs I run on. I won't lose her again.

It doesn't end in the park. As I race over the brown stubble of grass I keep my attention locked on her, all the while feeling the eyes of the few kids there tracking me as I go by. Ryan, not far behind now, is silent again as he struggles to keep up. Or maybe he sees the other children as well. The air's blistering and shimmers off the play equipment, too hot to touch. The world is quiet, the only sounds my wheezy gasps and the crunch of feet on the grass. No birds, no cars, no voices.

Just like last time she's suffering in the heat too. I've been catching up to her and now I can't be more than a couple of metres away. Her skin is flushed bright-red, as her dress, the same thick fabric she always wears flaps heavily as she runs. It's the exact opposite of what anyone would wear on a day like this. It's stupid. She gasps as she stays ahead of me, her breathing quick and mouse-like. I know better but I call for her to stop. Of course she doesn't. She glances back in my direction then turns and disappears through a solid hedge. Despite my exhaustion, I'm not too tired to notice how unbelievably green it is in all the burned summer browns of the park.

'This way,' I yell out to Ryan and he nods, his face beetroot-red and slick with sweat. I push through the hedge following the footsteps of the girl, surprised at how little resistance there is. Instead of the dense thicket of branches I'm expecting, it's only a couple of centimetres deep.

I've got no idea where I am. I try to get my bearings as I study the gently curving street I've stumbled onto. It's a strange mixture of residential houses and old semi-industrial lots. Sydney is full of these suburbs in transition but this is different. The homes seem to be as empty as the overgrown blocks and warehouses. Then I spot her again. She's waiting for me; so sucking up the stifling air I plod after her as Ryan falls through the bushes. He lands badly but I can't wait for him.

Ahead, the girl must be exhausted as well because her running is ragged and uncoordinated. She squeezes past an unlocked gate to a large grey warehouse in the middle of a sea of brown and yellow weeds. I follow, desperately dragging down as much air as my lungs will allow. My whole body screams at me, exhausted and abused. I have to stop, doubling over at the fence as I get lightheaded. Moments later Ryan turns up looking as bad as me. His pale blue shirt is plastered to his chest with sweat. When I can breathe again I turn to look at the girl, but she's gone.

'She went into the building,' I say.

He looks at me, hair flat and slick, blue eyes fierce. 'Come back to the hospital with me now,' he gasps.

'The girl,' I say, pointing to the warehouse, 'she's in there somewhere.'

'Alice, you're imagining her.'

I couldn't have heard that right, not after all this. 'We've been chasing her,' I say, but my voice trails off as he shakes his head, drops of sweat falling freely.

'The only person I've been chasing is you,' he says. 'There isn't any girl, Alice.'

'You're lying.'

'I'm telling you the truth.'

Ignoring my own pain I run across to the building and try to get in. She has to be inside, I know it, but the huge wooden door hasn't been touched in years. I test a boarded-up window next, hoping to find a plank loose enough to squeeze though, or at least loose enough for a girl to squeeze through. Nothing. Running the length of the warehouse, I check everything I can think of, searching for an entry point. Every door or window I find is rusted, locked, boarded or broken. There's no way in.

I've got nothing left in me. I ache from the run and God knows what I've just made worse from the accident. I go back to where Ryan is waiting, still panting quietly in the unrelenting heat.

'Screw you,' I say eventually, feeling betrayed.

What had I been expecting? That everything would open up and become clear? That I'd find the girl and she'd tell me the secret to making Manhattan go away? I shake my head, a bad move because the motion brings on a new wave of dizziness. Some quiet part of me laughs. This is it: I'm officially insane.

'You need to return to the hospital,' he says, 'before they start looking for you. If they find out you've run away then you won't get a choice about Mayfleur.' I don't look at him. He shakes his head and pulls out his phone. 'I have a duty to you,' he says quietly. 'Come back with me now or I'm going to have to call the police.' He tries to catch my eye. 'Alice. This isn't a joke.'

'Go to hell,' I say, knowing I'll head back with him anyway.

49

CONNECTIONS

Last night changed everything — Sydney is a code, and the girl is the key. Olen's just going to have to wait. That's what all this comes down to.

I've been standing here for over an hour, waiting, trying to ignore the cold. This isn't Sydney and I won't let myself be pushed around like she does. The kid will come to me, I know it. When I think about how close I came to repeating the cycle Other-me has fallen into, of chasing and losing and chasing again — No. I'll follow her in my own time. Even though I can't explain how I'm so sure, I'm certain she's coming.

When I catch a glimpse of her green dress I'm not surprised — but that still doesn't stop my heart from thundering. Things are syncing, moving in the way they should be. This block inside is breaking down and the girl, ghost, whatever she is, is the answer. I don't run. Instead I jam my hands in my pockets and slowly walk after her. I won't question what's happening — just accept it, because if I stop and think about how insane all this is I'll scream.

Keeping pace I let her go ahead and lead me to wherever

it is she needs me to be. For a moment I lose her in the crowd but refuse to run. I keep telling myself she wants to find me and it's true, because seconds later there she is again, waiting. Sydney-me hasn't figured out the girl needs us.

The crowds of pedestrians and shoppers are thinning as we turn down another street, so close and cramped it's more an alleyway than a road. A single lane runs down the centre, butting up against businesses and wrought iron fences. Brownstones bear down on us from both sides. For some reason it reminds me of the overgrown shortcut in my dream. So many parallels.

I make myself slow down, refusing to hurry. I want to grab her and force her to talk to me, but I keep my distance as we pass some jewellers and a small architecture firm before exiting onto a larger road. She disappears from view for a second but I turn the corner and stop.

I stare for a second in complete confusion, not understanding what I'm looking at. Then I get it. Fuck.

I don't know what I expected, but it wasn't this. My girl joins another, also dressed in green. The dress is a uniform. The kid I've been following turns to speak to her friend and now I can tell she's not the one from the dream. I was so certain. Stunned, I stare at the building they're walking towards: a perfect, snowbound copy of the school she'd lead me to in Sydney.

I need a cigarette.

I WATCH a trickle of girls dressed in the green uniform turn into a torrent as they explode from a bus pulled up beside the fence. They shuffle through the gates and into the warmth of the hallways and classrooms inside. It's so normal, so weird.

'OK,' I say to myself, knowing I'm talking aloud. Another coincidence, another mirror. The building, a prim and proper freestanding brownstone sits well back from the ornate iron fence at the sidewalk. The sign on the gate reads, St Francis. Sounds exclusive.

A short woman stands guard at the door, greeting the girls as they go in. Her face is weathered but vibrant in the way only old people can pull off. Her ample skin is pulled into creases, highlighted by a natural blush. She says something to some of the older girls as they rush past, then calls out sharply to a couple of others, who come running. A younger kid, reminding me of my own girl, walks by, looks up at her and smiles. The woman's no doubt a teacher, and reaching out gently touches her back, propelling her through the double doors.

I smile in sympathy, catching myself by surprise. Crushing my cigarette into the snow I feel ruffled and unkempt. I've got to go in: I'm here for a reason, even if it's not clear yet. So I suck it up and merge with the throng of girls climbing the steps.

The woman by the door eyes me warily, her smile for the students pulling into something more neutral and cautious. There'll be no getting by her. I turn back to the street, noticing for the first time parents waving their daughters goodbye from the gate.

'Hello,' says the teacher, nodding to one of the older girls as she goes past.

'Hi,' I say. What now? Shit. I didn't think this through.

She squints at me for a moment, some unreadable expression on her face. 'Are you a parent?'

'No,' I say, 'I was hoping to speak to somebody. I'm thinking of sending my own daughter here.'

She looks at me with exactly the kind of expression I'm expecting. 'Usually,' she says, 'you would call ahead and arrange a meeting.'

'I tried,' I say, 'but you know how things are.'

'You better leave,' she says.

'Listen,' I begin, but I can already tell the way this is going to go. I had a taste of it in Sydney. The teacher crosses her arms and scowls. Some of the girls walking past glance at me quickly before looking away.

OK, I know when I'm beat. I'll try something different. I'm about to leave when a wrinkled hand falls on my shoulder. I glance back into a face that almost but not quite, seems familiar.

An ancient teacher pulls out a pair of equally ancient, wide-framed glasses and, without putting them on, holds them in front of her eyes. She nods, pocketing them. 'I thought so.'

'Excuse me?'

'You're Alice,' she says. 'Alice Van de Korte.' To the other she says, 'It's all right Bridgett.' And with that she guides me into the school, brushing past her. 'You're the one who went away.'

My heart's racing.

The staff room smells of cinnamon as the old teacher closes the door behind us. She takes off her coat and drapes it over the back of a chair and indicating I should sit, moves quickly to a kitchenette and starts making tea — all this without saying a word. She seems completely in control; I can't find a way to break the silence. The room's empty and I have my pick of chairs, so I choose a comfortable-looking one next to a small table and sit down. The wall opposite me is plastered with notice sheets, timetables and various prints. Half buried beneath blue and green xeroxes, an orange poster advertises last year's production of MacBeth.

'It's a funny thing, I always said,' she says from the kitchenette, 'how some people stick in your head more than others.' She walks over and places a mug in front of me. 'And you've been one of them.' She waits for me to reply then shrugs when I don't say anything. 'I'm Anne. Mrs Bedford to my students.'

'I'm Alice,' I say eventually.

'Yes. That's established, dear.'

I study the woman as she sits, looking for something more than a vague sense of familiarity, some sign I might have known her from my childhood. Anne arches one of her eyebrows and sips her tea, a trace of patient amusement on her face. She's old enough to have been my grandmother and then some, but there's a strength about her that I like. No one could deflect that gaze. Mrs Bedford's classes would be quiet, I'm sure.

'How do you know me?' I ask, touching my mug.

Anne turns her mug gently in her hands. 'Really, Alice. I would have thought it obvious. I was one of your teachers here.'

'I don't remember.'

That gaze again: stern appraisal. 'I'm hardly surprised dear.'

I clamp down on my excitement. 'Why do you say that?'

'You were a very good student, I recall,' says Anne leaning forward, 'not naturally academic, but you applied yourself. Made friends easily.' I can imagine those words sitting on a report card. 'But when you returned to classes after your illness, you'd changed.'

'You know about that? Changed how?'

Anne sits back, putting the mug on the table. 'It was so sad, especially for you. You didn't recognise anyone, you couldn't focus on anything; you were unsettled, buzzing around in your own head. It troubled your classmates so much we had to separate you. We did our best but I can't imagine how it must have been for you.'

I'm hearing the history of a stranger. 'I don't remember any of that,' I say.

'It doesn't shock me,' says Anne with a disdainful sniff. 'I told the headmistress you needed individual attention, special tuition, that kind of thing. You weren't going to reintegrate into school life without more time to adjust, but she didn't listen.' She throws up her hands. 'What do you do?' She takes a moment to recompose herself, drinking some tea. 'So Alice, why are you here?'

How to answer? I followed a ghost from my dream self's life? Right. I glance again at the memos on the wall, the colourful artwork, listen to the muted sounds of hundreds of girls going about their morning, getting ready for class outside. 'I'm not sure,' I say eventually. 'I didn't remember what happened before I caught meningitis, but something's changed. This seems —,' I search for the right word, 'important.'

Anne nods. 'Memory can be a strange thing. Works in odd ways. With you for example,' she says pointing, 'what stays with me most, before the time you became ill, was that you always seemed happy here. You were no angel, let's get that clear.' I smile. 'But you had a luminosity about you.' I struggle to connect with this information. 'That was the saddest part for me,' she goes on, 'I remember the last day I saw the real you.'

'Real me?' I echo the words quietly.

'It must have been no more than one or two days before you caught meningitis. It was a Friday and Mr Canders was picking you up. You turned from the car and waved to me. Almost as if you were saying goodbye.' Anne shakes her head, her eyes watery.

'Olen?' I ask from a long way away.

'Yes,' says Anne, reaching for her mug again. 'I spoke to him once or twice. He was the only person your parents trusted to pick you up from school. Personally I didn't like the man.' A bell rings over the loudspeaker and she looks up. 'Well, there's my cue,' she says.

I take the moment to collect my thoughts. 'It's strange,' I say.

'What, dear?'

'You don't seem that surprised to see me.'

She stares at me for a good while. 'You'd be surprised how many former students pop in, now and again. Looking to firm up their memories, reconnect with their past, so to speak.'

'Well,' I say, 'guilty as charged.'

She gets up and I stand with her. 'Are there any records I could read? Something from my time here?'

'Talk to Karen in Administration, she'll help you out.' We walk through the door straight into a surge of girls moving down the corridor. The small bubble of quiet from the staffroom evaporates under the stampede. Anne stops and faces me. 'Alice. It's been good to see you again.'

I almost wither under her simple searching gaze. 'And you too. Thank's for helping fill in some blanks.'

'Good luck with whatever it is you're searching for.' She

waves and disappears into the tide of bodies, leaving me without a reply.

It takes ten minutes but I find the school's Administration room hidden at the end of a maze of corridors. After a minute of typing queries, Karen looks up, grinning. 'Found it,' she says and prints me out a report. Holding the paper in my good hand I thank her and leave.

Flicking through the transcript I push open the double doors and step outside. It's like the album in so many ways, details about a little girl who's still a stranger.

My phone rings again and I fish it out. It's Mother. This time I take the call.

50

HOME HISTORY

I hold on to my transcript all the way to the house, where Mother is waiting. It was never a home. Mollher glances at me in the rear-view mirror as he drives the car slowly away over the cold gravel of the drive. It sounds menacing. I flick him the bird — the guy gets under my skin.

Jeane's waiting for me in the Screw-up Room. It's a small library off the main entrance that my parents used to council me in when I screwed up, which was a lot. It's crammed with books I doubt anyone's even bothered reading, and way too hot. The tiny fireplace on the north wall is stacked with wood and pumping out waves of blistering air. I could be back in Sydney. Walking through the door I ditch my jacket and drop into the soft leather of a couch. Mother is tired, her eyes are dark and baggy and she looks gaunt. She's showing her age. The atmosphere's frosty, despite the heat.

I place the transcript on the table in front of me. 'Why didn't you tell me about St Francis?' I ask.

She doesn't even glance at it. 'Hello Alice,' she says, 'or don't we do that these days?'

'Well?'

Mother nods, not much more than a twitch of the head. She accepts my discovery like it's no big deal. A small hope I didn't even know I had fades when I realise the way this is going to go. 'I'm not prepared to have any conversation with you until you admit you need some help,' she says.

'Well, you can stop patronising me. That would definitely help.' I fish around in my bag and pull out a cigarette, blowing smoke into the room. 'And unlock my accounts, that would help also.' Tearing off some of the pack I flick it into the fireplace, feeling the pressure of the last few days. 'And get your monkeys off Gabe. I know you're trying to shut him down.'

At that moment Mollher chooses to make his presence obvious at the door, hovering in the frame like a muscled-up blob. Jeane glances his way then shakes her head, dismissing him. It's not the first time I wonder if something's going on between them. She leans forward and traces the profiles of her eyebrows. It's something she does when she's either tired or stressed, and she does look tired. Haggard even.

'Listen to me Alice,' she says, 'you might not believe it, but we love you.' I stay quiet. 'St Francis's was never a secret. When you recovered from your illness...' She stops herself, lost for a second to the white light of memory. 'You were only out for two days.' Her tone is odd, almost plaintive, 'But you had forgotten most of everything that had come before.' Her composure cracks under the weight of the recollection. She stares at me; caught between defiance and desperation. 'I'll do anything I have to do to make sure you don't end up in a ditch somewhere. I'm not apologising for that.'

I push myself back into the couch, looking for an ashtray. There's nothing so I tap some ash into a small flower arrangement. It's petty but the woman has a habit of pushing my buttons too. 'Get off Gabe's back and we'll talk,' I say. 'He doesn't deserve it. I lean forward, trying to catch her eye. 'Something's happening to me. It's important.'

Mother blinks through the blue coils of smoke. 'That something you're describing is a breakdown.'

'Get away from Gabe.'

Jeane reaches over and plucks a cigarette from my pack. I never knew she smoked. 'All right,' she says tiredly. She motions for the lighter. 'We tried returning you to the school of course, but you'd forgotten not only the work but also your friends. You were hysterical. We had to take you out of that environment; it was the kindest thing to do. You know the rest. We organised for you to be home-schooled and you were given the best education we could give you before you went to college.'

'I remember lessons in the old house,' I say. 'It's murky. I haven't thought about it in a long while.'

Mother regards me quietly through a haze of her own smoke. 'What made you remember the school after all this time?'

'I couldn't say,' I reply eventually. I'm not ready to tell her about the girl. 'I'm remembering things in Sydney too. I just kind of found my way there.'

'Your father and I have organised for you to go to the clinic. Discretely.'

'What?'

'The clinic. It's not officially open yet but there's a space for you.'

I can't believe what I'm hearing. Someone's playing someone, but who? Are they using Olen to get to me or is this some kind of double bluff? 'Take it, Alice,' says Jeane, the intensity in her voice surprising me, 'take this chance. We love you. You may not think so and I know we were never good parents but we really did try. Come back and let us help you.'

I close my eyes and attempt to hear the sentiment behind the cliché. 'Tell me about Olen,' I say.

'Pardon?'

'Olen. I want to know what he's got to do with the family.'

'I don't understand. We're talking about you.'

'We spent time with him when I was young, right? I don't remember him. If you want to help me, then help me with this.'

Mother nods, as if piecing together things in her mind. 'You want to understand why you reacted the way you did at the party?'

'Yes.'

'Drugs, Alice. Your bloodstream is full of poisons. You might have acted like that with anyone, it was only a matter of time.' She shifts, switching to the attack smoothly. 'And you can't tell me you don't suffer other blackouts, hallucinations, whatever you want to call them.'

I let her say her piece without interrupting and she mistakes my quietness for agreement. 'Of course you can't.' Some of her pallor has disappeared in the rush of emotion. 'You don't even know who you are, hiding like you do. You and your,' she waves her hands angrily, on a roll, 'attitude. You're killing yourself and you're too pig-headed to see it.'

'I want to get better,' I say at last and it's true. The words feel like they're coming from someone else, surprising me. 'I really do. But I need to know about my past, back when I was only one person.' So strange. For a second I'm echoing another person's voice. I almost reach out to her. Jesus. Where is this coming from? I clamp down on it quickly, but not before she glimpses something in my face.

Jeane wipes her eyes angrily, staring at me for a long time. She's looking at me, but not at me. She's searching for someone. 'You are one person.'

'Then tell me about Olen.'

She sighs, shifting a burden. 'All right. Olen was a good friend,' she says. 'It didn't start that way. Your father was in banking before health, did you know that?' I tell her I do. 'He wanted to break into something new and started looking around for opportunities. He heard about Olen and his financial troubles and did a deal. He paid off his debts and purchased the business, including the building and patents. He kept Olen on as an administrator. The man was a great doctor but a bad businessman and it took your father to put the pieces back together the right way.'

'So Olen was always a friend?'

'No. He was bitter at first, then grateful. Mattiew understood he was a good man and kept moving him up in the company as it grew. We became close after a while.' There's something in her tone that makes me look at her. Jeane glances away. 'He was family.' She flicks the exhausted butt of the cigarette into the fireplace and leans over to take another one. 'We were so small when all this started. Such a tiny company.' She glances at me. There's something in her expression.

'You and Olen were lovers?' I ask, somehow unsurprised.

Jeane shrugs. 'Your father had other interests. We trusted him. He helped us build the business. Of course we became close.' Even now she can surprise me. I marvel at the inevitability in her voice, the sheer dispassion.

It's kind of funny in its own twisted way. 'Olen — surgeon, inventor and fuck-buddy.'

Jeane takes a drag of her cigarette. 'Well, whatever you want to call him, he saved your life.'

'What do you mean?'

'We were away for the week on business. We'd asked Olen to take care of you while we were gone. He recognised the signs straight away and got you into hospital. We came right back of course, but we almost lost you. It took you two days to wake up.'

I sit very still. 'So all you know is what Olen told you?'

She blinks. 'What are you saying?'

I stand up, crossing my arms. 'I hate it. I don't remember this; I don't remember him. I don't have a beginning.' My voice, it's so whiney. Again, I hear the almost-echo in my head, someone speaking the words before I say them.

She examines me closely. I can almost see her lips forming a question. She starts to say my name, but changes her mind, walks around the table and tries to hug me. It's uncertain and uncomfortable. We separate but she refuses to let me go. 'Honey, you do. We kept your things from when you were a child. They're in the old house.'

'You still have the house?'

She smiles and for the first time there's a flicker of warmth. 'I could never let it go.'

'Show me,' I say.

51

THE OLD HOUSE

Mollher brings the car to a stop in front of a place I haven't thought of in years. He opens the door for Jeane, refusing to meet my gaze. It's a dead giveaway. We walk under bare elms to the house. I follow Mother as she unlocks it and leads the way into the large foyer where she turns on a light switch, evaporating the shadows as rows of hidden globes spill warm light from the ceiling.

Memories flood back.

Studying quietly by myself. The parties and functions of my parents as they steadily grew their influence. Echoes of laughter and chatter through the rooms, the rare and quiet family dinners. Arguments and jokes and the dusty randomness of things I thought I'd forgotten. We moved out to the mansion when I was ten. It's so strange to be here again; almost like I'm back inside a landscape half made up of memory.

'I had no idea you kept it.' I say quietly.

Jeane's voice is distant, the sound of someone lost in

their own memories. 'This was a good house,' she says. 'We had some special times here.'

It's cold, not freezing. The lights work. The rooms are dusty but not decrepit. There must be a caretaker to clean it now and again.

'Your father wanted to sell it but I wouldn't let him,' she says in that same tone. 'The house was good to us.'

I leave her to walk through the rooms, many still furnished, white dust shrouds making strange, anonymous shapes. The place is large but still on a human scale. Not like that mausoleum my parents now call home. We tour the ground floor then slowly make our way upstairs towards the bedrooms.

With every step I take, every room revealed, the house becomes more familiar. The creak of a door and the off-coloured patch of a wall where a portrait once hung all come back to me like forgotten friends, but there aren't any answers.

I go to my old bedroom, bare except for a shrouded bed and a neat stack of cardboard boxes. It's unremarkable, real but belonging to another person from another time. A small plastic doll sits on the cover. It stares at me.

Mother joins me at the door.

'Why did we leave all this here?' I ask as she enters the room.

'These are the things you didn't want any more,' she says. 'When we moved you weren't interested in taking much with you to the new house, but I couldn't throw them out.' She walks over to a box and pulls the tape from the cardboard. 'You never formed strong attachments to things.'

I join her and we move a couple of boxes to the bed. I know this room, how the light used to come through the wide windows in the morning, the sounds it made as the rest of the house settled at night. It's strange to be here again. I tear open a flap and poke at old clothes, plush toys I vaguely remember, some more photos.

I lay out five or six of the polaroids on the floor and lean in close. They're faded, yellowed with time, most blurry and not particularly worth keeping. All the real family pictures are housed safely at the mansion, except for my own small album. Three of the pictures are landscapes, a hilly place I can't remember going to; one of a pet dog we used to have, long since gone. Ringo, we called him. The fifth, a badly framed family portrait. The Van de Kortes standing with Olen in front of the door to this house. I scoop them up and drop them back into the box where they spill like cards over some old baby clothes.

'What are you looking for?' says Jeane.

'I don't know,' I say, walking over to the window. Below, the street seems cold and empty, the black lozenge of limo sitting like a smokey shadow. 'Everything is wrong.' I put my hand against the glass. 'I can touch things, but nothing feels real.' I look at my palm, pink from the pressure, and compare it to the other one — still bandaged.

I open another box and pull out a brittle finger painting I probably did when I was three or four. Primary colours, big bold sweeps and splashes fill the yellowing paper. 'In Sydney,' I say, 'there's this girl. Sydney-me thinks she's a ghost.'

Mother shakes her head. 'No one died, Alice.'

'I'm seeing her here too.'

She accepts this information without comment, but I know what she's thinking. I've lost it. 'Why did Olen leave?'

She hesitates a moment before answering, then puts the toy back into the box. 'Your father was furious when you became ill. It wasn't Olen's fault of course. It was just one of those things, but he took it personally. The transfer was in everyone's best interest.' Her emphasis on the last two words hint at politics mostly invisible until now.

'It seems like everything's been patched up,' I say carefully.

The bed creaks as Jeane sits, shrugging. 'Water under the bridge. When he asked to come back, Mattiew agreed. You can't hate someone forever, life's too short for that kind of grudge.'

I turn away from the window. 'He asked to come back?'

'Yes, when he heard about the plans to demolish the original clinic.' She stands, brushing fine dust from her coat. 'He was insistent.' As I absorb this, she beckons. 'Follow me.'

I shut the door to my old room without looking back and trail her down the wide wood-panelled hallway. Mother stops at a new door and fishes around in her pocket for a key, finally finding the one she's searching for. This particular room is a mystery to me; it was the only place I was never allowed into as a kid. Despite all the years, there's a glow of anticipation.

'This was Olen's for a while,' says Jeane. 'Before he left of course.' I walk past her into the room, which is about the same size as my old bedroom, with a view through the window onto a bland patch of brickwork. It's cold in here. There are some chairs, a desk whose legs peak out beneath a cover. Grimy windows. The air is musty and I can see the dust is thicker than in the other rooms. Whoever occasionally looks after the rest of the house never makes it this far.

'He was over so often when we first renovated the clinic,' says Jeane as she stands in the centre of the room, 'it was like he was a member of the family. We eventually set this up for him.' I'm surprised it took me so long, when I finally get it. This house is a museum. Mother has taken a snapshot of her life and this is her shrine to it; packed and covered, closed off from the rest of the world and this office is the heart of it all. Hermetically sealed. I have to smile tightly at the irony. If this place holds secrets and memories, they're not mine.

Jeane's phone rings and as she checks the number on its screen, she's torn between taking the call in private and leaving me in the room. 'Give me the key,' I say as it keeps ringing, 'I'll lock up.' She answers the phone, passing over the old brass key as she puts her hand over the mouthpiece, walking down the hall.

As the sound of Mother's voice grows muffled, I turn on the spot and try to imagine the gaunt figure of Olen, younger and more driven, working at this desk. The old clinic was never luxurious, but at least it had been big. Being here must have galled him. I wonder why Jeane didn't know that, or perhaps she did. Whatever it was that had powered their relationship, it wasn't love.

I pull the shroud from the desk, revealing a bare, functional surface, little more than a table with drawers running down one side. Scraping the chair I sit down and open one of the drawers at random. Something rattles as I move it, but it's only some paperclips and plastic binders. I reach in and push them around, feeling the grit of wood shavings and dust when my fingers touch cold metal at the end. I pull out a couple of old keys.

The sound of footsteps grows louder and along with it Mother's voice. On impulse I pocket them before throwing the shroud back over the desk. I meet Jeane just as I'm locking the door.

'So Alice,' she says, looking at me speculatively. 'This is where you grew up. You didn't suddenly pop into existence.'

Her expression softens. 'Please let us help you. Let me take you to our clinic, there are programmes that can make you better. It's ours, you'll get the best treatment in the world.'

I touch the keys in my pocket. Something has gone full circle. 'All right.'

52

CLINIC

It's not an intervention, not quite. As the sun sets flamboyantly beyond the clinic I know what I'm walking into. Outside the final sounds of the bulldozers fade away, the last of the workers power down their tools. I sit in a slightly uncomfortable green chair, Olen in another facing Mattiew and Jeane who are sitting at opposite ends of a couch. Mollher fills the door like a bouncer.

'We want to keep this private,' says Mattiew.

'Sure,' I say, 'why not. I'm big on low profiles.'

'It's for your own good,' said Jeane.

'Yeah. No problem.' The words don't come out quite as sarcastically as I'd intended.

Olen leans towards me, his blue eyes inscrutable. Now I'm here, I wonder: is this my doing, or have I been manipulated by all three of them? As the minutes wear on, there's something unspoken in the room, something I'm not across. Whatever it is, it sits there, somehow defining our relationship. This is a bad idea. Maybe Olen has told them everything. The old man catches me glancing at the windows. 'They're still behind schedule.'

'All right,' I say, 'how about we get down to it? I'm a fuckup and you want me clean. Got it.' I look at my parents, sitting as far from each other as their own internal decorum allows. 'And I just want to live a normal life.'

'Alice,' says Olen. 'This isn't about judging you. I understand how difficult coming here is for you.' I bite back my reply, aware of the keys in my pocket. The truth is I do want to be here, if being here is going to give me my answer. If what he'd said before was true then there may be a way to wake up once and for all. My parents appear anxious as he turns to them. 'Alice and I have had some conversations ahead of our meeting here.'

'What the fuck?' I get to my feet. I should have known. Then he looks at me so only I can see and actually winks.

'Alice!' hisses Mother. Mollher stirs from the corner, tensing.

Olen holds up a calming hand, silencing her. 'Alice wants this as much as you want it for her. And I care for her too. We've agreed on a course of mild sedatives to help her get through the first days. But you need to understand this can only work if it's voluntary. We will be trying short sessions to begin with and based on how they pan out, we'll take it from there. We have a long-term plan, but the important thing is to play things day by day at the outset.'

'Bullshit,' says Mattiew. 'I want this straightened out now. This needs to be done properly.' He stares defiantly at the old doctor.

'This,' says Olen carefully, 'is how to do things properly. Alice and I have an understanding.' He looks at me, his face conveying something I can't parse.

'Yes,' I say quietly, taking my seat again. 'I'm over this crap. I'm done with it.'

'One day and one night at first,' says Olen. 'And we'll take things from there.'

'And turn on my accounts,' I say to them. 'I'm not going to be blackmailed.'

Jeane nods. 'All right.'

There's a moment of silence, punctuated by a final banshee wail from the siren at the demolition site. The theatrics of the moment aren't lost on me: the whole meeting has the air of a performance. I get the impression everything was decided before. This is just the final touch to make it all seem real.

'Then all that's left is to sort out the administrative side,' says Olen, 'which we can do without names. After that we can get to work.' Jeane nods, sharing a glance with me. I nod as well, but this isn't an agreement. It's just a truce.

53

WE ARE NOT THE SAME

Ratbone's curled up in a tight ball on the pillow next to my head. He smells rank, probably been hunting birds again. He senses my movement and starts clawing as he purrs. 'Shoo,' I say, pushing him off. 'Stupid cat.'

Later as I stare at myself in the mirror, I decide I'm not going to work or visit Ryan today. I hurt like hell from the accident. As I brush my teeth I scrutinise the woman in front of me, still dressing in that childish Donald Duck T-shirt. I've never really liked my own body, always too fat or too thin, always just short of what my other self seems to have naturally. 'Bullshit,' I whisper. Over there, she's not so special either but despite all that I do like her hair. I take a deep breath, take off the nightshirt and stare frankly at my body.

'Fuck. It,' I say the words slowly, relishing them, owning them. This isn't parroting the kind of thing I'd say over there, this is me speaking. I realise a horrible, simple truth: I define myself by being her opposite. I'm not me. I'm just not her. The harder I push back against her the more I become her shadow. And the joke of it all is that she's me. I'm her. Whatever.

I don't flinch from my reflection. Fine-boned face, beautiful eyes, fullish lips. I'm a bit pale but healthy enough, toned through all the walking I do. In New York, I'm skinnier. I stare at the dark bruises across half my body — it had been such a near thing. Instead of staring at myself in a mirror I could be dead.

Fuck. It.

I open the cupboard and reach for a pair of scissors.

JUST FOR A CHANGE I've decided to wear a T-shirt and old jeans. The summer dress is in the bin, along with the grandma bra I usually wear. It feels, well, different.

Ignoring the heat I go back to Lavar's apartment block. I'm not going to walk away from the mystery, not when it's almost killed me. Real or dream, I don't care anymore; I will find out who the hell that girl is. Or at least prove this guy is a flake. 'Nothing is real,' I hear myself quoting Lavar as I look up at the block, half hidden behind its palm trees. Well I'm real.

I knock on the door, pushing my hand through my hair by reflex. It's so weird being short. I try again. I can hear the muffled sound of a radio inside, but there's no answer. I call out, tapping against the thin wood and listen for a response. Still nothing. On a hunch I reach for the handle, which turns easily. I know I shouldn't go in, I really do, but the radio's playing so he's probably home. And I'm not going until I get answers. I announce myself one more time before pushing open the door.

The lights are off and the curtains are drawn, filling the

flat with blooms of sunlight. I'm blinded for a moment by the sheer whiteness of everything and as my other senses go into overdrive to compensate I'm hit by a blast of some sort of pine-scented cleaner. The place is sparse but I never picked him for a clean freak.

I can still hear the radio as I glance around. With my eyes adjusted to the brightness, the room is almost like I remember, though somehow emptier. I can't put my finger on it. I call out for Lavar but he doesn't answer. Moving out of the lounge I walk down a small hallway and glancing into a bedroom I'm surprised to find a single bed made up with military precision. The sheets are turned down with razor-thin creases and the pillow is perfectly positioned. Again — that vacantness. The space is empty, not just of an inhabitant but of a personality. There are no pictures on the walls, no bedside tables, no shelves. It's a room with a bed in it, that's it.

I'm going to at least find that damn radio. I mean, who leaves their door open and radio switched on if they're not at home? 'Hello?' I call out, feeling more like a criminal with every step. 'It's Alice Brundford.' I pass another room as sterile and deserted as the first, then get to the kitchen area. Damn.

A round table is set for breakfast. On it, a plate of toast lies next to a toppled mug, which trails coffee in a drying stain over the tablecloth and floor tiles. An empty bowl sits in the middle next to a box of cereal, unopened. I walk around it all, stepping over the spill, not wanting to touch anything. I find the radio at last, behind me, a small white utilitarian thing filling the apartment with chatter. One of the chairs has been knocked over. Lavar, my clairvoyant left in a hurry.

What had he seen to make him run? Maybe someone

broke in, but nothing obvious is missing. All the easy to take things are still here: the TV and computer game from the lounge were there when I walked in. And nothing's been broken. Now, I definitely need to go. I should have gone with my gut and never opened the door. Another thought takes hold, this one much harder to shake — what if the thing he'd seen coming was me?

'Shit,' I say to the radio. If I'm correct and he's run rather than stay and meet me, then he probably is the real deal. Maybe he's been right about the other things as well.

54

RETURN

So it comes back to the girl again. The second I started talking to Lavar about her he freaked out. Since I can't find him, I'm going to try and find her. No more waiting. Manhattan-me has it right. She's getting somewhere.

I don't have any trouble finding the building she lead me to before. The warehouse sits alone towards the back of an industrial block, surrounded by compacted, oil-stained dirt. A lot of trucks once came here. There's one massive roller door at its front, now rusted shut, with rows of cracked yellow windows behind wire mesh along the walls. It's obvious even from where I'm standing, I won't be able to climb in — there's nothing to hang onto, no guttering I'd trust to take my weight.

I walk past the gate then duck under the chain-link fence that seems more symbolic than functional. Keeps the cars out, maybe. Weeds, gangly and brittle-dry under the sun, claw at my legs as I push through, which makes me thankful for the jeans.

The fact the girl lead me here is important. More than

important, judging by the connection I'd made with the school in Manhattan. I wonder at that and what it means for us both. Before I can ponder it too deeply, something flickers at the limit of my vision and I spin round, heart beating fast. Great, now I'm jumping at shadows. It's stressful being here, half expecting to see that green dress, even though I'm looking for her. Before, she came for me. This time I'm coming for her.

Despite my new resolution, I'm unsettled. The disappearance of Lavar gnaws at me as I walk slowly down the length of the building. I pass another two doors, both locked — one painted over with graffiti, before circling around the back. The rear of the warehouse is a bland red-brick, coloured with faded markings, almost as if the local gangs had lost interest in it too. The ever present long grass pushes up against the wall, covering the lower part in tangles of yellow and brown. There's a spot where the dry tufts are uneven, and I slow down as I notice something.

The more or less straight line of weeds bulges outwards near the corner, almost like they're growing around an obstacle. My heart beats faster as I go to the spot and start pulling the stringy plants away. A couple of seconds later and I'm staring into a small basement window, open wide enough for a child to climb through. I kneel and rip out the remaining grass, clearing space.

As I wipe the sweat from my forehead, I accidentally smear some dirt across my face. It smells strange, a weird mix of oil and another scent, something sweeter. The smell is distracting and although I can't say why exactly, unsettling.

Back to the window frame: a brittle dry grey wood that threatens to splinter under any real pressure. Although I can't figure out how, if she got in anywhere, this would be it.

Beyond the glass, there's a dim twilit basement full of shapes and shadows. I don't expect the window to move, but I give it a go anyway. I put my hands under the frame and attempt to ease it further open. No use, it's stuck. Swearing softly, I try again, pushing and pulling against the ancient wood gently, hoping to break through the seized action of the hinges. There's a sound like a branch snapping and I let go, falling backwards into the weeds.

When I look again, the window's cracked — in fact one part has completely broken away. Slowly I become aware of a sting in my hand. I must have cut it on the glass when it shattered.

Surprisingly red, a thin line runs knife-straight across my palm, a perfect copy of my other injury. I sit staring at it for minutes, thoughts strangely empty. Of course I'm cut, a part of me whispers. We're the same person, after all. On autopilot I pull out some tissues and do my best to stop the blood, which is already congealing in this weather. It's so red. I watch the drops fall, forming tiny black circles at the centre of minute craters in the dust. I should go home and get it seen to. I'm not a self-mutilating rich kid out to prove herself.

Then I look at the window again. The girl wanted me to see something here. OK. Things are coming together. We both know that. This means it's working. That's what I tell myself as I wrap my hand in my T-shirt, snap off the loose wood, smash out the remaining glass and carefully, carefully climb into the basement.

The room is cramped, dark, dry and horrible. On the far side there's a metal door, patchy with half peeled paint — the only exit. A small pile of dirt that's blown in from the open window across the years has spawned a few sickly-white plants. Their flimsy, almost translucent leaves strain to catch whatever dim light makes it down here, filtered first by the weeds, then the dirty glass. I ignore the pain in my hand and let my eyes adjust. Despite my thundering heart it's right to be acting at last. I'm doing my part. There will be something down here; I know it.

I look around, slowly beginning to make out the mouldering wrecks of old wooden chairs piled up against a wall. There are tables and desks as well lying in a twisted, almost sculptural tangle of furniture. It takes a moment for me to figure out everything is smaller than it should be, that it's been built for children.

My foot bumps into something soft and yielding and I leap back with a scream, which the room amplifies into a nightmarish wail. I shut up, that sensation of rightness I had before evaporating with the sound of my own fear. God, I'm trapped. Cursing myself for being so stupid, I turn to the window, trying to figure out how to get out. It's too high to jump.

I step on that thing again, and forcing back my nervousness bend down to get a better look in the half-light. It's a toy bear, its fur matted and clumped together with dried mud. I pick it up and spot a hint of a patched jacket under the grime. The teddy bear is ancient and filthy, smells of the weather and hotness and darkness. It's horrible and pitiful. I want to drop it, but don't. Instead, I imagine it here in this place, abandoned and lost, and clasp tighter.

Still holding the bear I walk the few steps to the door, the only other way out. My sense of purpose has fled and all I need is to escape. I try the handle but like all the doors aboveground, it's locked. I breathe out slowly as the pain in my hand goes to a whole new level. Leaning against the cool metal I let myself slide down the length of it to the dirty floor.

A sound.

Muffled.

Almost not there at all. And a whiff of roses, that other scent in the dirt.

I leap up, electrified and on the verge of panic as I scuttle away from the door, breathing hard, barely suppressing a scream. For a nightmare few seconds I pace around the room, mind whirling, claustrophobic and caught in a loop of fear, but I force it down, managing to bully the spiky terror into something I can handle. I'm here for a reason. The girl wants me in this place and point-by-point, I make myself remember my mission. I run my hand through my freshly cut hair, now dirty and oiled with basement dust.

Slowly, I go back to the door. I am meant to be here. There is a purpose to all this. But that still doesn't take away the fear.

I lean into it and strain to hear past the percussion of my pulse. Nothing at first, then gradually, as if I'm imagining it, comes the sound. Someone laughing. No. I push my ear against the cold metal. Not laughing. Crying. A child crying.

Ignoring the fear I yank at the door, setting loose a shower of plaster. I slam myself against it then pull back again, straining to break the lock. I yell. It could be the girl behind there. The image of her trapped and crying beats at me. I grab the handle, frustration cracking my voice and blurring my vision. Taking one of the wrecked chairs I smash it into metal.

Time breaks apart into slices; a scream, a flash, the blood in my hand greasing the wooden leg of a stool. I become nothing but broken shards, just like the glass above.

I'm still screaming when something clamps down on my shoulder. I spin in horror, distantly surprised to discover I'm still holding the bear.

'Alice, it's me.'

I blink through tears, voice almost gone, reduced to animal sounds.

'Alice!'

I stop. It's Ryan, outlined by the spill of light from the window. 'Alice, you've got to get out of here.'

I calm down enough to speak but my voice is ragged and hoarse from all the screaming. 'What are you doing here?'

'Jen couldn't find you. She called me.' I had a feeling this is where you'd be.'

I put my head in my hands. 'Just get me out.'

Ryan begins to stack the broken furniture under the window, helping me up when there's enough to climb.

'I'm sorry.'

'You don't need to keep saying that.'

I sit hunched in the seat, and in the cool air-conditioned atmosphere of the car the road sounds muffled and underwater-like. Trees and houses roll past as if nothing had happened. Beside me, Ryan's holding the wheel with both hands, not relaxed. His shirt's stained from the dirt and effort of getting me out of the basement and into the sun.

'Sorry.'

He shakes his head.

'You said you didn't see her,' I say, fighting off a sense of displacement. Outside the cabin, the world's turned second-hand and muted.

'That's right,' he says after taking the time to carefully turn onto my street. He's driving cautiously and I wonder how shaken up he actually is. 'We have to get you back on track,' he says. His voice is grim.

'The girl is real,' I say weakly. 'I heard something behind that door.' I stare at my hands, still grasping the teddy bear. I have no say in the matter: they cling to the dirty thing in a death grip.

'No you didn't,' He says and I'm shocked by the anger in his voice.

We pull up in front of my house and Ryan turns off the car, swivelling to face me as the engine ticks in the heat. 'Do you know how I found you?' I shake my head. 'I followed the screams. You tell me, do you think that's a sign of someone who's got things under control?'

I look at the bear again. It's disgusting but I refuse to let it go. I force my attention from the toy.

'Listen to me Alice, I care for you,' he says, measuring his words. I can read the cost of what he's saying in his face and I start getting scared all over again. 'But as a doctor I've let the lines blur. 'Tomorrow, we need to talk. Your sister as well.'

'Keep Jen out of it.'

'Alice, she has to be there. She has power of attorney.'

'Pardon?'

Ryan tries his best at a reassuring smile, but his heart's not in it. 'Technically, she's your guardian.'

I shake my head, wondering if this is some sort of test. 'That's impossible.'

'No,' he says, his features creasing even deeper. 'You were the one who told me, remember? Which is why she needs to be involved.'

'Don't be stupid,' I say, but my voice is barely a whisper. The emptiness I'm experiencing is fast turning into dread.

'Alice,' he says, 'ask her if you want. I'm sure she'll be able to show you a copy of the order. I've seen it myself, it has your signature.'

'Bullshit,' I whisper.

Behind us, a horn blares. Jen pulls her car into the drive and steps out.

'Ask her,' says Ryan, acknowledging her with a nod.

'This is fucked,' I say and step out of his hatchback and into the blast-furnace of the day. Jen opens her mouth to say something but I walk by without a word. As I get to the house, Jen leans into Ryan's car, deep in conversation. I shake my head and still grimly hanging on to the bear, go inside and shut the door.

55

DETOX

It's a surprising morning. The sun's unusually strong and even though the air's still cold the light has a spray of colour. A warm red highlights the frost, a colourful backlight that makes the blues deeper and the shadows mysterious. I pay the driver with my reactivated card and grabbing my overnight bag, walk a few steps over the gravel to stare at the demolition site. It's also caught up in the unusual light; the broken walls and piles of rubble looking mysterious and in a weird way, ancient. I smile to myself and pull out a cigarette, flipping closed the lighter when I'm done.

A man in a casual white shirt waves to me from the entrance to the clinic.

'Mrs Hilben? He calls, walking up to me.

'That's me,' I say, playing along. Mrs Hilben. This whole cloak and dagger thing's strangely fascinating.

The orderly, whose name is Joel, delivers me to Olen's office, where the old man invites me to sit down.

'It seems as though things are gaining their own momentum,' he says.

I stare at him cautiously. 'Second thoughts?' he asks, noticing my expression. 'My offer still stands. In fact,' he continues, 'it seems events have aligned.'

'How?'

He smiles. 'Your parents need what they would think of as a result and you need an answer. Both of these, requirements, I can help with. They are the same thing.'

There's a small vase of white roses on his desk and I feel an odd echo of my other life intruding again. Next to the flowers, a framed photo of Olen and my parents. I crane my neck to see the picture better and Olen, noticing, obliges me by turning it around. 'I will personally guide you through this, Alice,' he says.

'Is that your promise to them, or to me?' I ask.

'To you.' He looks me squarely in the eye, apparently leaving no room for doubt. 'We need to put one demon to rest before tackling another, don't you think?' He moves to replace the frame and fumbles it heavily to the desk. Quickly picking it up, he takes care to return it to its original position. But not before I notice a piece of paper peaking from behind the backing board, dislodged in the fall. I glance away before he catches me staring at it.

'So,' he says. 'We'll get a start today. What I said before still stands. You need to go into this thing clean or there will be complications. So the detox is for real. Agreed?'

'Agreed.'

He nods as if everything's been settled and leans back in his chair. 'Are you ready for this?' He seems to struggle for words for a moment then, 'And your other self, does she know this is happening?'

I shrug at his bizarre question. 'Yes, everything. And vice versa.' I laugh, more a quiet exhalation. 'She's losing it.

Strange thing is — she says exactly the same about me, but hell, this chick's going apeshit if you get what I mean.'

'No, not really.'

'Well, she's trying to follow this girl. A ghost maybe. What's weird is I've been seeing her here too. She lead me to a school. I went there when I was kid, but I never remembered before she showed me. What do you make of that? It's a total headfuck, right?'

He stares at me for a long moment. 'St Francis.' It wasn't a question.

'Yes.'

'I used to drop you off there sometimes, for your parents.'

I keep forgetting almost everybody knows more about me than me. 'I heard,' I say.

He leans forward, looking at me with a keenness that goes beyond simple interest. 'Maybe you have things the wrong way around. You are starting to remember your past. Perhaps, this ghost girl you followed, you first saw here. It's no surprise such a powerful image would manifest in the dream as well.'

'Image?' I ask quietly. 'Of what? Then who is she?'

Olen smiles again, but there's not a trace of warmth in his expression. He looks disappointed. 'Come on Alice. You must know.'

I shake my head, stop. I stare at him. He nods minutely in encouragement, a teacher waiting for a slow student to grasp an idea. So who was the girl in the green school uniform, the same as I used to wear? How could I possibly know the child, a stranger?

But she's not.

Something shifts inside and I realise I must have understood all along.

'She's me.' I say those words so quietly, they're only a breath.

'There,' he says through a smile that isn't a smile, 'not even ten minutes and already we're making progress. Congratulations.'

HERE BUT NOT HERE. I sit mute and still throughout the compulsory medical check. I let the staff, who are painfully efficient and polite, prod and measure, sample and collect. I piss in a jar.

I replay everything I remember about the girl, hoping for context, but if she's myself, then that makes me the stranger. Which, I guess, might be the message. Closing my eyes I try to think of something else, someone else. For no reason, Jordie comes to mind, not Gabe. He's there, not much more than a simple presence in my life, but I wonder how the kid gets on, what he does with his time, what he wants to be. I can't even say for sure if he even goes to school.

As Mrs Hilben I get through most of the day in a daze, thinking about the girl. There's a group therapy session at some point, me and a bunch of strangers sitting in a circle, sharing. I surprise myself by making up a complete history for her; a divorcee, one kid (who wears a green school uniform and haunts her dream persona — that part I leave out), living off a small trust fund. I don't like Mrs Hilben, but even that fits in with the others' self-loathing well enough to ring true. So in between mousey offerings of her own experiences, I get to be left alone.

The one distraction is the demolition work just visible through the windows. My attention's drawn back to those earth movers and the almost beyond-hearing whistles of the supervisor. It somehow carries over the grind and shudder of falling masonry and heavy treads. The destruction is magnetic and it's at one of these moments Olen stops by the door. I shift in my chair and he acknowledges me with a small nod, a fellow conspirator.

Later, after the session has broken up Mrs Hilben finds herself talking to a skinny addict called Mari. Mari's OD'd three times this month but I find myself not giving a shit. Her tone is all last chance and quiet desperation. I tune out. I catch Olen's silhouette standing at the fence separating the demolition site from the clinic and I turn from her mid sentence, staring through the window at his back.

It's night before I get a chance to unpack, which I do by upending my bag on the bed. A change of clothes and some toiletries spill out onto the bedcover. I'm in what's called the Azure Suite. They're so into colours here. It's an okay-sized room, complete with double bed and decorated with freshly cut flowers. The room reminds me of something between a small hotel suite and a day spa. I make a note to myself: when I wake up in Sydney I should look into trying to get into the rehab market.

There's a soft knock on the door as I pick up a remote for the TV, flopping onto the bed. It's Olen.

'Alice,' he says, 'checking in to see how your first day went.' I do a so-so sign with my hand. He sits on the duvet next to me. 'Mrs Hilben was quite a hit. Very cooperative, very open.'

'Yeah,' I say, 'some people are built for confession I guess.'

'My offer is genuine,' he says, 'but you have to make an effort.'

I rub my neck, getting rid of the tension that came along

for the ride today. 'The only thing I have to do is prove to you I'm clean.' I roll up the arms of my sweater, stick out my tongue. 'And I'm doing that. Cross my heart. You can check.'

He nods like what I've said doesn't matter. 'We do. You have an opportunity here,' he says again, but I shake my head, cutting off the spiel.

'I'll do my bit, you do your bit. When do I start the treatment?'

He rubs his mouth as he thinks about it. 'Soon, in fact as soon as your bloods come in clean. The medication is here. I'm waiting on you, to be frank.'

'Then don't wait. I'm up for it.'

He puts a hand on my shoulder, but I shrug it off. I don't like how he's getting so touchy-feely all of a sudden. 'You don't have a choice in this matter. I'm doing this to help you, not to risk your life.' He stands. 'Take advantage of what's here. It's a second chance, not something that comes round too often for most people.'

I lay back on the bed. 'OK,' I say tiredly. 'But answer me a question.'

He turns at the door. 'Shoot.'

'What happened on the day I got sick?'

He stares at me for a moment and I can tell he's been expecting this. 'I picked you up from school and noticed you had a high temperature. You started vomiting and when I spotted the rash on your arm I took you directly to the hospital. I called your parents and the rest you should know. It was a close thing.'

'So you saved my life then.'

He angles his head. 'Yes. I did what anyone would do.'

I look closely at the remote for a second before turning my attention to him. 'So why did you leave? My folks owed you big time.'

He smiles. It's like looking into the face of a museum exhibit. 'I didn't run, if that's what you're implying, but I had my reasons for leaving.'

'My mother?' He almost flinches, though I can't be sure. 'And so now you're here again.'

He opens his hands. Nothing to hide. 'As I said, this place is a second chance. Good night, Alice.' He shuts the door and I flop back down on the bed, wondering.

56

BETRAYED

I can't say why, but I seek out the bear the second I open my eyes.

I sling on some clothes and storm though the house, opening the door to the backyard where I go over to the small tin shed left over from Dad's time and find what I'm looking for buried in a mess of tools. Jen calls out for me as I head back but I ignore her. As I step out into the street I know how I look. My hair's standing up in sleepy knots and my tracksuit's all crumpled and ugly. Truth is — don't care. I walk with purpose, carrying the crowbar.

Two bus connections bring me to the long curving road that ends in the cul-de-sac bordered by the park. I'm going back to the warehouse. That door is coming open. I march past the slides, the sand pit, the empty playthings, the air pungent with white summer roses, as I focus on my goal. I've been given the challenge and I'll get it done.

As I push through the growth of hedges I almost stumble down the lip of the small retaining wall again, startling an old couple who jump at my sudden appearance.

They stare at the metal in my hand and back away warily. Not my problem.

Ryan's waiting for me. I notice his car before I find him standing near the corner of the building. 'There's no girl, Alice,' he says. 'It's just you. Put down the crowbar.'

I wipe the sweat from my eyes. The sun's hidden behind a smoggy brown smear of cloud but the heat is as relentless as ever. 'Why are you following me?' I say.

'You're obsessed.'

I hold on to the iron, gripping it the same way I gripped the teddy bear yesterday. 'Looks like you are too,' I say angrily.

He shakes his head, his hair oily with sweat. His shirt is stained dark under his armpits. He's feeling the day as well. He walks past me and opens the door to his car. 'Get in. Let's go back to your house.'

'Jen told you I would be here,' I say.

'She didn't need to.'

I stay put, gripping the warm iron of the crowbar even tighter than before. My injured hand stings from the sweat in my palm, knuckles white with pressure.

'Alice,' he says again, leaving the car and coming over to me. 'Give me that damn thing. Do you realise you're walking around with a weapon?'

I shake my head. He's not going to put me off. 'I need to get into that room.'

A flicker of green.

I spin in time to catch a glimpse of the girl running behind the building and leap after her. Dropping the crowbar I push everything into a sprint, leaving Ryan behind. I skid on the fine dirt as I round the corner, finding her standing at the basement window, face flushed, angry and alive with emotion. She's no ghost, no image. This child, whatever she is, is as real as me. I grab her arm and sensing her body's heat through the fabric of her sleeve, refuse to let go.

'Who are you?' I pant between breaths.

The girl, wide brown eyes teary, her features lost beneath streaked dirt and those purple bruises points with her free hand. I take too long to understand. When I turn, Ryan's already coming around the corner. He has to be able to see her now. My emotions flare with relief and a thousand other things. 'What's your name?' I ask her.

She screams and startles me enough for me to lose my grip, but Ryan lashes out and catches her arm roughly. The girl jerks back like she's on a string as he clamps down with his other hand. 'She's real,' I say, half pleading, 'we have to help her.' But Ryan won't meet my eyes and turning wordlessly, begins to carry her away.

I watch for a second, not understanding what I'm seeing, then chase after them. He's halfway to the car by the time I catch up, yelling for him to stop.

'I'm taking her to a hospital,' he says, holding her tight against himself to keep her from struggling. She screams again and claws at his face leaving ugly red lines down his cheek.

'But she's real,' I say, crumbling as all the old weakness return.

'I can see that,' he shouts, 'and she's been abused. Now help me get her into the damn car.' I reach for her then pull back. 'Alice,' says Ryan, forcing reasonableness into his voice, 'we can talk about what this means later but right now we need to get this child to hospital.' He reaches the car and puts her gently into the rear seat. The girl rakes his face a second time and he leaps away, slamming his head into the door frame. 'Help me, will you?' he shouts. I stumble back, in my own way wordless as the girl. Ryan puts a hand to the scratches on his cheek, glancing at me. 'OK, you were right,' he says, 'get in.'

As I climb into the seat next to her she starts screaming again. The noise is an assault. Backing away I realise that she's not looking at me. I follow the direction of her eyes: she's staring towards the basement, hidden behind the building. She turns to me and mouths the word, Go. Ryan calls to hurry things up and this triggers another bout of screaming from her. I back out of the car.

'Alice?' he says, but I can't answer.

'Fine.' He slams the door firmly and climbs into the driver's side.

As they drive off the girl leans across the back seat to stare at me through the rear window. I stand there a long time alone, frozen in the heat, victorious but beaten.

He wasn't surprised to find her.

I walk along the warehouse to the crowbar sitting heavily in the dust and pick it up. It's oddly hot in my hand, heavier. Still holding the iron I glance again at the basement window, seeing the stubs of yellowed glass jutting from the frame.

I inch myself past the brittle splinters, wary of their razor edges, until my feet balance precariously on the stacks of chairs below, left over from yesterday's escape. The room is colder than last time. The girl is gone. The door's still there. This is where she wanted me to be.

I try the door. Locked and unchanged. The thing disgusts me; the faded red studded metal, pimply with scabbed paintwork and rust. I flick away a few loose curls of rot and put my ear to the surface, straining to listen. There's something there at the limit of my hearing. It's not a voice this time. It might be the echo of traffic from the street outside, but the sound is different — mechanical and rhythmic. The metal's icy, cold as my dream of Manhattan. There's no sense in putting this off, and I ready the crowbar.

I try to lever it against the hinges with no luck: the door's frozen tight. I swear. Hefting it in my hands I go for a different spot instead but the metal bar slips from my fingers and crashes, ringing onto the concrete floor. I pick it up. Try again. This time it shrills as it scuds out of the gap near the join, filling the room with a metal on metal screech.

'Shit!' I yell. 'Fuck!'

I grab it from the ground once more and attempt to jam it into a small gap, leaning all my weight on the iron. My feet lose their grip on the floor and I slide away, rolling onto the dirt. Picking it up I start hammering it again and again, ignoring the pain as it tries to break free from my hand. Scraping and punching, I lose myself in a fog of violence until I just fling the iron at the door in desperation, crying out as it bounces straight back and hits me. I fall, crippled for the moment by agony in my leg. Goddamit! As I lean against a chair I kick the crowbar so that it scuds over the concrete. I'm so close.

Eventually I make myself stand and face the window, turning my back on my goal. It's beaten me for now. I hate it but I have to return empty-handed. At least they'll have to admit the girl is real and I'll get a chance to talk to her; that's something I suppose. I kick the iron once more for good measure and begin the climb, emptied and exhausted.

Walking heavily into the lounge room, my mind's blank, beyond exhaustion. Jen's there waiting and races up to hug me the second I get in. 'Did he tell you?' I ask.

Then she gets this strange expression and stands back, her hands halfway between clasped and relaxed. 'What is it?' There are other people in the room. Two men, both dressed in similar shirts and jeans. Ryan is here too. He closes the door behind me. He stares at me, face heavy with some emotion: not sadness, but something very like it.

'What?' I ask, looking between Jen, Ryan and the others. One of the men glances away.

'Alice,' says Jen, 'we have to do this.'

'Do what?' I ask again, feeling the world cave in. My throat tightens and breathing becomes impossible as Ryan steps forward.

'Alice,' he says, 'we need you to come with us.'

'No,' I say. 'Ryan, you took the girl to hospital. Tell them.'

He stares at me — looks me right in the eye. 'There isn't any girl Alice, we've been through this.'

'No,' I whisper.

Jen shakes her head. 'Alice, you're going to get hurt.'

'It won't be permanent,' says Ryan calmly, 'but you need to come with us to Mayfleur.'

I stare at him. 'Why are you lying? I'm not going back,' I say, struggling to breathe through the growing panic attack. I hate how weak I sound.

'Alice, you could have died in there,' says Ryan. 'It's only by luck that I knew where to find you.'

Jen walks over to me, attempting to hug but I back off. The world's falling apart.

'Alice,' says Ryan, 'you have to do this. It'll work out, trust me.'

'Turn your face,' I yell, rounding on him. 'She scratched you. Show me the rest of your face!'

Jen looks at Ryan, who shakes his head. 'Alice, there's no girl.' He turns, left then right. His cheeks are untouched. It's like it never happened.

He nods at the two men, who approach me cautiously. One of them has a taser. They take me by my arms and I let myself be lead away quietly until I reach the door, then I start screaming.

57

BREAKING IN

It's three am exactly. The soft blue light of the alarm clock fills the room, as a blinking dot counts down the seconds; magicking the time between them away like it's not real. I sit up shaking in the bed, my body still in the throes of reaction. I'd screamed and run. And then the taser. Images of my nightmare induction into the Mayfleur Hospital roll in my memory: the glazed faces of the patients, my cellmates, the sedation.

I rub my neck, confused. Everything's broken; the failing symmetry of my personal time had now collapsed entirely. I almost never wake at night in either of my lives; the act of going to sleep is also the act of waking. I never sleep.

Ryan betrayed me, the prick. It's all a dream I know, but it still hurts, hanging around like a stench, even though I'm wide awake. Who knows what caused it, why he behaved the way he did? Unless she really was imagining the girl. But I don't know how that can even be possible — can a dream hallucinate? Real people hallucinate. I put my head in my hands, shaking, more lost than ever.

The moment slowly passes, then wearily I swing myself

out of bed. I don't want to go back to sleep. Especially now, knowing where it's going to take me. Grabbing some clothes I go to the small bathroom, where I stare at myself in the mirror. The woman who stares back at me is closer, now that she's cut her hair short. The colour's different and so are her eyes, but I could have been looking at my twin. Who's also in a clinic. The symmetries keep on rolling. 'Who is it?' I ask quietly, 'You or me?' As I stare at the mirror I wonder whose reflection is the real one. Only one way to find out.

The medication Olen's talking about won't be stored in the clinic's pharmacy. I quietly leave the room and walk down the carpeted hallway towards the administration section of the building. A thought strikes me and I go back and retrieve the keys I'd brought with me from his old desk. The hallway's dimmed but it's easily bright enough to find my way around. At one point I hear the sound of approaching footsteps and hide in a photocopying room long enough for them to pass. As I wait for the soft tread to go away, the urge to laugh is almost overwhelming. I feel like a spy.

His office, close to the front of the clinic, is near one of the session rooms I remember from yesterday. After making a wrong turn I turn around and eventually find it in the half-light. I try the handle and to my surprise it opens easily, swinging inwards into the darkened room in an open invitation. He's either slack on security or pathologically confident. I know which of the two I believe.

I don't want to risk drawing attention to myself by turning on the lights. Instead I drop low and inch my way through the room until I find the window that overlooks the demolition site, drawing the wooden blinds to let in whatever light there is from outside. The room transforms into a landscape of blue shadows and the pale outline of his desk. The objects on its surface are ghostly and indistinct, but as my eyes adjust I'm able to pick out the picture frame. I grab it and turning it over, pull out the piece of paper I noticed before. Holding it against the window, I can see that something's been written on it, barely visible in the faint glow of the security lights at the site. After another few seconds I make out a series of numbers and letters in Olen's precise hand. A code to a safe. It's so obvious I almost shake my head.

Finding the safe proves to be much harder than I expected. I eventually discover it set into the floor under a removable square of carpet. More by luck than skill: one of the cleaners must have left an edge of the square lifted after they'd vacuumed the office and if I hadn't felt the bump in the floor I'd have missed it altogether. The safe sits beneath the window, next to his old-fashioned globe. I kneel down as close as I can get and taking advantage of the light that spills in through the window, study it.

The locks and T-shaped handle are inset an inch and a half into the body of the safe, where a circular dial sits next to a traditional key-lock. All of this opposite a heavy gunmetal grey hinge. I wonder. I give myself a moment to steady my nerves before pulling the keys from my pocket. Surely it won't be this easy. As I bring the keys closer to the light, I can see without even trying them that they're not going to fit. I put them back in my pocket. It would have been too good to be true. Magically convenient even. Dreamlike.

So it's with the faintest sense of relief that I get up and go back to his desk. The keys will be different, but the man hiding them isn't. I open first one drawer then another, my fingers searching their backs for cold, hard surfaces. On the third drawer I find a key, stuck loosely to the wooden interior with tape.

The safe opens on my first attempt. It pushes down inwardly near the door's centre point, not around what I can now see are fake hinges. I reach into the metal container, which is deeper than I expect, my fingers touching a number of documents, something that feels like a computer hard drive and then finally, a small pill bottle.

I remember Ryan's betrayal and worse, Jen's. They don't exist, I know that, but that doesn't stop it getting to me. It's time to put them down. I pop the lid and taking one of the pills, swallow it dry. Could Dream-Alice's mirror of a life ever have been better? What the hell. It doesn't matter. I swallow another pill, close the lid and replace the container into the safe.

I get as far as the door when the first of the cramps grips me, doubling me over in mad, unexpected pain.

I stagger to my feet, my skin breaking out in a sweaty rash as I stumble from the office. I look up to see one of the night nurses walking past, then he stops, noticing me. 'Hey,' he says to someone, 'need some help here.' I glance at him, an excuse forming on my lips when the words catch in my throat. The man's face is odd. It seems longer than it should be. He starts asking me what's going on but I recoil at the stink of his breath, rank and sweet, the smell of rot and dead things. His teeth jut yellow and dirty, his tongue a black shape rolling disgustingly in his mouth.

I back away from him, doing my best to ignore the agony in my stomach and run. My body pings and stabs with strange, almost random pains, as I force myself through a doorway and down a freshly carpeted corridor. Perspective seems liquid, the indoor horizons confusing me and tripping my feet, which are suddenly leaden. Everything throws my balance off-centre.

Thoughts come fast and panicky and no amount of rationalising is going to help. I turn a junction in the hall to see three more nurses: two women and a man talking quietly. Their faces, long melted versions of themselves, turn to me like grotesque sunflowers, their calls low and sneering. I run back the way I came.

I'm trapped between that first nurse and the others. Their voices, full of droning sarcasms and insults, go ahead of them filling the air with a buffeting stench; malign, playful and so full of intent. I moan something low and pleading, then make for a fire escape door.

Slamming down on the door release I push through the exit, triggering a cascade of strangely distorted alarms. I emerge seconds later into a cold concrete stairwell with flights of steps in both directions. A door bursts open below, echoing like an explosion between the concrete walls. The only way is up and I run, taking three steps at a time, hands hovering over the cold grey rails in case my balance gives out entirely.

My foot comes down on something hard and I almost trip. There's a toy fire engine at my feet, cheerily red in the sea of concrete. I round the landing and see a doll lying abandoned on one of the stairs ahead. Someone shouts from the stairs a couple of circuits down; their sneering cynical voices half laughing. Careful to avoid the doll I run on, willing the cramps in my gut to go away. I can see the door to the roof and I focus everything on getting to it, stepping over a growing litter of kids' toys.

I burst onto the roof of the clinic, searching the shadowy boxes of the air conditioning plants for a place to hide. Something coils angrily inside and I stumble to one knee, feeling like I could puke. My hand lands on a rag doll, a lanky woollen thing, its face long and extended. I drop it with a small cry and pick myself up.

The rooftop is full of toys. Dolls, bears, cars, balls, windup things, plastic doll houses and more, all lying scattered around the gravelly surface as if they'd just been left there, ready to be picked up again. I pick out weird details. The hair on one of the dolls is braided wrong, the wheels on a car crooked. The toys are clumped and gathered around poles and boxes of machinery that line the roof. They look like they've been washed up on a tide. A sound snaps me back to the moment and I run towards the shadows, trying to get as far from the door as I can.

Using the light from the open fire escape to see, I try to hide at the farthest point of the roof — a ledge at the corner that overlooks some of the parking lot below. It's no good. Some of them see me and point with long, broken limbs. I look for a way out but I'm too near the edge already. I think about trying to run past them when a flickering, faceless Olen emerges from the shadows. Too close.

I hold out my hand to ward him off; a stupid gesture even as I make it. Somewhere, there needs to be a voice: calm, quiet, sensible, telling me that this is a trip, a side effect of the drug. But the only voice I can hear is my own, begging him to leave me alone. 'Go away,' I breathe, 'please.'

Olens' faceless face almost shimmers as he regards me with eyes that I can't see. He's reverted, become the thing I first saw at the party. I back away, bumping into the ledge at the edge of the roof.

'Don't jump,' he says, 'you really shouldn't jump.' His voice, somehow coming from that nothingness, leers, drips, invites.

'Leave me alone!'

Several monstrous orderlies appear behind him, long-limbed and apelike, their torsos now stretched as thin as their faces, slab jawed, slack eyed, pallid and taunting.

'What have you done to me?' I scream. Think I scream. The world is spinning and perhaps it's only a whisper.

'Nothing,' the thing that's Olen says, 'you've done this to yourself.' It turns to the others, gestures, almost as if to an audience. Then back to me. 'What a shame.' I step onto the ledge. Somewhere nearby, a doll falls three stories to the ground.

'Oh no,' drawls the Olen monster. They're everywhere, with more coming from that open door, shambling their way towards me in clots of shadow. The wind isn't strong, but it gusts. My hands have gone numb, my feet stumpy extensions with no feeling. Something moves at my side. One of the nurses has snuck up on me and I step away.

But my foot comes down on nothing. I scream as Olen lunges towards me. And then I'm falling and it's black and cold.

TIME FLIES

Muddy sounds. Strange light. Liquid images.

Flashes, strobes of white on black, bright against dark. It's the nightclub, or the bath, or the alley or rose-dappled shadow.

And noise, so much there's almost no hearing it, a wall of voices, opinions, theories, recriminations, sarcasms, gentle whispers, laughter and politeness.

The shadows go, leaving only the white.

It's not like waking up. I blink at the silhouettes crossing the frosted window and slowly realise I'm here. I must have been daydreaming or something.

There's a mark on my hand, the faintest feather of red on my palm. I stand still, recognising the shop but confused. I don't remember coming here today. Trying to put the morning together in my head is a struggle; I'm sluggish, different. I place the knife down on the jarrah workbench and take a moment to breathe in the scent of the flowers, letting the rich confusion of dirt and perfumes ground me. The fridge ticks and hums quietly to itself, the computer fan purrs, water drips. I stare at the wicker chair near the front window. It seems to be missing something important.

My quiet contemplation is interrupted by the jangle of the bell as a man walks in, red-faced and gleaming with sweat from the heat outside. He dumps a circlet of white roses heavily on the counter and the scent is so overpowering I take a step back. I recover slightly, putting on my most professional smile. 'Can I help you?'

'I hope so,' he says, unhappy. 'I ordered a wreath of lilies for today and this is what turned up. Who puts roses in a wreath? The service is in three hours. I need it fixed.' I blink, fighting a sense of déjà vu.

'I'm sorry,' I say, 'are you certain it came from us?'

The man, late thirties, overweight and uncomfortable in his warm suit is the image of exasperation. 'Of course I'm sure. I spoke to Alice someone or other. I paid by credit card. Check it, the surname's Armbrost.' He points angrily and his agitation seems to be out of proportion to the problem. 'Don't try and duck out of this.'

My chest tightens with the beginnings of an attack. 'I need this fixed right away,' he says. 'There's no one else who can do it, all the other florists around here are out of stock.' He leans forward, claiming territory on the counter and my pulse begins to race, throat tightens. I'm dizzy. 'So you can take this back,' he jabs the wreath towards me, almost pushing it into my hands. 'And give me what I ordered.'

'I can order the lilies right now,' I say, doing my best to sound normal, 'but they won't be here for an hour.'

'Not good enough,' he says.

I'm not sure how I can sort this out. I wish Jen was here,

she'd know how to handle it. 'I can offer you a refund, if you like.'

'I need the lilies, not a refund. I should be getting ready for the funeral now, not stuck here arguing with you.' He slams the counter causing me to jump. 'Jesus.'

My heart's beating so loudly I wonder if he can hear it too. What makes all of this worse is the sensation I've played it out before. It's so strong. The angry customer, the pressure of a mistake. It's like a set piece.

'So how are you going to fix it?' he demands, face growing redder. I stare at him as I struggle for words, light-headed. The angrier he gets, the more of a caricature he seems to be. Thinking gets strange and difficult; something wants to be remembered, another distortion, some metamorphosis I've seen. But the harder I try to recall it the less I can until all I'm left with is the memory of having a memory. Why can't I be like Other-me?

'I want you to do something about this right now.' He leans further forward across the counter. I know he's going to grab me, but he doesn't. Instead he jabs his finger down on the wood, stabbing it with his nail. 'Fix. It. Now.'

Slowly, calmly, as if there's all the time in the world I feel myself going away. There's a coolness, a distance, a kind of serenity. I pick up the knife, its blade now dewy from droplets of water. 'Get away from me,' I say quietly. I sense the plastic handle rasp across the cut in my palm, an annoyance. The man glances at the blade, expression frozen.

'I want —,' he begins, but I push the knife slowly in his direction and he stops.

'Go away.' My eyes meet his and measure him fully. The blood in his face drains, leaving a cadaver mask in its place. I'm looking at a corpse. 'Get away from me now.' I jab the blade forward again, forcing him to dance back out of its range. He puts up his hands as he backs off, eyes darting between my unblinking stare and the tip of the steel.

He turns and runs for the door, slamming it so hard the bell falls off.

I'm still holding the knife in front of me when Jen's hand gently pushes my arm down. I turn slowly, moving as if my muscles have locked up. In time I look at my big sister. 'Jen?' Jen takes it away and puts it out of reach behind me.

'It's OK, babe,' she says.

'What's happening?'

She shakes her head, smiling through a deep sadness. 'Come on, let's take a walk.'

'I don't know how I got here.'

'It's OK,' she says again.

'What about the shop?'

'We're done with the shop for now.'

She takes me to a park. That she would do this strikes me as strange, but as we sit on the swings I let my eyes close for a moment, feeling more relaxed. I enjoy the rhythm of the light and shade as I swing through the shadow of a tree. The sensation is body deep and soothing, quieting the voices arguing for attention inside my head. Hanging on to the chain links I see the park's deserted.

'Jen,' I say, 'there's something wrong.'

Jen studies me from the other swing, moving in slow arcs. 'Alice,' she says. 'There's nothing wrong. Do you remember Mayfleur?'

I push my feet out and go higher. 'I went there when I was a teenager.'

'Yes,' she says carefully, 'but you've been back since then.'

'Back?'

'A few times.' She stops, sitting still in her seat as I slow down, looking at her.

'What are you talking about?' I ask quietly.

'You've been out a bit over a week,' she says and I can tell she's gauging my reaction. 'You were there for a couple of months before that.'

'And before that?' My voice sounds faint even to my own ears.

'Before that,' Jen says, 'four months.' She smiles, gives me the look she uses when she's tiptoeing around something hard. 'We think this last time might have been it. You're getting better. Really.'

'I don't remember,' I say, numb.

'You're on some pretty heavy meds, darling, trust me. Sometimes you,' she pauses, looks around as if to find someone to help her get through this, 'sometimes you just, you know, blackout.' Her expression turns painfully optimistic. 'But that's OK — because you're on the mend. It'll all come back in a couple of hours, believe me.'

I rub my head, my fingers travelling on autopilot over my stubbly scalp, not short but bald, mapping the strange contours they find. They ride across small ridges that seem so unfamiliar, without hair. 'What the hell?'

Jen can't meet my gaze. 'We had to do what we had to do, Alice.'

I stand up from the swing, both hands rubbing my scalp. 'What did they do to me?'

Jen grabs me and stares at me hard. I can see her searching for something; she's looking for her sister and isn't sure she's seeing her yet. 'There were therapies.' She holds up her hands. 'They weren't invasive, but you'd started to pull your hair out. They needed to cut it to stop you from hurting yourself.'

An impression comes back, murky and frustrating. Another hint, full of potential. 'I cut my hair,' I said, my tone echoing the faintness of the memory.

Jen shakes her head. 'Honey, that's what you keep saying but...' She breathes through some personal recollection. I wait while Jen, usually strong and optimistic, bottles away her demons. Maybe for the first time, I wonder what the toll of living with me has been. I'm shocked I've never thought about it before, and it leaves me feeling small. 'But honey,' Jen says after she's collected herself' 'you haven't had the dream for two weeks now. We think you might be,' She searches for the word. Her lips begin to form the shape for cured. Instead, making some internal compromise, she says again, 'better.'

'Better? What did you do, lobotomise me?'

Jen shakes her head. 'Of course not.'

'No.'

I wait for the anger, the shock, or any one of the other emotions that storm through my inner life, but I'm calm, almost serene. It's a different coolness from what I'd experienced at the shop, a disconnection that's nothing to do with fading out. It's not that I don't know where I am and what I'm doing, it just doesn't matter.

'It'll pass,' says Jen at my ear. 'You're a little disoriented from the drugs. It comes and goes. They're still working out the right doses.' She shakes her head, the echo of a smile crossing her face. 'Alice, it'll be OK.'

I nod.

That night, as I curl up with Ratbone already asleep on the bed, I wonder. The scent from the rosebushes in front of my window keeps me awake for a long time. I hate roses.

59

3AM

As I blink owlishly in the almost complete darkness of the bedroom, I'm confused. Then I hear the purring. 'Holy shit,' I whisper. I roll over the covers, startling Ratbone who complains with a strange, uncatlike squeak before jumping free of my legs, which I fling out of bed.

I stare at all the familiar shadows in astonishment, leap to the light switch daring the room to vanish. As I squint against the painfully bright bulb I scan my bedroom like it's the very first time I've seen it. 'Holy, fucking shit!'

I scream out loud as I pelt towards the bathroom, exploding through the door and hammering on the lights in one fluid move, momentum banging me up into the basin with a yelp. My own elation stares right back at me from the mirror. Jen's footsteps thump down the hall.

'Alice, what's wrong?'

I turn to her when she arrives, struggling to see her through a sudden deluge of tears.

'Alice?'

'It's me,' I say. 'I'm here. I fucking woke up fucking here!'

I fling myself at her, sweeping her into a massive hug and spin around. Jen grins wide and crazy, holding on as we turn a wobbly circle, bumping into things and laughing.

She slows us down eventually and looks at me closely. 'So, no New York?'

I shake my head like a child, grinning. 'Nope.' Grabbing her by the arms I spin her around one more time. 'I went to bed last night and woke up this morning in the same place.' It's so crazy I can't believe it. I make a wordless, breathless sound. 'Holyfuckingcrap!' Then I start spinning again, pulling Jen with me and yelling until we both crash into the towel rack. We burst out laughing, lost in my happiness.

Slowly, we stop. 'Jen, take me surfing.'

'What, now?'

I nod. 'Right now.'

I'M BABBLING and don't care. I cover everything as we walk across the cold sand of the empty beach. Waves break darkly offshore, filling the morning air with the sound of artillery fire. 'He told me about these new anti-psychotics,' I say, struggling with the light but awkward shape of her old surfboard, 'so I broke into his office and took a few. Then everything turns totally fucking batshit and I wake up at the shop yesterday.' Jen walks quietly beside me, arms around her own board as she listens.

I pause, taking a moment to breathe. The predawn light paints the sea in deep, brooding greens and blues. Everything is different, more alive.

'So,' says Jen as we reach a point on the beach and rest, 'someone from your dream told you to stop dreaming and you did?'

'It makes perfect sense,' I say, 'If it's got to happen anywhere, it's there, right?'

Jen puts her board down. 'I'm not going to say I get it.' She studies me in the growing light. 'You know you haven't dreamed of New York for over a week, right?'

'I don't fucking remember that part at all,' I admit, catching something in her reaction. 'What's wrong?'

'Nothing, babe,' she says, 'but you want to ease up on the f-bomb a bit?'

'Prude.'

Jen laughs. 'Fuck yeah.' She smiles at me as she sits and listens to the breakers. 'Alice?'

'Yeah?'

'You don't need to rush things.'

I sit on the sand next to her and give her a small hug. 'I know.' I breathe deeply, inhaling the ocean smells. 'I don't understand why I can't remember the last week. Shit, right now I can't even remember being at Mayfleur, but what the hell.' Jen's expression darkens for a second. 'All I know is I'm here, now. And, I'm going to take that.'

She nods. 'One day at a time?'

'Something like that.'

'So, how about getting wet?'

I stand up and help her get to her feet. 'That's what we're here for.' I pick up the board and look into the brightening expanse of ocean. The waves are visible now, massive curls of water exploding down on the break. Foam sprays into the air, red-lit and glinting diamond-like in the first rays of the sun. 'Wow,' I say.

'We won't be going that far out,' says Jen, half smiling. 'Not yet.'

I nod and start changing into Jen's spare wetsuit.

Minutes later as we walk towards the water, I look over at my sister. 'Jen, how did I get to Mayfleur?'

'You agreed you needed to be there,' she says, 'you, me and Ryan talked about it one night — the whole night. You didn't think it was a good idea; you fought like hell to tell the truth. In the end you came round.'

We wade into the surf and the first cold water surges up to my knees. 'Shit,' I whisper.

'You OK?'

I try to smile but can't. My face becomes as pale as the foam that washes around me and just like that I'm scared all over again. I back away from the water as a hint of my own shadow stretches ahead of me, daring me to go further. 'I can't,' I say. 'I'm sorry, Jen, I can't do it.' The backwash sucks at my legs, forming liquid rills that collapse and churn in the sandy water. The cannon-fire waves get louder. I shake my head and turn away from it all, retreating back to the loose dry sand of the beach.

'Don't worry about it,' she says walking beside me, 'you can't expect two miracles in the same day.'

I nod, not trusting myself to speak.

'One step at a time, remember?' With a smile I give in to her optimism. 'So,' she says after a while, 'you don't mind if I —?' I wave her on. No sense in wasting the morning.

Leaning across to kiss me on the cheek, Jen turns and wades back into the sea, her slick wetsuit figure seal-like and lithe in the waves. I sit and run my fingers over the sand, enjoying the texture. Behind me the sun inches upwards through a scattering of red-bloomed clouds, sending long blue shadows across the beach and into the water. Jen's turned into a silhouette against the wall of greens and churning dark that is the ocean. I watch as my sister ducks under the foam and pops to the surface, red hair slicked, vital and alive and literally in her element. She waves, straddling the board. I wave back.

I smile. Jen's right. One day at a time. As I think this, something inside unwinds. A tiny tremor, barely there at all, but for the hint of greater change.

I'M GOING EXPLORING. Driven by this calm curiosity I'm intrigued by the places I live in, familiar yet changed by my waking. I know how strange that sounds but it's true. Everything's the same, except now there's a stamp of truth to it all, which is all the difference in the world. It's like seeing things for the very first time.

I stay at the beach long after Jen leaves, walk the small paths under the growing heat of the day. I watch people flocking to the water, some content to play at its edges, others plunging deep and far, past the waves to the place where the swells move like muscles. Out there, the pure daylight blue changes into a deeper, more mysterious colour. I catch a bus, one of the newer air-conditioned ones and sit staring out the window as it drives around the smaller streets and larger arterial roads, making its stops with gas-compressed hisses. For no particular reason I get off at a random stop and wander through a strange, oddly empty park before winding my way back towards the house. I'm touching base with reality, after all this time. I don't know exactly why I go to the places I do, but it feels familiar and right to do it.

There are gaps in my knowledge; I've been warned to expect that. It's an odd sensation to be partially amnesic, to have gulfs in my personal timeline. My time at Mayfleur is a blank, as are the days after I left. Jen's told me not to push;

these memories will come back in their own time and in their own way. I'll remember to bring it up with Ryan.

It's so good to just be me, one person with one life; a crazy luxury no one else will ever understand. I feel the heat in the air, the sweat in my pores. My stubbly scalp prickles under the rays of the sun, a sure sign sunburn's on its way. It's a tiny, real life annoyance. I open the door to my house and go to the kitchen to fetch a drink of water. Small, domestic things.

In the shower that night I make a point of washing my buzz-cut with a medicated shampoo, ignoring the sting of the soap as I wonder how long it will take for my hair to regrow. Maybe a wig? No, the idea of wearing a disguise is wrong; I've had enough of illusions. As the hot water courses over me I can't quite bring myself to believe I'll be waking in the same bed I'm going to sleep in. Maybe I'll dream, a normal dream. I wipe a circle of steam from the glass, enough to see through to the mirror. But it's my hand, not my face that catches my attention. I turn it over to examine my palm — the old cut fresh again and an angry, painful red.

A flash of memory takes me to the warehouse and I remember cutting it on the broken glass of the basement window. I touch it and wince, wondering if I'll need to wrap it in something. Then I get it. If Jen had been telling the truth, the wound should have had months to heal.

I stand under the tap until the hot water runs out, lost in thought. Then just lost.

IMMORTALITY

She lied to me.

A false dawn lights up the eastern sky with a hint of fire and promise, the almost-there sun brightening the air above the sea. It catches the clouds, which are ponderous, heavy and anvil shaped. They glow with it, all purple and steely grey; great big airborne mountains threatening thunder and rain later in the day. I can't wait. Right now though, it's just hot.

I'm wearing my loose tracksuit as I slowly swing the detector coil back and forth across the cool beach. I meditate on the dolphin sounds it makes, the whistles and groans of buried treasure talking to me from under the sand. They want to be found, these little lost things underneath.

I try to keep my thoughts still as I walk, only stopping when the signal gets strong enough. Digging, I take a moment to examine a small, rusted locket the detector's picked up. I drop it into my bag and pulling off the headphones reorient myself. The usual early risers are walking or surfing, everyone staking their territory in their own way.

The machine squeals again, surprising me with such a loud signal, so much stronger than the others. I jump, shocked at the sound. It's lucky I'm not wearing the headset. I sweep the coil back and forth, pinpointing the source, kneel down and dig some wire from just under the surface. I grab a loop and pull at it, following it into a low clump of leathery beach plants.

Wires like this are common. It's probably a relic of an old fence, exposed by a recent high tide, but I'm curious. Still kneeling, I follow the rusted curves through matted roots then out again until it submerges itself into a mound, burrowing away from the growing light. I push the sand away and yank the wire, sensing something give. I'm not prepared to let it go without seeing what's at the other end. A bulge forms and I scoop out a hole, the salt irritating the cut in my palm as I pile mounds higher and higher in dim light. Coiling a loose loop of the rusty metal around my hand I brace myself and wrench hard. Something explodes free and I fall backwards, showered by icy wet clumps. I rub the grains from my eyes, at first not even recognising what I'm seeing.

It's heavy, cold and limp; a dead thing in my hands. I pull off clumps of seaweed and brush loose the remaining sand, untangling it from the wire. Lifting it up, exposing it to the growing light something inside me falls away. It's a rag doll mermaid, its long plaited red hair still wet from the ground.

I CAN HEAR Ratbone yowling before I walk through the door. As I go in I'm confronted by the cat, his back arched, fur fluffed and eyes wide. 'Shh,' I say, trying to calm him, but he backs off, fixated on my bag. I reach inside and hold up my discovery, feeling the damp knots of wool. 'You don't like it either, do you?' I say. 'Me neither, but I'm keeping it anyway.' I lean the metal detector on the wall and go to my bedroom, where Ratbone lays down flat on the covers, his eyes locked on the doll. 'Why don't you stay here and guard the room?'

I search for a place to put it then spot the bear, the ugly toy daring me to throw it away. I can't, like I can't throw away the mermaid-doll resembling Jen. Looking at the teddy bear I remember the building, the basement, the girl again. And that Jen lied to me.

I put them together. For some reason they are better like this, the bear, with its bedraggled jacket and round glasses next to the Jen-like rag doll. I wonder what she would make of it. It's hard to explain, but a part of me whispers I'm doing something wrong, staring at those broken, dirty, toys.

I move quietly through the house, aware of the subtle snoring coming from Jen's room. I can't confront her. I don't even know her anymore. I keep myself busy with the small stuff, preparing for the day, covering the hundred little things that need doing before going to work, but my heart's not in it. I check back a couple of times on the cat, who still refuses to settle. Ducking into the room on my way out, I stroke his fluffy, static-charged fur gently, feeling the snap of miniature lightning under my fingers. 'You be good now, crazy cat,' I whisper, experiencing something too much like loss. Before I leave I glance at the toys on the bookcase making a last minute decision to put them into my bag.

I think I'm saying goodbye to things.

I can't say why Jen lied, or what Ryan is doing, but I don't want to be here anymore. Funny really, after all this time I would have thought I'd head straight for the airport and get a ticket, just like those other times I've tried. It's not going to happen that way. Instead, I might hop on a bus, simple as that. There's no real destination in mind, maybe south to Melbourne. Try my luck there and start again, but before that, the shop. One more time at least, then I'll understand what to do.

Things are quiet all over: not many cars on the road, not many people on the street. Which is good. Today of all days, quiet is good. Somewhere in the background of my mind, things are rearranging, connections breaking and remaking. And below everything else — a small, tingling sense of urgency. I glance at the heavy clouds above, and realise this strange experience is anticipation.

The phone's ringing as I unlock the shop, a hollow sound in the green-filled space. I go to the counter and answer it, surprised our old-fashioned answering machine hasn't triggered. The voice on the other end of the line is quick and efficient, telling me Ryan needs to cancel the appointment for the day and I've been rebooked for tomorrow, if it was OK with me. I don't want to see him again, so it's fine.

I replace the receiver, which is a ridiculously antique thing, back into its cradle. I wonder why I've never seen it that way before, but the old beige plastic is prehistoric. As I round the counter I notice other things, equally ancient. Light fittings, switches, the electric cash register. It's not as if we'd chosen retro for the decor, they're just old. It shouldn't bother me, not now, but the shop is different, not perfect anymore.

I lean on the workbench and stare at the window, stretching out to pick up the pruning knife. I examine the blade carefully before slowly and lightly drawing it over my palm. I push harder, watching my skin growing taut before breaking, a tiny bead of bright-red blood pooling around the tip of the knife. I remember doing this before, using the pain to prove I'm real, but now I can't believe in it. I wince as it starts to sting, then after a second hurt like hell. The phone rings again and I expect it to be a customer. Which is why it takes me a few seconds to react to the strange breathing on the line.

'Alice?' The voice is tight and breathy, I can hear the tension in the clipped, almost strangled way he says my name.

'Yes?'

'Alice, this is Lavar.' There's a pause. 'I don't know if you remember me.'

His name means something to me, but I struggle to recall what it is. Even as he speaks I sense other memories falling into place, the earlier sensation of urgency heightening to a point that's just short of physical. I glance at my hand, intrigued by the vibrant, almost painted on redness. It hurts but I don't care. It doesn't matter.

'Lavar,' I whisper, 'the psychic?' There's laughter, an empty, defeated sound.

'Yeah,' he says, 'that's me.'

I go to push back my hair, surprised again at the stubble there instead. 'You went missing.' More memories are coming back.

'I need to see you,' he says.

'Why?'

'It's to do with your dreams.'

'What about them? You can tell me over the phone.'

Again, the laughter. As much as it sounds like it's coming from a crazy man, there's no menace in it. The sound is the quiet voice of someone laughing at themselves. 'Where are you?' I ask.

He tells me. I more or less know the place and with the same sense of connections reshaping in the back of my mind, agree to meet him there. As I hang up, I glance at my bag and its ugly cargo of toys. I throw in the knife.

61

UNDERPASS

I have to be careful; people can get into trouble here. A graffiti-tagged metro train surges past the station with an explosive clatter of rolling stock and blast of hot wind. As I shield my eyes from the sting of dust, the air's filled with a stench of ozone and harried electrics. I stare at the sky. The clouds still hold their promise of a storm. Even now the humidity is oppressive, plastering my blouse to my skin in uncomfortable folds. The air, once the stink of the train is gone, smells a different kind of electric.

I'm at a concreted-in bank of a small creek, turned ad-hoc marina for local fishermen. An untidy string of fibreglass boats sit still and quiet in the low water, their prows tied like a bunch of faded balloons to fence-post pilings. It reeks of dead fish.

Lavar's standing in front of an underpass at the end of a concrete path. Half in shadow, he spots me too and waves. It's a furtive, jerky motion. I grasp my bag tightly against myself and nod to him, then not knowing if he saw that, wave as well. As far as secret rendezvous go, this one needs some work.

When I get to him he looks scared. I'm the one who should be scared. He falls back into the shadows of the underpass. What little I can see of him in there freaks me out. His face is white and mottled with clumpy growths of a beard coming through in patches. His eyes are the thing that worry me though. They're dark, baggy and wild. Dad used to read me books about trolls and dank things living under bridges. Not so good, dwelling on those stories right now. His clothes are filthy, white shirt yellowed and torn in places, and as I get nearer to him I smell the rank stink of sweat and other things. I slow down as I near the entrance.

The underpass isn't much more than a small concrete tunnel, wide enough for three people with a low ceiling and a single old-fashioned fluorescent tube. The walls are missing graffiti, which is strange. It's disturbing that a place can be so invisible, forgotten. I follow the pathway down a final slope leading to the mouth of the tunnel and stop. I'm not taking another step 'So,' I say. 'What's going on?'

He stares at me from the darkness, fascinated by the bear and doll poking up from my bag. 'I know who you are,' he says. I wait for him to go on as he leans against a wall and lights up a cigarette. His hands are trembling violently. 'You are the Devil and God and nothing all at the same time.' I shake my head, attempting to hide the fact he's scaring the hell out of me. How could I have been so stupid to come here?

'What makes you say that?' I say, instinctively trying to buy time as I look quickly behind me, thoroughly aware I'm alone with him.

He taps his head, smiles with dead eyes.

'Listen,' I say, 'you need some help.' He laughs at that, drawing shakily on the cigarette.

'It was stupid,' he says at last.

'What?'

'Running. I knew it the first second I met you. You can't run from the Devil.'

'I'm not the Devil.'

'OK.' He doesn't argue the point.

His words are chilling. I hold my bag in front of me as if it's some sort of shield, slowly backing away. What the hell am I doing here? What did I expect he could tell me? I have a flash that I'm going to die in this place and all of a sudden I care a whole damn lot about living. 'Look,' I say, 'I've got enough fucked up stuff in my life and I don't need any more. I'm sorry you...' I wave my hands vaguely, trying to capture what he's become before giving up. 'I thought you had something to say to me.' I take another slow step backwards. If I try and run for it, he'll chase me.

He reaches into his pocket — I freeze. It's not the gun, a black snub-shape he pulls on me, it's his expression that makes me stop. 'I had to meet you again,' he says. His voice is calmer now and that scares me even more. I feel the blood rush away from my head in dizzying surges. 'What do you want?' I whisper.

'What we all want, a second chance,' he says in a strange echo of my conversation with Olen. There's a powdery grin on his face, 'But it won't work. See?' He points the gun at me and fires.

The gunshot sounds like a branch snapping and there's a muffled impact behind me. I open my mouth, paralysed by shock — while Lavar, his arm outstretched and aiming the pistol directly at me, fires a second time. The bullet misses again, glancing off something metallic to my right. I raise my hands to him.

'Please don't.' I can't run. I want to but I can't.

He emerges from the shadowy tunnel, white face

blotched with red; cigarette hanging stupidly from his lips, stinking and torn. He's a nightmare come to destroy me. His eyes are glassy, tearful, pupils so wide they're almost completely black. I need to run, but my body betrays me like it always does. All I can do is cry and watch as he raises the gun, now stinking of spent powder, to my forehead. The tip of the barrel burns. 'Please,' I beg.

He fires.

I don't have time to close my eyes, so I catch his expression as the bullet jams. He's not surprised. Beyond the used-up smell of him and shaking husk of his face, there's a detached, intellectual assessment. It's the look of a doctor discovering some new, horrible disease. 'See?' he says again.

I don't see anything. I stare at him. 'I had to try though.' His tone has become almost conversational. He laughs weakly.

I find something of my voice. 'What do you mean?'

'You're immortal,' he says without any inflection. 'You can't die. I could fire every bullet in this gun and I'd miss. I could stab you but the knife would break.' He starts crying. 'You never know until you try, though.'

I start shaking. 'You're not making sense.'

He falls to his knees, whatever clarity he had now gone. 'I'm sorry,' he says, his voice choked with emotion. 'I had to be sure.' He stares up at me, holding his hand out. 'Can you make me better? Make me, me again and better?'

I back away, my legs finally figuring out how to move. 'I don't understand what you mean,' I say in a whisper. My emotions have tripped full circle and I'm almost sorry for him. If I wasn't shaking so much. 'You need to put the gun down.'

'You can't die,' he says between bouts of shivers. 'I needed to know for sure. But I can.' He turns the weapon around, puts the barrel in his mouth and pulls the trigger. The gunshot is masked by the sound of an express train thundering over the tunnel.

A red mist appears behind his head and he drops. I stand there, frozen to the spot looking at his body. Whoever Lavar was, he's gone, but his words buzz and sting my mind like wasps. A train passes, water laps quietly, boats bob against each other and the day goes on as usual. I reach up with a trembling hand and wipe away something from my face. My fingers are bloody. On the ground in front of me, the corpse of Lavar stares up at the clouds, his expression still locked at that point of understanding. I make a sound, some wordless, meaningless choke as I shake all over again.

My blouse is stained pink and it reeks of the strong iron tang of blood. I start shivering and soon it turns into a full body quake threatening to pull my legs from under me. I fight it, forcing myself to walk step by jerky step up the rise to a patch of burned brown grass nearby, where I collapse to my knees. My mind is a cloud of confusion and fear, disowning what I've just seen. But I keep replaying it, moment by horrible moment. I stay that way until something hot and wet slaps my neck and I jerk.

There's no one around, the creek and its tiny moorings as deserted now as when I arrived. I look up at the sky, my face blank and accepting. Above me lightning flashes inside the storm clouds, lighting their blue-black edges with a searchlight glare. Thunder rolls slowly all around and rain, heavy and relentless, begins to fall.

And it's still hot.

62

RAIN

I'm cut free of things, almost weightless.

The rain comes down like hard stones. It hammers off rooftops, batters the solid baked soil, smashes and steams on the black bitumen roads as it evaporates. It cools quickly too, turning icy after the first few drops. The city goes dark in the storm causing streetlights to turn on, their cones of light visible against the cascade. I've left the glassy-eyed corpse of Lavar behind me. I don't care who finds him. He said I couldn't die, but no one's immortal. No one who's awake at least.

The rain has thrown the city into confusion and cleared the streets as drivers wait out the squall. I eventually catch a bus, an old stuttering diesel that should have been retired years ago. I pay the driver for my ticket, noticing I'm the only passenger before taking a seat near a window. As the bus' wipers screech and shudder across its broad windscreen, smearing the water but not removing it, I wonder how he can see anything at all. Tail lights from the cars ahead transform into bizarre Rorschach patterns, street lamps become odd dribbling eyes.

The cloth seat stinks of old sweat and rain and the window next to me is fogged from the humidity. I need to talk to someone. I stare at the rag doll in my bag, its red plaits so similar to Jen's and have to fight back a sense of connection that's been growing more urgent, even through my ordeal with Lavar. The stink of the seat, the percussion of rain, the traffic; all serve as distractions. I grab the plastic handle at the end of my seat until my palm tingles, forcing me to focus on my body and its demand to be believed. I can't manage it.

I've missed my chance to run, if I ever had one. I try to unravel the lies but they're too dense. I need to talk to someone, someone who can help, but if this is all a dream, then it's all me anyway. Everything's me.

The last of my confusion drops away, washed clear like the rain on the windscreen. I remember the girl again and that Ryan took her. The child is me and she's my way out.

THE LANDETH CENTRE'S car park is a lake with inch high swells howling across the surface launching spray into the dark air. I splash through it fighting hard to stay upright in the gale, doing my best to shield my eyes from the sting of water. The building's a bunker in this storm and most of its lights are out. I pray Ryan is here.

I burst through the doors; I'm shocked by the contrast of quiet and warmth in the reception. Cold rivulets fall from my clothes and pool on the floor. For a wheeling, out-of-control second I begin shivering, suspecting I might faint. I force it back. There's no time for that anymore. That weightlessness is still with me, pushing me on. If I'm finally going mad, then OK, but I know what I have to do.

Ryan is in his office because in my world, he has to be. He looks up as I push through the door, putting down the book he's reading. 'Alice,' he says, covering his surprise.

I glance around, half expecting to find another patient, but I'm alone with him. 'I need you to tell me what's going on,' I say, beginning to shiver again despite myself.

He gets up quickly. Guiding me to one of the chairs he goes into the small bathroom adjoining his office, returning with a towel. 'Here, get warm,' he says sitting. His eyes are large, framed by his circular glasses, his hair scruffy as if he's been raking his hands through it moments before. As I wrap the blanket around my shoulders he seems younger than ever. The Klimt on the wall behind his desk glints as a spear of lightning flashes through the sky. I look out the window at the storm.

'The weather's broken at last,' he says.

'Ryan,' I say looking at him, 'you need to tell me the truth.'

He takes my hands and leans in close. For a second I think he's going to kiss me. 'It's just a storm. A bad one, for sure, but nothing we haven't had before.'

'The truth,' I say. 'I saw a man kill himself. He tried to murder me.'

He raises his eyebrows. 'What? Did you know him?' He thinks for a moment. 'You called the police?'

'It was Lavar, the clairvoyant I told you about. He figured it out. He wanted to prove it to me.'

'Prove what to you?' His voice takes an edge.

I stare at him. I'm not going to let him escape this. 'This really is the dream. I don't think you're real. I don't think anything here is real.' The cut on my hand stings fiercely, as if the mere fact of the pain will change my mind. I hold on to his hand, ignoring the ache in mine. It's bad enough believing you're dreaming. How much worse must it be to realise you were someone else's imagined thing? Poor Ryan.

I feel him freeze. 'Alice,' he says after a second, 'we've been through this.'

I lean down and pull out the bear, the girl's bear, her ugly drenched toy with its round glasses, exactly like Ryan's and patched jacket, exactly like Ryan's. 'I don't know why,' I say, 'but this is you somehow, isn't it?'

He tenses even further. He lets go of my hand and stands up. 'Of course it's not.'

'Olen said the girl was an image of myself,' I say, 'and he's right, isn't he?' He doesn't answer me, so I stand up as well, looking closely at his young face. 'This bear was hers.'

'Alice,' he says, 'you are quoting a fiction from your dream, talking about a girl who doesn't exist. How do you expect me to respond to that?'

I examine the ugly thing in my hands, and next to it, the mermaid doll with Jen's hair. 'Just tell me the truth.' He shakes his head and stares out of the window. The rain lashes at the glass and I turn to face the noise. 'If this is the dream, what's it for? Why won't you help me?'

He moves to my side. 'We are all helping you, the best way we're able, but we can only help you as much as you are willing to help yourself. Alice, we need to get you back to Mayfleur. The treatments were working, you'd put all this behind you. We can try again.'

'I don't believe that happened,' I say quietly, refusing to play his game any more.

'There are records,' he begins, but stops himself. 'You genuinely think this isn't real? You've decided at last?'

I look at him. 'Yes.'

'Well, if you're dreaming,' he says reasonably, 'why don't you choose to wake up?'

I stare across the car park lake, through the rain smashing against the window. 'I've tried. I can't'

'There's a simple explanation for that.'

'This is the dream,' I say again.

He reaches across to a tall bookshelf and grabbing the tennis ball, starts tossing it from hand to hand. 'So if you think I'm a figment of your imagination,' he says, his voice cool reason, 'why come here?'

'I trusted you,' I say quietly. 'Why did you lie to me?'

'Alice, I've done nothing to betray your trust.'

I look at him again, trying to figure out if there's a soul behind those glasses, someone real or something I've somehow magicked into life. The idea is horrible and claustrophobic.

'Where did you take the girl?'

He bounces the ball sharply off the wall and catches it. 'There is no girl.'

'Fuck it Ryan, I saw you drive off with her. I didn't imagine it.'

'Alice,' he says calmly, his tone patronising, 'calm down.'

'Don't fucking tell me what to do.'

He throws the ball again and snaps it from the air.

'Stop that,' I say.

He glances at me before turning away. 'I'm not going to indulge you any more,' he replies, throwing the ball once again. I follow it as it leaves his hand and bounces back, his fingers grabbing it mid-flight.

'Stop it. I want to see the girl.'

'She isn't real.' Bounce. Snap. The ball punctuates his words like a slap.

'You are not real.'

He shakes his head. Bounce. Snap. 'We are not having a

rational conversation Alice.' Bounce. Snap. 'Listen to yourself.'

'Ryan!' The sound of the ball is more than a distraction. With every beat I find it harder to think.

'I am not going to be party to your self-destruction.' Bounce. 'The girl is imaginary.' Snap. He stares at me, all traces of his happy easy-going nature gone. 'We need to start again. We need to get you back to Mayfleur.' He throws the ball.

I snatch it from the air. 'What did you do to her?'

'Alice,' he says, anger surfacing. 'The child is a symbol. She's not real.'

I shove him. 'Why are you doing this to me?'

He steps back before striding over to his desk where he picks up the phone.

'Who are you calling?'

He ignores me, jabbing buttons. There's a moment as he studies me, some expression on his face I can't begin to identify before he calls security. I hurl the tennis ball at him; it misses and bounces harmlessly off some cardboard legal boxes. 'You're all fucking symbols!' He begins to say something but I reach into my bag and snatch out the blade, twisting so that I'm behind him holding it to his neck. He drops the handset. 'What did you do with the girl,' I yell, 'I need her!'

'Why?'

'Because she knows how I can wake up.'

'How do you know that?'

I don't. I just believe it. I tell him that. As I hold the knife against his throat, I realise there's no coming back from this. I either get to her, or from here it will be a trip to Mayfleur, or worse. They'll drug me and I'll lose. Ryan senses some of what I'm thinking because he struggles slightly under my grip.

'Alice!' He risks trying to turn, but I hang on to him solidly.

'I saw you take her,' I say quietly. 'I don't want to hurt you, but I will if you don't tell me how to find her.'

He struggles for a second longer, stopping only when the edge of metal bites into his skin. 'Alice!'

'I'm serious,' I say. 'Stop lying.'

He tests the blade one final time again before slumping slightly as sheet lightning slithers through the storm clouds outside. 'Alice,' he says, 'don't go somewhere you can't get back from.'

'That's the whole point,' I say, eyes tearing. 'Take me to her.'

'This isn't you, Alice' he whispers, minimising the movement of his throat.

'This is exactly me,' I say. 'New York-me, Sydney-me, I don't think I can tell the difference anymore. I can't die here. You can.' I twitch the knife, drawing a line of blood and he gasps. I hate to do it but he needs to believe me.

'Alice,' he says, 'think about it. Think about the logic. If this really is a dream then it's not you doing the dreaming. You are as much a creation as everything else. If you wake up, then you die.'

I pull the blade a little harder. 'Where is she?'

Without warning he starts struggling, tries to duck and push away but I hang on. There's a brutal, short-lived fight before he finally gives in, panting and wincing at the line of blood at his neck.

He slumps. 'All right.'

I sag as well. That's it, the last of the illusion gone away.

I'm not vindicated, just relieved and at the same time, heartbroken. 'So take me to her.'

'It's complicated. She's in a hospital.'

But at the end of it all, I'm tired. 'Ryan, why did you lie?'

He puts his fingertips to the edge of the knife and pushes gently, just so. He doesn't struggle and I don't resist, instead allowing him to turn and face me. The skin under his Adam's apple is red and bleeding and I feel bad about hurting him. 'I don't know who she is,' he says as I allow him to push the blade further away. He could snatch it if he wants, but instead he leaves it in my hands. 'If I'm honest, she scares me, but it doesn't mean this is a dream.'

'Take me to her now, Ryan.'

'I can't...'

'Please.'

He takes my fingers in his, looks deep into my eyes, defiant and defeated at the same time. 'If I do this, I'll lose my license. I'll be taken off your case.' The words sound scripted and I don't know why he's still clinging to it. But he waits for me to acknowledge this. 'We've gone as far as we can go. But whatever happens after you meet her, swear to me you'll go back to Mayfleur. That you won't run.'

I nod. It doesn't matter. The girl is my last chance anyway.

'I promise.'

63

THE GIRL AND THE STORM

We drive without speaking. It's too noisy; the cabin's filled with the sound of the rain and the wet sluice of tyres as the car ploughs through the storm. Everything's watery. Ryan's face is lit by the glow of the instrument panel, a washed-out green that makes him look like a drowned man. I start to ask something then stop myself, letting him focus. I don't know what there is to say now, anyway.

I begin to recognise roads and ask him exactly which hospital she's in, but he shakes his head. After another few minutes of driving, he tells me it's not Mayfleur, if that's what I'm worried about.

I hate that I pulled the knife on him, but I couldn't figure out any other way. What a fucked up thing to do though, he doesn't deserve it. I've wrecked whatever trust there may have been between us. Then I catch myself. He's a dream. It's so hard to let go of what used to be real.

Ryan steers his hatchback through a pool of water on the road and the car bucks as it kicks up dirty bow waves littered with cans and other rubbish. I twist in my seat to catch the name of the street but miss it in all the spray. 'Where exactly is this hospital?' I ask. Maybe I've made another mistake and he's taking me to the cops.

'Close,' he murmurs. He's distracted.

But he's not doing that. As we pass a row of houses I finally know where I am. 'Ryan?' He doesn't look at me, instead flicks on the indicator and turns into the muddy lot of the abandoned warehouse.

Except it's not abandoned. I lean closer to the windshield staring at the building, its windows blazing with warm light made liquid by the sweep of the wipers. It's somehow softened and stretched under the weak beams of the headlights. The watery illumination has turned it into some sort of cold-weather mirage. I glance at Ryan, but his face is expressionless. After a weird, still moment he blinks and glances at me. 'We're here.'

We open the doors into the icy rain. Ryan walks around the car, his feet sinking deep into the oily mud. He takes my hand and his touch is gentle but cold. 'She's here,' he says with a strange, glassy look. If I had any doubts about this being the dream they're gone. With every second he seems to be growing more disconnected and confused. More puppet-like. More like a toy.

I stare at my bag, which is soaked like the rest of me, filled with the bear and the red-haired doll. What's life going to be like without Jen, my optimist best friend big sister? Ryan tugs my good hand. 'This way.'

He pulls me gently and I follow him to the back of the building. A rose-scented gust of wind buffets us both and he turns to me, an uncertain smile on his face. I glance down through the broken window, now clear of glass into the space beneath. It's lit with a cold white light. 'Where are we, Ryan?'

'At the hospital.' His voice is distant, disconnected.

I kneel in the freezing mud. Other than the stark illumination the room is exactly as before. The same jumble of abandoned furniture piled against the wall gives me a haphazard staircase down. I begin to lower myself into the basement but pause as a figure emerges from the dark. It's Jen, her face tight and struggling, like she's fighting hard to remember something. I try not to cry as she walks up to me, looking as lost as Ryan. She opens her arms wordlessly and hugs me. I don't know what I can say, so I just hug her back. We separate at last and I kneel, dropping through the window.

The girl's waiting, still dirty but clear of emotion. She holds out her hand and I take it and draw her to the rusty door. I pull back on the handle expecting it to open easily, shocked to find it still locked. I turn to her seeking an answer but she stares at me, waiting. It's still up to me. I look around, wondering what I've missed when I feel something in my pocket. The girl stands at my side patiently as I remove the keys I'd taken from Olen's office in my old family home in Manhattan. I don't question the impossibility as the first one I try fits perfectly.

The door opens easily, which is a surprise. The room on the other side is utterly black, but I know there's something there. The sound I heard before, that machinery noise is clear now. I'm terrified and grip the girl's hand tighter. She pulls me on as I draw back in fear, but she's strong. It's pointless fighting it. This is what I'm here to do. Everyone's played their part and now it's my turn. So despite my heart beating wildly, I let myself be lead into the darkness.

And in the instant before everything goes away, I hear her say, 'Thank you.'

IT'S some sort of maintenance room.

It's bright, lit by heavy-duty incandescent bulbs high in the ceiling and so, so hot. Sweltering and stinking of old rot, the bare concrete floor is damp and warm under my feet. Remnants of dirty wallpaper hang from the walls in horrible shreds. I can see a window that's been blacked out with paint, but it's peeled away in places, allowing a view of roses scratching against the glass from outside. Nearby there's a hiss of steam and those machines again.

The girl is here. She's slumped on a water-stained mattress in the corner of the room. Above her, a poster that's almost completely come free from the wall. My eyes are drawn to the floor in front of her. Lined up near the rags of bedding in a row are her toys. Not only the bear and the mermaid-doll, but a cat, a fat business man and a worried looking scientist, who might be Lavar. All of my Sydney family. I walk over to her and kneel down. The mattress stinks of mildew.

'Where are we?' I ask.

The girl looks up at me, expression tense and wired like she's waiting for something. She nods at the poster behind her and I stand and push back the corners that have come loose so I can see it. It's old and rubbed bare in places, but the sails of the Sydney Opera House are clear against a cloudless blue sky. I let the tattered edges drop back down, steeling myself. 'I want to go there one day,' says the girl.

I kneel by her side again. 'Why are you here?'

'I'm going to get out of here,' she says, her face determined. 'And then I'll come back and get him.'

'Who?'

A hollow clank echoes through the room. With a protest

of metal on metal the door shudders open. The girl tenses behind me and starts shaking, her breath quick and faint. Ignoring my fear, I put myself in front of her as a figure emerges from the blackness.

God I'm in a nightmare.

It's tall, something made out of darkness, too-long limbs clicking under janitor's overalls. Its face is a pale, shimmering blob from the neck up. It carries a bowl and next to it on a tray, the long slender shape of a hypodermic. The girl's hand seeks my own, crushing it in panic. 'He's going to make me sleep again,' she says, 'he always makes me sleep. Help me.' But I can't. My breathing is almost as fast as hers.

I do my best to fight back my terror at this faceless, almost-formed thing. I want to ask her how I can help her, but the words catch in my throat, squeezed shut in the grip of a panic attack.

The man-shaped monster takes a step closer and the girl runs. She leaps from the mattress and throws herself around it, bolting for the darkness behind the door. The creature spins to follow her, an arc of gruel spraying from the bowl before he drops it and chases after her. Ramming my legs down by force of will, I launch myself a heartbeat later, following the thing as it vanishes into the gloom.

I burst through in time to hear a panicked shriek and a splash. Sliding on something, a tile, I crash into the low edge of a sunken pool. Stars of pain explode in front of my eyes as my shin cracks with the impact. The girl screams again, her voice bubbling as she flails in the water. As my vision adjusts to the dark I can make out the figure laying on the edge of the pool, leaning over. One of its arms lunges after her, grabbing her collar.

'Get off her!' I scream, running over to the thing, which turns its head towards me at the interruption. I ball my fists and hammer at it, feeling soft flesh underneath the overalls. With a massive shove I send the monster sprawling then jump in after her.

The pool is dark and freezing and the cold stabs my nerves with icy knives. For a moment I hang there, shocked into stillness, then ignoring my fear, dive deeper into the water. The pressure pops my ears and I'm screaming in my own mind in the panic to find her. Finally, with lungs agonised and starved of oxygen I have to come up for air. I push back with small, strong arms, fighting my body's demand to open my mouth and try to breathe water.

I surface, choking. And there above me is the monster. 'Alice,' it hisses, 'there's nowhere to go.' Its hand slams down on my head and grabs my hair. 'Leave me alone!' I scream in the girl's voice. 'Get away!' But it's not going to leave me alone. Bubbles and snot pour from my nose as I go under again, my body twisting in an agony of cold and panic. It hauls me half out of the water. It's never going to let me go.

How many days have I been here? I don't know any more; I've given up counting. My dream of Father and Mother bursting through the door and saving me is gone. The monster's killed them, it said. I'm alone.

'Alice,' it says, the monster voice so mocking, so falsely caring, 'you need to get out of the water or you'll risk hypothermia.' The monster pretends to be a man, but I know better. I start getting sleepy and the sting of the cold isn't so bad now. Then I think about my bear and Jen-doll and the cat. I'd forgotten to take them with me when I ran. That wasn't fair. They don't deserve to be locked away in that room forever. 'Alice!' it shouts leaning further in, its body half over the black water of the pool. Its face isn't a blur. It's wearing layers of stockings to hide its features, just like a robber.

But it can't disguise the truth of what it is, no matter how hard it tries to hide its features.

'No,' I say and yank at the stockings. My fingernails scratch over the slippery surface but catch, tearing through enough to show what's beneath.

Shocked, the thing with Olen's face rears back as I push my head away so hard I rip free of its grip. The near freezing water wraps me like a blanket and takes me to the bottom of the pool, in darkness.

64

WAKING

My mouth is dry and tastes like metal and all I can smell is an acrid stink of burned electrics. It must be the after-effects of the drug. There's a sound at the door, a quiet turning of the handle and a nurse enters. I pretend to sleep but not before keeping my eyes open long enough to check she's normal. She fusses around the room then checks my temperature. Small, routine things that don't seem important. She leaves quickly but I hold back another minute before sitting up. Everything is tight and painful. 'Olen,' I whisper to myself, 'you bastard.'

Edging out of the bed I stop only to gather what I need before throwing on some clothes and hurrying out. I enter the hallway, waiting for an orderly to pass before walking as confidently as I can through the reception area and out into the cold, sunlit day.

The day's brighter and crisper than any I remember; everything's heightened and even my footsteps crunch crisply on the gravel. I half expect to hear sirens or something, but there's nothing. Risking a glance back, I can tell no one's following and I'm surprised at the ease of my, what? Escape? I remind myself I haven't done anything wrong: this isn't a prison. Whatever that prick Olen was planning hasn't worked. Then an image comes to me and it's all I can do to stop from running. There are monsters in the shadows.

Now Sydney is truly gone, now I know what's real, there's a nothingness inside me. Even when things were at their worst here I always had that escape to cling to, the thought none of this might be true. But it is. Now, there's no more waking up, no more escaping from here to there. This is it.

Walking into the sunny morning I wonder where to go. I turn on my phone and make a call as I leave the grounds, aching but for the first time in control. Maybe things are going to be OK after all. Which is when my legs give way and I grab on to a fencepost as I'm wracked by sobs.

That stinking hot room with its poster of Sydney was a memory.

THE FAMILIY MEETING

I'd always thought when I finally learned the truth everything would somehow snap into place and be all right. It's not like that. Now, my body doesn't seem to trust anything any more.

There's a kind of shadow hanging over me, and even though it's warmer than its been for ages I'm cold. This is real but something inside doesn't want to believe it. Things seem painted on, stage-like. All the pretend years of my other life in Sydney have made me untrusting.

They're waiting for me. The mansion is different now. It's so familiar, so understood, but this time I see the flaws that have always been there: a small ridge of dirt in the drive, ugly and brown in the snow; a tiny crack in one of the pillars near the entry; a mound of slush on the steps. The imperfections of reality. It still stands proud and unsubtle in the cold light and colder dusting of snow, but now it's diminished, just a house not a monolith. I can almost read the politicking, the manoeuvrings embedded in the architecture, the uncompromising statement it's meant to be, now revealed as something flagrant, obvious, maybe even childish.

My parents are waiting for me, faces set, ready for confrontation in the Screw-up Room. I pass it and tell them to join me in the big library. When they get there I sit down, drawing out a cigarette and lighting it with shaking hands. They pull up a couple of chairs, stiffly formal and expectant. The silence stretches on as the yet to be started conversation fills the air with a weird potential. I put out the cigarette, furious and paralysed and trapped and almost free. I can feel it.

'What the fuck did Olen do to me?' I spit it out. Angry barking words.

Mattiew glances at Jeane, who seems as always startled at my outburst. I know better. The reaction is a set piece, just part of her repertoire.

'What are you talking about?' she asks.

'What happened to me? He took me somewhere.'

Mattiew shakes his head and a silence drags out between us for the longest time. 'It wasn't Olen.'

'What do you mean it wasn't Olen?' My voice quavers and I hate myself for it.

Mother stands up and sits next to me, holding my hand. There's something happening under all that carefully applied makeup; I can feel the clamminess of her touch. Her other hand beats out a small nervous rhythm on the leather, her fingers faintly alive with motion. 'Alice,' she says, 'we couldn't tell you.'

'Tell me what?'

Jeane stares at me and opens her mouth for words that struggle to come. The mask is down. I've seen pictures of prisoners of war with expressions like hers. 'You were kidnapped when you were five.'

I shake my head, but it's not in disagreement, just reaction. Her words confirm my memory of the room. She goes silent, drained by the admission. Another silence stretches out between us, filling the space until it's unbearable. Eventually I stare at them. 'The meningitis?'

'You never had meningitis,' says Mattiew.

'So why lie about it? Why didn't you tell me?'

'Because it doesn't work,' says Father angrily, his face for the briefest second revealing a glimpse of grief. Then it's gone, his own mask much better than hers. 'It doesn't work,' he says again, 'because you keep forgetting.'

I light another cigarette, hardly tasting it. 'I would have remembered if you told me.'

'But you don't. We've tried to tell you what happened,' says Jeane, 'but you kept repressing it, forgetting it.' She looks to Mattiew for support. 'Again and again but every time you forget.'

I blink through the smoke and shake my head. 'Don't lie to me,' I say quietly.

Father looks away, faced flushed. 'It's the goddam dream,' he says, 'the insane fucking obsession you have with Sydney. That's what they think.'

'They?' I'm numb. My world has changed again and as usual I didn't see it coming. 'You should have told me,' I whisper. Images and memories reshuffle as I try to make sense of everything.

'We did, so often,' says Jeane, 'but in the end it was always something you'd need to remember by yourself.'

'That's ridiculous.'

'Ridiculous or not, it's the truth,' says Mattiew. 'We tried for years to tell you. You'd accept it, or not, but it always went the same way. Eventually the dreams would start and you'd forget all over again.'

I rub my head, swimming in the memory of that room, the heat, the fear. Of him telling me my parents were dead, the steam and empty noises from the space beyond, always black and terrifying. And of pulling at the mask and revealing the monster behind the monster. Images whirl and I feel physically sick.

Mattiew leans forward staring at me, his eyes searching. 'You think there is a psychologist we haven't used, a therapy we haven't tried? You think what, we abandoned you to your own devices and didn't care? What parent would do that to their child?'

'Bullshit.'

'Bullshit?' He shakes his head momentarily lost for words.

Jeane squeezes my hand even tighter. 'And you've remembered again. Darling, this is wonderful.'

Therapies? It's another world, another life, another Alice looming up out of nowhere. Wasn't two lives enough? Now they're telling me there was someone else, another me. Another Alice Van de Korte who sometimes, just sometimes, comes back to them. I can see it in their eyes now; the fearful, coy hope, too beaten down to be more than a glint. It's so clear. I might have the same body, but they're waiting for their real daughter to return.

Why don't I remember? I look though the window to the snowbound garden outside. It's always winter. My mind pushes back and makes the thought slippery and hard to grasp, but I stick with it. It's always winter. How can that be? I try to remember another season, but the images are flimsy and feel invented. A part of me crumbles. How can this not be real? My conversation with Lavar returns with brutal clarity. And New York as well, he said. Both lives a dream. Which means I knew, some part of me must have understood the truth of my life. Sensations of sessions with doctors, FMRIs, blood samples and talking — endless talking, echo faintly in my mind. They're shadows on the periphery of memory, almost real enough to grasp.

'But this isn't the dream,' I say quietly.

'Of course it isn't,' said Jeane, her eyes wide and moist.

Sydney had been there for a reason. It had been my escape from that room and the memories it contained. So what is this? It's like I'm staring into a well with my own reflection peering back up at me from the depths. Except it isn't a reflection, it's the real me. I'm the fake, the incomplete thing. The filter.

The weight of memory presses. It's too much. I slam my hand down making the ashtray jump and spill over the marble. Jeane starts. A genuine reaction this time. 'Fuck it.' I am who I am right now. Whoever else there is lining up in the deeps of my mind can take a ticket and wait.

'Screw your breakthrough,' I say at last. 'It was Olen.' Even as I say his name my heart pounds. I can't accept I let myself get so close to him and his experimental drug.

Then I get it.

Olen had taken me as a child and now he'd almost done it again. He manipulated me. The pills weren't anti-psychotics. I roll my tongue in my mouth, the smoke and tobacco unable to mask the residue of that other taste. A whisper in my mind wonders at that. Olen's face leers at me, huge and distorted, backlit by the lights on the clinic roof. The drugs I took sent me over the edge, precisely the opposite of what he told me they were. And me, so full of my own cleverness, had allowed myself to be manipulated into taking them. I look down, stunned by the attack and by my naïvety.

'Olen took me,' I say. 'There was this room and he kept me in it. It was him. I know what I saw.'

'Alice,' says Jeane, 'you can't rush this in all the excitement. It's natural some memories get confused. Olen found you.'

'Don't tell me what I remember!' I pause for a second. 'Found me? What you mean?' My mouth is still bitter and electric, tainted by the residue of the drugs.

'The kidnapper left you at the clinic,' says Mattiew and again the mask slips, his face stoney, lips white, 'and Olen was the first to find you there.'

I shake my head. It's not right.

'We paid as soon as we could get the money,' says Jeane, 'but it took a while.' Her voice becomes a whisper. 'We didn't know what was going to happen.'

'Took a while? How long?' I'm numb: memories of the room, the squalid stink of it, the oppressive heat, the window with the view of roses and the poster, all jostling.

'Ten weeks.' Mother's voice is small.

'Why did it take so long to pay?' I ask. Ten weeks of being drugged, of being alone and thinking everyone I loved was dead. Ten weeks of losing myself to the dream.

'It was complicated,' says Mattiew. 'We didn't have the money. We'd invested everything in expansion and we were past our limit.'

'Why didn't you sell something?' I can almost feel her. There's someone else now, someone looking on. She's on the edge of my awareness, someone almost like me. She's only a voice at the moment, a whisperer, a rememberer.

'It wasn't that simple,' says Mattiew.

'It was Olen,' I say at last.

'Don't be ridiculous,' says Jeane, but there's an undertone in her voice hinting of doubt and secrets. Did Olen use her, became her lover to get to me? 'We saved the man's career. He'd be bankrupt if it weren't for us.'

'He tried to do it again,' I say, 'he tried to kill me at the clinic.'

Mattiew sits back. 'Alice, are you hearing yourself right now?'

'That fucker tried to send me mad.'

He crosses his arms. 'Why? Why would he want to do that?'

'I'm figuring it out. I was waking up from Sydney and the reason I was waking up was because I was remembering what he'd done to me. He wanted to shut me up.'

Mattiew shakes his head and Jeane looks away from me. I can read their minds. They're losing her. Their Alice is slipping away again and being replaced with me: the broken thing. So I go on. It's all or nothing. 'He told me he could get me some new drugs, not on the market yet, that would stop the dream entirely.'

Mattiew shifts in his chair. 'Do you realise how illegal that is? Why would he risk his entire career, even imprisonment to do something as insane as that?' He rubs his head; annoyed, frustrated, a mess of emotions. 'So where are they?'

'I took them.'

'These drugs, they were just laying about in the clinic?' He looks incredulous.

'Of course not,' I say, feeling cornered. How did this turn around so quickly? 'They were in his safe.'

'That you found open, full of this top secret drug no one else has heard about presumably and works better than anything else on the market.' Mattiew stares at me and I wear the full force of his anger. For an instant it softens, replaced by something else entirely. He shakes his head.

And there it is at last. I'm not his daughter. Somehow in his mind, I'm the one who's taken her and won't let her go. He thinks I've stolen her away just like his kidnapper. Maybe it's true. 'And how did he get this drug? Did he tell you?'

'From our company,' I say quietly. What an idiot I am. Olen's played me from the start.

'We don't have a pharmaceutical arm.' Mattiew says quietly. 'It's time I showed you something.' I watch as he pulls a phone from his pocket. 'Olen sent this through last night.

'Mattiew, don't' says Jeane.

He ignores her, turning the handset so I can see. Blue-black and grainy, the video is a composite of security camera vision. The footage follows my path as I run through the corridors of the clinic, screaming madly at the serious-faced orderlies and nurses trying to subdue me.

The pictures cut to an even grainier wide angle of me on the roof as I race from shadow to shadow, mincing over imaginary obstacles, stopping to examine things clearly not there. I close my eyes, remembering the ghoulish faces and rotten, stinking breath of my pursuers, knowing what the security vision would show next. On camera, I run to the edge of the building and teeter on the concrete lip. I scream at someone off-screen then fall, only to be caught as an arm lashes out and grabs me. Olen is wrenched to the ground by my weight, but he's saved just in time by an orderly who almost dislocates his shoulder as he catches us both and begins hauling us back.

Mattiew shuts off the phone. 'He saved you. How does that fit in with this plan to kill you?' The words sting but he says them without malice. 'That wasn't you being abducted. It wasn't you being attacked. It was your life being saved from whatever toxic shit you'd pumped into your own veins.' He stands.

'I know what I remember.' I say it so quietly it's not even a whisper. 'And I know what he did.' I turn away. 'The man is evil.'

'You are going back to the clinic,' says Mattiew evenly.

'No.' I want answers, not redemption. I get up to leave. There's no family here. They're still waiting for their daughter.

66

DEMOLITION

Nothing is OK. I've come back to my place, unsettled, unresolved. It's just a destination now, not a home. The apartment could belong to anyone. I stop at my portrait on the wall and feel guilty that I haven't spoken to Gabe. There's too much to deal with there. Even as I look at it I'm beginning to understand a decision I made a long time ago.

I go to the window and stare out through the winter light to Central Park. White-shrouded, clean, still busy with ant-sized heavy-coated tourists and regular walkers. As I turn away I imagine it blooming into life, the snowmelt feeding the grass and trees and beds of flowers. The people, the day trippers and cyclists and joggers and kids and clowns and vendors and the whole beautiful mess of it. Water that isn't ice; the warmth of the sun.

Later I find myself in my room staring at the box of old photographs. The thought of Olen eats at me as I spread out the photos in a messy pile. Two-dimensional faces look back blindly, people caught in moments, snatched out of time and context, made random. I pick up a photo of me, Mother and Olen in front of the old building. It almost looks like a family portrait. I shiver and flick it aside.

I twitch at the memory of his hands in the water. And those eyes. I'm alone now, isolated by his easy manipulation. Who'll believe my story against his? He even has that security vision to support him. I'm irrelevant.

I examine the snapshot of the three of us in front of the clinic again. Father said Olen had found me there. I stare at the picture. Of course he had. That's where he'd kept me. Behind the self-conscious smile of the girl in the photo stretches a row of neatly trimmed rose bushes.

I NEVER THOUGHT I'd be coming back here. The afternoon is dissolving into evening as I walk down the long drive to the clinic. I know the cameras will be picking me up but I'm not acting suspicious. A walk like I belong here. Maybe I do.

It's getting cold. As I arrive at the fence that separates the new clinic from the remains of the old, the setting sun is swallowed by clouds. The demolition work is almost done. The main three-storey building is gone now, reduced to tread marks in the mud. Random pieces of broken masonry lie scattered along the paths the machines have chewed into the ground. The only parts still standing are the utility rooms. Steel beams line the site next to the wreckage, left for last by the demolition crew. They disappear into the remaining brickwork like a ribcage, the corpse of a giant whale slowly being eaten away.

With all the mess it's probably too late to find anything. But then, whispers the quiet new voice, Olen would never have kept me in the main building anyway. There's only one place where I could have been. A huge dirt-spattered bulldozer rolls through the blazing glare of the site lamps, its scarred metal bucket raised high on its way to start the final demolition.

I check to make sure no one's watching before dropping to the frozen mud and forcing myself under the fence. The wire tears at my clothes but I ignore it and push through. Standing, I take a moment to gauge the best way to the site. Most of the demolition crew are working at the other end as they pile up huge mounds of rubble, separating the salvage. That leaves only the one bulldozer to work on the remaining walls. I decide to chance it and race towards what's left of the building in a wide arc, avoiding what lights I can.

I arrive panting and dizzy from the run. Stepping over a low pile of smashed masonry I climb through a ragged hole in the wall of the outermost building, finding myself in the dark. I swear quietly, fishing around in the gloom for my lighter. Should have brought a flashlight.

The room is long and narrow, its depths lost to the weak flicker of light. The rumbling of the bulldozer outside dislodges tiny drifts of masonry dust from the weakened walls. My breath is foggy from the cold, my body still aches from the after-effects of Olen's drug and I have to fight back a sudden feeling of hopelessness. I can't say exactly what I'm expecting but I need to find out for sure; to know the dream is also a memory. I've got to see the room. I understand I won't be able to convince anyone else, but that doesn't matter.

The bulldozer smashes through a wall in an adjoining corridor and the building shakes with the violence of it. Shit. I glance at the exit for a second then turn to the dark. If I leave now I can never come back.

I push though a jammed door and find myself in a short

hallway ending in a T-section. Mould grows up the crumbled plaster, so rotted away in places the skeletons of wiring brackets and wood panels are revealed beneath. The place stinks of damp and rot, not winter smells at all. I choose a direction at random but it quickly turns into a dead end with iron beams and bricks filling the space and blocking the way. Forced to backtrack I find another door illuminated by the dying light. There's a word stencilled on the wood, but it's too faded to read. I force it open with a squeal of rusted hinges.

It takes a moment but when it finally arrives the sensation of familiarity is overwhelming. Even though I can't see the end of the chamber I know exactly where I am. I'm standing on a mezzanine, with an iron staircase ahead of me, running down to the next level. Windows sit evenly spaced along the length of the ground floor, admitting enough of the faded outside light to show the long empty lap pool below.

I climb down the stairway, my footsteps echoing loudly in the room as the cold metal shifts under my weight. My breathing gets shallow as I half expect the tall, monstrous figure of Olen to loom out of the darkness. I turn around but the lighter's flame does almost nothing to add to the light. Instead, the space seems darker, the flicker of illumination drawing out long, attenuated shadows from the dimness. I start shivering but force myself onwards as somewhere above me the bulldozer crashes through another wall.

I lean over the pool, empty for years now. As I strain to see in the murky light I move the lighter around but can only make out faded blue tiles, many of them missing. I know it's the same pool. Images from my dream memory flash through my mind; the coldness of the water, the frantic, desperate fight, the slow, slow descent. My mouth is dry. It really happened. It really happened here.

I get back up and carefully make my way down the length of the pool, finding a door at the end of the room marked 'Utilities.' I put my hand against it, knowing what must be on the other side. The metal is cold and dead, but I can remember the sweaty heat of the pumps, the hisses, drips and surges of water. Not loud, but loud enough to muffle the cries of a little girl. I turn the handle.

The ground shakes and I reflexively drop to the floor as the wall at the top of the mezzanine explodes inwards, the huge teeth of the bulldozer's bucket bright amidst clouds of dust. Glass shatters and sprays over the empty pool and the room is filled with shrapnel as bricks and structural beams give way.

I choke, heaving for breath in the near darkness. The clatter of the debris falls away, replaced by the regular beeping of the machine as it reverses for another run. I'm out of time. Something solid and heavy cracks behind me with the sound of masonry stressed beyond breaking point. I could run now, maybe even make it to the stairs and get out before the bulldozer attacks the next section of wall, but I can't. Instead I scrabble around in the darkness until my fingers find the lighter. I open the door.

'Oh Jesus,' I whisper as I stare into the dark of the room. The mattress has been removed, the poster disintegrated, but it's the same as I remember. The window has even clung on to some of the black paint, the view not onto roses in bloom but headlights from the heavy machine as it manoeuvres above. As the rumble of its engine grows louder I dash through the exit, heart explosive and near panic as all my fears come back at once. But I hold on, riding the terror instead of letting it overwhelm me. The lighter is burning my hand but I make sure I look at everything.

Dust begins sluicing from the walls, resonating with the bass thrum of the machine's engine when I spot the remains of the toys. I can't see them clearly, but their outlines are right, the mermaid-Jen doll, the bear, others; toys he must have randomly collected for me from the clinic in some strange concession to humanity. The bulldozer sounds as though it's right above me now. I've seen enough. Its headlights shine bright through the window, heading straight towards the room. I run, make it as far as the door before skidding to a stop. Racing back into the place that created half my life I scoop up the doll and bear.

There's an explosion of bricks and dust and metal and glass and my screams are lost to the noise, just like all the times before.

67

COLD

Cold.
I'm breathing.
Dark.

I open my eyes.

Snow falls gently down around me and I find I can move. I push at the rubble pinning most of my body, then jerk back my hand as it presses against something sharp. Across the room, which is now roofless and lit by the second-hand glow of demolition lights, the area by the door has collapsed completely. If I hadn't turned back, I'd be dead.

For a moment I freeze, remembering the bulldozer. But the sound of its engine is gone, shut down for the night. I shiver as a combination of shock and cold settles over me. Ignoring the pain I turn to find something I can use as a lever, beginning the long, painful process of digging myself out. The pain is intense but it doesn't matter. I have what I came for.

68

LAST STOPS

I spend most of the day asleep. Truly asleep. When I wake I know what I have to do.

The afternoon is bleak and almost snowing. Winter. Always winter. There are days when it is crisp and beautiful and sparkling with whiteness but this isn't one of them. The statue of Alice is icy and alone in the grey.

I rest my gloved hand on the worn metal, feeling the cold bite through the fabric. She's lost her magic. Even my namesake had to wake up in the end.

I stay there despite the snow falling gently around us, a decision clear in my mind. As the warmth of my body goes away I imagine for a second I'm also made of bronze, unchangeable, just like my winter. The idea's tempting and as I stand there alone under the frozen sky I finally accept my choice and say goodbye.

WALKING SLOWLY down the corridor I favour my left leg as I do my best to ignore the bruises and a pulled muscle. My body's been reduced to a mass of painful twinges and protests. Sounds of a console game echo down the hallway long before I get to the apartment. I adjust the leather tote bag on my shoulder as I arrive, explosions and sharp rattles of machine-gun fire filling the air as I knock. I wait for a break in the action and knock again. The sound cuts off, war suspended, replaced by the more disturbing click of multiple locks. Jordie's face, bleary-eyed and unfocused, appears. He blinks slowly as he comes down from whatever Nirvana the game put him in, before unlocking the rest of the door.

'Hey Jordie,' I say, 'is Gabe in?'

'Yeah,' he says and lets me in, pointing towards the kitchen.

Gabe's voice floats out from another room. 'Who is it, eh?'

I walk through the cluttered lounge, overwhelmed by the smell of weed as I step over a toppled pile of vinyl records and wind my way past a couple of dinner plates on the floor. A radio plays somewhere nearby but its music is swamped by the firefight that Jordie resumes.

Gabe's at the tiny Formica kitchen table with his feet up. It takes a moment for him to lock in on me, the features of his face slightly out of step with one another as he smiles and waves me to the remaining chair. I move a box of Chinese take-out and sit, dropping my bag.

'Baby,' he says, drawing back on the joint. He offers it to me and I reach out, taking a drag. The smoke is acrid. I pass it back and breathe out slowly. 'Did you find the girl?' he asks as the fighting in the other room dies down.

'Yeah,' I say.

He stares at me — carefully neutral. 'And?'

'I'm leaving, Gabe.'

'Fuck babe.' He puts the weed down and rubs his head. 'Give me a second, eh?' He gets up and splashes some water onto his face from the kitchen sink before returning by way of the refrigerator with a couple of beers. He offers one to me but I say no.

I put my hand over the top of his can, stopping him from opening it. 'Listen, Gabe.'

'Why?' he asks. 'What happened?'

'Listen to me Gabe. This is important.' I look away for a moment and wonder how to say what I have to say. 'I always fuck things up, right? Well, I'm tired of it. I can't do it anymore.'

'Hey baby, everyone fucks things up. That's life.'

I shake my head. 'Gabe, just shut up and listen, all right?' I take his head in my hands and gently force him to see me. 'I used you and I'm sorry for that, OK?'

He blinks. 'You mean sex? Shit, that's no thing.'

'Not about that. About my family. Everything.' He watches me in silence. 'So what I'm saying, is I'm sorry.'

He stares at me in smokey confusion. 'What?'

'Listen you idiot,' I yell, 'I'm fucking apologising for messing up, OK?'

'Ah. Well, whatever babe, we're big bad grownups, eh? It's the universe, or some such crap.'

I lean over and grab the bag, dumping it on the table. 'You've got to do right by Jordie.'

He sits up at that, his eyes clearing as a flush of anger darkens his face. 'Don't go criticising my boy. He's all right. He's a good kid and he's doing OK.'

'No, that's bullshit and you know it.'

'Say again?'

'He's going to end up staying here forever if you don't do something about it.'

Gabe stands, instantly sober. 'Well listen to you, Miss Reformed. Coming down all righteous now. Fuck!'

'Jesus Gabe, calm the fuck down. You're a good person. That's what I'm telling you. I'm going to help.'

'How, by getting another big-ass TV?'

I unzip the bag and pull out tight bundles of cash. 'This,' I say with my voice trembling slightly, 'is what I owe you.' I pull out more notes. 'This is interest.' He sits, face slackened by the amount of money I'm putting on the table. 'This, is to get you and Jordie into a better neighbourhood.' I retrieve a final clip of notes and place it down. 'And this is to set up a studio. You've got a great eye.' I stare at him, pleading silently for him to understand what I'm saying. 'Do it right, Gabe. Don't fuck it up and blow it all. I know you're a good person.'

He stares at the money.

'And these are for Jordie.' I reach into the bag and pull out a pile of Treasury Notes, lay them on the table next to the cash. 'There's enough to get him through college if he's careful.' I stare at him. 'Give him a future, Gabe.'

He starts to say something. Stops. Tries again. 'Where did all this come from?'

'It's mine.'

He grabs my hands. 'What are you doing, baby?'

'I'm saying goodbye.'

'I'm not taking it.'

'Then give it to the boy.' I remember something. 'Be there for Jordie,' I tell him. 'I know what growing up without parents is like and it really sucks.'

'Alice, you're freaking me out, eh?'

I nod, my face set in a kind of calm agreement. 'Yeah Gabe.' I kiss him. 'I've got to go.' I glance out the small window at the snow outside.

'Baby, this is very fucked.'

He tries to stop me leaving but his heart's not in it. He knows I've made up my mind. It makes it even harder to do what I have to do, but I go anyway. Finding Jordie on the way out I hug him.

I TELL the taxi driver to wait as I step onto the icy sidewalk, breathing in the stale odours of the neighbourhood, smelling the familiar piss in the air. All of it feels older though, the tenement door fronts faded, footpath littered with plastic bags and the spill of garbage. I wrap my coat tightly around myself and make my way past a reeking overturned dumpster, surprised at the intensity of the stench. I spot the wrecked car that marks the entrance to Rene's house as I also search about for the kid, but no one's there.

The place seems abandoned and as I push open the door I wonder what I'll find. Maybe one of Rene's competitors had enough or maybe he just shut up shop.

The familiar blast of heat is enough to tell me someone's here. I take off my jacket, feeling some consolation in the routine shock of the sweatbox atmosphere. As I stand in the hallway there's a stink in the air, something lingering beneath the usual incense and smoke, sweet and rotten. I jam my hand to my mouth and almost leave, but where is there to go?

I push on down the hall, wilting as the heat and humidity soak through my tee, feeling dirty just by sharing the same air. The door that had opened onto the old couple before is ajar and I nudge it open further. I turn on the light and have to stifle a small gasp of surprise as the kitchen flashes into life, revealing the man sitting in a chair, apparently asleep. Behind him the pantry is open but I glance away, not before seeing something hung up on a hook. I tell myself it's a pig. The old man stirs as I slam the door shut.

I find Rene in the main room. He's staring wide-eyed and stupefied at the television in front of him. The blue grey light of the show paints his features corpse-like, his huge, jowly face slick with sweat, the bulk of his thin singlet and track pants wet and stained. I gag at the stench of it. Either side of him the albino woman and midnight man sit jammed into their own corners of the couch. They're not the lithe, feline creatures I remembered. The woman is awake or at least conscious and acknowledges me with a slow blink before looking away as if embarrassed. They seem older, the lean and toned muscles of their bodies turned paunchy. The stink of decay is almost physical.

'Alice, my dear.' Rene nods at me. 'So sweet.'

'Rene,' I say.

'Come back to join our little party after all?'

I shake my head.

'Pity. It's in dire need of some joie de vivre in my opinion.' The woman stares at the floor, apparently mortified to be there. 'So my lovely, what can I do for you?'

'I need something special.'

He laughs, a massive unappealing sound that wakes the man next to him. 'Alice, you always need something special.'

I hold my ground, despite the heat and the stink and the fear in this room. Something has happened here, changed badly. Or perhaps I'm seeing it as it's always been. 'I need something for a very long trip.' I feel ridiculous using a metaphor but it's part of the rules here. And right now, I just want what I've come for and to be out.

His eyes widen slightly as he shifts his huge bulk, disturbing the others. Something in his face becomes animated and aroused. 'And, lovely Alice, how long do you imagine this journey will last?'

I meet his gaze. 'I don't know. A long time.'

He leans forward, the couch protesting as his weight crushes down on different springs and cushions. The man and woman retreat further into their corners, fearful. Rene looks up at me, his mouth wide and amphibian, his eyes even wider. There's a bulge in his pants. 'Well well well. So you're finally leaving us?'

I stare him down.

He nods to his male companion and whispers something in his ear, nipping it playfully as he slides off the sofa with evident relief. 'You'll have to excuse Michael. He's filling in.' He laughs again.

'Where's Ezekiel?' I ask.

Rene makes a moue. 'No longer with us, I'm afraid. The times, they are a changin'.'

The man, Michael, returns moments later from another room carrying a small plastic bag which he hands over to Rene. He glances at me before leaving, followed by the eyes of the woman who's obviously jealous of his escape. Rene hefts it, his pudgy fingers pushing into the powder inside. He stares at me searchingly and nods.

'This much,' he says, using his free hand to indicate an amount of the drug, 'will put you on the moon.' He smiles, something like a fond memory crossing his large, sweaty face. He opens his fingers some more. 'This much will keep you there forever.' He tosses the bag to me which I catch with a fumble. 'And any more, well, that's a different kind of choice altogether now, isn't it?'

I stare at the bag. 'Will it hurt?'

He laughs again but doesn't answer.

'How much?'

Rene shifts, focuses on me with a strange intensity. 'Last one is always free, lovey.'

THE BAG SITS in my jacket pocket as I stare out the taxi window into the sunset of another winter day.

I call Olen and tell him I want to meet him. He has enough dignity at least to not try and hide his surprise. He recovers quickly though and switches smoothly into doctor mode, welcoming me back to the clinic, applauding my good sense. I hang up, then call my parents one final time to say goodbye.

69

THE BUTTERFLY'S DREAM

Olen sits formally behind his desk, face stern but caring, every bit the concerned father figure. I close the door behind me quietly and sit in the chair on the other side of him. The room's been cleaned again, taking away the clues he'd so carefully left for me to discover. The picture's gone, the carpet's smooth. I'm hot, like the blood in my veins has turned electric, demanding to be noticed. My body's waking up now, so long after the mind.

'Why?' I ask quietly.

He stares at me, his eyes tired but unable to hide a glimmer of victory. 'Alice, you need to understand you are in a very fragile situation,' he says calmly enough.

'Don't talk to me about my situation. You fucking created it.'

He leans forward and steeples his hands on the desk. 'One thing we have to learn, Alice, is each of us is responsible for our lives. You were traumatised as a girl and created a fantasy world to escape to.'

I shake my head unable to believe what I'm hearing.

Instead I pull open my bag and yank out the teddy bear, slamming it on his desk, watching him follow the spill of dirt and grime falling from its matted fur onto the polished wood. I sit the mermaid doll next to it. Olen's eyes widen slightly as he stares at the ancient, ruined toys.

'You know what these are, don't you?'

He pushes back from the desk, distancing himself. 'Why are you here, Alice?'

'I want to know why you did it,' I say, voice tight.

'Did what?'

'You're going to force me to actually say it?' I slam my fist down on the table, knocking over the doll. 'Why you kidnapped me, you fucking dick! Why you used me and drugged me.' Then lowering my voice, 'You could have killed me.'

'I'm not a murderer.'

'No one believes me, you've seen to that. Just tell me the truth.'

He laughs and the sound is gentle and refined. 'With all the ways we have to listen in to conversations these days, to record voices?' He shakes his head and stares at me pointedly. His face makes his voice a liar. 'Alice, I still don't understand what you're talking about.'

So I pull out my knife. I'm replaying the symmetry of my dream when I attacked Ryan, knowing this will be the last mirrored moment of them all. He backs away as I go around the desk and put the blade to his throat. Was it always going to come to this? I wonder if part of Sydney had been some sort of training ground, a practice realm for when reality demanded I act.

Olen staggers back but I keep pace with him, holding the knife so the keen edge grazes his skin. 'Don't think I won't,' I whisper.

'What do you want me to say?' he gasps between breaths.

'Tell me why you did it!' My own voice is harsh, my breath coming in bursts.

'You can't get out of here,' he says trying to move back further and stopping short at the wall. 'They already know you're a danger to yourself.'

I lean in close, my mouth almost brushing his. I smell his aftershave. 'Who says I want to get out of here?'

'Alice, you're not a killer.'

I raise my eyebrows. That's a big assumption to make right about now. 'Tell me why you did it.' I push the knife and he gasps, his Adam's apple bobbing furiously as he swallows in a dry throat. I can see the clamminess of his skin, the drops of sweat forming on his brow.

'All right,' he chokes. I ease back the pressure on the blade, satisfied at the line of bright red on its metal. 'The money should be mine.' His voice intensifies with emotion, something beyond fear. 'I created that ventilator and your father took it from me.'

'He paid you.'

'He was a leech.' Olen spits out the word. 'I developed a machine that could save hundreds of thousands of lives and all he did was circle like a scavenger, a vulture stepping in at the last moment, taking all the glory. I deserved more.'

I back away despite myself. 'It was about money? You kidnapped me for money?'

He shakes his head, scornful. 'You say that as if it's nothing. Only the rich like you can afford to live poor. You don't know anything about struggle.'

I leap at him and bring the knife high. 'Struggle? Do you know what you did to me?'

His eyes betray him: he does. 'It wasn't only about the

money, although it was useful.' He's breathless, excited with fear and adrenaline, his smooth and controlled tones cracking to reveal a hint of the monster underneath. 'Not at the end anyway. I wanted to take something from them. Something that mattered.'

I push harder on the blade, seeing another trickle of blood. A kind of deep cold fury grips me now, colder than the winter outside. 'So why did you let me go?'

He looks away. 'I won. That bastard Mattiew first lost his wife and then he lost you.' I try to say something but I can't. He sees me hesitate. 'You know it too, don't you? His daughter's dead to him. She died when she was five. You — you are just damaged goods.'

I bring my knee up into his groin and he falls, crooning in agony. I bend over but he pushes back with unexpected ferocity and I reel into the table spilling ornaments and a stack of pens. He hobbles to his feet, face locked into a cold snarl and reaches for me, but I roll away knocking into a bookcase. The case rocks with the impact, spilling journals and hardbacks.

I stand and turn, shocked to find him holding the knife. I advance, hesitating as he flicks it deftly.

'I'm not a fighter,' he says breathing hard, 'but I know exactly where to cut.'

I can barely hear his words over the rush of my pulse. 'Why couldn't you just leave me alone?'

He shifts the weapon in his hand as he gauges the weight of it. 'When I heard the clinic was to be demolished I had to return.' He passes the knife to his other hand and starts feeling behind him for the door. 'Not that there would have been evidence.' I back away further from his reach as I search for a weapon, grasping a paperweight. I edge myself in front of the exit and in range of the blade, counting on the fact he won't attack unless I provoke him. 'But I needed to make sure.'

'And then I turn up.'

He twitches, ever so slightly.

'And you go to work on me all over again.'

'You were breaking through. You said so yourself. I had to do something.'

I shake my head as the coldness takes me to a place beyond rage. 'Well you won. I'm mad; you proved it. No one believes me — and you get away with, what, nothing? You didn't get anything.'

He looks at me with a shadow of a smile and the force of his eyes is mesmerising and intense. 'I don't think of it that way. I took something, just like I said. I took you.'

I leap at him again and feel a cold pain slice across my arm before landing the paperweight. I pull back at the last second and soften the blow. He's right about one thing; I'm not a killer.

Here I am. Alice, dark-haired, green-eyed and infinitely tired — staring at nothing. Take away the exhaustion and soul-deep sadness and I could be beautiful, I think.

The room is in shadow. I sit on the carpet, separate from everything: bigger than everything and smaller than my own skin. I'm wearing a suit made out of myself and I wonder if I might simply fall inwards and never stop falling.

Someone groans.

'There's this story,' I say, my voice a whisper, 'It was on a Kung Fu rerun or something. Very Zen. You'll appreciate it. An old man went to sleep and dreamed he was a butterfly. And the butterfly, when it slept, dreamed it was an old man.'

I kick at Olen, a shape in the shadows. He says something to me but I'm not listening and the words are noise. 'So who was dreaming who, that's what I want to know.'

I punch the Olen shape playfully. 'Don't answer. It's rhetorical.' I lean over to the dark lake that is my bag, pull out a syringe full of Rene's gift and uncap it. The liquid inside the plunger is black in this light. Motes swirl within.

There's a sense of things concluding. I tap the needle and watch as a bubble worms upwards.

'Time for you to find out, yeah?'

70

LAST WAVE

The sand is deliciously cool under my toes. The air's clean and fresh, redolent with the scent of growing things. A salty breeze tussles my long hair as I walk down an infinite beach, swinging the metal detector in slow, wide arcs. There's no rush. Time is anything I want it to be right now. Ryan's beside me, barefoot, trousers rolled up, happy to share the companionable silence as I listen to the sounds in my headphones. Out past the break, Jen sits on a yellow surfboard in the bright, almost Caribbean waters. She waves.

I smell the air, enjoying the sun. 'I could stay here forever,' I say.

Ryan smiles. He's wearing his glasses now, looking very much like the doctor bear I had in my bag. Not an old decayed toy but new and clean and plush, the friend I'd needed and finally come back for, no matter how childish it was. I take the headphones off.

The machine whistles as the detector coil discovers something hidden in the sand. I kneel and dig into the pristine white grains, cupping my hands, savouring the fineness of this perfect world.

'You know,' says Ryan, 'it all started like this.'

'I don't remember.'

He kneels beside me. 'It was beautiful for a long time. It's nice to see it this way again.'

'Why did it change?'

'I can't say, not really. Maybe you wanted more than we could give. You knew something wasn't right and kept pushing, making it as real as you were able.'

My hands find an object in the sand. 'Why didn't you ever tell me?'

'You made us to be an alternative, a different truth. We don't have choice, like you. We just weren't able.'

'But the girl, you lied about her.'

He looks away for a moment. 'We might not be real,' he says, 'but we can still feel. She terrified us. We didn't know exactly what she was, but we all saw the hurt and we wanted to keep that from you.' He looks at me. 'We truly didn't know.'

'It's all right,' I say, and pull free a small bouquet of tulips. As I shake the flowers gently the fine white grains fall away like water, leaving the red and yellow petals spotless. I lean into them and let the scent wash over me.

'A trip to the park,' I say, eyes closed. 'It was spring and I don't think I was much over four or five. On the way back we stopped for ice cream and Mother took me into a flower shop. I remember.' I open my eyes. 'It was beautiful. Like a magical forest, I thought.'

Ryan smiles.

I place the flowers and the memory gently into the bag and walk on, taking his hand. As the minutes fall away and wear into something without time, I stop along the beach, kneeling as I dig out more trinkets, more memories from the sand. I don't need the metal detector now.

The sun finds a spot in the sky and stays there. The clouds, far distant puffs of white, drift like imagination. And the ocean, a gentle living tableaux of blues and greys and greens and purples, waits patiently for me under the painted sky.

I walk with Ryan to the water's edge, our footprints marking a path back to the horizon. I halt a final time and plunge my hands into wet, almost gravelly sand. This memory's elusive and I have to push deep. I hit a cool patch, stretching my arm down as far as it can go until I'm laying down. And there at the limit of my reach I find what I'm looking for. My fingers curl around the object and pull it cold and dripping from the hole.

Wet sand clumps to an object the size of a large stone. I wipe it with my blouse then holding it to the sun, look at the snow globe with fascination. 'A dancer,' says Ryan, squinting at the figurine inside the ornament, now bright and delicate in the light. I shake it gently and tiny white specks begin to swirl about the figure.

'I always loved dancing,' I say quietly, 'I even wanted to be a ballerina for a while.' I smile. 'Like what girl doesn't, right?' Ryan smiles back. 'One time my parents took me to the ballet and I got this. I think it was the happiest day of my life.' I tip the globe and it begins to snow again in that perfect little world.

'I'm sorry,' says Ryan, his attention captured by the snow globe. 'I only did what I did to protect you. We all did.' He rubs his mouth and a glimmer of the old Ryan returns as he smiles lopsidedly.

'Thank you,' I say, ignoring the part of me that knows this is a dream; that knows I'm just talking to myself.

He grins as he pulls a tennis ball from his jacket pocket. 'Don't thank me too soon. Wait until you get my bill.'

I laugh and take a swipe at his arm. The moment passes. 'What happens to you now?' I ask, placing the globe in the bag and turning my attention fully to him.

'We stay. We fade.'

I face the sea and Jen waves again. Ryan gives me a hug before cleaning his glasses on his shirt, harmless as a teddy bear. I hug him back. 'Thank you.'

'You have to go.'

'Yes.'

I wade into the water, cold and bracing.

I dive in.

And surface next to Jen, who pats her board.

'Room for two,' she says.

I nod and climb on, somehow finding the balance and coordination I'd never had before. There's no fear anymore, only a great sense of expectation and curiosity. I try to find the shoreline but it's gone, replaced by a vast endless ocean that wraps around the horizon. I've got so much to tell her but I can't think of anything.

'I always knew you'd be leaving one day,' she says smiling at me sadly. 'You were too tough to hide forever.'

I look at my sister. Pretend or otherwise, it doesn't matter. I open my mouth, but she puts her finger to my lips. So instead we sit there on the board in the water watching the horizon, sharing silence.

After a time, I glance at her. Jen winks back. 'Ready?' she asks.

I nod. 'So let's catch a wave.' I feel the board move under

me as a deep swell forms behind us. 'I'll ride this one,' I say to her, 'then I have to go.'

Jen grins. 'Less talk, more walk, babe.'

The swell grows and we push off into the curving blue.

71

THIS TIME FOR REAL

I can see how it will be: a bright spring sunrise reflects off the windows of the Van de Korte Hospital, showering brightness over the site of the former clinic — several stories below and separated by a green swathe of gardens.

A nurse enters a private room, which is awash in flowers and get well cards. She draws the curtains and takes a moment to admire the view, absorbing the sunlight before turning to her patient. A Cander's Ventilator stands by the bed, working away quietly, keeping the man alive.

The nurse rearranges one of the bouquets and checks his vitals. Satisfied everything's well she leaves the room in sunlight and closes the door on Dr Olen Canders, leaving him to his dreams.

I'D FORGOTTEN my eyes are brown. I snap shut my compact as I stand under the great steel beams of JFK and pay for my ticket with cash. The woman types rapidly into her bookings terminal and flashes a smile at me. I smile back easily.

'So that's one way to Sydney, Australia?'

'That's right.'

I hand over my passport and lean back, letting the atmosphere wash over me. The attendant finishes processing the transaction and hands me the boarding pass stuck between its pages. 'The flight leaves in three hours,' she says. 'It's a long haul after LA, so plenty of chance to get some sleep.'

I smile, thank the woman and walk away — looking for a place to wait for the flight. I've packed light, only a change of clothes and toiletries in my carry-on. Almost. I pull the zip and stare at the ragged but now cleaned teddy bear and Jen doll. I know I'll let them go one day. I've already done it in every other way.

'Ah fuck it,' I say to myself, and stop worrying. I walk through the terminal until I find a good view and stand watching the planes take off into a perfect spring sky.

AFTERWORD

Thanks so much for reading Undreamed. If you enjoyed this story please think about writing a review. Reviews really do matter.

If you enjoyed this, you can download the prequel, UNBE-LIEVER for free.

I love to hear from readers and you can find me on my website at: pwesternpittard.com So, thanks once more. Hopefully we'll meet again.